Praise for *The Ten Thousand*:

"Very rarely does an author manage to leave
you heartbroken while still allowing you to
have enjoyed the book you've read... Kearney
captures all the best parts of fantasy and
combines them together with grit and realism
and enough blood to drown a horse."
- *Fantasy Book Review*'s
Book of the Month

"Not only were my expectations met, but they
were surpassed... energetic, powerful and not
for the faint of the heart, *The Ten Thousand*
is a novel that brings together a great piece
of history and Mr. Kearney's extraordinary
storytelling skills with superb results."
- *Fantasy Book Critic*

"This is a engrossing and exciting read that I
couldn't put down. Kearney's battlefields are
bloody and churned and fascinating to read."
- *SF Site*

CORVUS

PAUL
KEARNEY
CORVUS

SOLARIS

This omnibus first published 2010 by Solaris
an imprint of Rebellion Publishing Ltd,
Riverside House, Osney Mead,
Oxford, OX1 0ES, UK

www.solarisbooks.com

ISBN: 978 1 906735 77 7

10 9 8 7 6 5 4 3 2 1

A CIP catalogue record for this book is available from the
British Library.

Designed & typeset by Rebellion Publishing

Printed in the US

For Marie

This book would not have existed without the patience and hard work of Jon Oliver and John Jarrold, and I am hugely grateful to them both for their encouragement and their sheer professionalism.

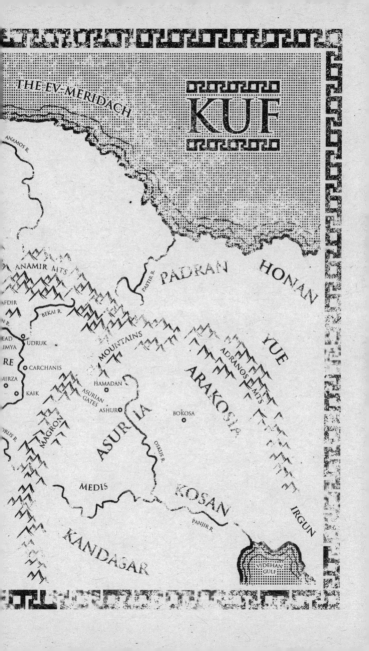

PART ONE

THE SPEAR BY THE DOOR

ONE
THE QUIET WATER

As ALWAYS, HE halted on the crest of the last ridge. Leaning on his spear, he looked down in the gathering blue-shadowed dusk and something like a sigh ran out of him.

Before him, the land poured down in darkening folds and hollows until it met the flat shadow of the glen at the river-bottom. A flash of red there, as the river glanced up at the last light of the sun. Then the mountainsides all around seemed to crowd together as if huddling against the night, and the valley was blanked out, like a conjurer's trick. But in the midst of that quiet darkness, he could see a light burning, steady and yellow.

The spear creaked under his weight. The leather straps of pack and shield dug into his shoulders. The heat of the day broke past him, a warm passage of air rushing down to fill up the cool darkness of the river-bottom below. He closed his eyes as the air kissed the glimmering sweat on his forehead, and turned, straightening.

Behind him, on the northern slope of the ridge, a long line of men sat by the side of the track. Every one of them was burdened with packed cuirass and strapped shield. Every one had a spear in his fist. They looked up as he turned to them, and their eyes were pale glitters as the sunset shattered across the mountains behind them.

"This is me," he said. "I leave you here."

Word went down the line. The men rose to their feet in a ripple of movement, like a snake shivering itself awake down the length of the track. Three burdened figures at their head made an arrowpoint of burdened shapes. One of them bore a banner, a staff of yew wood with a tattered flag that rippled idly in the breezes of the dusk. Upon its tattered face could just be made out the snarling, stylized muzzle of a dog or wolf.

"We'll call on you before the first snows," the banner-bearer said, a massively built fellow with a battered, craggy forehead and eyes like shards of blue glass below it. He grinned, showing broad yellow teeth, some of which had been ornamented with silver wire.

"No, you won't. You're full of shit, and you've too much gold in your pouch. Don't spend it all at once, Kesero. And keep a wind-eye open for those fellows from Machran; Karnos, especially. The New Year comes, and you're looking for jobs again."

"And you, Rictus?" another of them said. He was

younger, a long, lean, red-haired man who would have been pretty as a girl were it not for the deep scarred hole below his left eye which dragged the lower lid downwards, unbalancing his face, giving a him a look at once mocking and mournful.

"What about me?"

"Will we be seeing you after the turning of the year?"

Rictus paused. His gaze swept down the track over the scores of men who lined it silently, all of them looking up the ridge at him. The last of the sun caught his eyes and flashed back out of them in a red glare. He was a big man with a shock of yellow hair veined grey, broad in the shoulders, long in the arm, and there was not an ounce of excess flesh on his face. As his lips thinned, so the outline of his teeth could be seen behind them, and an old seam of scar tissue paled out from his lower lip and down his chin.

"I'll wait for the New Year, Valerian, and see what Antimone brings me," he said at last, making the words lighter with a smile.

Valerian hitched his pack up higher on his shoulders. "Well then, here's to Hal Goshen, boys," he said, his lop-sided face like two halves of different masks. "Here's to red wine and wet women. I'll come up with Kesero, Rictus, and dig you out of your burrow before the snows bury you too deep."

He raised his spear above his head and pointed it towards the east. "Dogsheads!" he cried, and the word was caught up by the mountains and flung echoing around the high country. "March on – we can make ten more pasangs before Phobos rises."

Behind him, the long files of men started out, taking a stony track along the crest of the ridge with the last light of the sun on their backs. Valerian held out a hand, and Rictus shook it. Then the big, crag-faced bannerbearer, Kesero, did the same. They led the line of burdened figures off, and Rictus stood and watched them go. As the men passed him on their way east, they each and every one nodded at him. A few struck their spears against their chests in salute. By the time the rearguard had gone by it was almost fully dark, and the stars were glimmering overhead in their tens of millions.

A dark shape uncoiled itself from the shadow below Rictus and stood to become a compact, black-bearded man with a face as sharp as a fox's nose.

"Well, are you going to stand there until Phobos finds you, or are we to get on home?" the man asked waspishly. He yawned, and rubbed his eyes.

"It's all downhill from here, Fornyx," Rictus said. "Tonight you'll sleep in a bed with a fire at your feet."

The two men set off down the ridge to the glen below, from which the sound of rushing water could now be heard. They moved quietly, and their sandaled feet ate up the downslope with the steady pace of men who have been marching all their lives.

"You're not retiring. You just tell them that to mess with their heads," Fornyx said, picking at his teeth with a thumbnail as he walked.

Rictus strode along in silence, eyes fixed on the single point of light in the widening glen below them.

"And if you were," Fornyx went on, "Why bury

yourself up here in the hills? It's a hard scrabble up this high, Rictus." When he received no response, he went on, "Any city in the Harukush would shower you in gold just to have your spear planted on their walls. You could live like a king, had you a mind to."

"We have no kings," Rictus said quickly. "And me, I've no wish to set myself up as one. Damn it, Fornyx, don't you ever shut up? You love these hills as much as I do. And besides, there's enough gold buried under Andunnon's hearth already."

Fornyx grinned, looking more vulpine than ever. The top of his head barely reached the taller man's shoulder, but the muscles in his arms and legs were like corded wires, and he kept pace with Rictus's long stride without obvious effort.

"I find conversation an amusement, and if no-one will talk to me, then I'll amuse myself until they do."

"Well, amuse yourself in silence for a moment, will you? Stop here."

They halted, almost on the brim of a mountain river, which fell flashing from a rocky bluff to the west and ran along the bottom of the glen, foaming and purling in its stony bed. Rictus breathed in the cooling air deeply.

"Smell the pines?" he asked. "There's still garlic growing on the far bank, and thyme, too. I wonder how the barley did this year."

"The same as it did last year, I shouldn't wonder," Fornyx said with a snort. "Aise and Eunion will have the place blooming, as they always do. Come, let's cool our feet." He began splashing across the silver-flashing river.

Rictus watched him go, smiling slightly. In the hanging woods that carpeted the upper sides of the glen, an owl hooted as though it, too, wondered what was keeping him. His hand went up to his neck, and there at the lip of his cuirass it brushed against a cord of rawhide upon which hung a wolf's tooth and a rounded fragment of coral. Then Rictus began to wade across the cold, fast-flowing river in Fornyx's wake.

THE DOGS CAME out barking as they approached the eaves of the farm, but their barks changed to delighted yips and whines as they caught the scent of the two men. Big, brindled hunting hounds, they bounced around Rictus and Fornyx like pups, tongues lolling happily. A square of light opened into the night, dazzling, wiping out the stars and making the glen around them into depthless black space.

A woman stood outlined in the threshold, firelight and lamplight flickering out behind her along with the laughter of children. She snapped a word to the dogs and they calmed down at once, grinning happily. The laughter within ceased. Rictus stepped up to the door.

The woman who confronted him there was tall, iron-coloured in hair and eyes. She was wrapped in a finely spun woollen shawl the same saffron hue as the light behind her, so that she seemed bathed in bright warmth. She had a long face, strong-jawed as a man's, and as she saw Rictus and Fornyx her eyes widened a trifle, but that was the only way the face changed. She reached back inside the house and produced a shallow dish.

"My lord. Welcome home," she said, a voice as low as heather honey.

Both Rictus and Fornyx took salt from the dish and tasted it. "Antimone bless us all," Fornyx said.

"Aise," Rictus said. And he bent to kiss the woman on the forehead.

She stood aside. "Come in. Since you sent word from Nemasis we have been expecting you, this month and more." A slight pause, long enough to be noticed. "It's late, but there's still some supper to be had."

Rictus had to stoop to enter the house, and he blinked as the lamplight and woodsmoke within pricked his eyes.

A long, low mountain farmstead, built and flagged with stone, thatched with reeds from the riverside. It had a hearth the shape of a beehive opposite the doorway, from which floated the faint fragrance of baked bread. Oil lamps hung from the rafters, suspended by silver chains – he had brought those back from the Avensis siege, fifteen years ago – and the heavy pine table and benches he and Fornyx had hammered together with much drunken profanity some decade before remained, darkened with age and use.

There were unfamiliar touches though: a new loom stood in the shadows of the north wall, and a bronze-hinged chest had replaced the old one he had stored his scrolls in for as many years as the house had stood.

And the people had changed also. Eunion came forward from his place by the fire, touching his fist to his chest. He rose more stiffly than Rictus remembered, and there was even less hair on his skull, but the lively intelligence in the dark eyes was the same.

"You are welcome home, master," he said, still using the term although Rictus had freed him many years ago.

"Are you well, Eunion?"

"As well as always, sir. The lady keeps the life in me."

The newcomers dumped their gear on the stone floor, unclipping the fastenings on their armour. Eunion took the black cuirasses from their backs one by one and set them reverently on the cross-shaped stands at the gable wall. The rest of their gear followed, until it seemed that there were two helmed and armoured men squatting in the shadows there, scarlet cloaks on their shoulders.

Aise had already disappeared out the back door and they could hear her clapping her hands for the slaves. Rictus thought to stop her – he wanted no fuss – but then thought better of it. It was her household, after all, and well over a year since he had been in it.

"Well, aren't you going to speak to me?" he asked the two slim, upright figures by the fire. "Don't you know me?"

"Always," one of them said, and then sprang forward into his arms. He spun her round, laughing, breathing her in, feeling the litheness of her youth against him, then set her down and stared at her.

"Gods above, Rian, you're taller still – will you never stop growing?"

"Not until I'm as tall as you," she retorted. "One day I'll look you in the eye."

"You always look me in the eye." He kissed her, cupping her face in his big, spear-calloused hands. She had his eyes – he had been told – and the thick black hair of her mother's youth. "How many summers are you now – thirteen?"

"Fourteen," she corrected him scornfully.

"I'll bet they've been trooping to the door in line to marry you," he said.

"Yes, but none of them are rich enough – and I want a man who can read!"

Both Rictus and Fornyx laughed.

Aise returned with the two household slaves, Garin, a stocky man in his thirties, and a girl, a new one Rictus had not seen before.

"Where did you get her?" he asked Aise, frowning. It was he who decided on the buying and the selling of the slaves, part of the duties of the master of the household. "What happened to Veria?"

"She fell pregnant by Garin here, and lost the child. After that she mooned around and was no good for anything, so I sold her. I bought this girl, Styra, in Hal Goshen, at the big market."

"Hal Goshen –" Rictus bit off his words, having seen Aise raise her chin in that combative way of hers, as though readying for a blow. Now was not the time.

He looked at Garin, who was busy stacking fresh wood and turf by the fire, but the man had his slave face on, stony blankness. He and Veria had been a couple, a unit that Rictus would not have broken. But even now, he was more sentimental about these things than Aise had ever been. It came from memories of his own loss, perhaps.

"Father, you haven't said anything to Ona," Rian said in a whisper, squeezing his hand.

"Yes, yes – come here girl, I won't bite you." Aise had soured his mood somewhat, and it showed in his voice. Ona approached him as a mouse might a hawk. He held out his hand to her – his other was still on his eldest daughter's waist.

"Ona? It's all right. Come here to me."

His youngest daughter had grown up also, into a freckle-faced child with hair the same shade as horse-chestnut and great green eyes. She was seven – no, eight years old now. Rictus gathered her into his free arm and pulled her close, remembering how she had ridden screaming with laughter on his shoulders the previous autumn, and the three of them had come home from the woods with a basket of mushrooms, and beech leaves in their hair. He held his daughters in the circle of his arms and felt Rian's breath on his neck, Ona's stubby hands gripping his arm, and it seemed to him only then that he had truly come home.

THERE WAS GOOD food laid out for them, despite the lateness of the hour. Garin built up the fire until it blazed like a lamp and the new slave, Styra, laid the table with the glazed plates Rictus and Fornyx had brought back from some long-ago coastal campaign, bright red earthenware decorated with dolphins and octopi.

There was barley bread and goat's cheese, black olives and green oil, and slivers of cured ham from the pig they had killed only the month before. Garlic dug up from the riverside, and purple onions to make the eyes water, and fresh thyme to scent it all. And wine, the thin yellow resin-flavoured wine of the highlands. Rictus and Fornyx fell on the food like starved dogs, and for a while the house was silent save for their grunts of appreciation, and the crackle of wood in the fire. At last, though, they were sated, and pushed back from the table with something between a grunt and a groan.

"Last year's wine, lady?" Fornyx asked.

Aise nodded. "We put by six amphorae, and five are still full. We don't drink wine much when the master of the house is away."

Rictus stood up from the table, stretching. He ruffled Rian's black hair as he passed her, and adjusted the midnight gleam of his cuirass where it was displayed on its stand at the eastern gable. He ran his fingers through the transverse horsehair crest of his helm, and touched the leather mid-grip of his spear.

For a while he stood there. Fornyx was coaxing Ona onto his knee – she had always been his favourite, perhaps because his own daughter had been russet-haired. Aise was clearing the table, and Eunion and the slaves had left for a last look in on the stock, what there was of it. The farmhouse was settling back into the interrupted routine of the night, having made space for Rictus and Fornyx within it.

"Where did you go this year, father?" Rian asked, joining him before the sombre panoply of his armour.

He remembered this summer's fighting, the endless marching through the dust, the incompetent wrangling of the men who were his employers. Blood blazing scarlet in the withered grass. A man with his guts spilled out, trying vainly to keep the flies off them. His men singing as they slew. Rictus closed his eyes for a second.

"It was nothing much. A lot of running around in the hills about Nemasis. Scarcely real soldiering at all."

"What about your men? Are they   are they all alive?"

"Not all of them, my honey. That is war; not everyone can come back from it. But we sang the Paean over the pyres of the dead, and gave the losers back their kin, and so settled the thing."

"And is Valerian all right?"

Rictus looked at her with eyes only half amused. "Valerian is all of a piece, the same as ever. Don't tell me you still carry a lamp for him, my girl?"

Rian blushed, and her face seemed to bloom like a flower. "I was curious, is all."

"Well, you may see him up close ere the winter comes. He and Kesero have promised to visit before the snow closes the passes."

"Really?" Her face lit up – a daisy touched by the sun. She reached up and put her arms about his neck and kissed his scarred chin.

"Really. Now get to bed, and take your sister with you. It's near the middle of the night."

"In the morning I'll show you a new cave where Eunion says the bears sleep."

"Yes, you do that – now off to bed."

OVER THE YEARS the farmhouse had been enlarged and extended. Once it had been no more than a long room with a rude firepit and a single crooked doorway covered by a flap of goatskin. That had been in the early days. Back then Rictus and Fornyx and Eunion had clinked up the walls themselves, stone by raw stone, and used willow withies to support a turf roof. Aise had cut the turves herself, handing them up to the men as they perched on the walls above.

That first winter had been so cold that all four of them had huddled under the sheepskins together at night, so close to the fire that the wool was singed black, and wolves had prowled and snuffled just outside the door.

Since then, the place had expanded with almost every year – near on twenty of them. And in that time, Rictus had fought in fifteen campaigns, missing all but a handful of summers and springs here.

Andunnon, he called this valley of his – *The Quiet Water* – for as the river curled round the glen bottom beyond the house, so it broadened in its bed and became a sleepier, brown thing with trout as tawny as freckles flitting shadowlike in the sunlit depths. It had also been the name of his childhood home, far north and east of here, near the burnt ruins of what had once been a city.

Now, Andunnon had blossomed from a single stone hut into a farm proper. They had cut back the brush and tamed the tangle of wild olive trees on the western slopes, planted vines to the east where the glen caught the best of the sun, and harvested barley in the flat rich soil of the valley floor. Bread, wine, and olives, the trinity of life, they had made here. And children, to carry that life on after them. It was more than Rictus had once ever dreamed of having. And it had cost no blood to build.

The farmhouse had annexes and extensions grafted onto it now: rooms for slaves and visitors, and for Fornyx, whose home this was also. It had become an ungainly, ill-planned sprawl of stone and turf and reed-thatch which nonetheless seemed as much part of the landscape as the river which bounded it. The farm had settled into the earth itself, part of the seasons as a man's hand is part of his arm. No matter how far Rictus marched, and how many men's eyes he took the light from, this, here, was where he belonged, and where his spirit found what peace his memories allowed.

Fornyx had staggered off to bed, the potent yellow wine singing in his head, and now Rictus joined Aise by the dying fire, the hounds lying sprawled and content at their feet. She had snuffed out the lamps, all save one cracked little clay bowl which would light their own way when they retired, and between its guttering light and the red glow of the sinking hearth she seemed almost youthful again, the lines hidden, the strong bones of her face brought out by the shadows.

Rictus could see Rian in that face, and Ona, and the boy who had been born between them and whose ashes were now in the earth and air of the valley itself. He reached out his hand and Aise looked at him with that guarded smile of hers and let him take her fingers in his own.

"Well, wife," Rictus said.

"Well, husband."

The wind was picking up outside, and Rictus knew from the whistle in the clay-chinked chimney that it was from the west, off the mountains. It would bring snow with it soon, perhaps even tonight. He almost started to ask Aise if the goats had been brought down to the lower pastures yet, but caught himself in time. She would have seen to it already, as she saw to everything while he was away.

"The sow had a litter of six," Aise said, withdrawing her hand. "We slaughtered two, sold the rest down in Onthere. We lost two kids to the vorine, but in the spring Eunion and Garin found a den north of Crag End hill, and killed the vixen and her cubs. There have been no more of them about since then."

Rictus nodded.

"We had a good pressing, a dozen jars. I made that olive paste you like, with the black vinegar from the lowlands – we got a skin of it when I sold the pigs."

"You should not have sold Veria," Rictus said quietly.

Aise's face did not change.

"She was discontented, harping on about her dead baby, and she was unsettling Garin with her keening."

"A dead child is no light thing," Rictus said, heat creeping into his voice. Aise seemed not to hear him.

"I had to go into the chest for gold to make up the difference, but Styra is a better prospect. She's young, she has good hips, and Garin will father a child on her soon enough." She paused. "Unless you would prefer to plough her furrow yourself."

Rictus looked at his wife in baffled anger, searching her face in the red firelight.

"I don't fuck my slaves, wife. It is something I have never done."

"I was your slave; you fucked me," Aise said coldly.

Something like a chill went down Rictus's back. They had gone straight back to the old caches of forgotten weapons stored in their hearts, and unearthed them all sharp and glittering again.

"It was different then – we were different. Gods below, woman, I will not go over this again the very night I appear back home. You are the stone I have built this life here upon. What's done is done."

"And through the year's campaigning, do you have some camp girl service you at the end of the day?"

"You know I do, on occasion – I'm a man. I have blood in my veins."

"When you left, you said it was a summer campaign, no more – and here you are with almost a year and a half gone by. You said it was over, Rictus. No more soldiering. You said you would put aside the scarlet and stay here with me."

"I know."

"We need no more money– we have everything here a man could want."

"Except a son," he snapped. And the instant he said it he could have slapped his own face. Such stupid warfare, as fruitless as the year's campaigning.

Aise stared into the fire, seeming somehow to wither before him, though she did not move.

"I should not have said that – I had no cause," he said, reaching for her hand again. She gave it, but it was limp in his fist; obedient, no more.

"Men want sons," Aise said lightly. "That is the way of life. It's how they make themselves remembered. A daughter leaves the house, and she becomes someone else's family. A son continues his own." She faced Rictus squarely, her face as blank as a blade. "You should take another wife."

"I have a wife."

"I'm past bearing children now, or as close as makes no matter. And you are no longer young either. If you want an heir you must father one on some decent woman – it would not do to have a slave as his mother."

"You were a slave once," Rictus reminded her sharply. "Do you think that matters to me, after all this time?"

She smiled, and in her face there was both bitterness and a peculiar kind of happiness, as if a memory had lit up her eyes.

"You freed me. You would have no other but me. I do not forget, Rictus. I will never forget that."

"Then let's go to bed," he said, tugging on her

hand like a child intent on its mother's attention. It was like pulling on the root of an oak.

"No; I will bide here awhile with the dogs. Go you to bed – there's a dish of water to wash in."

"There was a time when you would have washed me yourself, Aise, and I would return the favour."

"We are not youngsters, Rictus, coupling like dogs every chance we get."

"We're not dead yet, either," he snapped, and he rose, the anger flooding his face. He seized his wife by the arms and drew her to her feet. Her eyes met his, blank as slate. With something like a snarl he hoisted her into his arms and strode across the room, the dogs whimpering at the mood in the air. He kicked open the door that led to their bedroom – there was a single lamp left burning in it, and his muscles locked as he prepared to toss her onto the bed.

But he stopped, arms tight about her spare frame, she tense within the embrace as a man's face stiffens before a blow.

A neat, ordered space. She had laid out a fresh chiton for him, and the battered sandals he always wore about the farm. There were the year's last flowers, fresh-cut in a jar – the deep aquamarine jar he had brought all the way from Sinon, a lifetime ago – she had always treasured it, for the memory. Clean linen, a jug and ewer, all set out as she had set them out for him these twenty years and more, sometimes under a roof, sometimes under the ragged canvas of an army tent, and sometimes under nothing but the canopy of the stars. His anger drained away.

He laid her gently down on the willow-framed

bed, his face harsh and set. Then he kissed his wife on the forehead, her own features unreadable in the shadow he cast before the lamp. He stood over her a moment, a dark giant, an interloper filling the room with his bulk and the smell of the road, the stink of the army. Then he turned and left, closing the door behind him.

THAT FIRST NIGHT back in his home, Rictus slept on the floor before the dying fire, wrapped in his scarlet cloak with the dogs curled up around him for company.

TWO
THE GOAT AND HIS EAGLE

As Rictus had predicted, the snow came that night, drifting down soundlessly in the black hours. He rose well before dawn to poke the ashes of the fire into red warmth again and toss kindling upon the pulsing glow of the embers. The dogs rose beside him, stretching and yawning. Old Mij licked his face and would not leave him alone until he had had his ears well scratched, while Pira, the young bitch, rolled on the floor, arching her back like a cat.

He opened the door, shivering in his well-worn cloak, and in the pre-dawn dark the snow stretched grey and unbroken across the valley before him. Above the lip of the mountains red Haukos still sailed, but his brother Phobos had almost set.

Rictus crunched barefoot across the virgin snow, the dogs trotting after. In the blank whiteness only the river seemed dark, prattling noisily to itself.

Rictus's eye was caught by tracks in the snow – a hare, and heading down to the brim of the river was the spoor of an adventurous vole not yet ready for its winter sleep. The dogs snuffled along the riverbank, lapping at the water.

Rictus knelt beside them in the chill mud and dipped his hands in the flow, dashing the water about his head and neck. The bite of it made him gasp, but brought him fully awake.

When he returned, the household was coming to life. The fire was a yellow roar now, and Aise was tending a pot suspended above it; barley porridge, by the smell. The new slave, Styra, was bringing in more wood and Fornyx was sat at the kitchen table, last night's drinking dragging down his face.

"You're too damn sprightly looking," he told Rictus. "You don't drink enough – never did. Lady" – this to Aise – "Would there be any more of that fine yellow wine to chase down the humours?"

"Porridge will serve you better," Aise said, and clicked a bowl down in front of him.

"Where are the girls?" Rictus asked her. She did not look up from the pot as she replied.

"Out milking the yard-goats. They'll be in presently. Eat, husband, while there's heat in it."

He ate standing, out of long habit, scooping up the glutinous stuff with his fingers, until he caught Fornyx's meaningful look, and took a horn spoon off the table instead.

The girls came in with pails of warm goat's-milk, chattering like starlings, though Ona went wide-eyed and silent when she saw her father standing in his red warrior's cloak. Eunion was close behind them, wrapped in the greasy sheepskin he'd worn in cold weather since Rictus had first known him. All at once the kitchen was alive and crowded and noisy, the table framed by faces, the tick and clatter of earthenware. Fornyx joined in the morning banter with Rian as though he had never been away, and the dogs sat silently behind the two girls until their patience bore fruit in the form of bread crusts soaked in milk.

Rictus remained standing by the door, his spoon circling his empty bowl mechanically. He watched them without a word, like some guardian apparition, and felt an inexplicable ache near his heart. This was his family. He had brought it together, had made it himself. The girls were of his own blood, and the others were so bound to him by memories and the sharing of the years that they were as good as kin.

Why, then, did he sometimes feel that he was on the outside of it, looking in?

EUNION HAD BEEN a tutor of literature before Rictus and his men had defeated his city's army in battle. A tithe of the defeated citizen-soldiers had been sold into slavery as part of the negotiations which had concluded the war – some petty little affair away to the west of Machran – Rictus could no longer even remember the name of the city that had hired him to battle Eunion's people.

The defeated had drawn lots, to see who would be sold, and Eunion had simply been unlucky. He had a beautiful singer's voice, and he knew every ballad and lay of the western lowlands; for this, and his learning, Rictus had purchased him, to preserve him from the slave-agents who picked like crows in the aftermath of every battlefield. A simple decision, made on the whim of the moment. It had kept Eunion from the mines, and had gained for Rictus the friendship of an exceptional man, as upright and decent as it was possible to be in this fractured world.

Fornyx had taken scarlet with a brute mercenary centon while still little more than a boy. He had been badly used by them, made into a camp servant. Rictus's own centons had destroyed them in a hard, bitter fight near the Kuprian coast. It had been autumn, the campaigning season almost over, and the two little armies had fought in a rainstorm, churning the ground beneath their feet into a mire in which the wounded were trampled and suffocated.

When the battle was over, Rictus had discovered the boy Fornyx busily smashing out the brains of his own centurion with a stone. He had recognised the look in the boy's eyes – had seen it in the eyes of a host of others like him up and down the war-torn cities of the Harukush. Once, his own face had looked the same. So he recruited the undersized Fornyx into the ranks of his own centons, and in time the boy had become a man, and had proved more faithful than any hound, though possessed of an acerbic wit that could ignite men in a roar of laughter or set them at each other's throats in the time it took to drink a bowl of wine.

There had been a woman, in later years, and a daughter, but these had been killed by goatmen while travelling to join Fornyx here, at Andunnon. It was the only time Rictus had ever seen his friend weep, as they burned the pitiful remains of his family on a hasty pyre. After that, it was as though some light had gone out of him.

Not until both Rictus's own daughters had been born had Fornyx regained some of his old flash and fire, as though Rian and Ona were in some way a reparation for the wife and daughter he had lost. He had lived at Andunnon ever since – Aise had insisted. Fornyx was senior centurion of the Dogsheads, second in command. He was a natural leader, accustomed to commanding the most hard-bitten of men. But Rictus's daughters knew him as Uncle Fornyx, who brought them back trinkets from his travels and told them tall tales that made them squeal with laughter.

He was the closest thing to a brother that Rictus had ever known.

AND THEN THERE was Aise. Rictus watched her sit by the fire as was her wont, eyes softening as she listened to Fornyx elaborate on one of his preposterous yarns at the table, and the girls listened agog.

Aise was the spoils of war, a slave-girl given to Rictus in part-payment for a debt. He had been hired by a poor highland town to defend it through a long winter from the ambitions of its more prosperous neighbour. The job done, the town had little in the way of coin to pay with, and so had given over what it could – cattle, pig-iron, wine, and slaves.

The tall, beautiful dark-haired girl who carried herself like a queen had caught Rictus's eye at once, something the town elders had no doubt been counting upon. She was indeed a beauty, but it was not that which had drawn Rictus to her – he had seen beautiful slave-girls by the thousand in the course of his campaigns. No, it was the way she held herself, the stillness that seemed to be about her.

In the first few weeks of his ownership, Rictus had not even attempted to bed her. He had seen what rape did, and though there were many men who regarded it as simply a part of the process of warmaking, he hated it with a cold fury. He had killed his own men for it before now. Instead, he treated Aise with courtesy, almost as though she were his guest. He was not even sure why.

At least, it was not something he could have put into words that made sense – even to Fornyx. But it was around the campfires in those early days that he had looked at the faces about him: Fornyx, Eunion, and then Aise, and had come to realise he had found something rare here, or had a chance to. A kind of wholeness perhaps.

He was not without self-awareness; he knew, deep down, that he was trying to recreate the family he had once lost, years before in Isca's fall. But that did not mean he was wrong.

When he had first bedded Aise, it was because she had come to him of her own accord, and that had made her even more singular in his eyes. They joined together out of curiosity and a kind of mutual hunger. Perhaps she, too, had been trying to recreate something of a previous life, one she had lost forever.

Less than a month later, Rictus freed both Aise and Eunion, while Fornyx rolled his eyes and the other centurions took bets on how long the pair would stick around.

And that had been twenty years ago.

AISE LOOKED UP from her bowl at him. Her magnificent mane of hair was bound up tight at the back of her head, iron-grey right through now, and there were dark lines running from the corners of her nose. The shapeless long-hemmed chiton she wore made her almost sexless, and her hands were raw-knuckled and coarse with the work of a highland farm. But her eyes were the same, that sword-edge grey so rare in the lowlands. Like himself, she had the eyes of a highlander.

A bubble of laughter burst round the table, Eunion throwing back his head like a boy. Fornyx rose, wiping his mouth, the joke still in his eyes. "Ah, you're a whimsical lot, to see humour in the tale of my mishaps. Lady, I thank you for the food – I believe I'll go look upon the day outside, and perhaps add something to the flow of the river. Will you join me, brother?"

Rictus cast one more look at his wife, but she was clearing the table, issuing orders to the girls and to Eunion, calling for the slaves. The machinery of the farm was ticking smoothly. His return had barely made it pause.

"I'll join you. I'm not needed here." The flat ugly tone of his voice made Aise stop and look at him once more, but whatever she was thinking remained tucked out of sight behind her eyes.

The sun was up over the mountains now and the valley was a sharp-edged glare of white and blue. The dogs crunched through the thin snow-crust, sniffing at invisible trails of scent. Rictus stood beside Fornyx as the smaller man pissed into the river, eyes closed and smiling.

"Give her time," he said to Rictus, then walked upstream before kneeling in the snow to wash.

"Time for what – to begin missing me?"

"We were away a year – more than a year. She is mistress here, Rictus. Then you come home and throw things out of kilter. It'll take time, but you'll both come to it in the end – you always do." More quietly he said: "Every year the same."

"I heard that, you little squint."

"Well, good. Listen to yourself – fretful as a child. In three days Ona will have her arms around your neck, Aise will have a kiss for you morning and night, and Rian will still think her father a god among men."

"I'm a fool, perhaps, thinking of retiring, of staying here year round."

"You're a fool, certainly, but not because you lack the love of your family. You're a damn fool if you think you'll ever find it enough in life to herd goats and plant barley."

"It was good enough for my father, and he was Iscan."

"It's not Isca." Fornyx straightened, puffing. "Phobos, that water's cold! Rictus, that red cloak on your back is all you've ever known – Antimone's pity, you were the leader of the Ten Thousand! And for good or ill, you always will be. I'd bet you a year's pay that the next war you come to hear of, you'll be moist as a girl to get your legs around it."

"And what about you, you black-bearded little weasel – have you no hankering to settle yourself and –" He almost said it. *Watch your children grow up.* It was in the very air between them.

"If I have a home," Fornyx said, grave now, "then it is here. And the day you hang up the scarlet I will do the same. I would serve under no other but you."

"No-one else would have you."

Fornyx grinned. "Don't be too sure. To have been the Second of Rictus of Isca, that counts for a lot in this world." He hesitated.

"I do envy you, though."

"Envy me what?" Rictus asked. It is Aise, he thought. It has always been Aise. But Fornyx's next words surprised him.

"What you saw, in your youth. The places you marched, the world you wandered across. You were part of a legend, Rictus, and you saw sights few of the Macht have ever imagined. The land beyond the sea, and the Empire upon it. For all of us it is nothing more than a story, or the words in a song. But you were there. You fought at Kunaksa. You survived the charge of the Great King's cavalry, and the long march home. I would give anything to have been part of that."

"I've heard many men say the same thing, usually while drunk," Rictus said. "But never you."

"I thought I had too much sense. We know war,

you and I. So I know what it must have been like –
like some black dream of Phobos. But to have been
part of that, to make history – that would have been
something."

Rictus remembered.

The shattering heat of those endless days on the
Kunaksa hills, the stench of the bodies. The shrieking
agonies of the maimed horses. And the faces of
those who had shared it with him. Gasca, dead at
Irunshahr, not much more than an overgrown boy.
Jason, whom he had loved like a brother, who had
come through it all only to be knifed in a petty brawl
in Sinon, within sound of the sea.

The sea. How he had loved it, in his youth. And
he remembered the remnants of the Ten Thousand
shouting out in joy at the sight of it. That moment,
that bright flash of delight was carved in stone
within his heart.

"It was a long time ago," Rictus said, a thickness
to his voice. "Half a lifetime, almost. The march of
the Ten Thousand is nothing more now than an old
man's memory."

Fornyx spat into the river. "It's more than that,
and you know it. Just as you will always be more
than some highland farmer with a spear beside the
door. We trail our past with us wherever we go,
brother, especially those of us who wear the Black
Curse. It is what we are."

They stood side by side as the valley brightened
further around them and the birds in the hanging
woods above filled the air with song.

"It is what we are," Rictus agreed at last.

*   *   *

THE SNOW WAS a morning wonder which was gone by mid afternoon, save where the shadows of the trees protected pockets from the sun. That first day back, Rictus tramped the borders of his little kingdom with a hazel staff in his hand and a bronze knife in his belt to cut the bread and cheese and onion that Aise had packed for him.

He and Eunion and Rian trudged up the tawny hillsides to the open country beyond the woods, and there stood like royalty to survey the speckle of the goat-herd as the hardy animals ranged across the last of the year's good grass. Like everything else, the herd had grown while Rictus had been away.

The mismatched trio sat on the grass as the wind surfed it into waves around them, and as the time wound to noon they munched on red onions as if they were apples. The dogs lay to one side, bright-eyed and watchful, and Rian's chatter washed over Rictus half-heard, tugging his mouth into a smile now and again as he caught the gist of it. Chiefly, though, he sat enjoying the sound of his eldest daughter's voice, and he would now and again grasp her hand in the depths of the yellow upland grass, as if to make sure she were real.

Voluble though Rian was, it was from Eunion that Rictus received the clearest version of the year gone by. There was indeed a bear's den in the slopes of Crag-End hill, hidden in the brush and juniper that swamped the northern slope. Bears were semi-sacred to the Macht, respected for their strength and ferocity, but the occupant of this particular den was elusive and, for now at least, best left alone.

The vorine had hardly been seen in the valley since the killing of the vixen and her cubs, but wolves had been glimpsed in their place, scouting the hills. The bear would sleep through winter, but the wolves would not – something to be considered.

The billy goat, wise, wicked old Grenj, had had a fight with an eagle, a sight Eunion had never seen before nor heard tell of. Rian mimed the struggle as she described it like some tale out of legend: one hand the eagle, the other, valiant Grenj. Anyone else would have seen some portent in the goat's killing of the eagle, but to Eunion it was a fascinating natural phenomenon, something to be stored away and analysed. And as if summoned by the story, Grenj himself ambled past them amid his harem, with his regal spread of horns and cold yellow eyes. As good as a hound for protecting his own, Eunion said, though he was old now – another winter might see him done.

"When he is, we'll put his horns up here on a pole," Rictus said. "It's what they used to do around Isca when I was a boy. To keep his spirit here."

"He'll live for years and years," Rian protested. "He must, after such a feat."

"I hope he will," Rictus said, kissing the top of her head. "You're right – he deserves to."

"And your campaigning, master – how went that with the year?" Eunion asked. "It was Nemasis, was it not, that hired you?"

Eunion loved to hear of the goings-on in the wider world, and he was one of the few men who could dissect them with intelligence. Rictus looked down at Rian. She was sat, chin on knees, between them, rubbing Mij's belly with her bare toes. He caught Eunion's eye, and saw the apology in the older man's face.

"It was a protracted campaign," he said gruffly, and he set his hand on his daughter's nape as though to comfort her.

"There was little fighting – one or two clashes south-west of Machran. But they were stubborn, the Vengans. They have good land around that earth-walled city of theirs, and they would not admit defeat even when we drove them from the field. So it became a siege of sorts."

"A siege!" Rian exclaimed, as though this were some marvellous revelation.

"A rarity, in this age," Eunion said. He rasped one hard palm across the white bristles on his chin.

"A rarity, thank God. And in winter, too. We sat there all through the coldest months of the year, and ate the country bare all around while the Vengans sat in their city and starved. They made a sally at the turning of the year, and that was their mistake. We took the gatehouse, and then it was all over."

"And the terms?" Eunion always wanted to know. It came of his own fate in life, perhaps.

"What did you do to them?" Rian demanded. His own eyes, in his daughter's face, looking up at him.

"Well, the Nemasians had been made to freeze in camps half the winter instead of sitting at home with their wives, so they were not disposed to mercy."

Rictus was reluctant to say more. He had no wish to convey to his daughter, or to this good, gentle man beside her, the carnage and chaos that had concluded the campaign.

"Did Venga survive?" Eunion asked, tight-lipped.

"Yes. She lost most of her good land." And most of her sons and daughters, Rictus added to himself, thinking of the hopeless lines of shackled children filing up the roads towards the Machran slave-markets.

"Our own casualties were light, not above fifty for the whole episode."

"Fifty? That's nothing – you barely fought at all," Rian accused him.

"Hardly at all," Rictus agreed, though something in his face made Rian set a hand on his knee in obscure apology.

"And what news from Machran, master?" Eunion persisted. "We've been hearing stories down in Onthere and Hal Goshen, but they are so garbled as to be little better than myth. Have you heard any more about what is happening in the east?"

Rictus frowned, rubbing his right thigh just below the hem of his chiton. There was a pink scar there where a Vengan arrow, almost spent, had smacked into his flesh the year before. It had been a long time healing in the winter camps and it troubled him still when he sat awhile on the cold ground, as he did now.

The east, where this new thing had arisen, this prodigy. It was all anyone had ever asked him in his travels – what word of the east? What is he doing now? This apparition, this phoenix of war.

"It's hard to separate myth and fact when it comes to talking about the east," he said at last. "I know he is well inland from Idrios now, and I heard word that Gerrera and Maronen had fallen to him."

"It's true, then – he does head this way!" Rian exclaimed, and she lifted both her hands as though to catch a posy.

"If he has Maronen," Eunion said tersely, "then his next step must be Hal Goshen."

"That is my thinking also."

"Master, Hal Goshen is barely –"

"I know," Rictus said curtly.

"What does he want, father?" Rian asked.

Rictus shrugged. "Some say he aims at nothing more than overlordship of all the Macht cities. But that's absurd." He spoke over Rian's head, meeting Eunion eye to eye.

"When we were in Machran, Karnos was talking of invoking the terms of the Avennan League, and this time I think the core cities will respond. If that happens, Machran can field an allied army of maybe forty thousand, a force the like of which the Harukush has never seen before. This would-be conqueror cannot match that. He will see sense, and pull in his horns." He wanted Eunion to agree with him, to treat the thing as Rian had. But the old man would not oblige.

"Is it true what they say about him, that he is little more than a boy?" Rian asked, with a wide grin.

"He's young, by all accounts, but it would take more than a boy to do what he has done these last three years. He has a dozen cities under him now, and rules them as King in all but name."

Eunion nodded thoughtfully. "*Corvus*, he calls

himself. That's an old word indeed. I wonder how he dug it up. It denotes a black carrion bird, a raven or suchlike."

"It's what he's called. His true name, no-one knows, or he has not seen fit to tell it, at any rate. But whatever his name is, he has an army of twenty thousand in the field this year, and it swells with each fresh conquest. When he takes a city, his terms are so lenient that its citizens are almost glad to fight for him afterwards. He enslaves no-one; he confiscates no land or property. All he wants are men to hoist spear in his ranks, and coin to finance his campaigns. He makes war feed upon itself."

"I hear tell he reads like a scholar," Eunion said with a curiously wistful smile.

"I don't know about that. Folk say all manner of nonsense about him." Rictus stared at Eunion. From his daughter, he might have expected it, but it disappointed him to see the old man caught up in the stories, the weave of myth that was thickening about this Corvus. He had experienced something like it in his own life, and knew how baseness could squat behind a legend. "I've also heard that he grows wings by moonlight, that he is the son of Phobos himself, that he's not even one of the Macht, but some kind of demigod. You of all people, Eunion, should not believe all you hear."

The old man smiled again.

"I know, master. But sometimes men need the stories." He set a hand on Rian's head. "We all do. It is what set us apart from the beasts."

They felt his anger. Rian shrank from him towards

Eunion, which made him angrier still. In silence, the three stared across the foothills to where the dark forests ended at the hem of the mountains in the north and west. Last night's snow lay on the peaks; they were white as a dream of winter.

"I've always scoffed at signs and portents, not thinking them worth a rational man's time," Eunion said, "but were I a peasant from the hills –"

"A strawhead?" Rictus asked, mocking, bitter even.

Eunion inclined his own bald pate. "That is a word I've not heard for a long time, living up here. But, if you like. If I were an uneducated highlander, I might read something into old Grenj's defeat of the eagle."

"And what would that be?" Rictus asked, frowning again.

"The upset of normal things. Something new in the wind – a change for us. For all of us. For all the Macht."

"You read a lot into a goat's good luck," Rictus said coldly. He did not like to hear Eunion talk like this.

"Forgive me, master. This boy conqueror, this... phenomenon. I don't think he is going to leave the world without making a mark on it much larger than the one he has henceforth. And if I read you rightly, you believe the same. Fornyx let slip you are thinking of hanging up the scarlet. Is it true?"

Rian's face upraised to him, open and delighted. "Father! Is it?"

"Eunion, you leap like one of these damn goats from one subject to another."

"I think not. I think there is a connection there."

Rictus said nothing for a long time. He bit into his

onion, the crisp sting of it flooding his mouth, and then chased it down with a lump of creamy goat's cheese.

"This Corvus is making war on us," he said. "And it is a war like we haven't seen before; he does things so differently. Do you know he has cavalry in his army – not as scouts or foragers, but as part of the main battle line? He is, as you say, a phenomenon."

Rictus breathed in deep, smelling the tang of the pines on the wind, the close-to smells of goat and onion and the wool and sweat of his own body and those beside him. The grain of the world itself, this quiet emptiness of the highlands. A place apart, it had always seemed to him, beyond the concerns and confines of the lowland plains, the cities, the politicking of men.

He set one arm about Rian's shoulders, and brought her tight to him, until he could smell the lavender and thyme that Aise always layered in the clothes chests.

"Father –"

"I've been a soldier all my life, Eunion. I've carried the Curse of God near a quarter-century and I have seen men kill one another in every manner in which the act can be conceived. It is part of life.

"For me, it has been a trade, a calling for which I find I have an aptitude, as other men can make music or build with stone and marble. I accept that. I have carved my life around it. But there is something else in the wind now. Things are going to change.

"I think that to carry a spear in the times to come is to fight in a war without end."

He bent his head, and kissed his daughter's black hair.

THREE
FIRE IN THE NIGHT

AUTUMN BIT DEEPER. Walking in the woods was like strolling through a blizzard of dry, copper-coloured leaves, rattling in the wind, circling and twining in fathomless dances. The earth itself was growing colder under their feet, whilst the sky was a tumble of pouring cloud, light and shadow chasing across it in endless patterns, following the sunset.

Aise had grown thinner. In Rictus's arms she felt light and spare and angled with bones, her skin white as ivory where the sun never saw it.

She had always been a modest woman, something Rictus knew to be rare in those blessed with a face and form such as had graced her youth. His second night home she took him by the hand and led him to their bed without a word, and they joined within it like two polite strangers, until at last she seemed to come to life under him with grudging moans, and her hands pulled him deeper into her. When he was spent, they lay in the dark of the wind-wreathed room and their faces were so close that he felt her lashes brush his cheek as her eyes opened in the darkness. Her fingers ran down his flank, as though reacquainting themselves.

"What was this?" she asked as she settled on a ridge of scar. "It's new."

He frowned. "I don't remember. A knife, I think. It was nothing."

She found the arrow-pock on his thigh, and her fingers circled it gently. "So many wounds."

"War's accounting," Rictus said. He lifted himself off her with some reluctance and they lay side by side in the bed. "I have always been lucky that way. Antimone has spared me."

"Or Phobos," Aise said. "They say the god of fear looks after those who do his work in the world."

Rictus set a hand on her flat belly, as taut as a girl's despite the three children who had bloomed within it. "Is that what you think of me, Aise, after all this time?"

"I know that when I see you in that black armour and the red cloak, with the helm hiding your face, I am afraid. There is something in your eyes, Rictus. Perhaps it is what has made you what you are. It changes only when you look upon Rian."

Rictus took his hand away from her warmth and knuckled his eyes. "You and Fornyx. Sometimes I wonder if either of you know me at all."

She raised herself on one elbow and moved closer to him once more, until they were skin to skin, and the wetness at the crux of her thighs was leaking onto his hip. Even in the dark, he knew she was smiling down at him.

"Perhaps, husband, we know you better than you know yourself."

Her mouth sought his, hungry now. She straddled him with sudden energy, and their second coupling had real joy in it, like some flash of memory, a moment from the past when she had more flesh on her bones, and he fewer scars on his.

THUS, DAY BY day, his other life claimed him, and Rictus's spirit began to attune itself to the quiet routine of the farm.

He and Fornyx chopped wood until their palms blistered, beat the last of the hazelnuts off the trees with long staves whilst the girls ran squealing around them, trying to catch them in withy baskets, and dug in the hard clay plot beside the house for beet and turnip. They threw themselves into the work of the farm with such gusto that Aise complained the slaves were becoming lazy, but Rictus loved to come back into the house at dusk, stiff and filthy with the day's labour, to find the fire blazing and the girls at the table and Aise baking flatbread on the griddle. He would seize his wife into his arms and kiss shut her protesting mouth until she put her flour-whitened hands on his shoulders to push him away.

More often than not Rictus and Fornyx would have wine after dinner, and Eunion would sing a song of his youth, or go over some past campaign from history that the two men had never heard of.

He had taught Rian to read, and was now doing the same for Ona, so every evening after they had eaten there would be his low singer's voice in a murmur with Rictus's youngest daughter, the two of them heads together in a corner with a single lamp, puzzling out the words on a scroll.

And then there would be bed, Aise and Rictus always the last to go. Sometimes Rictus held back to stand at the beehive hearth alone in the last red light of the fire, savouring the warmth of the flagstones under his bare feet, the smell of bread and wet dogs, the creaking of the roof beams over his head as the wind rushed down from the mountains to stir the thatch. On still nights he could hear the river trundling endlessly in its bed, and owls calling from the woods on the valley sides.

He did not think often of the gods as a rule, except when going into battle, but there were times when he stood there in the quiet house with all the people he loved most in the world sleeping about him within the broad stone walls, and he would raise his head to quietly thank Antimone, goddess of pity, for allowing him this.

He did not think on Antimone's other face, or dwell upon the fact that when she donned her Veil, she was also the goddess of death.

THE FIRST REAL snows came, knee-deep in the space of a night, and along the margins of the river the ice fanned out in brilliant gem-bright pancakes. The goats were now down in the valley itself, Fornyx,

Eunion and Garin herding them from the high pastures while the dogs trotted on the flanks of the flock and sniffed at wolf-tracks in the snow.

Now the wolf-watch would have to begin, the menfolk of the farm taking it in turns to stay out at nights beside the flock, huddled by a fire in the lean-to on the western valley slope with the dogs for company.

Rictus and Fornyx took the first night's watch together, for while bringing the goats down from the highland pasture, Fornyx had found the tracks of an entire pack quartering the hills, and the tracks led south. So the two men set by a store of wood in the lean-to during the day and as darkness fell they donned their old scarlet cloaks, took up their spears and shouldered a skin of wine against the bitterness of the night. Rian's demand to come along was firmly rebuffed, and Rictus kissed his womenfolk one by one before shutting the farmhouse door on them and standing by Fornyx's side in the chill darkness underneath the stars.

"You have the most stupid grin on your face," Fornyx said. "I can see it even in the dark. Didn't I tell you how they would come round?"

"You're short and ugly," Rictus retorted, "but do you hear me bring it up? Come on, dogs."

They crunched through the frozen snow, the two hounds padding beside them, transformed into lean, predatory shadows in the starlight. Once, Rictus held up a hand and they both paused to listen. The half-frozen river had been muffled and there was barely a breath of air moving in the valley. They could hear the creaking of their own bones, and the soft rush of blood in their throats as their hearts beat, like the sound of a panting dog.

There it was, far off: the faint sad song of the wolf. The hounds beside the two men growled, low in their chests.

"A bad sign, so early in the year," Fornyx said in an undertone.

"Mark of a hard winter to come, my father always said. Phobos, it's a heavy frost falling. Let's get that damned fire lit before our feet freeze to the ground."

They trekked through the brittle snow to the shelter and Fornyx set about lighting the fire; he was far and away the best of them with flint and tinder. The goats – twitchy, fey creatures up on the high pastures – seemed here almost pathetically glad to see their masters, and the flock gathered in front of the hut, a dark blot on the snow. Soon the firelight picked out the ranks of the nearest, and their cold eyes reflected the flames at the men and dogs in the lean-to.

Fornyx stood stamping his feet up and down in front of the fire. He and Rictus had stuffed their sandals with rabbit's fur, which was singed by the flames as they stood there, an acrid, campaigning smell.

"You think the passes are still open?" Fornyx asked.

Rictus cocked his head to one side. "Maybe. It'll be worse up there on the high ridge. It depends which way the wind blows the drifts."

"I'll bet Valerian and Kesero are still down at the sea in Hal Goshen, in some tavern with their bellies full of cheap wine and their laps full of some cheap tart's arse."

Rictus smiled. "If they've any sense."

"You know that Valerian and Rian –"

"I know. I'm not blind."

"She's of an age now, Rictus, and Valerian's a good man, for all his antics."

Rictus opened his hands out to the firelight with a curt nod. "I know Valerian's worth, as well as anyone."

"But –"

"But he wears the scarlet."

"He doesn't have to wear it all his life."

"He won't be wearing it if he wants to marry Rian. I would not have her live the life her mother has led."

"You have given Aise a good life, Rictus," Fornyx said quietly.

"It would have been better, were I a man like my father was."

Fornyx threw up his hands. He knew better than to pursue a matter once Rictus had invoked his father's memory. "Reach me the wineskin, will you?"

They sat out the night, taking it in turns to doze once the middle part of it was past. They talked desultorily of old battles, old comrades, and the attractions of various women they had known. They hardly noticed when the snow began to fall again, a grey veil beyond the firelight that paled the sleeping goats and brought into the valley an absolute hush, as though the world was awake and aware, but waiting breathlessly for some happening.

The fire died down, and in the snowbound silence they heard again the high, distant call of the wolf.

The goats stirred uneasily at the sound, dislodging snow from their backs so they became piebald. Now that the flames were low, Rictus and Fornyx could see how bright was the light from the two moons. Cold Phobos, his face as pale as pewter, and warm Haukos his younger brother, whose light tinged the snow with a pink like watered wine. Both moons were full in the sky, and around them the ice crystals in the air arced in a double halo of rainbow light.

"Fear and Hope, both full in the sky together. It's an omen, Rictus," Fornyx murmured. They were both staring aloft, spellbound.

"I don't believe in them," Rictus growled, but he, too caught some of the sense of wonder, a feeling that they were standing on the threshold of some change in the world.

"I've seen it maybe four times in my life, and every time it was on the cusp of new things."

"Ach –" Half angry, Rictus turned away. He hated talk of omens and portents. His life had leached all sense of the numinous out of him. He believed in what his hands could do and his eyes could see, and though he invoked the gods in prayer and thanks it was as much a reflex as anything else, a grace-note. He did not believe –

"Fornyx – look there, on the ridge to the south. Do you see it?" He crunched out of the last dimming glow of the firelight and stared across the fields of snow to the dark woods of the hills above, and beyond them, the high ridge which marked the entrance to the valley, maybe six pasangs away. There in the moon-drenched dark was the light of a single fire, as steady as a candle-flame in a glass lantern.

"I see it." Fornyx joined him, shivering. "It's a campfire, up on the side of the ridge. They must be deep in the drifts up there, whoever they are."

"Valerian? Kesero?"

"Too close. They know this valley – for the sake of six pasangs they'd have marched through the night, knowing a warm bed was here waiting for them. Whoever is up there, Rictus, does not know Andunnon."

BEFORE THE SUN came up, Rictus and Fornyx were back in the farmhouse. The rest of the family rose to gape as the two men methodically armed one another, hauling on the black cuirasses which were Antimone's ageless gift to the Macht, belting on their swords and strapping bronze greaves to their shins. The girls clustered around their mother, round-eyed, and Eunion, after a moment's shock, unearthed his own hunting spear. Rictus saw this and held up a hand.

"No, no my friend. You stay here."

"What is it, Rictus?" Aise asked calmly, her arms around Ona's shoulders, her face white and fixed as a statue's.

"It may be nothing. Fornyx, tie up that damned loose strap at my back, will you?" The two men checked one another over, tugging on straps, tightening buckles.

"Shields?" Fornyx asked.

"And helms. We may as well look the part."

Ona began to cry.

Within minutes, the Rictus and Fornyx of the farm had vanished. In their place now stood two heavily armoured mercenaries, their eyes mere glitters in the T-slits of their helms, the scarlet cloaks of their calling on their shoulders, shields on their left arms, spears at their right. They had become men of Phobos, the god of fear.

"Stay in the house," Rictus told the others. "If we're not back by mid-morning, pack some things and head for the north, up in the hills. Make for the old shepherd's bothy on the high pastures. This may all be for nothing, so do no thing that cannot be undone." He caught Eunion's eye. "Keep them safe, you and Garin, until we return."

Eunion nodded, swallowing convulsively.

Rictus stared at Aise, then Rian, a blank mask, unknowable. The face of death. Without another word, he ducked out of the house, and Fornyx followed him.

THEY COULD SMELL woodsmoke on the still air, the only smell in the white snow-girt morning. Without speaking, they trudged uphill into the woods, shields slung on their backs, spears at the trail.

After two pasangs they doffed their helms and halted to listen. The snow had stilled the woods, the birds, the river itself. The trees were silent and listening with them. A cock pheasant creaked and coughed away to the west, the sound carrying like a shout.

And then the other sound. Men's voices, and something large making its way through the snow and the brush above them.

"I count four, or could be five," Fornyx said.

"Five," Rictus said. "And at least two horses."

"We should have javelins, or a bow."

Rictus smiled with sour humour. "We wear the red cloak and the Curse of God. They'll piss down their legs at the very sight of us. Helm up, brother, and guard my left – you're quicker on your feet than I am."

"Every time you say that. Just once, couldn't I –"

"Fornyx." This last came out of Rictus's mouth in a whispered hiss. Fornyx grimaced, ducked behind a tree and donned his helm. The two men nodded silently at one another, grasping their spears at the mid-point.

They could make out men talking now, strange accents, a bark of laughter, and the truckle of air through a horse's nose. The trail down the hillside was buried in snow, but still made a clear way through the trees, a white ribbon uncoiling across the slopes of the forest.

Up close now. They could smell the sweat of the horses.

Again, the cock-pheasant rasped, as though counting down the moments. Behind his tree, Rictus breathed deep and even, as his father had taught him in boyhood, as he had in turn taught so many men who had fought under him.

The spear-grip in his hand was more familiar to him than the feel of his wife's breast. The black cuirass was feather-light on his back. The world was a bright slot of light. He had known these sensations all his life. They were what his life was about. They were what made him alive.

He stepped out from behind the tree.

THAT FIRST MOMENT, counting bodies. How they are standing, what is in their hands, what they are wearing – the weak points. Who is the leader? Deal with him first.

They were soldiers, all of them. He saw that at once, despite the dun-coloured cloaks, the winter-gear. They had swords – the heavy curved *drepana* of the lowland cities – hung at their hips, and from the pommel of the nearest horse hung three bronze helms, like outsized onions. But no red cloaks on display – they were not mercenaries.

The men froze as Rictus and Fornyx materialized in front of them, gleaming faceless statues of ebony and scarlet, spears held easily at the shoulder. Rictus's eyes flicked back and forth within the helm-slot. He breathed out a little, relaxing somewhat, looking at the deeds and intentions of their eyes. No need for death, not right away.

"Good morning, lads," he called out, the bronze robbing his voice of tone and warmth. "What's up here for you in the snow and the hills this time of year?"

One of the men edged closer to the lead pack-horse, where a bundle of javelins was slung. Rictus stepped forward two paces and levelled the aichme of his spear at the man's throat.

"You'll not be needing those, friend. Not today."

A black-bearded man held up his hands in the air.

He had a broad, likeable face which was at once good-humoured and sinister. He might have been Fornyx's younger brother.

"The Curse of God, here in the middle of nothing and nowhere – now there's a prodigy! Lower your spear, brother. We mean you no harm. We are merely travellers, on our way to better things,"

Rictus cocked his head, the spear stone-steady in his fist. He was aware of Fornyx at his left, breathing quiet clouds of breath into the still air. No-one else was stirring – they had sense enough for that, at any rate. One brisk movement would resolve the morning in carnage, and they knew it.

"Who are you?" Rictus asked the dark-bearded man.

The man bowed his head, grinning. "I am Druze, and these are my friends, my comrades in arms Grakos, Gabinius, and a couple of other rascals. We were seeking the quickest way to Hal Goshen and seemed to have gotten ourselves turned around in the night. Our apologies if we have trespassed upon your ground. We mean no harm. We may take a rabbit or two out of your woods, but that's all."

He was lying. The straight road to Hal Goshen lay up along the ridge, impossible to miss. Only an imbecile could wander off it, and this man was no fool. Rictus knew that just by the sloe-black twinkle in his eyes. He was not afraid, either, or even apprehensive. That was worrying.

One of the man's friends trudged down the slope from the rear of the party, also holding up empty palms. This was a smaller fellow, and slender. He wore the short woollen chlamys of the mountain folk, with the hood pulled up so his face was hard to make out except for a bright gleam of the eyes as the sun caught them in passing.

"Perhaps you would like us to turn back," he said, setting a hand on Druze's shoulder. The nails had been painted scarlet some time ago, but the paint had worn and flecked. He looked as though he had been scrabbling in blood.

"If you do, then I cannot see us arguing with two men such as yourselves. Even the five of us are no match for two Cursebearers. So consider yourselves the victors." A smile under the hood. "There is no need for blood to be splashed on such a bright morning."

"Agreed. Turn back out of this valley, and we will part in amity," Rictus said. He lowered his spear but kept his left shoulder towards the strangers, the shield covering him.

"So be it," the small man said. "Though, if I could, I would like to know the names of those who turn us back on our tracks."

"You think me a fool?" Rictus asked lightly. They were all young, these five men, and the speaker perhaps the youngest of them all, yet their gear had seen much service, and they stood with the easy, yet alert poise of trained soldiers. These were no mere citizens. Something about all this was wrong.

"I hear tell that Rictus of Isca lives in this glen," the hooded youth said. "He's a much storied man, and a Cursebearer to boot. If I were to encounter him, I'd like to know I had, just for the telling of the tale later."

"Cursebearers do not just spring up out of the ground, especially so high and far from civilized life," Druze added, spreading his hands like a reasonable man. "You cannot blame us for being curious."

"Perhaps Rictus prefers to keep himself to himself," Fornyx said.

"He has every right to do so," the hooded man replied. "Believe us when I say we wish him no ill. I have been reading stories of the Ten Thousand since I was a boy. It would be a banner-day in my life, were I to meet their leader face to face."

He raised his head, and for the first time looked Rictus eye to eye. "You have my word on that."

His face was pale, and there was something odd about his eyes. But before Rictus could quite grasp it, the youth had lowered his gaze again.

"Phobos," Fornyx cursed.

"Go left," Rictus murmured out of the corner of his mouth. These young men were not going to back down. The morning was going to end in blood after all.

Louder, Rictus said; "Leave now. No more questions, no more talk. Leave, or die here." Both he and Fornyx raised their spearheads to throat height and assumed attack stances.

Not one of the men moved. The hooded youth sighed, reached into his sleeve and brought forth a cheap wooden flute, the kind soldiers whittle for themselves in their encampments.

"I will not fight you, Rictus," he said calmly – he was too calm. Even as Rictus and Fornyx advanced, neither he nor any of his men stirred, but the youth put the flute to his lips – they were as red as a girl's –

and played a shrill melody, a fragment of a marching tune Rictus had heard half a hundred times before.

And instantly, the forest came to life all around them.

Men rose up out of the snow, from behind trees, out of the brush. They had been lying under white cloaks, hiding in the thickets. Their appearance set the woods alive with frightened birds.

In a moment, Rictus and Fornyx were surrounded by dozens, scores of armed soldiers, blue-faced with cold. Some had bows, others javelins, and yet more unsheathed their drepanas so that cold iron glittered in the snow-brightness.

They stood silent and watching, like legendary warriors brought to magic life out of the very soil of the earth.

"Damn," Fornyx said. "The little bastard."

There was the white, draining shock of it, the knowledge it was all over, his whole life finished at last.

So this is how it ends, Rictus thought. For me, for Fornyx, for all of us. He thought of Aise and the girls, and what would happen to them now, and he fought down the automatic impulse to charge, to skewer this flute-playing boy and drown him in his own blood. He had to buy time.

"Stack arms," he said to Fornyx.

"My arse," his friend snapped, wide-eyed with fury behind his helm.

"Do it, Fornyx."

The two men stabbed their spears butt-first into the ground so that the sauroters buried themselves. His right hand free, Rictus took off his helm, and the cold air bit his face.

"You have us at a disadvantage," he said to the flute-player. "And you have my name right. I am Rictus, and this here is my second, Fornyx." He looked about himself, heart thundering, face stiff with the effort to keep it impassive. But he managed a little flourish of contempt.

"You think you brought enough men?"

The youth reached up and threw back his hood. He was smiling. He walked down the slope as though descending the steps of a palace, until he stood so close that Rictus could have reached out and set both hands about his throat.

His eyes were weirdly pale, a shade of violet that did not seem quite natural. He had black hair past his shoulders, as gleaming black as a raven's wing, and his white skin had a sheen of gold about it.

He was as beautiful as a maiden, but had the scar of an old sword-stroke at the corner of his left eye.

"I have wanted to meet you for a long time, Rictus of Isca," he said.

"I am called Corvus."

FOUR
MEN OF PHOBOS

It is a fine line, sometimes, Rictus thought, between guest and hostage. The key to it is left unspoken, buried in courtesies. The fist inside the glove.

They were escorted back down into the glen of Andunnon as though the men about them were for their own protection, and the strange youth who called himself Corvus walked beside them, as though he were a friend of theirs. Some of his companions relieved Rictus and Fornyx of the weight of their shields, helms and spears, but they were allowed to keep their swords. Courtesy.

"This is a beautiful place," Corvus said, as the woods thinned and the column came out into the open sunlight of the valley bottom. "A man could be happy here. I do not wonder that you wanted to keep your home a secret, Rictus."

"I am curious as to how I failed in that regard,"

Rictus said tartly.

The youth nodded. "There's a lot to be said between us. I hope you will perhaps count me a guest here and not an intruder. It is no part of my intent to harm you or your family."

"If talk were commerce, all men would be rich," Fornyx said, and spat into the snow. "A guest does not bring a full centon of warriors to test his host's hospitality."

"If I had brought any fewer, you would both have fought me," Corvus said, holding up one long-fingered hand as though to catch something. "I had to take away hope of winning to make you listen to what I have to say."

"They're a patient bunch," Rictus said, gesturing to the ranks of soldiers who marched on all sides. "How long were they buried in the woods?"

"They are my Igranians," Corvus said. "From Igranon in the high eastern Harukush. It's so cold up there they think this is a mild spring in comparison. They are my light troops, my foot cavalry. Druze is their chieftain, and one of my marshals."

"I hope they brought their own bread," Fornyx drawled. His tone was mocking, insolent, but his face was white and drawn as a fever-victim, and his fist was knotted on the hilt of his sword.

"In this valley, my hounds stay on the leash," Corvus said gravely.

THEY MADE GOOD time. As the column approached the farm, they saw that Aise and Eunion had not yet left. Garin and Styra were in the front yard packing up bedrolls. The two shrank together as the long line of armed men came into view and began splashing across the shallows of the river. Then they bolted like hares, sprinting for the north. Corvus swept an arm forward and at once the dark smiling fellow Druze led off some two dozen of his men at a run. They skeined out into two lines that flanked the farmhouse and surrounded it. The two fleeing slaves were tripped up, pinioned, and prodded back down the valley towards the house. Rictus and Fornyx looked at one another. These Igranians' discipline was almost as good as that of the Dogsheads. High mountain tribesmen they might be, but they had been well-drilled.

The main body of the centon halted short of the farmyard and stood there in rough ranks. Corvus turned to Rictus.

"Call to your family. Tell them there is no need for alarm. I've brought good food and wine on the horses – if you will permit me, Rictus, I would like to dine with you this morning." The sun caught him full in the face; his skin seemed more colourless than ever, and his eyes were as pale as tinted glass.

THE HOUSE WAS in disarray, blankets, pots and lamps all askew, things strewn over the floor in the panic of packing. It was dark inside as they entered – the fire had gone out – and Aise, Eunion and the children were in a huddle at the far wall. Eunion had his old boar spear levelled, and Aise was clutching a hatchet.

"Wife," Rictus said, his voice harsh, "get the fire lit, and clean up this mess. We have guests." A cup broke under his foot as he strode over to them. He set a hand on Ona's head and touched Aise's shoulder. Softly, he said, "This is not what you think." He wiped a tear from Rian's cheek, her face white and defiant in the gloom.

"Father, are they here to kill you?"

"They're here to talk, my honey. And we must be clever about this. Set the table and light the lamps." To Aise he said nothing, but they gripped each other's hands bone-tight for a long moment.

"Do as your father says," Aise said at last, her voice as hoarse as a crow's. Her gaze did not leave Rictus's face. "He knows best. We are in his hands."

Outside again, Rictus spoke to Corvus and his waiting men. "You might want to give them a moment. They've had an unsettling morning."

"My apologies," Corvus said, grimacing. "Grakos, unload the horses. Druze, the men may stand easy and break out their food. Then you will accompany me inside, as soon as Rictus here is willing to extend an invitation." He bowed slightly to Rictus.

He had old-fashioned manners, a kind of courtesy that Rictus had not seen for a long time, as though he had stepped out of an earlier age. His accent was strange also. Rictus had heard Machtic spoken by men from every corner of the Harukush, and a few from beyond it, but he could not place this Corvus at all.

"What is this, some kind of game?" Fornyx demanded. "We are your prisoners – what's all this talk of invitations?"

"I mean everything I say," Corvus said mildly. "If Rictus does not wish us to enter his house, then we will remain outside. It'll be colder, mind."

Fornyx shook his head, torn between anger and sheer bafflement.

"I'm willing to let you in," Rictus said, with the ghost of a smile. "My wife may have other ideas though." Despite himself, he was beginning to believe that this strange young man meant what he said.

"We've brought good wine, Minerian from the western coast," Druze said. "Inside or out, it'll still taste better than anything you can drink within a hundred pasangs."

"Minerian? You hear that Rictus?" Fornyx said. "If we're to die, at least our bellies will be thanking us."

"Let us not talk of death today," Corvus said, and a coldness came into his pale eyes. For a moment he seemed a much older man.

AISE DID WELL. She had always been good at bringing order out of chaos, and she had never been anything other than level-headed even in the most brutish moments of their life together. When Rictus finally, formally invited Corvus and his companion Druze into the farmhouse, the place was as neat and ordered as if this were any other morning of the year. The fire was a yellow blaze in the hearth, and the good lamps had been hung from the ceiling beams and were burning sweetly. There was food and wine on the table, and the two dogs were being held back in the corner by Eunion. Their low sing-song growling was the only discordant note in the proceedings.

Aise came forward bearing a dish of salt. She had piled her hair up on her head and was wearing the sleeveless scarlet chiton Rictus had bought her one drunken night long ago, when they had both been young and full of fire. Her eyes were made up with kohl and stibium; it recalled something of her old, heart-stopping beauty, and it brought Corvus and Druze up short. Corvus bowed to her as though she were a queen, lifted a pinch of salt to his lips and said, "Antimone's blessings on you and your house, lady."

"You are most welcome," Aise said, and Rictus loved her in that moment for the pride and the courage of what she had done. If they were all to die today, then he was glad he had seen her like this one last time.

"You must be seated – I have –" but Aise trailed off. Corvus had gone straight to the corner and had knelt down in front of the dogs.

"What beauties what these are. Release them, friend. They have no quarrel with me." Startled, Eunion let go his grip on the hounds' collars and they sprang forward, sniffing, growling, baring their teeth and licking Corvus's face, alternately. He laughed, sounding like a little boy as he played with their ears and scratched their flanks. Old Mij rolled over like a puppy, tongue lolling.

Rictus caught Druze's eye and the black-bearded man shrugged with a wry smile. "Dogs, horses, he has a way with them."

"And men?" Fornyx asked.

"You'll find out. It's what we're here for."

Corvus rose, the hounds dancing around him as though he was their long-lost master. "Forgive me, Rictus. I have not yet met the rest of your family."

Ona stared at him silently, sucking her thumb – she had not done that for years. Rian, in her pale, defiant pride, looked every inch a younger version of her mother – a woman, no longer a girl – and Rictus felt a jolt of pure fear as Corvus took her hand and kissed it.

"Your household is filled with beauty," he said to Rictus, his gaze still fixed on Rian. "You are a fortunate man. Druze, the gifts."

Druze set a skin of wine on the table, and then a net of oranges and fat lemons from the far eastern coast.

"Let's eat," Corvus said briskly.

IT WAS PERHAPS the strangest meal Rictus had ever shared. They sat about the long pine table and passed the dishes up and down it to one another in perfect amity, as though there were not a hundred soldiers squatting outside, as though Corvus was a family friend who had chanced by.

Rictus and Fornyx sat in their black cuirasses, which lent a certain sombre glory to the proceedings, and Druze poured them all cups of the good Minerian as though he were the master of ceremonies. There was little in the way of talk, until Rian, having ripped her bread to shreds on her plate, said; "Are you really him? The Corvus we hear about, the man from the east?"

"I am he," Corvus said, sipping his wine.

"How do we know that? You don't look like him – you could be some bandit who's trading on his name," Rian said defiantly.

Corvus looked at her. His red-lipped smile was like a scar across his face. "What does he look like, this Corvus you've heard about?"

"He's – he's tall, for one thing. And he rides horses, I hear tell, and leads an army of thousands, not some mountain band of brigands."

Corvus set a hand on Druze's shoulder. "I would not call my Igranians brigands, lady. At least, not any more." The two men grinned at one another. Druze leaned across the table, black eyes shining. In a mock whisper he said, "We were once, it's true – it is in our blood. But things are different now. There's no money in banditry anymore." And he laughed as if at some private joke.

"You're too young to be the man in the stories," Rian persisted.

Corvus shrugged. "Ask your father about the truthfulness of stories. The farther the truth travels, the less it becomes the truth. That's the way of the world. I was brought up with tales of the Ten Thousand and Rictus of Isca who brought them home from the land beyond the sea. He was a hero, a giant of myth to me – when I was a boy. But your father is a real person, one solitary man who sits here drinking wine with us. Every legend begins with the ordinary and the everyday, as the acorn begets the oak."

"You're too short!" Rian exclaimed, colour rising up her face. Aise set a hand on her arm. "Enough, daughter. You will eat in silence now."

Corvus seemed to have taken no offence. "My mother was a wise woman, like yours," he said. "She always told me that a man is as tall as he thinks he is." He raised his cup to Rian. "And besides, lady, I am tall in the stories, am I not?"

The stilted meal ended, and Aise led the girls out of the room, Rian still smouldering. Eunion took himself off to a corner where he affected to read a scroll, though he fooled none of them; he was as prick-eared with curiosity as a bald-headed cat. Rictus, Fornyx, Corvus and Druze remained about the table, watching one another, until finally Fornyx, who had drunk deep of the superb wine, rose with an irritated hiss of breath and turned to Rictus. "Get me out of this damned thing, will you?" And he slapped at the black cuirass on his back.

"Let me," Corvus said, rising as swiftly as a dancer. And before Fornyx could protest, he was working on the clasps of the armour, opening them with sharp clicks. He lifted the cuirass off Fornyx and held it in his hands a moment.

"It amazes me, every time I touch one of these," he said. "The lightness of it, the strength inside. What are they made of, Antimone's Gift? Do you ever wonder, Rictus?"

"Gaenion made the stuff of them, they say," Druze put in. "Out of the essence of darkness itself. And because she wove them into chitons for us, Antimone was exiled from heaven, to watch over us in pity, and to take us behind her Veil in death. I've heard it said that the life and fate of the Macht are woven into them in patterns we cannot see." Druze had a

wide, broad-nosed face, that of a farmer, and he had
the olive colouring of the eastern tribes. But his eyes
missed nothing, and the hilt of the drepana hanging
from his shoulder had seen much use.

Corvus was turning the cuirass this way and that
to catch the fire while Fornyx stood looking at him
owlishly.

"You see the way it takes the light sometimes – a
gleam here or there. And yet at other times it will
reflect nothing, but will be as black as a hole in the
earth itself."

Fornyx took his cuirass back, swaying a little.

"With all the conquering you've been doing, I'd
have thought you would have one of your own by
now," he said to Corvus.

The strange youth's face hardened, became a pale
mask. "I have one," he said softly. "I choose not to
wear it."

"Why so?"

"A man must earn his right to the Curse of God,
Fornyx."

Fornyx snorted, and then wove his way to the end
wall where he placed his cuirass on its stand there.
He set a hand on it.

"They do not care who wears them," he said over
his shoulder. "They fit your bones like a second skin,
whether you're fat or thin, tall," he turned round
with a sneer, "or short."

Corvus seemed all at once to grow very still, and in
the room the only sound was the crackle of the fire,
and the breath slowly exhaling from Druze's mouth.

"Rictus, your friend has savoured too much of the

wine," Corvus said quietly. "He forgets himself."

"I forget myself, do I?" Fornyx snarled. He strode back to the table. "You short-arsed little fuck – how about I break you in two over my knee?"

Rictus stood up. "Enough." One look halted Fornyx in his tracks.

"We've played your game," he said to Corvus. "Now I want to know your intent. Are you here to kill us, or make some kind of offer? We're mercenaries, not seers. Be straight, and get it over with."

Corvus nodded, and some life came back into the mask-like face. He really was as fine-boned as a girl, Rictus thought. It did not seem possible he was the man who had been conquering the cities of the eastern coasts for going on three years now, the unstoppable conqueror of rumour. A leader of armies.

And yet, when one looked in the eyes... There was a coldness there, an implacability.

Corvus stood by the hearth and splayed his long white fingers to the flames, the nail-paint on them black in the firelight. It was barely midday outside, but here in the farmhouse it might have been the middle of the night. There was the low murmur of talk from the men beyond the walls, but no wind in the valley. The Andunnon River was a mere liquid guess of noise.

Corvus turned around. He was smiling.

"It is very simple," he said. "I am here to hire you, your friend Fornyx, and your men. I wish you to come and serve in the ranks of my army."

Rictus took a seat, squirted more wine for himself into a clay cup, and methodically filled cups for them all. Druze raised his in salute before sipping at it, black eyes as watchful as those of a stoat. Fornyx sat down beside him, the two dark men looking more than ever like children of the same father, though one was hefted with wide-boned muscle, the other as lean as a blackthorn stick.

"Mercenaries pick their employers," Rictus said. "They choose their contracts, and vote on them. You may wish to hire us, Corvus, but that does not mean you can."

Corvus approached the table, lifted a cup, and studied the trembling face of the wine within.

"Oh, I think I can," he said softly. "Druze, tell him."

"Your senior centurions, Valerian and Kesero, are guests of our army as we speak," Druze said, flapping a hand in apology. "Your centons have been rounded up and are in our camp outside Hal Goshen."

"Prisoners," Fornyx hissed.

"Guests," Corvus corrected him. "I have already broached my terms of employment to them, and they find them agreeable. But they want to know your word on it, Rictus of Isca."

There it was. The glove slipped off, the fist shown at last. This slender cold-eyed boy held Rictus and his family in the palm of his hand.

"What if I said no?" Rictus asked.

Corvus looked back down into his cup. "This is a harsh world. A man must do what he can to safeguard those he loves. And he will do what he must to make the life he has chosen for himself. I know that Karnos of Machran has approached you and your centons with a view to employment – employment against me. The Dogsheads are renowned across our world – how many are they now, Druze?"

"Four hundred and sixty two," Druze said instantly, "Not including those present here."

"Four hundred and sixty two men, only – but those men have been trained by Rictus of Isca. Their prowess, their very name – your name – is worth ten times those numbers of ordinary spearmen. And if Karnos sees sense, and offers you, Rictus, overall command of the League's field-army, why then, my work would be doubled. The leader of the Ten Thousand, at the head of the Avennan League's army – think on it! You would light a fire in the Harukush, one that might consume my ambitions forever."

Corvus was smiling now, tight-lipped, and in the firelight his high-boned face did not seem entirely human. His eyes caught the flames like those of a fox.

"So you see why I am here."

Rictus's voice rasped like gravel out of his mouth. "What if I take employment with none of you – what if I wish to stay here and till my land and live out my life in peace, here in this valley?"

Corvus nodded. "Your centurions have told me that you have spoken thus. You think of hanging up your spear, of following a plough, herding goats, laying down that scarlet cloak." He paused. "You have loyal friends, Rictus. They almost convinced me."

Slowly, he tipped his cup and poured a thin stream of the ruby wine onto the tabletop. It spattered and pooled like fresh-spilt blood.

"For Phobos," he said. "A libation." He placed his hand in the wine and then raised it, palm outwards.

"We are men of blood, you and I, Rictus. Sons of Phobos himself. You can no more set aside your nature than can I. In the times to come, you will don that cloak once more, you will heft a spear, and you will follow your calling. Do not try to tell me different. I see in you the restlessness that I have felt in myself all my life. If you join with me, you will be a part of great things; you will live your life as it was meant to be. You will have a part in the changing of the world. And I will keep faith with you forever. This I swear, to Phobos himself." Then he looked Rictus in the eye.

"If you do not join with me, then I will do what I must. You will die here today. But I promise you that you will die alone. Fornyx here will be spared – as will your family – and your men will take service with me. Your name will have a place in the story, but your part in it will be over. Today." He smiled a little, and in his face there was something genuine – an earnest regret.

Then he turned away, and at once his eyes blazed like those of a hungry animal.

"I will let you think on it. And I will see you outside when you have made up your mind. Druze, let us go."

Druze rose and opened the door, letting in a blare of white light and the chill air of the world outside. He and Corvus went out, closing the door behind them. For a few moments Rictus was blind in the dimness of the farmhouse, his vision flaring with afterimages. It seemed that not only his eyes but his mind was reeling a little with what he had been told. As his vision returned, he drank deep of his wine.

"Modest little bastard, ain't he?" Fornyx said, sitting down heavily.

"A phenomenon," a voice said, and both Rictus and Fornyx started. It was Eunion, forgotten in the corner. He rose stiffly now and approached the table with the scroll still hanging in his hand. The dogs whined as they picked up the mood of the room.

"A slave's gift," he said with a tight smile. "To have oneself overlooked."

"A gift I find myself wishing I had," Rictus conceded.

"You think he means what he says?" Fornyx asked.

It was Eunion who answered. "He means it, master. He means all of it. He is a man who has a certain picture of himself in his head, and he will do anything to keep that picture real. Such men are the most dangerous of all to know. They are not pragmatists, but dreamers."

"His dreams have taken him far," Fornyx said sourly, running his fingers through his beard. "Rictus, we're in a corner here – we'll have to go along with the little fuck, for now at least."

Rictus sat rolling the wine around in his mouth. He was curiously detached. He felt that he had never in his life tasted a cup of wine so completely, enjoying every nuance of its taste. There were complexities within it he had not guessed at, far beyond the run of his own mountain vintages.

Something else – this Corvus knew him, knew him well enough to prod at the weaknesses in his makeup. Not just the veiled threats to his family and his men, not just a crude leverage. One gained men's obedience that way, but not their loyalty.

Corvus had lifted a curtain and made a promise of something greater beyond it, and Rictus knew, without question, that if this slender, terrible boy gave his word on something, he would keep it. Because, as Eunion had said, he was a dreamer, and to break his word would destroy some picture he held of himself in his mind.

Rictus looked at his friends. "We can trust him," he said. "I know it."

Fornyx let out a low whistle. "You're going to do it."

"It's that or death – why not?" Rictus replied. He stood up, the wine loosening his brain. Looking around the homely room, he realised that this place had always been a refuge for him, and he hoped it always would be. But Corvus had been right – and Fornyx too.

He would live and die with a scarlet cloak on his back.

FIVE
THE ARMY

HAL GOSHEN. IN old Machtic the name denoted a gateway, and in the centuries since men had settled there, that was what it had been, commanding a gap between stone and water.

The Gosthere Range, a jagged, rocky, bare-headed line of high hills or low mountains, threw out a long spur here, some two hundred pasangs from north-east to south-west. At the end of it, on a wide flattened knob of high ground, the city had been built. It overlooked the ancient highway that connected the eastern portion of the Harukush with the western, and was a scant fifteen pasangs from the sea.

The lowland ground between coast and mountain had been fought over for generations, and was the root of Hal Goshen's prosperity. It had deep, black soil which might yield two good crops a year, if the weather were kind, and down on the shore to the south were scores of fishing villages and small towns whose menfolk counted themselves citizens of the city on the hill, and voted in its assemblies. The port of Goshen itself was the largest of these, linked to the hilltop city by a fine road. It had one of the best natural harbours on the southern seaboard, and a prosperous fishing fleet was based there.

An army travelling west across the Harukush would find the land narrowing between the mountains and the sea, until the grey tufa walls of Hal Goshen were before it, like the cork in a bottle. To drink the wine of the west, that cork would have to be popped.

A company of men stood on the high ridge northeast of the city and halted there to take in the wide sweep of the world before them. It was bitterly cold, and snow was blowing across the ridge in clouds as hard and heavy as sand, pluming off the peaks of the mountains behind them in long banners across a pale sky, blue as a robin's egg.

Corvus seemed to feel the cold more than most. He was buried in a thick cloak, highlander's felt, and held the hood close about his mouth.

"There she lies, the door to the west. I hope we shall not have to knock too hard," he said.

Rictus scanned the open country to the south of the city, the scattered farms, so much closer together than in the highlands. A taenon of earth here would be a mere tithe of the expanse a man would need to support a family in the high country. Even with autumn well into its stride, the place had a prosperous, comfortable look, lined with vines and well-spaced olive trees, the woods cut back, the wetlands drained, neat tufa walls everywhere; a thousand years of labour or more. A tamed landscape, this; a fat pigeon waiting for a hawk.

"It does not seem to me that the men of Hal Goshen are much panicked by your army," Fornyx said. Snow had greyed his beard and eyebrows. He looked pinched, almost as grizzled as Rictus.

"Our camp is eight pasangs back to the east," Corvus said, his gaze fixed hungrily on the city. "But they know we're here. They closed their gates eight days ago, and brought what provisions they could within the walls. The road to the port has been cut by my cavalry."

"I see no burnt farms or uprooted vines," Rictus said.

"That is not the way I make war," Corvus told him. "I mean to possess this city, and the lands around it. I do not intend to capture a wasteland."

"Then how do you feed your men?" Fornyx asked, genuine surprise in his voice.

"Trains of supply wagons are sent to me from my eastern possessions," Corvus said. "That is why I am able to keep campaigning with winter coming on. We do a certain amount of foraging when we are on the march, but in general I find that it is best not to despoil a country whose inhabitants you wish to conciliate."

"It could be argued that a man whose farm is burning is more apt to listen to reason," Fornyx said.

Corvus turned his strange pale eyes upon him. "I have found that there are two ways of dealing with men. Either you treat them with respect, or you kill them. Anything in between merely breeds resentment and the desire for revenge."

"Your world is a stark and simple place," Fornyx said.

"I sleep well at night," Corvus retorted with a grin.

Rictus listened to their exchange without a word. He was thinking of Hal Goshen. For twenty years he had lived close by – Andunnon was barely sixty pasangs away, up in the Gosthere hills. He knew the men inside those tufa walls, had sat at their tables and drunk their wine. Phaestos, the Speaker of their Kerusia, had hired him more than once, had eaten in Andunnon, hunted with him. He and Aise had been to the theatre there, to see *Ondimion* acted. Her scarlet dress had been bought in the city agora.

It was from the port of Goshen that Rictus had taken ship for the Empire, so long ago. The sea had been black, then, with the ships of the Ten Thousand.

He had no wish to see this city besieged, assaulted, or watch its people broken and enslaved. This was too close to home, to the memories that spanned the web of his life.

"Your reasoning is sound," he told Corvus. "Hal Goshen and its surrounds can muster some four thousand fighting men, maybe two thirds of them spearmen. They have no chance. If we inform them of that fact, then I don't believe that it will prove difficult to make the Kerusia open the gates."

Corvus nodded, watching Rictus's face closely. "That would be my take on it also. Of course, it would be better if this were pointed out to them by someone they know. Someone they trust."

Rictus looked down at the hooded youth, frowning. "Indeed."

Fornyx broke in. "Well, what say you we go take a look at this army of yours first? I want to see what all the fuss has been about."

AN ARMY'S CAMP usually announced itself on the wind, with the stink of men's excrement. That, and woodsmoke. As they tramped down from the high land to the plain below they were able to take in the smell on the breeze, and at once it brought back to Rictus a spate of memories.

In all the fighting he had done since returning with the Ten Thousand over two decades before, he had never been part of a force greater than two or three thousand men. The inter-city conflicts of the Macht were small-scale affairs, conducted almost to a kind of ceremony. Sieges such as that of his last campaign were unusual.

The fighting men of two cities would line up in the summer, well before harvest-time, and crash into each other with all the tactical refinement of two rutting stags. Often the battlefields they fought upon had been fought over by their fathers and grandfathers, cockpits of war since time immemorial. One side would win, one would lose, and the victor would dictate terms. It was rare that such an encounter would lead to the extinction of a city as a political entity – the Macht considered it vaguely impious to destroy a polity entirely.

There were special cases, however. Rictus's own

city, Isca, had been extinguished by a combination of her neighbours because Isca had drilled her citizens like mercenaries and made war on others with the intention of subjugating them entirely to her will, rendering them her vassals. To the Macht this was intolerable, unnatural. War in the Harukush was a bloody ritual, a way to make men of boys, and enhance a city's riches and prestige. It was not conducted with the aim of outright conquest.

And now Corvus had changed all that.

How the hell did he do it? Rictus wondered. Who is this boy and where does he come from? He had so many questions, and he had not yet admitted even to himself that part of the reason he was here was sheer, avid curiosity. He wanted to see how it had been done.

The camp of Corvus's army was huge, a sprawling scar upon the face of the countryside. Roughly square, it was perhaps twenty taenons of tents and horse-lines and wagon-parks, the largest encampment Rictus had ever seen in the Harukush. Fornyx halted in his tracks at the sight of it and ran his fingers through his beard. "Phobos! So all the bullshit is true, after all. You really have conquered the east, and you've brought half of it here with you!"

Corvus pointed out segments of the camp to them both.

"Those lines nearest to us are the conscript spearmen, citizens of the eastern cities who are here for the duration of the campaign. Behind them are my own spears, who have followed me since the fall of Idrios, two years ago. Druze's Igranians are encamped on the north side, and in the rear are my Companions, the cavalry of the army."

Rictus had seen large armies before. There had been over thirty thousand in the forces of Arkamenes, the Kufr pretender to the Great King's throne, and Ashurnan had brought several times that to the field at Kunaksa. This was the camp of many thousands, but it was not the army he had heard of in the stories – it was too small.

"How many men do you have here?" he asked Corvus bluntly.

"Enough for the task in hand. I have had to leave several garrisons behind me." Corvus cocked his head to one side in that bird-like gesture of his.

"The army you see here numbers somewhat under fourteen thousand."

"Phobos!" Fornyx exclaimed again, but Rictus was not so easily impressed.

"You had best hope then that Karnos does not marshal all the forces of the Avennan League against you."

"Numbers are not everything," Corvus said. "You of all men should know that, Rictus."

They walked down the descending slopes of the hills to the camp itself. There were mounted pickets out in twos and threes, unarmoured men bearing javelins, perched upon the tough hill-ponies of the eastern mountains. Closer to the mass of hide tents, spear-carrying infantry stood sentry. The Macht cities emblazoned the shields of their warriors with the sigils that denoted their city's name, but Corvus's soldiers all had the symbol of a black bird painted on theirs, their only concession to uniformity.

The nearest of them raised their spears and shouted Corvus's name as he was recognised, and it seemed to send a stir throughout the camp, as wind will usher a wave across a field of ripe corn. The hooded boy walking beside Rictus threw back the folds of his highlander chlamys and raised a hand as he entered the encampment of his army, to be met by a hoarse formless shout from the crowds of men who saw him arrive.

"They love the little bugger," Fornyx said, marvelling.

A tented city, with neat streets, the roadways within corduroyed with logs where the ground was soft. Latrines had been dug at every crossroads, deep slit trenches with men squatting over them. Fresh ones were being dug even as Rictus watched. There was discipline here, a level beyond that of the usual citizen-army.

An open space before the largest tent they had yet seen. A line of tall wooden posts with outspanning arms had been embedded in the earth along one side, like a series of gibbets.

"What's this?" Fornyx asked.

"The execution ground," Corvus told him. "And here is my tent. Rictus, I would be happy to make you my guest."

"Where are my men?" Rictus demanded. "I wish to see them."

Corvus nodded to Druze, who sped off. It had begun to rain, a cold drizzle clouding down from the mountains. "Come inside. They'll be here presently."

The tent was tall, a draped house of hides upon which the rain had begun to drum more insistently, with one entire wall lifted up on poles. There were braziers within, bright and hot with charcoal, a broad table covered with maps, a simple cot, and an armour stand hung with weapons and a black cuirass. Two sentries stood stolid as marble by the wide entrance, ignoring the rain running down their faces.

"This is home for me," Corvus said, discarding his sodden chlamys and spreading his fingers out to the heat of a brazier. A pair of boys, not more than fifteen, took the cloak and brought wine to the table in a jug of actual glass.

"After I took Idrios, I had it made – it took the hides of eighty cattle. In the past two years I have not slept under a proper roof more than a half-dozen times." He raised his head, smiling. "I like to hear the rain beat upon it."

He seemed to snap himself out of a reverie. "Drink – it's not Minerian, but almost as good. I eat at dusk. You'll meet the other commanders of the army then. We have much to discuss."

Rictus drank, admiring the glass jug, discreetly studying the maps upon the table. For the most part they showed the eastern Harukush: its rivers, its roads, its cities and towns. But there was one that portrayed the lay of the land all the way up to Machran and its broad hinterland, the ring of cities about it that were all members of the loose confederation known as the Avennan League, named for the city of Avennos in which it had been formed, over twenty years ago.

This boy standing at the brazier had in two years conquered his way across some eight hundred pasangs of the Harukush, and by these maps he now controlled at least a dozen major cities, as well as all the countless towns and villages in between.

Where in the world had he come from?

"I might have known I'd find you pair with cups in your hands," a voice said. It was Kesero, grinning so wide as to show every thread of silver ringing his teeth. And beside him Valerian, the ruined beauty of his lop-sided face alight with something akin to relief.

"Rictus – how went it at the farm – is everyone – is Rian –"

"My family is well," Rictus said formally, unsmiling. "Report, centurions. How are my men?"

They stiffened, raindrops streaking their faces. Fornyx stood silent beside Rictus. The two older men were both in their black armour with the scarlet chitons and cloaks of their calling. The rest of their gear had been carried for them by Druze's men, but they bore their swords, and looked every inch the hard-boiled mercenary centurions. Valerian and Kesero, by contrast, were clad in grey civilian chitons which had not been washed any time recently.

"The Dogsheads are bivouacked half a pasang from here, on the south side of the camp," Valerian said. "All are present with their arms on hand, awaiting your orders."

"We voted on it," Kesero said, his shaven head gleaming with rain. "They're sticking with you, Rictus. They've signed no contract, and will sign none without your say."

Rictus looked at Corvus. "I think we may be out of the territory of contracts. The game has changed."

"Something else to talk about," Corvus said. "But later." Druze and a pair of aides had entered the tent in the wake of Valerian and Kesero, and stood patiently. The Igranian was as lit up with curiosity as a kitten watching a ball of yarn.

"I must go. Stay here, Rictus, you and your officers. The pages will set up the place for the evening meal in a little while – until then you can have the place to yourselves." His gaze travelled over the four mercenaries. He seemed to waver for a second, then shook his head, and with a slice of his hand beckoned Druze and the aides out into the rain with him.

"The conquering hero leaves us," Fornyx said drily. "Grab yourself some of this wine, brothers – the boy keeps only the best on hand, it seems."

But Valerian and Kesero stood immobile, fixed in place by Rictus's glare.

"Tell me what happened," he said, in a voice as cold as the rain.

"We were in a wine-shop in Grescir when they took us," Valerian said. "Three parts drunk."

"It was just a little shithole on the way to Hal Goshen," Kesero put in. "We halted on the march to let the men fill their skins. They must have been watching the road. That black-eyed bastard Druze surrounded the place with what looked like a thousand men, then sent in word that they had you and Fornyx and were negotiating a contract with you."

"They gave us safe passage if we would follow them to their camp," Valerian said. "By the time we had formed up they had a thousand more on the hills outside the town, and cavalry too. What the fuck could we do, Rictus?"

"You could keep a better watch," Rictus said quietly.

"This fellow Corvus knows all about you," Kesero rumbled. "Your history, your family, the farmhouse. He must have had spies on every road from Idrios to Machran watching out for the Dogsheads these last few months."

"What about the men – how are they provisioned?"

"They're being fed by Corvus's quartermasters. They've even been issued tents and a place in the baggage train." Valerian shook his head. "It's all been organised, like it was set up for us weeks ago."

"I believe it was," Rictus said. "Corvus does not like to leave things to chance. I know that much now."

"So what's the play?" Kesero asked. "You want to try something, or are we to bow our necks to this boy and let him fuck us up the arse?"

Rictus looked at the maps on the table. Everything is deliberate, he realised. He left these here to let me see what he has done, what he has achieved and what he means to do.

What would this phenomenon be like in battle, with his strange ideas, his men on horses? Once again, the curiosity of it welled up in him.

"How stupid would it be, to let pride get in the way," he murmured, touching the map table, seeing the whole of the Macht countries laid out there before him like some picture of history already drawn. He thought of the petty, brutal campaign of the summer and the winter before it. The crass incompetence of the men who had hired him. And before that, the countless little quarrels he had fought in over the last twenty years, purposeless warfare, squalid little battles with nothing to show for them but the dead and the maimed and the enslaved.

How boring it had all been.

And he remembered Kunaksa, the terrible glory of those days on the Goat's Hills, fighting for the fate of an empire. Creating a legend.

"We could do worse things," he said, musing aloud. He regarded his two junior centurions with one eyebrow lifted. "You look like shit. How long have you been here?"

"Five days," Valerian said with a nervous grin. "We've been keeping ourselves to ourselves."

"Clean yourselves up – I want you in scarlet by the time we sit down with this fellow's officers. We're not going to look like some vagrant bandits in front of him."

"The same goes for the men," Fornyx added sternly, but there was a light in his eye. "We're professionals – this fellow Corvus, he's just a gifted amateur."

THE OFFICERS OF the amateur's army trooped in later that evening, as the campfires of the host began to brighten in the blue rain-shimmered dusk. Trestle tables had been set up, with narrow benches lining the sides.

A group of beardless boys waited on the diners. They were not slaves, and in fact held themselves with a peculiar nonchalance. They watched Rictus and his centurions with open curiosity.

The others were more guarded. These were mostly young men, Valerian's age. Corvus introduced them as the food was placed up and down the table without ceremony. Plain army fare: black bread, salted goat meat, yellow cheese and oil and vinegar to help it down. The wine was local; Rictus had drunk it a thousand times before. Apparently the best vintages were saved for special guests and occasions.

Druze was there, as chieftain of the Igranians, and a broad shouldered strawhead named Teresian was named as general of Corvus's own spears. Looking at his face, Rictus saw himself twenty years before, raw-boned, grey-eyed and withdrawn.

An older man, perhaps in his thirties, was named as Demetrius. He had one eye, the other a socket of whorled scar tissue – he was general of the conscript spears, the levies which Corvus had brought east from each of the twelve cities he had conquered. Rictus wondered how these men – there were some six thousand of them, by all accounts – felt fighting far from home for a man who had destroyed their independence. They were likely here as hostages for their cities' good behaviour as much as anything else.

But the real shock was the leader of Corvus's own Companion Cavalry. This fellow's name was Ardashir, and he was a head taller than anyone else in the room, with violent green eyes and skin a pale gold. His face was so long as to be almost equine, and he had dragged his long black hair into a topknot.

Ardashir was not Macht. He was Kufr.

It had been a long time since Rictus had laid eyes on a Kufr. From his own experience he knew that the other peoples of the world came in many shapes and sizes. He had encountered most of them in his travels, and while the Macht might lump them all under the same derogatory label, he knew better.

There were many castes in the Empire, but the highest were formed by those who came from the heartland of Asuria, who spoke the language of the Great King's court, provided his bodyguards and administrators. By his appearance Ardashir was one of these, a high-caste Kefren of the Imperial nobility. And he sat here at a Macht table, commanding troops in a Macht army.

Rictus found the tall Kefren studying him almost as intently as he was being studied. Ardashir smiled. "It is not often one finds oneself breaking bread with a legend. Rictus of Isca, I have heard your name in stories all my life, as have we all here. It lifts my heart to think that we shall be fighting shoulder to shoulder from this day on." His voice was deep, melodious, his Machtic almost perfect.

"Come, drink with me."

Rictus found his throat seizing up on him. The Kefren's face had jolted his memories. He remembered faces like that raging down at him in a line thousands strong, crashing in close enough that their spittle sprayed his face, their blood soaked his skin. He had trampled faces like that into the muck and mire of Kunaksa. He had not believed the memories could be brought back so bright and vivid while he sat eyes open and wide awake, and had to fight a momentary, overwhelming urge to spring to his feet. He bowed his head and choked down a cup of yellow wine.

The whole table was watching him; Rictus, leader of the Ten Thousand, thrown into panic by the sight of a single Kufr. He beat it down, grinding his teeth on the wine. When he raised his head again his face was as blank as a flint.

"You are a long way from home," he managed.

Ardashir bowed his head in acknowledgement. "A friend came this way, and I followed him."

"Ardashir's people make up most of the Companion Cavalry," the one-eyed man, Demetrius, said. "They were among the first to fight for Corvus, and have come all this way –"

"They are my friends, all of them," Corvus said, his high, clear voice cutting the older man short. "They have fought by my side on a dozen battlefields. The Macht have never been a people to appreciate the potential of cavalry, and a man does not become a horse-soldier overnight. To create a mounted arm, I had to look over the sea. Rictus, in your youth you battled your way across half the Empire. You of all men should be able to appreciate the valour of the people within it."

Corvus was taut-faced, staring at him. Here was a test, Rictus realised. He spoke to Ardashir again.

"I fought the Great King's Honai at Kunaksa, and the Asurian cavalry at Irunshahr. I do not have to be convinced of your people's prowess."

Druze leaned close to Ardashir and reached up to shake the Kefren by the shoulder. "Prowess or not, he still beat you, you big yellow streak of shit."

The table erupted in laughter, Ardashir laughing as loud as the rest. He clinked cups with Druze, the two of them as familiar with each other as any two fighting comrades can be. Rictus wiped the cold sweat from his forehead. He found Corvus still watching him, smiling without humour. Then the pale-faced youth raised his own cup to Rictus and drained it. It would seem the test had been passed.

"Rictus has drilled his Dogsheads to a level not equalled by any other troops I have seen," Corvus said, raising his voice. The long table fell silent instantly.

"They are only a half-mora of spearmen, but I intend that their example shall be followed throughout the army. Here and now, I name Rictus of Isca as one of my marshals, equal to all of you here. Demetrius, Teresian, you will consult with Rictus on the drilling of your own men. If we can field a phalanx that fights as well as did the Ten Thousand, then there is nothing in all of the Harukush that can stand against us."

There was a general buzz of consent, and Fornyx slapped Rictus on the back, leaning in close to speak in his ear.

"Congratulations, marshal. Before you let me kiss your elevated arse, look at your colleagues. I think you just pissed in their wine."

One-eyed Demetrius, and rawboned Teresian. They drank silently, looking over the rim of their cups at Rictus, and he realised that he had just made his first enemies in Corvus's army.

SIX
THE MAN AT
THE GATE

THE GREEN BRANCH got Rictus up to the city walls. It was snowing, a wet, dark snow that was the child of the decaying season. Impenetrable though the Curse of God might be, it held no warmth, and Rictus was shivering under his scarlet cloak as he stood with the olive branch held up in one hand, the blank pocked stone of the ramparts looming over him. There was activity up there on the walkway; he could see the conical gleam of helms moving, but as yet the massive city gates remained closed.

IT HAD BEEN a year and a half since last he had stood here, the tail end of the summer, just before he left for the Nemasis contract.

The gates had been open then, the sun warm and the land as rich and ripe as a plucked pomegranate.

The roads had been thick with people and handcarts and animals making their way to the Summersend market. For most of the country folk around about it was a once-a-year trip, to sell what they had grown and reared and woven, and in return to buy what they could not make for themselves on their farms. They would go home with the redware pottery that was unique to the city, or perhaps a new axehead, or a slave, or perhaps even a scroll of poetry to read aloud in the dark hours of the winter.

Hal Goshen was the hub of men's lives for sixty pasangs around, as much a part of the landscape as the mountains that reached white and remote on the northern horizon. It did not seem possible that a thing of such permanence could be taken away, erased from the world because of the will of one man.

But that might well happen now, if Rictus could not raise an answer out of these walls.

He tried again. "I am Rictus of Isca, and I am known to you and to your Kerusia. I am here to speak for the eastern general, Corvus, whose army is behind me." Nothing. His temper flared.

"Open the fucking gate, will you? I'm one man, and it's fucking freezing out here."

A snap of laughter from above. Finally there was the crack of a reluctant bolt, and a postern in the gate swung open, admitting a heavily cloaked figure. The postern slammed shut behind him.

"I hope Aise has the goats down from the high pastures," the figure said. "There will be drifts up there by now that would bury an ox." The man was lean as a whip, with long lank grey hair, and a gold stud in one nostril. When he smiled he had the white teeth of a much younger man – he had always been proud of them, Rictus remembered, and the effect his smile had on women.

"Phaestus," he said. "Thank the goddess. I was thinking it was about time I got an arrow in my neck."

"I have bows trained on you," Phaestus said, "not that they'd be much use against a Cursebearer. So it's true then; you and the Dogsheads have thrown in with the conqueror of the east."

"It's true, though we didn't have much choice in the matter."

The two men looked wordlessly at one another for a long drawn out minute. Rictus was a guest-friend; he had dined in Phaestus's home, brought trinkets for his daughters, and told tales of old campaigns to his son. The two men had hunted boar together in the hills, and had shared wine around a campfire, Fornyx making them roar with his filthy jokes.

"Ah, well, it seems he is adept at making men choose," Phaestus said at last. "Even you. What do you make of him, Rictus? Is he the all-powerful champion we've heard?"

Rictus thought of Corvus, the short, slight youth with the painted fingernails, and said truthfully, "Well, he scares me, as no man I've met ever has."

Phaestus looked genuinely shocked at this. "Phobos!"

Rictus grasped the older man's shoulder gently and led him away from the walls. "I come to bring you his terms."

"Does he have Aise and the girls – is that it?"

Rictus shook his head. "Listen to me, Phaestus. And look south. Take in what you see and be honest with yourself."

The white snow had blanketed the farmland south of the city, rendering it a blank field broken only by the outlines of walls, the barely discernable grids of sleeping vineyards and olive groves. But some four pasangs away from where the two men stood there was a black stain on the world, an ordered rash of lines that could just be differentiated into ranks of men, of horses. A massive host whose lines extended five pasangs from end to end, a distance greater than the width of the city they faced.

"He has twenty-five thousand men, Phaestus, every one of them a veteran, fed on victory. Do not try to tell me that your citizen soldiers can contend with that. I know what the strength of Hal Goshen is. I know your centurions and their drills."

"I don't doubt it. But Hal Goshen is not alone in this thing, Rictus. What of Machran, and the League? Karnos himself almost had you in his employ at the end of the summer, and you walked away. But the League will come to our aid."

"The League is too late. They've spent the last two years debating what to do about Corvus and have ended up chasing their own tail. There is no army coming to your rescue, Phaestus, so put that out of your mind. He has moved too fast for them. I tell you now in friendship: accept his terms."

Phaestus's face was as livid as his hair. "What are the terms?" he said.

"The same as those he has given to a dozen cities in the east. You must give up your independence and join him, accept him as absolute ruler. You must pay a tithe of all your wealth and income to his treasury, and you must send him five hundred spearmen every year to fight in his wars.

"You do these things, and Hal Goshen will not be touched – he will not even enter the city, but will appoint a governor." Rictus took Phaestus by the arm again, squeezing flesh down upon bone. "I have spoken to him of this. You will be the governor, Phaestus. You have my word on it. And if you prove loyal, then your son Philemos will follow you."

"He's establishing dynasties now, is he?" Phaestus snapped. "Petty little kings, to serve under him, the Great King of all. What are we now, Rictus, no better than Kufr? A free man bears his spear and has his voice heard among his peers – that is how the Macht have always lived."

"Times are changing," Rictus said, angry now, though not with Phaestus. "I warn you, as a friend, if you do not submit to him, he will take Hal Goshen, and he will destroy it, to make an example. You and your son will die and your womenfolk will be enslaved. Hal Goshen will disappear as Isca did. He will do it, Phaestus, believe me."

Phaestus looked at him with a mixture of wonder and contempt.

"The great leader of the Ten Thousand, whom I termed my friend. Rictus of Isca, reduced to the errand boy of a barbarian. Run back to him, Rictus, and tell him –"

"For Antimone's sake, Phaestus, don't come all high and mighty on me now. We stand in a cold hard world, and honour is something we leave for the stories. You are being offered something priceless here. There can yet be honour in what you accept, and you will save your city a nightmare."

Phaestus looked like a man in doubt as to whether he was about to sob or shout. He shook his head.

"I never yet truly understood the nature of a mercenary. You redcloaks are a dying breed, and we have made you into a kind of legend. But in the end, all that matters is the weight of the purse you are offered. What you consider honour, I spit upon, Rictus."

Rictus seized him by the throat, his grey eyes blazing. "Watch what you say, old man. You do not know of what you speak. Have you ever watched a city burn? I have. I have seen my people led off to the slave market, my family butchered. If your pride seeks to consign your own folk to the same fate then I swear to you I will make special effort, when your walls are breached. I will find you and kill you myself, and your precious son. And your last sight on this earth will be that of my men raping your wife and daughters." He tossed Phaestus aside as a dog will discard a dead rat.

"I came to you out of friendship. I advanced your name with Corvus because I knew you to be a just and honourable man, one who would rule wisely. You love this city, as do I. Its fate is in your hands now."

Phaestus rubbed his throat, eyes hot and white. "You think I would enjoy setting myself up as a tyrant, the slave of a greater tyrant? You do not know me as well as I thought you did, Rictus. And it seems I do not know you at all."

"Take his terms to the Kerusia, then – see what the other elders have to say, and put it to the assembly."

Phaestus's lip curled. "How did he buy you? Are you to have the pickings of his conquests? Antimone watches us, Rictus. Her black wings beat over our heads all our lives. You and Corvus will answer for what you are doing."

"I'll take my chances with the gods. You think on the offer I have made, and ask whether your ideals are worth the death of a city. Corvus expects answer before nightfall. If there is none, the army will assault your walls at dawn."

Rictus turned on his heel and walked away. Neither Phaestus nor the men on the walls could see the agony written across his face.

HAL GOSHEN CAPITULATED that evening. A leading elder of the Kerusia, Sarmenian, was proclaimed governor by Corvus. The city accepted a small staff of clerks from the conqueror's entourage, and agreed to forward provisions to the army for the remainder of the present campaign. Five hundred glum-faced youths wearing their fathers' armour marched out to join the army on the plain below, and were folded into Demetrius's command.

Of Phaestus there was no sign. He had relayed the terms of the city's surrender to the Kerusia, and then disappeared, fleeing Hal Goshen with his family, making for the hills. In his absence, and on Corvus's insistence, he was declared *ostrakr* by the Kerusia, before that body disbanded itself. Like Rictus, he no longer had a city to call his own.

It was perhaps the most efficient example of conquest Rictus had ever seen. Not a drop of blood had been spilled, and yet a great city had fallen. And with the fall of Hal Goshen, the way was open to the western heartlands of the Harukush. The cork was out of the bottle.

The army of Corvus shook out into march column next morning, a river of men that blackened the face of the lowlands. The great camp in which they had passed the preceding days was dismantled and abandoned – the leather tents, the field-forges, the barrelled provisions all packed up and loaded onto the waggons of the baggage train. Then the thing began to move. The clouds broke open and yellow sunlight made of their passage an immense, barbed snake slithering west, the endless companies passing by the walls they had not been called upon to breach.

In their midst, Rictus trudged silently at the head of his men, and his black armour reflected not a gleam of the autumn sun. He did not look back.

PART TWO

GRINDING THE CORN

SEVEN
SPEAKER OF
MACHRAN

KARNOS RAN HIS fingertip down the spine of the girl from her nape to the silky crease of her buttocks. She was wet there, and she shifted slightly under his touch, her white body arching up like a cat being stroked. His fingertip moved upward again, traced the geometry of her ribs, touched the side-swell of one breast. He brushed her ear-lobe where the dark tresses of shining hair fell over it.

"I don't care what Pollo said, you were worth every obol," he murmured.

A knock on the door.

The girl smiled as Karnos kissed her delicate ear. His hand ran down her body again, more urgent this time. A flare of base delight as she lifted her rump up in invitation.

Again, the knock – not so discreet this time. A rapping of knuckles.

"Fuck you, Pollo!" Karnos shouted. "I was not to be disturbed!" The girl stiffened beside him, and her eyes took on the blank slave-look. Duty had replaced arousal in a moment, though she remained stock still with her white buttocks up in the air.

"Master, my profound apologies, but there is news here that cannot wait. Kassander himself is here, and awaits you in the court."

"Kassander? Ah, shit," Karnos said. He rose to his knees in the bed, pushed the slight pale-skinned girl to one side and reached for his chiton.

"Get him some wine – have Grania bring it."

"I have already done so, master. He demands to see you at once."

"Of course he does," Karnos snarled, pulling his chiton over his head. To the girl he said, "Get out and clean yourself up." She scampered naked from the bed, leaving by a side-door. The hanging that half-hid it was still twitching as Karnos rose barefoot and said, "Tell him I'm on my way. And it had better be important – Phobos's arse, it's the middle of the night."

Pollo came in bearing a bronze lamp, shielding the wick with his long fingers. "Shall I call for the cook?"

"No, let's see what we have first. Light the way for me, Pollo. Kassander is an impatient son of a bitch, but even he doesn't turn out at this hour on a whim."

The two men walked along the passageway in a fluttering globe of yellow lamplight while their shadows capered around them. Pollo was a spare, elderly man with a broad grey beard. He wore a slave-collar, but it was chased with gold, and from his shoulders hung a himation of fine white linen.

Karnos wore a food-stained chiton of plain undyed wool. He was a broad, beefy man with a round paunch and a close-cropped black beard. His hair, worn long, was dressed with oil and he bore several rings on each hand. His bare feet slapped on the stone floor.

"Was he alone?"

"He came with an escort of spearmen, master, but they remained outside."

"Fuck – then it's official. Rouse the household and lay out my council robes, and a good cloak."

"Some food, perhaps –"

"Wine – lots of it. The good stuff. It must be bad news; no-one ever brings good tidings in the dark. We'll have it in the study. And have some sent out to the escort."

A wide space surrounded by pale-pillared colonnades, open to the sky. Karnos gritted his teeth against the cold. There was the rill of water from the courtyard fountain, the glow of the solitary lamp kept burning by the gate-shrine, and a brazier for the doorman, the coals dull and almost dead. Beside it stood a large shadow, red-lit by the charcoal, and to one side the slim shape of a shivering slave-girl, a glass jug in her fists.

"Leave us, Grania," Karnos said crisply. The girl fled, feet pattering on the chill stone.

"Kassander?"

The shadow resolved itself into a massive cloaked figure, as broad as Karnos but taller.

"You keep buying up all the pretty girls, Karnos. How many do you have stashed away here now?"

"If you want one, I'll lend her to you – now what's the news that has me shivering like a spent horse here in the night with Phobos leering down at me?"

Kassander drained his cup. "Word from the east. Hal Goshen has surrendered to him."

Karnos leant against a marble pillar, the last of the bedroom's warmth sucked out of him. "Ah, hell." He rubbed one hairy-knuckled hand over his face, and seemed to feel the weight of his years and the loom of the winter weigh down his very bones.

"I told them, didn't I?"

"Yes, you did," Kassander said. "You have been proved right at every turn. There's good in that – it means they may pay heed to you now."

Karnos raised his head sharply, a sneer splitting his beard. "You think so? Brother, you have a faith in the rationality of men that makes me wonder whether to laugh or weep."

"If this does not unite the League, nothing will. This could be good news, Karnos – it may be the turning point."

"Ever the optimist, eh? Who else knows this?"

"It'll be all over the city by dawn. I've already sent couriers to the hinterland, and the Kerusia is being waked as we speak."

"Come inside with me. My prick has shrivelled up like a raisin in this cold – or maybe it's your news has done it." Kassander followed him like an obedient bear, tossing his cup into the courtyard pool with a silver splash.

"Light, light!" Karnos roared. "Am I to stagger around in the dark in my own home? Bring a lamp there!"

Pollo appeared again. He bowed to Kassander, who nodded curtly in reply. "Master, your study fire has been lit, and –"

"Have my clothes laid out there, Pollo, and rouse out the stables. I want the black gelding warmed up and shining, my best harness. I'll be going to the Empirion with the dawn."

Pollo bowed again, handed his lamp to Karnos, and glided away.

The household was coming to life, slaves scurrying everywhere with lamps in their hands, unintelligible shouts emanating from the kitchens at the back of the house. Karnos and Kassander strode along the corridors, oblivious, until a heavy door was swung back to reveal a firelit room, littered with scrolls and papers, and a wide-eyed slave who bowed deeply, placed a tumble of clothing on the desk and fled, mumbling inanities.

"You've too many slaves," Kassander said, unlooping the end of his cloak from his arm. "They're underfoot like damned cockroaches. Can't you hire some free men to light your fires and groom your horses?"

"Free men have loyalties and families and worries of their own," Karnos said, sweeping the piled papers from two iron-framed chairs. "Slaves only have to worry about their job. They do that well, and they have no other worries in the world." He threw off his woollen chiton and stood naked in the firelight, then began to dress in the clothing the slave had abandoned.

"You'd have been Speaker far sooner if the world did not look askance at the harem you have here. There's jokes about you and your insatiable prick scrawled across every wineshop wall in the Mithannon."

"Insatiable, eh?" Karnos said with a grin. His head emerged from the neck of a black linen chiton. "I like that. The people love a politician whose vices are out in the open, Kassander – they know he has less to hide. Me, I love women –"

"Then marry one."

"Are you insane? No, no. I flirt with power and I fuck slaves. Good decent women are too dangerous for a man like me. And I'm near forty now – too old to be learning the ways of a wife. Have a seat. No, you make my blood run cold merely by mentioning it – and you know the regard I have for your sister –"

"She thinks the sun rises and sets on you, Haukos knows why."

"She is the very picture of a virtuous lady, a credit to your family. If I married her, she'd – well, you know what would happen. No, one day soon she will see sense and marry some other worthy fellow who will come home sober every night and plant her with babies. Enough." He patted down his fine chiton and stepped into a pair of beaten sandals. "Now where is the fucking wine? Pollo!"

The wine arrived, borne by an absurdly pretty girl whose tunic barely reached her thighs. Pollo stood over her like a stern father.

"Master, will that be all?"

"For now. We'll eat later – have the cook run up some of that good broth we had yesterday. And make sure no-one comes near this door, Pollo."

Pollo bowed and withdrew, as stately as a grey-bearded king.

Karnos sat down and poured two clay cups of wine. He stuck his fingers into his own glass and flicked a few drops into the fire. "For Phobos, the rotten bastard – a libation."

Kassander did the same with a big man's slow smile. "For Haukos, who has not turned his face from us yet."

"Your sunny disposition makes me want to puke," Karnos said. "What are the details of the thing, or don't we know them yet?"

Kassander leaned back in his chair with a sigh, making the ironwork creak under his bulk.

"The same story we've seen before. Scare the little people with the size of his army, offer them easy terms, and move on."

"He had only just arrived before their walls," Karnos said, punching his knee. "I thought we had time – Phaestus assured us he would hold out."

"Phaestus was overruled, and declared ostrakr. Sarmenian was installed as governor."

"Sarmenian! That rat-faced prick. I had him to dinner last month and he was full of shit about how Hal Goshen would halt the invader in his tracks. Bastard. He has a tiny cock, too; Grania told me."

"Whatever the size of his instrument, he now rules Hal Goshen as tyrant, under Corvus. But there's more, Karnos."

"I see it in your face. You're saving the best for last, you big fuck. Well, toss it at me if you must."

"Rictus of Isca was at Hal Goshen. He has thrown in his lot with the invader."

Karnos stood up. He set his wine cup on the desk, spilling some of the berry-dark liquid on the papers there. He stood before the fire and stared blindly into the flames whilst Kassander wiped up the spill doggedly with the hem of his cloak.

"Rictus," he said dully. "I would not have thought it of him."

"Who is the optimist now? Rictus is a mercenary," Kassander said, irritably. "He goes where the money is; and this Corvus must have a fortune in his treasury by now."

"No." Karnos turned round. "Rictus is one of the old-fashioned Macht. He believes in things. I thought I had him, Kassander. This summer, we spoke, and I thought I had him. Imagine, if we had lured him here to lead the army!"

"My imagination runs riot," Kassander said. "It's unfortunate you'll have to make do with Kassander of Arienus instead."

Karnos waved a hand at him. "Don't be a girl about it. You know damn well what it would have meant to have the leader of the Ten Thousand on these walls. Phobos! I never would have thought it of him."

"You're repeating yourself."

"A politician's habit – it keeps the mouth working until there's something new to say. Kassander, we must push this issue now, while the shock of the news is getting around the streets. If we argue it out in the Kerusia, Corvus will be at our walls before we've even managed to convene the assembly."

"Something tells me I have a role in this."

"You're polemarch of the army. For God's sake, he's ten good day's march from these walls – we don't have time to fuck around!"

Kassander sighed heavily. "You want me to call out the army on my own initiative."

"By dawn. We must have the streets full of men – we must wake up the people to the danger, and force the Kerusia's hand."

"I can do that – I can have the host called out, but it'll mean the end of your political career, you know that. You by-pass the Kerusia and they'll vote you down. They hate you anyway."

Karnos flapped a hand in dismissal. "I was voted onto the Kerusia by popular acclaim. If they throw me out of it they'll have the people to answer to."

Kassander looked into his wine. There was a silence in the room, broken only by the cracking of the fire. Olive wood was burning upon it, and the subtle blue fragrance of it stole about them in the quiet.

"You got me this post," Kassander said. "You made me polemarch, so I am tied to you. I owe you for it."

"This is not about calling in favours –" Karnos cried. Kassander raised his head, smiling. That slow, broad smile of the honest man.

"I know that. We have been friends a long time, Karnos. If I do this it will be for two reasons. Because it is the right course of action to preserve this city, and because you are my friend."

"The only real friend I have," Karnos said, with feeling. "After this the rest will desert me like rats running from a burning house."

"Look on the bright side; you'll still have your slaves to fuck."

MACHRAN WAS SIX pasangs from west to east, and three parts asleep. Even up in the Mithannon Quarter, the wineshops and brothels shut their doors for a few hours at this time of night. It was remarkable, then, how fast news could travel the narrow streets, how it lit up at window after window.

Kassander started it, storming into the dormitory of the city criers with Karnos's seal affixed to a Kerusiad edict and shouting them awake. Brass-voiced men with fast feet, the criers took to the streets within minutes, shouting the news at every crossroads they came to. Hal Goshen had fallen. The army was being called out. Every able-bodied man of the first and second property classes was to arm and make his way to the Marshalling Yards on the Mithos River.

By the time Karnos was mounted and riding to the Empirion, the streets were wide awake and teeming as though it were festival time. Men shouted at him as they thronged the wide avenue to the Amphion Quarter, many bearing shields and spears. He tugged his black cloak about him and rode on with a practised look of remote authority on his face, feeling as though he had just opened the gate on a fractious bull.

The Empirion was a vast domed amphitheatre which could house five thousand with ease. Nominally a theatre, it was also used for public meetings in inclement weather. Karnos had chosen it quite deliberately. He wanted a certain amount of chaos, a massed crowd to speak to. He was always best when addressing a mob. It was how he had become Speaker of Machran, though his father had been nothing more than a stallholder of the third class, unable even to afford a spearman's panoply.

The other members of the Kerusia, all scions of the oldest families in Machran, regarded Karnos with at best a certain patronising indulgence, and at worst with outright loathing. He was a man who got things done, who took on all the dirty jobs and accomplished them not only with relish but with a certain vulgar flair.

He was uncouth, foul-mouthed and ostentatious, but when he spoke, men listened. He could cajole a crowd, flirt with it, make people laugh and set them alight with outrage. Those who thought him ill-educated and uncultured had never seen his personal library, or heard him hold forth on drama or philosophy after dinner. He was careful to keep it that way. He was everyman. That was his charm.

Kassander had done his work well. Crowded though the streets were, there was a definite current of movement to the north and the Mithannon Gate. The levies were gathering, trusting that the machinery of the city was working with legal correctness. Hundreds of men were bowed down under the weight of their wargear, and every street was bristling with spears.

Karnos dismounted in front of the Empirion. One of the marvels of the Macht world, the dome was the height of fifty men, all in blazing white marble now tinted pink by the light of dawn, hewn block by block out of the vast stone quarries around Gan Cras and brought south on ox-drawn wagons with iron wheels. It was old as the city itself, though it did not look it. The white marble was inviolate, austere and dignified. Everything that Karnos was not.

They had lit the great flambeaux inside and the place was a shadow-textured stage humming with voices, row upon row of people lining the stone step-benches, those at the back some eighty feet above the performer's circle below. When Karnos walked in, a roar went up, a wordless chorus of interrogation, greeting, and cat-calling.

The middle-men of the city were on their way to the Mithannon. Those who were present here comprised the two extremes of Machran society. Small tradesmen, freed slaves, and ne'er do wells. And also the highest ranking families of the city: the Alcmoi, the Terentians, the Goscrins and half a dozen more. The menfolk of these families were not subject to the levy. They would don their armour when it suited them, and provide the officers of the phalanx. That was their privilege. Whether or not they had the ability to lead men in battle was irrelevant.

And waiting for Karnos in the circle, three of the more dangerous members of the Kerusia. Katullos, Dion, and Eurymedon. These three might have been Pollo's brothers, all grey-bearded and stern, the folds of their himations draped over one forearm in the classic style. They dripped anger; it shone out of their faces.

Karnos smiled. He opened his arms, halted short of the other Kerusia members, and breathed in deep the energy of the crowd.

Gestrakos had lectured on this very spot, postulating the existence of other worlds. Ondimion had staged his tragedies upon these stones. And here Naevios himself had plucked his harp, singing the songs that were now buried deep in the souls of the Macht, even the Paean they sang at the moment of death itself.

Some men made music, some built in stone. Some led armies.

Karnos – he knew how to work a crowd. It was the reason he had been put upon the world. This was his moment.

"Brothers," he said. And such were the superb acoustics of the Empirion that he reached the farthermost ranks of the crowd while barely raising his voice.

But he did raise it, along with his arms, outspread as though he would embrace them all if he could.

"Brothers! You know me – you know my name. I am Karnos of Machran, Speaker of the Kerusia. You put me here today by voting openly in the assembly of all free men at the Amphion of Machran, the first time in a generation that a Speaker has been so chosen. My brothers, you have honoured me beyond my deserts..."

He watched the crowd closely, alert to their postures, his ears pricked for the start of muttered conversations.

It was like reeling in a fish too heavy for the line. The mood had to be taken, massaged, guided and caressed to where he wanted it to go. A man could not storm the crowd – Katullos, the last Speaker, had tried it, and failed miserably.

"I have no family of note," Karnos went on. "My father hammered out metal at a stall in the Mithannon – I was born there, and I know those alleys like they were the veins in my arm. He put me to work cross-legged in the street, tapping out dints in people's pots for an obol a day before I was ten years old –"

A growl of appreciation from the crowd. They loved this stuff, the lower orders. Who needed rhetoric, when one could work on their sentimentality, the fellow-feeling of the urban poor?

"But he saw what was in me, and hired a slave for an hour every night to teach me to read and write, for he had no wish to see me back-bent and bowed and coughing up soot for the rest of my life."

The slave had been Pollo, a dark-haired, lanky young man who had found that teaching the bright, eager son of the street-smith was one way to dull the pain of his own servitude.

"When my father died, I sold his stall and his tools, and bought a single illiterate highland boy. I educated him in his turn, sold him at a profit, and never looked back."

That had been about the same time that the Ten Thousand had returned from their failed expedition to the Empire. Karnos remembered it well. A few centons of them had marched through Machran, invited by Dominian, Speaker at the time. The famous Rictus had not been there, but all the same, the streets were clogged five deep to see the heroes of the east in their scarlet cloaks.

Karnos still remembered the lean and hungry look on their faces, their eyes still fixed on some invisible horizon.

It was the first time he had seen the mob of Machran in full voice on the streets, and he had never forgotten it. What would it be like, to have that adulation thrown at him – or to have those thousands hang on his words? It had been the beginning of the slow fire of ambition that had burned in his gut ever since.

"But I will not bore you with my life story – you've heard it all before. Brothers, it is enough for me to say that I came from where you are."

His gaze swept the curved ranks of the amphitheatre. He let the statement hold the air a moment, saw a stir of restlessness, and plunged on.

"I am an ambitious man, that is true – were I not I would still be hammering pots in the Mithannon. But I am a man of Machran – this is my city. My life has been and always will be within her walls. I would never – *never* – do anything that would harm this place. I would rather die first." Now the richly clad men near the bottom of the circle stirred. He saw some smirk.

"And brothers, know this: I have never lied to you. You know I am no hypocrite. I like wine, women, and as much amusement as I can pack into my life – this I have never tried to hide –" Now the common folk were smirking, and a few laughed out loud. "Aye, we know that all right!" someone cackled, and there was a buzz of laughter.

He had to grip them again, quickly. "So I am here today with no pretences, no defences. I come to you with the truth in my hands, to give to you. It is your privilege to do with it what you will."

The baleful stares of the other Kerusia members present could almost be felt on his back. An irrational part of him twitched at the thought of a knife plunging into him, unseen, unexpected. The Empirion had seen it happen before.

He took a few steps forward, closer to the rising slope of the crowd, until he could smell the perfumes and scented soaps of those near the floor, and the unwashed miasma of those higher up in the dome.

"I hereby formally convene this gathering as an emergency assembly, gathered in time of war, to vote upon extraordinary measures taken this day by myself and the polemarch of the host, Kassander of Arienus." Phobos – now he had their attention all right. In the next few minutes he would either have saved his career or would be feeling that knife in his back for real.

"You have all heard of the capitulation of Hal Goshen, after an eight-day defence by its people and the leader of the Kerusia, Phaestus. The enemy of us all, Corvus the warmonger, is on the march as I speak, barely a fortnight from our own walls.

"Brothers, on my own authority, I called out the levies this morning; they are gathering now at the Mithos River. I did this with the full support of our polemarch, but without the consultation of my fellow Kerusia members. Hence, I acted illegally."

There it was. He had admitted it publicly.

"I hereby ask now for a vote on my actions. I did what I did for the good of the city and of us all, with no thought of my own position or ambitions – this I swear to you by Antimone's Veil. I ask now that you vote to retrospectively legalise the call-out, so that we can go on to organise an effective defence of this city against he who would destroy your freedoms forever.

"According to Tynon's constitution, in time of war, extraordinary assemblies may be called to pass laws by popular acclaim. Brothers, I need to hear your voices now. Forgive me for my infraction of our codes, and let it be written that I did so only in the city's interest – in your interest.

"Brothers, will you now formally legalise my actions of last night, the calling out of the army, and the convening of this assembly? Let us hear what you say. All in favour, say aye."

The dome roared.

Karnos struggled to be heard. "Those against –"

He could see the mouths of the well-dressed men at the floor of the circle opening, but whatever noise they made was drowned out by the thunderous wave of *ayes* that was still shaking the Empirion. He raised his arms.

"I declare the motion passed!"

The crowd kept roaring. Gobbets of food were thrown down from the topmost circles of the amphitheatre to land on the lower benches.

Men stood up. He heard his name called out by thousands, arms lifted to him. He stood and raised his own arm in salute.

I have you, he thought. *I have you.*

One of the other Kerusia members crossed the floor to stand at his side. It was Katullos, the bull-necked, grey-bearded patriarch of the Alcmoi family who had been Speaker himself at one time. He leaned close to be heard and said to Karnos:

"That was nicely done."

"Thank you."

"You are safe for now, my friend, with the mob shouting your name. Let us see how long it lasts." He set a massive hand on Karnos's shoulder in what looked like a friendly gesture. But Karnos could feel the fury in the grip of the older man's fingers.

"One day they will cheer the news of your fall, Karnos. And I swear I will be there to see it."

Karnos smiled at him with perfect affability.

"You must count on living a long time, Katullos."

EIGHT
THE OBJECT LESSON

DRUZE HALTED, PANTING, and held up a hand. He made the hand into a fist. At once the column behind him bifurcated, splitting to left and right of the road in a movement reminiscent of a shoal of fish. The men formed a line, caught their breath, and began weighing the heft of the javelins in their hands.

"Some stubborn bastard has decided to make a stand," he said.

The man to his right, a gangling thatch-haired youth with eyes the colour of cobweb, tossed his javelin up in the air and caught it again, out of sheer lightness of heart, it seemed.

"I hope so, chief. Antimone's tits, I hope so. The last good fight I had was with a whore in Maronen."

Druze grinned. He clapped the youth on the shoulder. "That's right, brother – and I hear she won."

A crackle of laughter ran along the ranks. The Igranians stood easily, tightening their belts, retying sandals, fingering the cruel iron points of their javelins. Each man carried a bundle of them, and these they now untied, checking the shafts for warp, stabbing them into the ground to clean the blades. They wore the felt tunics of the inner mountains for the most part, and rough wool chlamys whose folds they now tied up under their left armpits to leave their throwing arms free.

A pasang away on the road their path was blocked by a body of spearmen. These had formed up in four ranks and extended four to five hundred paces. At least sixteen hundred men, Druze thought, measuring them with his bright black eyes.

"They'll be out of Goron, that city on the crag to the west," he said. All humour left his face. He watched the enemy phalanx closely, noting their intervals, they way they stood, how they held their spears. These small details meant something. If spearmen kept their shields on their shoulders long before battle was joined, it meant they were nervous. If they left the ranks to piss or shit instead of doing it where they stood, it meant they were not well-drilled.

"These lads are not bad," he said, noting the stillness in the enemy formation, and the fact that slaves to their rear were passing water-skins up the files.

The flanks of the phalanx were protected by woods, half a bowshot on either side of the road. Hazel woods, stark with winter but with enough brush remaining to act as a concealer. There might be more men in those trees, hunkered down on the cold ground with the snow numbing their bellies.

"Send back word to Corvus," Druze said. "We'll hold here for now. Gabinius, take a couple of fists down to the treeline and see if there's anything more than rabbits in there. I want no surprises."

"You got it, chief." The thatch-haired youth sped off at a run, calling out to the men nearest him. Eight of them peeled out of the line and followed him down the roadside at an easy lope, black against the snow-covered ground. Druze blew on his hands.

"A cold day to die," he said.

DOWN THE VAST column, Rictus strode along with the tireless pace of the old campaigner. As far as the eye could see the road was choked with marching men in both directions, and from their labouring bodies a steam rose in the chill air so that they were marching in a fog of their own making. There was little to see except the backs of the men in front.

They were two day's march out of Hal Goshen, and Corvus was pushing the pace hard. The men's armour was piled in the baggage wagons and they carried only what they had to on their backs, using their spears as staffs. The Dogsheads were an unmistakable scarlet vertebra in the backbone of the army.

Horses cantering past on either side of the trudging infantry, like ghosts from a swifter world. A knot of them reined in, the snow flying from their hooves, the animals snorting and white-streaked with sweat. Huge horses, larger than any the Macht countries ever bred. Atop one, a gaudily cloaked figure raised a hand. The Kufr, Ardashir.

"Rictus! Corvus wants you and the Dogsheads at the front of the column at once. Get your gear from the wagons and arm up – we have work to do!"

The Kufr's long, shining face broke out in a grin, and as he sped off again his long black hair flew out behind him like his horse's mane.

Fornyx grimaced. "I was just getting ready to piss."

"Piss in your own time," Rictus told him. "Valerian, Kesero – break ranks, off the road. Time to earn our pay, brothers."

THE LINE OF the army's march had mushroomed out, formations wheeling left and right of the road and taking up position in extended ranks, out to the trees. This was the old Imperial road of Machran, which had come all the way from Idrios, and the cities along its length kept it maintained and cut back the brush and woodland on either side of it to foil the designs of brigands and goatmen. Rictus led his centons off the road and marched them smartly past the waiting files of the army, aware of the hundreds of eyes watching his red-cloaked men.

"Tighten it up, you plodding fucks," Fornyx quipped in an undertone. "Let's make it look good for the crowd."

There was a gap, where the vanguard had halted, and then beyond it were Druze's Igranians and a body of the Companion Cavalry. The personal raven banner of Corvus snapped busily in the wind.

"There you have it," Corvus said, dismounting and joining Rictus as his men reformed into line. "Goron's citizen's have decided to make a fight of it. Two morai of spearmen and a cloud of light troops hidden in the trees. Druze has sounded out the position; it can't be turned without a long flank march over the hills, so we'll pitch straight into it. You will assault with your Dogsheads, Rictus, with one of Teresian's morai following you in. Druze will flush out the woods with his Igranians, and when the line is ruptured, I'll take in the cavalry. Any questions?"

Rictus blinked rapidly, looking at the wall of spearmen ahead. Their shields were emblazoned with the *gabios* sigil for their city and their line had the not-quite-straight aspect of citizen soldiers.

It was a good plan – the boy with the painted nails knew what he was doing.

"I'll hit their left," he told Corvus. "Tell Teresian to take his mora in right, but slow, so I hit first. That'll scramble them for him."

"I'll link with you on the left as you go in, and cover your flank," Druze said. There was none of his mocking humour on display now; he was in deadly earnest. For the first time, Rictus warmed to him.

"All right, then. Let us join the Dance," Rictus said, the age old aphorism of the Macht going into battle.

"Now we'll see how Rictus of Isca fights," Corvus said. And he had on his face an expression of such bright, intense happiness that he did not seem quite sane.

* * *

THE DOGSHEADS FELL into position in minutes. On their right, Teresian's men took rather longer to dress their lines. These were Corvus's regulars, and Teresian himself was going to take the mora in. One thing about Corvus's officers; they all liked to lead from the front.

A few observations were exchanged between the two bodies of spearmen, with reflections on the chastity of one another's mothers and other witticisms, until Fornyx put a stop to it.

"Save it for the buggers up ahead, you mouthy bastards," he called out.

Rictus stepped forward of the line. For a moment he stood there, a black armoured statue in a red cloak, face hidden by the close helm, the transverse crest bristling in the wind. Then he raised his spear, and as the Macht behind him stepped out he joined the front rank, and the five understrength centons of the Dogsheads began their advance.

It began as a murmur, a hum upon their breath. But then Valerian struck out with the Paean, a lone, ringing voice in the midst of the phalanx. Others joined him, until the entire formation was singing it, the measured, mournful beat of the ancient melody keeping their feet in time. To their right, Teresian's mora joined in.

And to their front, the men of Goron took up the song also, so that the whole battlefield was singing it, as though the two sides were coming together in harmony instead of mutual murder. It made of the coming fight a proper thing, a ceremonial event.

For Rictus, the Paean was something different. He no longer joined in the singing, and had not since returning from the Empire all those years before. He had never forgotten the second day of Kunaksa, when the Ten Thousand had sung that song, believing they were marching to their doom but advancing anyway, to make themselves worthy of memory. It had kept them going that day, had reminded them of who they were.

He no longer liked to sing it when fighting against his own people.

The enemy line levelled their spears and began to advance to meet the Dogsheads.

"Shoulder!" Rictus shouted, and his own men brought the long spears up so that the wicked points of the aichmes were jutting out to their front. The files were six men deep; usually they fought eight to a file, but Rictus had wanted to lengthen the line somewhat, and they were still a deeper formation than the more numerous enemy.

The men of Goron had made an error, trying to cover all the ground between the woods. They had thinned out their centons, the classic mistake of amateurs worried about their flanks.

Rictus turned his head this way and that, taking in the positions. In a few minutes he would be in the middle of the *othismos*, and blind to everything except the man in front who was trying to kill him. He saw Druze's men going into the woods like a crowd of screaming fiends to his left, and saw the hidden skirmishers of the enemy rise out of the brush to meet them. His flank was covered.

"Charge!" he shouted. And the Dogsheads broke into a run.

They kept formation; they had drilled and drilled this a thousand times over the years. No citizen army could maintain their ranks at a run; they grew scrambled and ragged, lost the compact momentum that was the key to phalanx fighting. But Rictus's men were professionals, the finest of their calling. They ate up the ground at a fast lope, still singing, and smashed into the enemy formation with an appalling crash of bronze.

Shields smashing against shields. An aichme thrust past Rictus's eyes. Another went through his horsehair crest.

He gave a grunt as the weight of the men behind piled into him, lifting his feet off the ground for a moment. He jabbed out with his spear, ignoring the shrieking enemy spearman who was pressed up close to his face, stabbing into the third and fourth ranks.

He killed the file-closer with a jab to the eyes, slotting his spearhead into the man's helm, the blade grating on bronze and bone as he pulled it out again. Blood sprayed warm across his forearm. The stench of excrement rose as men lost control of their bowels.

The Dogsheads shunted backwards a huge segment of the enemy's line. Men went down, stumbling, disappearing in the scrum.

The enemy ranks became a formless mob of yelling figures, painted with blood, jabbing wildly with their spears. There was a sound like the clatter of a hundred blacksmiths at work. A broken spearhead arced through the air, the shaft a splintered flower.

The Dogsheads worked mechanically, stabbing out at eye-slits, naked throats, raised arms, picking carefully the flesh they wanted to ruin. This was *shearing the sheep*. A man had to stand in the ranks and take it. There was no running away for those at the forefront of the fighting. They lowered their heads into their shields and dug in their heels.

Rictus heard his centurions shouting above the clamour of the fight. "Push, you bastards, push!" Fornyx yelled, and the men in the rear ranks set their shields in the backs of the men in front and obeyed him.

Another shunt forward, the crushing weight of the men behind and the men in front.

Without the protection of his black cuirass Rictus would not have been able to breathe in that packed mill of murder. Men passed out and were carried upright in the midst of it. There were bodies underfoot now, abandoned shields, and the ground was being trampled into muck beneath them, becoming mired with blood and other, baser fluids.

"One more!" Rictus shouted with what breath remained in his bruised lungs. "Dogsheads, forward!"

He could feel it, like a sudden change in the weather. The men of Goron were faltering; the pressure to his front was growing less. He met the eyes of the man pinned against him, and saw the doubt and defeat in them. He grinned.

"You are a dead man," he said, and laughed.

The enemy line broke as the Dogsheads pushed forward a third time. First the men at the rear dropped their shields and ran, and then the panic spread. In seconds, the battle opened out. The enemy formation lost all order, became a mob in which every man thought only of himself. The pressure eased. The man pinned against Rictus backed away one pace, two, still looking into his eyes. He was a good soldier – it was why he was a file leader. He did not want to run, to drop his shield in shame and present his back to the aichmes of his foes. He was weeping.

Finally, when those behind him had left him, he turned to follow them, to run for the safety of his city walls. When he turned, Rictus stabbed him through the back of his neck, feeling the spearhead crunch through the man's spine. He went down bonelessly.

Rictus stepped over him. The entire enemy line was in flight. To the right, Teresian's men were following up with a chorus of wild halloos and shrieks of laughter: wordless, mindless noise, both exultation and relief. Rictus raised his spear, breathing fast as a sprinter.

"Halt!" He shouted. "Reform!"

The Dogsheads came together, tightened their ranks, and stood motionless amid a tide-wrack of bodies, piles of discarded shields. The men fleeing them were no longer soldiers, and not worth killing. The only way to catch up with them in any case would have been to drop their own shields. They had done enough.

Rictus stepped forward of the front rank, stabbed the sauroter of his spear into the ground and unhelmed, feeling the blessed chill of the winter's day ease his throbbing skull. Fornyx joined him. His black beard was matted with blood.

"It's always the third shove that does it," he said, and nudged a corpse with his foot. It was the man Rictus had speared through the neck. He wore a bracelet of dried grass about his wrist, the kind a daughter might plait for her father on a summer afternoon. Rictus looked away from it.

There was a thunder on the air, a tremble felt through the soles of the feet. Teresian's men opened up their ranks to the right, and through the gap came a torrent of cavalry, Corvus leading them with his personal banner snapping above his head. The spearmen roared as the Companions swept past, tall Kufr on big horses with bright coloured cloaks opening out from their shoulders like flags.

They took off after the fleeing men of Goron, a cavalcade of death, and began spearing them from behind as they ran. Soon the open ground leading up to the city in the distance was black with scattered bodies, and still the Companions hunted them, killing scores, hundreds, riding them down like greyhounds slaughtering hares.

"That is murder," Fornyx said, his teeth bared with distaste.

Druze joined them. His Igranians were running in the wake of the cavalry, looting the dead, spearing the wounded, clearing up like jackals in the wake of a pride of lions. He offered Rictus and Fornyx a wineskin. Bitter highland wine, like that Rictus made at Andunnon. Druze wiped his mouth. His dark face was shining with sweat.

"I know what is in your mind," he said, "but if you fight against Corvus, this is what happens. These men had only to stay within their walls, accept our terms, and they would be alive with their families today."

"War has its conventions," Rictus said. "One does not pursue to the death when the foe is beaten."

"He is different," Druze retorted. "His wars are different. It is why he wins them."

Fornyx took a long squirt of the wine and handed the skin back to Druze, his gaze never leaving the receding slaughter. "Yes, he's quite some general, our little Corvus. But it's one thing to beat an outnumbered band of citizens, something else to face up to the army of the League."

Druze nodded. "I know this. And you know what, Fornyx? He is looking forward to it. He wants it with all his heart. And the more men the League brings against us, the happier he will be. Sometimes I think his sire is Phobos himself. He has no fear."

"All men fear something," Rictus said. "Even if it's not death."

"Then he fears failure," Druze acknowledged. "More than anything else. More than death."

The cavalry reined in perhaps two pasangs to their front. A few isolated, running dots were all that remained of the sixteen hundred men who had faced Rictus in line what seemed like only minutes before. The city of Goron had just lost its menfolk. All of them.

"What will he do now, sack the city?" Fornyx asked.

Druze shook his head. "That is not his way. He cannot abide violence done to women or children. I think maybe something happened to him in boyhood, to his own people. It is the thing he hates most."

Rictus felt a strange relief. He had seen enough cities sacked before this, and not just his own. He loathed the vileness which came out in even the best of men when all the rules were taken away, when the basest of appetites were freely indulged.

"How did you come to serve him?" he asked Druze, wondering. The dark Igranian did not seem a man who had ever been defeated. He had the self assurance of someone always on the winning side.

"Corvus killed my father," Druze said simply. "He beat my people in open battle one fine day west of Idrios. His Companions rode us down like they did these men today."

"Phobos!" Fornyx exclaimed.

Druze smiled his dark smile. "My father was a fine warrior, but also a brigand and a braggart. I loved him, but I was not blind to his failings.

"He fought Corvus sword to sword, and fell. And afterwards Corvus gave him a funeral worthy of a king. My people are not city-dwellers. You would call them uncivilized, and you would be right; but they can appreciate greatness in a man just as you can. Corvus has it. And me, I wish to be there when it comes to full flower – for the adventure of it. I want to be part of the story."

Rictus and Fornyx looked at one another, and Fornyx's mouth twisted in a wry smile.

THE ARMY CAMPED that night outside the walls of Goron, their tent-lines greater than the city itself. During the afternoon, Corvus had had his men gather up all the dead from along the road and set them on a pyre, to be burned the next day. All through the night, the women of the city trickled down to the hill of bodies to keen and wail and mourn their husbands, their fathers, their sons, and their cries carried over the camp of the army like an accusation, as though Antimone herself were hovering overhead, black wings beating in the darkness, her tears falling unseen upon the snow.

Rictus was called to Corvus's tent some time before the middle watch of the night, and entered to find most of the high command there, seated around the map-table with clay cups in their hands, braziers glowing bright and hot about them. Corvus was striding up and down, his long black hair loose. In the uncertain light of the hanging lamps he looked like some beautiful exotic girl dressed in a man's chiton. The silver weapon scars on his forearms marred the image.

He greeted Rictus with that peculiarly winning smile, like that of a son who thinks he has pleased his father.

"Your men lived up to their reputation today, Rictus. That is the first time I have ever seen a spear phalanx keep its formation at a run. You have given Teresian's spears something to think about."

Teresian himself, a younger version of Rictus, did not seem particularly thoughtful. He stared at Rictus with veiled hostility, but held up a wine-cup in a grudging gesture of respect.

"We should not have had to fight today," Corvus said, resuming his pacing of the tent. "It was stupidity on their part – what did they hope to accomplish?"

Anger lifted his voice a tone. He sounded almost

shrill. "I have made an object lesson of the men of Goron – that example will travel ahead of us. I'm optimistic that we'll have no more futile stands before we come to the hinterland of Machran itself. It is there that the campaign will have its climax. Word has come to me that the Avennan League is mustering at last, and Karnos has persuaded all the cities to send contingents. The decisive battle will be fought soon, before midwinter."

"Karnos has done well," Demetrius, the one-eyed marshal of the conscript spears said, tilting his head to bring his eye to bear.

"He's quite the orator, it seems, and the Machran polemarch, Kassander, is an old friend of his – they work together like the hand and the gauntlet. All this is to our advantage."

"I fail to see how," Rictus said. "The League can muster thirty or forty thousand men if it has the time to muster them. We don't have half that here."

Corvus smiled. "But if those thirty or forty thousand are fairly beaten in open battle, the thing will be done at a stroke – all the hinterland cities will have been defeated at once."

"If they are defeated." Rictus was more puzzled than alarmed. Did this boy *want* to fight against hopeless odds?

Corvus seemed to catch his thought. "Where is the glory, Rictus, in beating citizen armies one by one in an endless series of petty battles? No, we will let them combine. Let them grow confident in their numbers. Once they have mustered, they will find the confidence to come out and meet us spear to spear."

"Glory," Rictus repeated. He looked round the other men in the tent, thinking of the morning's slaughter. That had been a petty affair indeed, but the women keening at the funeral pyre would disagree.

He shook his head. Maybe I am too old, he thought. I have forgotten what ambition was like. What it can do in a man.

Druze winked at him. Teresian was lost in his wine. Demetrius, the oldest, seemed as unperturbed as a stone. Rictus had heard his name before; he had commanded a mercenary centon years in the past, lost his eye fighting for Giron on the Kuprian Coast, and had gone east. To end up with Corvus.

And Ardashir, the Kufr marshal. He met Rictus eye to eye, and there was something surprising in his face. A kind of fellow-feeling. A sympathy. Then the Kufr looked away and Rictus was left imagining it.

"What is it you want?" he asked aloud. "What is all this for?"

Corvus stopped his pacing, his pale face lifted in surprise.

"An odd question for a sellspear to ask," Teresian sneered.

Yes, Rictus thought; one day you and I will have a reckoning, my friend.

"Not so odd," Corvus said. "And Rictus is more than a sellspear. Much more." He cast his gaze about the tent, and a silence fell in which the keening of the women out at the pyre could be heard as a rumour on the wind.

"He commanded an army once, the most celebrated army the Macht have ever fielded, outside of legend."

I commanded it by chance, Rictus thought. Because all the best men were dead. It was a whim of Phobos, no more.

But he said nothing.

"I was born outside of Sinon, in the land beyond the sea," Corvus went on. "Most of you here already know this. I have seen the Empire that Rictus marched through, or a corner of it – as has Ardashir. He and I grew up together, and whether he be Kufr or no, he is my brother in all things but blood." He stared at the men in the room deliberately, meeting their eyes one by one.

"Sinon is where the march of the Ten Thousand ended, where their epic came to a close." Now he looked at Rictus.

"Not in glory, but in squalor. When the last centons of these heroes finally straggled down to the shores of the sea, what did they do?

"They set about each other like squabbling dogs. They killed one another for gold, for insults given and taken on the long march west. They were riven into pieces before they even saw the sea. They were Macht, and they had defeated the armies of the Great King over and over in open battle. They had humbled an Empire, but they could not govern themselves."

A flash of something passed over Corvus's face, something between contempt and anger. It chilled Rictus's spine to look upon it. This boy, he was –

"That is the fatal flaw within the Macht," Corvus ploughed on. His face was a mask without colour, the strange violet eyes within it bright as those of some feral animal.

"Unless they face death from without, then they will spend their lives fighting each other – farmyard cocks all crowing on their separate dunghills. This is what we are, here in the Harukush, the poorest patch of stone in the world.

"In the Empire the Macht are a thing of legend and wonder, a tale told to frighten children. We are the fearsome beast of the night, the things which crossed the sea to wreak havoc, and then disappeared. I know – I have heard these stories across the Sinonian. But here –" Disgust crossed his face. "Here we are a million struggling dwarfs, all pissing and moaning about where we shall have space to shit."

He lifted his chin, stood straight. He was slight as a girl, but Rictus had no doubt in that moment that he could have killed any one of those in the tent who stood up against him. Men smelled fear and weakness, as surely as dogs did. And in Corvus there was none. He was a creature of singular determination.

"I am here to unite the Macht, to make of them one people, one purpose, We were put upon this world to rule it, and that is what we shall do. To make us all of one will, I must conquer all. I intend to bring all our people under one ruler."

He smiled with a moment's disarming irony.

"I will wear the black Curse of God, Rictus; on the day that I am named King of the Macht."

NINE
THE GHOST IN
THE TENT

"Phobos, what a damned awful stupid time of year to be in harness," Fornyx said in disgust. "My second winter campaign in as many years. This is no way to run the shop."

He and Druze stood in the mire with their cloaks over their heads and stared at the flat grey world of the rain. In the country to their front the water had gathered in broad sword-pale lakes in which the black outline of trees stood forlorn and stark. The mountains were invisible, the sullen shadow of the clouds gnarled over the north and west, the sky brought low to meet a colourless landscape. And the rain did its best to bring the two together in one new element composed of equal parts water and mud.

"Six day's march to Machran," Druze said with that sinister, oddly winning smile of his. "Or maybe not."

"And still he pushes us on, your lord and master,"

Fornyx said. "What did we make, day before yesterday – six pasangs? The baggage spent a whole day just travelling the length of the column – and as for the supply lines, well..."

"I wish it was snow," Druze said. "Snow I am used to. But this lowlander's winter of yours, it sucks at a man's marrow, neither one thing nor the other."

"You'll get used to it," Fornyx said with a grin. "You'll have to, if you're not to retire back to banditry in the hills."

"There are worse trades, my friend. My people, they have strong places carved out of the very rock of the world, back in the Gerreran Mountains above Idrios. We hole up in those in the winter like bears, eat ourselves fat and greasy and fuck our women until they walk bow-legged."

Fornyx snorted with laughter. "Not a bad way to pass the winter. Me, I like the idea of a fishing town on the Bay of Goshen, where the sky is blue all through the dark months and a man can sit at one of those wine shops on the water and stare out at the Sinonian while eating fresh octopus and grilled herrin."

They stared silently at the rain for a long while, their feet ankle-deep in mud.

"I have wine in my tent..." Fornyx said at last, grudgingly.

"We are here to watch the enemy," Druze said.

"Look at them – they're not going anywhere. The bastards are as mired in shit as we are."

Out at the limits of visibility it was possible to make out a shadow on the world, dark as a forest. Within that shadow were the lights of struggling campfires.

They covered the land for many pasangs. As the rain-curtain shifted and drifted aimlessly, it was possible at times to make out the lines of the enemy's tents, but that was all. There was no movement, not a single ominous snake of men on the march. The enemy army was as motionless as a felled tree.

"A cup or two would not hurt," Druze admitted. "All right, then."

"And a game of knucklebones perhaps – Kesero had one on the go when I left."

"Not for me. You red-cloaked bastards cleaned me out last night."

The two men turned and began making their slow, plodding way back down the long slope they had ascended in the morning. They were barefoot; the mud sucked even the most heavily strapped footwear off men's feet. Some two dozen Macht were standing in the rain waiting for them: half Druze's Igranians, the rest scarlet-cloaked Dogsheads of Fornyx's centon. One of these spoke up.

"Any more of this and we can float over the walls of Machran in fucking boats."

"That's the plan," Fornyx said. "Didn't you know? Back to camp, lads – there's nothing doing out here that needs watching."

The little band of men followed their leaders back along the flooded length of the Imperial road, wading through the cold water with the stoicism of those who have seen it all before. To the east, the vast bivouac of Corvus's all-conquering army sat like a flooded squatter's camp, motionless in the unending downpour.

* * *

RICTUS, ALSO, WAS staring at the rain. He stood in the doorway of Corvus's command tent and watched the rills of brown water curl and thicken about the corduroyed pathways of the camp. As far as the eye could see the horizon was an unending mass of brown tents. The latrines had flooded out, and the stink of ordure hung over them. This was no place to remain long. Men sickened when they gathered together in great numbers. It was as if they produced an air unwholesome to their own existence.

He thought of Aise and the girls. Up in the highlands the snow would be thick and deep, the world closed down in mountain winter. They were safe, now – nothing and no-one would be able to make it through the drifts to Andunnon until the spring thaw. There was that to be thankful for.

"Some warmth in a cup," a voice said.

It was Ardashir, the tall Kufr. He proffered the brimming goblet to Rictus with a smile.

"Corvus is out digging drains with his Companions, to set an example. He will be a while." The Kefren marshal was liberally plastered with mud himself.

"I did my turn of digging this morning," he explained.

Rictus took the wine. Thin, watered stuff, but welcome all the same. The roads had been washed out and the supply-trains were not making it through. The entire army was on half rations. Another reason they could not stay here.

"It would seem Antimone is on Karnos's side for the present," he said, sipping the execrable wine.

"Your Antimone, goddess of pity and of war. A strange deity. Myself, I believe that Mot, the dark blight of the world, is passing over."

"Different gods, same rain," Rictus grunted. He walked away from the uplifted side of the tent and stood at the map table. They were so close.

Some two hundred and thirty pasangs separated them from the walls of Machran.

That, and the army which Karnos had managed to cobble together with incredible speed to throw in their path. It was not yet the full muster of the League, but it was a respectable showing all the same. Perhaps twenty thousand men were encamped on the other side of the hill, enduring the same rain as their enemies, and he did not doubt that more would be marching in over the next few days, mud or no mud.

"We should hit them hard, now, before the other hinterland cities send their contingents," he said. "This waiting is... unwise."

Ardashir came to the table, towering over Rictus like a totem. "In this weather?"

"Men have fought in worse."

"I know they have, Rictus. But we talk not only of men. What of horses? Cavalry cannot operate in this swamp. We must delay now until the plains dry out. Corvus foresaw that this might happen. He talks of glory, and he means it, but there is always a stone cold reasoning behind what he does. Until we have hard ground to fight on, the army cannot go on the offensive. If it does, then it will simply be two bodies of spears slogging it out, and in that contest, numbers will be more telling."

"I had not thought of your horses," Rictus conceded, throwing back his wine. "It is not something a Macht would usually take into account." He looked the tall Kefren up and down.

"Tell me, Ardashir – tell me honestly – what in hell are you doing here?"

Ardashir grinned. He had a kindly face, but so elongated and strange did it appear that it was easy to miss the humanity in his eyes.

"Corvus is my friend, the best I have. I would follow him anywhere."

"That's not an answer."

"It's one answer."

Then Ardashir inclined his head. "Very well. Then know this; my father was Satrap of the province of Askanon, maybe ten years after you and your Ten Thousand passed through it. He was a good man, an honourable man, but even good men can have worthless brothers." The Kefren's face changed. It was if the bones of it became more pronounced; a mask that was truly alien – like those of the Honai that Rictus had faced at Kunaksa.

"He killed my father, took my sister – his niece – to wife against her will, and proclaimed himself Satrap. I was a child, smuggled out of my father's palace in Ashdod by our family steward. He took me to Sinon, where my uncle could not touch me, it being a Macht city. And there I spent much of my boyhood, in poverty. When Kurush our steward died, I was left alone. All that remained of the life before was this –" Here he unsheathed the curved sword which hung at his flank. It was a plain Kefren scimitar with an hourglass hilt, and set in the pommel was a small incised ruby. He rubbed his thumb across it. "Our family seal. This was my father's sword. All I have of him."

His face brightened. "And I met Corvus, playing on the shore outside Sinon one fine day some twelve years ago. He was an undersized child, half my height, but he was the leader of all the local boys, and he made me, a Kufr, part of his friends. I have never forgotten that." He looked down at Rictus.

"Corvus does not care about Macht and Kufr. He cares about friendship. Once he gives it, he will never betray you."

Rictus stared up at the tall creature who stood before him. He had learned how to judge men over the years, and to judge soundly. He knew that Ardashir was not lying. More, he found himself liking this quiet Kufr, this dispossessed prince who had followed his mad friend west in pursuit of an insane idea.

He looked down at the map table again, seeing writ across it the fate of his world, his people.

"There is Kufr blood in Corvus, isn't there?" he said.

Ardashir nodded. "His mother was a hufsa, one of the mountain tribes. But she was an educated and refined woman. You and I can see it in him, as can all those who have known a little of both worlds; but most Macht have never met a Kufr; they think we are all horse-faced demons with glowing eyes." He smiled.

"So who was his father?"

"I never knew him, and nor did Corvus. He had left or died before the boy was born."

Rictus looked across the interior of the tent to where the Curse of God, the armour that Corvus would not wear, sat perched on its stand like some amputated statue. A sudden insight went like a shiver down his back.

Corvus's father had been a Cursebearer.

He might have said something, but as if summoned by their talk, Corvus himself entered the tent, flapping the rain off his cloak and bantering with Teresian, who was with him. The leader of the army was as plastered with mud as if he had been rolling in it; his teeth and eyes gleamed out of a brown face. His smile widened as he saw Rictus and Ardashir at the table.

"Ha! Steering clear of the muck, are we? And winecups in your hands! Come, Ardashir, this is a disgrace; lend me a gulp, will you?" He drank deep out of the Kufr's cup.

"Not Minerian, Rictus, sorry to say. But it all leaves us in the same way, whatever the vintage – Teresian, pour us more. I swear I have mud in my very gullet."

Corvus's spirits seemed undimmed by the rain and the morass his army found itself in. He threw off his cloak and one of the page boys came forward from the shadows to catch it – Rictus had not even known he was there.

"Thank you, Sasca," Corvus murmured, and when he set a hand on the page's shoulder the boy's face lit up.

"What word of the Dogsheads?" Corvus asked Rictus, making for the banked red coals of the brazier and standing so close to it they could smell the singeing wool of his chiton.

"Fornyx and your man Druze report that the enemy camp is about as lively as ours – no coming or going. No-one can make a move in this weather."

Corvus seemed profoundly satisfied by this news. "Excellent. Ardashir, the supply train?"

"It's making slow progress some twenty pasangs up the road. The wagons are up to their axles and the oxen are dying on their feet. It will be at least another two days before it reaches us."

"Ah." Even this did not dim his high spirits. "Brothers, we must not let a little rain dampen our mood. There may be a way to have some fun out of this downpour. Teresian, the wine stands by you; pass it round, man."

Fun? Rictus thought. He looked at Ardashir and the Kufr shrugged.

"I feel the urge to get to know my enemies better," Corvus went on. "There they are over the hill by the thousand, and we have not so much as said hello to one another. This Karnos is a fascinating fellow, by all accounts – like you, Rictus, a self-made man of a certain age. I'm thinking I should get a better look at him."

"I know Karnos – I've spoken to him many a time," Rictus said. "He's a braggart, an upstart slave-dealer with a silver tongue."

"That tongue of his certainly has a way of getting things done," Corvus replied, still in a good humour. "Look across the way and name me one other member of the Machran Kerusia who could have got their levies out on the road as quickly as Karnos did. No, he's a man of some substance this fellow, not just a crowd-pleaser." He paused. "I think I would like a look at him."

"What shall we set up – some kind of embassy?" Teresian asked, narrow-eyed.

"We could pitch a tent between the armies," Ardashir suggested.

Corvus held up a hand. "I was thinking of something a little more personal. I want to get a look at him tonight."

They were all foxed by his words, and then it dawned on Rictus. "You want to enter the enemy camp."

Corvus cocked his head to one side, and flakes of mud fell off his face. He peeled off some more, held it in his hand. "Why not – covered in this, all men look alike."

"Corvus, my brother –" Ardashir began.

"Not you, Ardashir – no amount of mud could cover your origins." Corvus was smiling, but the humour had dimmed in him. He was in earnest.

"You, Rictus – will you come with me?"

A moment of silence, the rain drumming on the roof of the great tent.

"You think it wise?" Rictus asked evenly.

"I did not say it was wise. I said it was what I intended to do. And as you are one of my marshals, I should like your company."

Another test. Rictus held the younger man's eyes. Something like perfect understanding passed between them.

"Very well," he said with as much nonchalance as he could muster. "Shall it be we two alone, then?"

"The fewer the better. But I wish Druze to join us – he has a gift for escapades."

"And when shall we leave?"

Corvus stretched in front of the brazier so that its red glow underlit his face, making it seem less than ever like that of a normal man.

"We'll wait for darkness," he said. "And Rictus –"

"Yes?"

"We'll travel light. Your cuirass will stay here, and that scarlet cloak with it."

Rictus nodded. Both Teresian and Ardashir were protesting, claiming it was a hare-brained venture, unnecessary risk. They did not use the word *madness*, but it was in their thoughts all the same. Both Corvus and Rictus ignored them. The leader of the army and his newest marshal needed to find trust in one another, and they both knew it.

His life will be in my hands, Rictus thought, as mine has been in his. I have only to raise my voice in the enemy camp, and he will be captured, and this army of his will fall apart. He knows this.

He had to marvel at Corvus's audacity. This boy –

No; he was not a boy. That way of regarding him was no longer tenable. In fact he was no younger than Rictus had been when he had been elected leader of the Ten Thousand. Sometimes, with the selective memory of a middle-aged man, Rictus forgot that he, too, had been something of a prodigy.

He took off his cloak, and began unclicking the fastenings of his black cuirass. He stared at the other Curse of God in the tent, perched on its armour-stand like some silent ghost. Who wore you? He wondered. Were you one of us, who made the March beside me?

He placed his cuirass beside its fellow, and for

a moment all the occupants of the tent fell silent, looking at them.

These were the keystone of the heritage of the Macht. No Kufr had ever possessed or worn one of them in all of recorded history. Antimone's Gift was a black mystery at the heart of the Macht world. Sometimes, Rictus thought that if one could puzzle out the origins of these artefacts, then one would have unravelled the enigma of the Macht themselves. He had come to think, during the long march all those years ago, that the Macht were somehow not part of this world they inhabited. At least, they had not been here in the beginning.

And he knew, now, why Corvus hesitated to wear the black armour. He was half Kufr, and even his undoubted courage must flinch at the thought of a creature of Kufr blood donning the Curse of God.

Who knows? Rictus surmised. Maybe it will not even let him wear it. How would that look? So he lets it sit here, a temptation and a reproach.

And he suddenly had a blink of insight into the engine that drove Corvus on.

He wants to rule the Macht, because he wants to feel that he is truly one of them. If the Harukush acclaims him its ruler, how can he not be one of us?

Eunion was right, Rictus thought. He is a dreamer. But there is more to it. This is what drives him on, this thing gnawing at his guts. He has surrounded himself with fatherless boys and made of them a family. He wants to belong.

Perhaps that is his other secret; to take the orphaned and make them feel part of something again.

* * *

THEY LEFT THE camp at dusk, three mudstained men in nondescript woollen chlamys, barefoot in the chill suck of the mud, their hoods pulled over their faces like the *komis* of the Kufr. They bore the lowland drepanas that Karnos's troops would carry, and Druze had painted across his leather pelta the *machios* sigil of Machran.

The waterlogged plain between the armies had once been good farmland, and there were still the black thickets of olive groves strewn across it, but it had been inundated with the rain that poured down from the hills so that now it bore more of a resemblance to some wildfowler's marsh, a grey mere of dappled mud and ochre water.

Karnos had planted his burgeoning army on a low rise across the Imperial road, and the water had filled a ring around its foot so that it seemed like an island, or a vast moated fort, pasangs wide; and the cloud hung so low that it almost met the summit.

Eight pasangs to the rear of the enemy army was the city of Afteni, renowned for its metal-working. And behind that was Arkadios, and then to the west and south of that one of the great cities of the hinterland, Avennos of the Laws, where Tynon himself had lived and lectured for a time, back in the mists of the past. He had been the author of those codes which now governed nearly all the Macht cities. The origins of the Kerusia – the assembly that every Macht polity possessed – lay there.

Avennos was not the metropolis it had been;

both Avensis to the south, which had been its colony upon a time, and Arienus to the south-west had grown greater with the passage of the years. But Avennos was a part of the Macht identity as surely as Machran was. That, Rictus reasoned, was why Karnos had thrown his army so far forward, extending his supply lines and landing himself in the same muck as Corvus. To preserve that core of tradition. It was militarily unsound, but politically it could not be faulted.

The darkness drew in over the floodplain, a lightless black without stars or moons. The three men lurched from one footfall to the next, the muck seizing them calf-deep. Once, Drúze went on his face and the others had to halt and lever him free, haul him upright again. Corvus was seized by a fit of laughter, and after a contemplation of their absurd condition it flapped through them all so that they stood for a few minutes holding their mouths, leaning on one another like drunks.

"I'll lead," Corvus said at last. "I'm lighter than either of you clodhoppers, and I see better in the dark. Grab a hold of my cloak and try not to pull me on my arse."

They went on, their only frame of reference in that starless murk the subdued glow of the enemy campfires. Only a few were burning, fighting a losing battle with the endless rain. Usually a host like Karnos's would light up the night sky with its fires like a city at festival time.

Corvus halted, and Rictus felt the young man's iron grip on his arm.

"Sentries," he murmured, his breath warm in Rictus's ear. "We go right, cast around them."

The three made a laborious dog-leg about the sentries which only Corvus had seen. They were glad of the rain, for the sluicing hiss of it covered their lumpen progress. Rictus found his joints aching as they had not since the winter before, in the siege-camp outside Nemasis, and he felt again the ache of the arrow-wound in his thigh. The cold and the wet were always ready to recall his old scars, as though in league with his ageing body to remind him of his mortality.

They waded as quietly as they could through knee-deep freezing water, clenching their chattering teeth shut, and began to hear other sounds than the rain ahead. Men's voices, a low hum of talk, and the chink and gleam of lights glancing through the gaps in leather-canopied tents. The ground rose under their feet, became marginally drier in that the mud was only ankle-deep.

"Here we are," Corvus said, as unconcerned as if he had led them into his own back yard. "From here on in we straighten up and look like citizens. Perhaps we should go under different names. Druze, you look like a Timus to me."

"Boss," Druze said, "I would follow you to the far side of the Veil if you asked me, but don't try to make me laugh. It's not one of your gifts."

"I fall short in that respect," Corvus admitted, and they saw him grin under his hood. He seemed as light of heart as a boy who has found a peephole in a bathhouse wall.

"I wonder if Karnos's tent is as big as mine. What think you, Rictus? You know him better than I."

"I think Druze's accent and your face will give us away in a moment. Let me lead, for Phobos's sake, and both of you keep your mouths shut."

Corvus nodded, and in an entirely different, clinical voice said, "Count the sigils you see. I want to know which cities have brought up their levies."

They walked through the camp as brazenly as though they belonged there, Druze wiping the muck off his pelta so the Machran sigil shone out white in the firelit gaps in the dark. The camp of Karnos's army stank worse than their own, and Rictus put out of his mind thoughts of what his bare feet must be treading through.

Men were crowded in their tents, huddled around guttering clay lamps and foul-smelling tallow candles. Some resolute souls were keeping campfires going, atop each the familiar villainous black shape of a centos, the great iron pot fighting men had eaten from since time out of mind. There was a toothsome smell on the air amid the baser stinks; Karnos's men were eating stewed goat, ladling in mounds of lentils and onions to eke out the meat. Lowland food; the smell of it brought back memories of a dozen old campaigns to Rictus.

He had to shake his mind into the moment; the scenes before him were so familiar that the sense of danger was dulled.

He stopped short when he caught sight of the *namis* sigil on some shields, painted in blue. These were men of Nemasis, with whom he had fought only the summer before. The gap-toothed man with the shaven head was Isaeos, the idiot whose bumbling had cost lives and lost months in Rictus's last contract. He bent his head into his hood as he passed by.

The mismatched trio of filthy strangers wandered through the camp without challenge, three more nameless Màcht in a sea of them. Rictus stopped counting sigils after he reached twenty. Every city of the hinterland was here, and yet the camp was not big enough to accommodate their full levies. Some must have been sending token contingents, no more. Even among the members of the Avennan League, there were hostilities and rivalries. Karnos had done well to come so far with so many.

No-one challenged them. Rictus was not surprised. He had known citizen armies all his life. They would fight like lions when the time came, but the idea of camp discipline was beyond them; one might as well try to herd cats.

After only a few weeks with Corvus, he had begun to take for granted the efficiency of the army on the far side of the plain, to view it with even a trace of indulgence. He had all but forgotten that his Dogsheads were the exception, not the rule, and that Corvus had made something surprisingly different out of his own host.

Once again, he found himself looking at this Kufr half-breed from a revelatory new angle.

Kufr. Now that was something to factor into things.

The three interlopers grew in confidence, emboldened by the black night, the rain and the muck-stains which made them almost indistinguishable from every other man in the camp. Rictus accepted a squirt of wine from a good-natured drunken fellow with the *machios* sigil tattooed on his arm, and went so far as to ask him where Karnos's tent might be found.

"That fat bastard?" the man cried. "He's still in Machran with his cock up some slave-girl's arse. It's Kassander you want, friend – he commands here. What are you, some kind of messenger? Fucking rain – ain't it a bitch, eh?" He staggered off, plashing through the muck with the bullish determination of the drunk who knows where he wants to go.

"The more I hear of this Karnos fellow, the more I like him," Druze said with his thick black brows beetling up his forehead. "Had I the choice –"

A woman's scream cut across him, shrill and terrified.

"I said," Druze went on, "Had I the choice I'd much prefer –"

"Shut up," Corvus snapped. "Rictus, where was that?"

Rictus pointed down the haphazard line of tents. "It's not our concern, Corvus. There's nothing more to be seen here."

He was ignored. Corvus strode off on his own in the direction of the scream.

"Oh, shit," Druze muttered, and grasped Rictus by the arm, taking off in his leader's wake. "Rictus, for Phobos's sake, get a hold of him."

Corvus moved like a black, silent raptor through the tent lines, with Rictus and Druze trailing him.

He had thrown back his hood, and his eyes caught the light of the campfires and reflected it back a violent green.

He pulled back a tent flap, and out of the interior blew a blare of lamplight, the stink of men's sweat, and something else, something high and keen and bitter in the night.

Fear.

TEN
BLOOD AND BLUFF

KARNOS WOKE WITH a start. He had barely been asleep anyway. Some gaudy dream of standing talking to a crowd, and the men he spoke to were all cheering him, shouting his name, and sharpening knives.

Subtle, he thought with a mental grunt. Phobos, how is a man to live like this, for weeks at a time? I am Speaker of Machran. I made this army – I created it out of nothing. It is here by my will.

He turned in the straw, snarling and tugging his cloak about with him. They could at least have made me some kind of bed... there are ticks in this straw.

He scratched his crotch violently, and cursed aloud. Awake now.

In all seriousness – how does a man live like this? He thought of his well-stuffed mattress in Machran, and little Grania in it with her white skin and soft mouth. Or that new girl – the one with the lovely arse.

Here he was, one cloak to his name, lying on tick-infested straw with the damp of the ground creeping through it.

He opened his eyes wide.

The lamp was almost out of oil; a blue, guttering blossom pulsing round the wick. It was almost wholly dark in the tent.

What in hell was that?

He heard it again; a distant uproar, men shouting. He was used by now to the sound of the interminable quarrels, the fights that flared up out of nowhere; these were the background noises of the camp. But this was different; more urgent.

He sat up, adjusted the lamp so the end of the wick had a last drop of oil to suck into, and as the light strengthened, he scrabbled through the straw which lined the tent floor, fumbling for sandals, sword; anything which might orientate him to this strange and new place the night had found him in.

The tent flap was flung open and he saw a black silhouette with fire behind it.

"Some trouble over at the eastern end – might be nothing, but it sounds ugly. Want to come along?"

Kassander's voice.

"Fuck it, yes. I'm awake now anyway. What time of the night is it?"

"The bad time, when men are tired but not quite asleep. This may only be a brawl."

"I said I'm coming," Karnos snapped, hopping into his sandals with his sword slung over one shoulder. "Help me with my cloak, will you? Phobos, what a life."

In a camp this large, Karnos felt like a tick on the hide of some great unknown beast. He had never truly tried to imagine what a host of some twenty thousand men might look like; he had merely totted up the numbers as they came in. If they stood eight men deep in battle array their line would stretch around three pasangs.

It was as though a new and noisome city of leather and shit and woodsmoke had been planted on the world, and here he was in the middle of it, one more face in a teeming sea of them.

This was not like holding forth on the floor of the Empirion – the rules were different here. Walking through the camp, he was accorded a certain amount of affectionate regard from the Machran host, a level of curiosity from the men of the other cities, but should a Cursebearer chance by, their eyes would be drawn to the black armour instantly, with a degree of awe that was almost religious.

I must get one of those one day, Karnos thought. It would perfect the image. Or redeem it, maybe.

He was a wealthy man; in the past he had tried to buy Antimone's Gift from Cursebearers down on their luck, but his offers had been rebuffed with such contempt that he had given up on the exercise. Once a man had one of those things on his back, it seemed it took up some space in his soul. Death was all that would make him part with it. It was one of the gauges of a city's greatness; how many Cursebearers it had as citizens.

There will be a few on the ground before all this is over, Karnos thought. I will talk to Kassander about it.

The two of them picked their way through the camp lines. The men had been sheltering in their tents, grumbling their way into sleep, or sharing a skin of wine, or rattling a game of knucklebones. Now the place was stirring again, and the paths between the bivouac lines were filling up with yawning, bad-tempered crowds, wondering what was causing the racket.

"I bet it's the Aftenai again," Kassander muttered. "A more bloody-minded set of fractious bastards I've never seen."

The noise rose – men were fighting, it was clear now. They heard the clash of iron, and someone shrieked, a death-scream.

"Phobos!" Kassander cursed, and he began to run.

RICTUS FELT THE man's blood spatter warm across his face as the drepana took the fellow's arm off above the elbow. He was unused to the heavy lowland weapon; it felt like a butcher's cleaver in his grasp, made for chopping and slashing.

He had the end of his cloak wrapped round his left arm, and threw it up in the next man's face, making him flinch long enough for the drepana to arc round again and open his belly. A stink of shit and hot meat as his entrails flopped down his legs into the mud, entangling his feet. The man tripped up and gave a high-pitched scream, rolling in the ropes of his own insides.

"Now," Corvus snapped, "back to us."

Rictus turned in the space he had made and darted between Corvus and Druze. The Igranian's pelta had been chopped in two and hung bloody from his arm. In the other his sword described a vertical circle as neat as a juggler's flourish, and another one of the enemy went to his knees, wide-mouthed in disbelief, and then fell flat, cleaved open from collar to breastbone.

Corvus leapt in with a flash and took down a third. "Machran!" he shouted. "Machran to me!"

A gap opened up in the ring that surrounded them and they were through it in a moment, slashing to left and right, out of the firelight and into the rainswept dark. Rictus tripped on a guy-rope and went on his elbows, only to be seized upright by the scruff of his neck and shoved onwards. Even in that instant, he found himself startled by the brute strength in Corvus's thin frame.

More men running at them, weapons in their hands. They were in the midst of a massive, congealing mob of bewildered figures, all shouting at once. The wounded were squealing behind them, and torches were being lit from the campfires. The rain hammered down on their faces and their legs were drained of energy, nothing more than mindless sinew hauling on the bone.

Rictus thought his chest was about to burst. He could not speak. Corvus and Druze both grabbed him and half-dragged his burly form through the tent-lines. An animal growl rose out of his throat; anger went white hot through his limbs and restored some sense to his head.

"Get the fuck off me." He shook away their helping hands.

Men shouted enquiries at the trio, unsure. Druze

tossed aside his split shield and tucked his maimed arm in his cloak, bundling up the fabric around a slash which had laid him open to the bone.

"Knucklebones," Corvus said loudly, panting. "Cheating bastards tried to rob us. They're still at it back there."

"Halt and identify yourselves," some officious prick yelled at them.

"Kiss my arse. We have a hurt man here – go stop that fight back there," Rictus shot back.

"Hold your ground!"

There were too many around them, crowding as men will about bad news or a quarrel. Rictus reversed his drepana and punched the officious prick low down in the groin with the wooden bulb of the weapon's pommel, then shouldered him aside. When the man next to him protested in snarling outrage, Corvus laid the flat of his sword against his temple, and he went down like a dropped sack of sand.

"Out of our bloody way."

They were through again, into the darkness, a tight, determined knot moving with a purpose, like an arrowhead plunging through the bowels of an ox.

KASSANDER BENT AND held the lamp up as he entered the tent. Karnos followed, mastering the impulse to retch at the stench within.

"What in the world happened here?"

The bloodied man in the torn chiton was holding the flesh of his forearm onto the bone, gore dripping in black strings from between his clenched fingers.

"He came in here like something sent by Phobos. He had a white face, and eyes, eyes like –"

"What happened to these men?" Kassander asked patiently. The inside of the tent was a charnel house, chopped-up corpses steaming as the heat left them. The back of the tent had a rent slashed in it from top to bottom.

"We had a girl, a slave girl the mess had gotten from the wagon-park. We were taking turns on her and he came in out of nowhere – General, his eyes – they were not those of a man. He came in here like a storm, killing right and left. There were others with him. They grabbed him as he was about to finish me off, cut open the back of the tent, and then they all went out that way. They cut us up like we were rabbits on a block, general. They were not men at all."

The man was in white bloodless shock, his lips blue. "Go to the carnifex," Kassander told him. "I'll talk to you later. What's your name?"

"Lomos of Afteni, your honour."

"All right Lomos, get out."

"Wait – where's the girl?" Karnos demanded.

"She ran. She's all right. It was just some fun, General, I swear."

"Go – go on – get that looked at."

Karnos and Kassander squatted on their haunches amid the carnage, the lamp's light lending a flicker of mocking movement to the bodies. Karnos counted five men there. It was as close as he had ever come to violent death in his life thus far, and while his stomach was still heaving, his mind studied the scene with a revolted fascination.

"Drepana wounds," Kassander said, moving the lamp this way and that. "The strawheads use stabbing swords. We must find that girl – perhaps she was not a slave at all, and had relations in camp – it has been known. Come, Karnos."

The camp was bristling like a kicked anthill now. The two men emerged into the rain to find that something was still going on, out near the eastern lines. A fully armed centurion with a transverse crest halted in front of Kassander.

"General, we think the enemy is behind this – there are infiltrators in the camp, and they've been raising hell. We have men hurt and killed all over the eastern end."

"Phobos!" Kassander hissed. He scraped a hand through his hair and turned to Karnos. "This makes no sense."

"Is it the precursor to an attack, you think?" Karnos asked. His heart lurched in his chest. Only a few days before, the notion of battle – real warfare, with himself in the thick of it – had seemed like the stuff of distant and slightly absurd conjecture. Here, in the chaos of rain and firelight, with other men's blood soaked into his feet, it was real and terrifying.

"We must turn out the army, just in case," Kassander decided. He turned to the centurion, noticing the *alfos* sigil on his shield. "Are you from Afteni?"

"Yes, general – these are my men butchered here."

"Pass it along the lines – the men are to arm and stand-to. I want them formed up on the eastern side, by centon." He turned to Karnos, his big, good natured face something entirely different now.

"We must gather the Kerusia, and rouse out all the contingents at once. There's no telling what this presages."

Karnos nodded. "You're the soldier, Kassander."

"You're the man who got us all here, brother. It's your job to talk to the other city leaders. We must assemble the army at once."

RICTUS, CORVUS AND Druze collapsed in the sucking mere some half pasang from the enemy camp, and lay in the freezing water, utterly spent.

"It must be near daylight," Rictus said. "We have to get on, or we'll be stuck out here like cockroaches on a tabletop when the sun comes up."

Corvus was wiping blood from his face with the corner of his sodden cloak. "Agreed. Look at them, Rictus; you see what we have done?"

There were torches lit all over the enemy camp now, travelling up and down it like fireflies. Even out here they could hear the surf of noise on the hill, men's voices raised in an angry clamour.

"Reminds me of stoning a hornet's nest when I was a boy," Druze said.

"It was madness," Rictus said, turning to Corvus. "By rights, we three should be dead in there, or captive."

"I saw your face when you looked in that tent," Corvus said, unabashed. "There was a time when you would have done the same thing. You wanted to, tonight."

"I have learned to think of the consequences of my actions."

"I have learned to trust to my luck sometimes, Rictus. And it has held. Phobos watches over me. He brought us out of there."

"It was insane," Rictus persisted.

"If a sane and sensible life includes walking past rape without blinking, then I would rather be dead," Corvus said, and there was a cold menace to his words that made Rictus and Druze look at one another.

He wiped his eyes with his cloak hem. "Sneer if you will, Rictus."

"I am not sneering." Rictus thought of the sack of Isca, of Ab Mirza in the Empire, the excesses of the Ten Thousand.

Once, I was the same, he thought.

"It may be expedient to tolerate what revolts you," Corvus said, "but where does that leave you, in the end? Better to die fighting for what you know is right and wrong."

"Black and white," Rictus said.

Corvus smiled. "Indeed. Druze, my brother, how is that arm?"

"It stings a little." Druze's face was pinched with pain.

"Then let's get you back home." Corvus put his arm about Druze's shoulders and pulled him close, then kissed him on his forehead.

"You took that blade for me," he said.

They staggered through the marshland with the adrenaline of the fight still singing in their nerves. It brought them another pasang or so, before draining away, leaving them wrung-out and thick-headed. At least that was how Rictus felt. Corvus began to talk again, as easily as a man lingering over his wine.

"Twenty sigils; that's the hinterland cities plus a few more. I saw the *alfos* and hammer of Arienus there, and Gast and Ferai – even Decanth. But they are not sending their full levies, or Karnos's army would be twice as big. Druze, give me your arm – that's it.

"It means they're holding back. Even now, they are not fully combined. Perhaps they do not rate their own danger as high as they should. I want them all in front of me, the men of every great city of the Macht. If we are to help our friend Karnos gather them all in his ranks, we will have to twist his tail a little more – more than we have done tonight."

"Boss, I think you went over there looking for a fight," Druze said.

"Perhaps I did. Did you see their lines? Amateurs, ankle-deep in their own shit, half-drunk most of them, their sentries gathered around fires and blind to the dark. At least we got them out of their blankets for a night."

He looked back. A grey light was growing in the air, Araian making her slow way up the back of the clouds to the east.

"Dawn is coming, and they're forming up on the brink of the hill – look, Rictus – they'll be all morning at it."

A black line was growing across the land, thickening and lengthening with every minute. Spearmen, moving into battle array.

"It would be rude not to respond," Corvus said, his pale grin back on his face. "When we get back, I think I'll have to turn out our lot to say hello."

Rictus looked at him sharply.

"You mean to bring on a battle?"

"Why not? Warfare is half blood and half bluff, Rictus. Karnos does not know what we're about, so he's taking the sensible route; he'll stand his men there in the rain for as long as he thinks we're about to come at him. Last night, the curtain went up. Now I intend to amuse the audience further."

WITH THE RISING of the sun, the clouds that had blanketed the sky for so many days finally began to part and shift, as though Araian had become impatient and was peeling them back to see what had become of the world. The rain petered out, and as the light broke broad and yellow across the flooded plain between the two camps it was caught by the pools of standing water and set alight in dazzling flashes of rippled reflection.

The curtain rises, Karnos thought. You would almost think he had planned it that way.

He stood uncomfortable and self-conscious in his panoply, acutely aware that there was not a single dint in his shield or scrape on the bronze greaves strapped to his shins. He had bought a layered linen cuirass in Afteni years before, the best of its kind, the belly reinforced with iron scales, the wings painted crimson and inlaid with black niello work. It had seemed splendid and martial back then; in this camp it now seemed brash and ostentatious when worn amid thousands of heirlooms and hand-me-downs, scraped and patched and rebuilt after numerous campaigns.

Men received their panoplies from their fathers; some were decades old, rebuilt and repaired time and again. The bronze breast-plates could be older still. But Karnos's father had never been prosperous enough to belong to the ranks of armoured spearmen that formed the backbone of every citizenry.

I am Karnos of Machran, he told himself. It may be that I am not much of a soldier, but it is I who have created this army, and I hold it together. They sneer at me as the slave-dealer from the Mithannon, but it is I who am cheered by the mob of Machran. I have done what none of them could do, for all their noble heritage and their bloodlines and their ancient heirlooms.

He turned around. Some two dozen men faced him, all in full armour, six in the Curse of God. This was the military Kerusia of the Avennan League, and it comprised the fighting leadership of the greatest of the Macht cities. They were all here today in some form or other: Ferai, Avensis, Arienus, even great Pontis from the south, whose membership had been for decades considered purely nominal. They had all brought their citizens to this hill, perhaps not as many as they might have, but they were here.

Kassander was here too, and his smile warmed Karnos, brought him upright in his heavy war-harness. He had never before been so conscious of his girth: amid these lean, ascetic-looking aristocrats he looked soft; even Periklus of Pontis, twenty years older, seemed more athletic.

But he spoke for Machran here, and the seven thousand spears she had sent to the field. His city was more populous than any two of the others combined, and had once been the seat of the ancient monarchy that had ruled all the Macht. The names of those kings had been lost to history, but the legend of them remained, as did the pre-eminence of Machran itself.

"The enemy moves," Karnos said, raising his voice to be heard over the marching phalanxes on the slopes below. The tents were emptying like a decanted jug, pouring a sea of men out onto the plain of Afteni.

"Last night it seems he conducted a reconnaissance of our camp. Today, he has set his troops in motion. It would seem that his numbers have been exaggerated; we outnumber him three to two, and what is more the ground is too soft for his cavalry. The odds favour us, brothers" – how that word almost stuck in his throat – "and while not all the promised city levies have yet joined us" – he paused, looking his sombre audience up and down with a hint of accusation, a note of disappointment – "we have the power here to defeat this Corvus where he stands. He has made a mistake, one which we must make fatal."

"You mean to fight here?" Glauros of Ferai asked. "Today?"

"Today."

"The ground may be bad for horses, but it is too wet for spears also," Ulfos of Avensis said. "Can you see our morai advancing through that muck?"

Kassander spoke up.

"Corvus is a soldier of great talent. His strength is in manoeuvre. His troops are better drilled than ours and thus more flexible. We must bog him down and bring our numbers to bear.

"This place, at this time, we can rule his cavalry out of the equation, and we cannot be sure of doing that somewhere else, or at some other time. We have a unique chance here. Citizen levies put their heads down and push; it is almost all they are trained to do. We do that here, and our numbers will soak up anything he can throw at us. We have the soldiers of twenty different cities here who have never fought together before – brothers, we cannot let this thing get complicated.

"We advance on a long front, into the floodplain, and there we fight this Corvus to a standstill. It will not be pretty, and Phobos knows there are many standing on this hill today who will be on the pyre by nightfall, but it is the surest way to take our kind of fighting to the enemy."

There was a silence as this sank in. They respected Kassander; he had been a soldier all his life, a mercenary in his youth before old Banos had brought him in to train up the Machran city guard. But his present position was due to Karnos, whom they despised. Karnos could almost see the wheels turning in their heads as they stood there cultivating their patrician aloofness, Katullos among them.

"Let this not be about politics," he said. "Whatever you think of me, consider the position as it stands.

We are here, brothers" – this time the word came easier, for he was sincere – "we are here to preserve the liberty of our cities and our institutions from a tyrant. All else is an indulgence."

He caught Katullos's eye, and thought he actually saw a flicker of approval there.

"There are men of Hal Goshen in the ranks across the way, and Maronen and Gerrera and Kaurios. These have been conscripted into this Corvus's army against their will, their cities enslaved and their treasuries emptied. How hard do you think they will fight for the invader?

"We have but to hold the line, and they will see what way their freedoms lie. Without his cavalry, this Corvus is nothing but a master of slaves." There were a few arch looks at this, from those who knew him. Karnos, whose wealth had been built on the backs of slaves. No matter – he had them now. He and Kassander had swayed them. Thank the goddess.

There would be a battle today, the greatest fought in the Harukush for generations.

And he, Karnos, would have to be in the middle of it.

His own rhetoric had led him to overlook this.

As his father had used to say, with the fatalism of the poor; you want to eat bread, you got to grind the corn.

ELEVEN
THE FLOODED PLAIN

RICTUS STOOD AT the forefront of his men with his helm cradled in one arm. His shield was leaning against his planted spear in the front rank. All of the Dogsheads were in battle-line, shields resting against their knees, helms off, enjoying a last feel of the air on their faces, a look at the sky.

They were back of the front line, and the ground was a little drier here on the rising slope leading east along the Imperial Road to the camp. Up front, the ranks of spears had already trampled the sodden earth into an ankle-deep mire simply by getting into formation. Most of the men were barefoot despite the chill of the day, for the plain ahead of them would suck the best-strapped footwear off a man's feet in a few minutes of fighting.

In front of the red-cloaked mercenaries, Corvus's army had shaken out into battle formation, a line of infantry some two pasangs long.

Not long enough, Rictus thought. He'll be outflanked on one side, maybe both. What the hell does he have in mind?

The cavalry had left their horses back in camp and stood beside the Dogheads. There were some two thousand of them under Ardashir, the orphaned prince. They were shieldless, armed with lances and drepanas, clad in the short corselet of the horseman. They were not equipped for phalanx fighting; against a line of heavily armoured spearmen they would be massacred.

Though it had to be admitted, they did lend an exotic sort of variety to the sombre, mud-coloured army. They seemed to vie with one another to own the gaudiest cloaks and most outrageous helmet-crests. And most of them were Kufr, head and shoulders taller than the Macht, their skin seeming almost to glow in the pale autumn sunlight. Ardashir their leader stood out in front of them, leaning on the long, wicked lance of the Companions, his cloak folded around him.

Corvus was on horseback, riding along the front of his troops and making a speech that Rictus could not hear. The men clashed their shields in response to it, and a full-throated roar travelled the length of the line.

Nine thousand heavy spearmen, over half of them conscripts from the conquered cities of the eastern seaboard led by one-eyed Demetrius, the rest dependable veterans under young Teresian. On their left, two to three thousand Igranians under Druze, whose left arm was in a sling, but who was not going to miss this for the world.

As if he could feel Rictus's contemplation, Druze turned around, out on the left, and raised his javelin in salute, his dark grin visible even at that distance. Rictus raised a hand in return.

On the right, nothing. Corvus had his right flank up in the air, and that was the flank held by Demetrius and his conscript spears. It was as though he was inviting them to collapse. True, the dismounted Companions were there to the rear, but they would not be able to stop a serious rout.

Across the flashing gleam of the waterlogged plain, the army of the Avennan League had almost finished shaking out its line. They had been at it for hours now; the men's freshness would be gone.

It was one thing to set up a line when a single city's troops were involved, when the men knew each other and their officers. It was quite another to co-ordinate the interlocking phalanxes of twenty different cities, with their own rivalries, their petty politics, their vying for prestige and advantage. Rictus had seen it on a small scale over a lifetime of warfare; he could imagine what a colossal pain in the arse it would be to command twenty thousand half-drilled citizen soldiers with their own ideas about how they should be deployed. Even Demetrius's conscripts were better trained than the spearmen he saw standing in half-dressed lines opposite.

But they had numbers on their side. More than that, they were fighting for something they believed in. That counted for a lot in war. It was why the Ten Thousand had been victorious at Kunaksa; the choice had been to win or die.

Fornyx blew his nose on his fingers and flicked the snot away. He was still angry about the antics of the night before, about fighting here in this swamp, about being held in the rear.

"Well," he said, "you got your war."

"Yes, I got it," Rictus answered.

"What does the little bastard intend to do, do you think, Rictus? He was closeted with Demetrius and Teresian all morning. You think he means to give battle?"

"Truthfully? I don't know. He won't refuse one – that's not in his nature. But look at that ground, Fornyx – you want to advance across that?"

"It's not fit for man nor beast," Fornyx grimaced.

"Well, then I suppose Corvus has a plan."

"That's all right then."

Corvus had travelled the length of the line from north to south. He halted now in front of Druze, and bent in the saddle to speak to the chief of the Igranians. They saw Druze nodding, and Corvus set a hand on his shoulder, then cantered through the open formless crowd of the skirmishers, raising a hand to acknowledge their cheers, pointing at one or two of them and reining in to exchange witticisms which set many of them roaring with laughter.

"He can work a crowd, the little bugger, I'll give him that," Fornyx admitted.

Leading a line of mounted aides like a kite trailing its tail, Corvus cantered over to the Dogsheads and reined in. Like Rictus, he had not slept at all the night before, but he looked fresh as a bridegroom.

"At least it's not raining," he said, dismounting

and clapping his horse on the neck with great affection.

"You think they're going to join battle?" Fornyx asked him bluntly.

Corvus smiled. "Brother," he said, "before the sun climbs to noon, they're going to be right in our laps."

DRUZE'S IGRANIANS MOVED out, an orderless crowd of ambling men picking its way across the flooded farmland like a great herd of migrating animals. It still wanted some two hours until noon, and the sun was at their backs. There was no urgency to them; they were like men strolling home after meeting at the assembly.

Rictus could see them talking amongst themselves as they advanced, and lightly armed as they were, they did not break up the soft ground as a formation of spearmen would. He saw them as a mass of dark speckles on the land, swallowed up here and there by the sunlit glare of the lying water.

"Stay by me," Corvus said to him, his face grave now, eyes fixed on the enemy line only some two and a half pasangs away, the tented camp rising like a mud-coloured city behind it. "I want your Dogsheads ready to slot in anywhere along the line."

"What's Druze to do?" Fornyx asked him.

"He's going to pick a fight."

The Igranians picked up speed, like a flock of birds all of one mind. They were moving out to the south, to threaten the enemy's right flank; the unshielded side.

There was a corresponding ruffle of movement in the lines of spearmen there; a row of bronze shields caught the sun one after another in a series of bright flashes. Then Druze led his men in to javelin range – a hundred paces, maybe – and Rictus saw their right arms go back, their bodies arced for the throw. It was too far away to see the missiles go home, but the glitter of enemy shields catching the sun came and went, flickering like summer lightning upon the sea.

"That's really going to piss them off," Fornyx said, with a grin of sheer relish in his beard.

"I thought they needed a prod," Corvus said. "The morning's a wasting."

There was always something almost joyful about watching a battle from a distance, Rictus thought. First, you were glad you were not there, in the middle of it with the iron tearing at your own flesh. But it could almost be like a sport, too. One could study the moves of the players with detachment, see the evolutions of the phalanxes with a clear eye, rise above the packed murderous terror of the othismos and survey things with real clarity.

And with a flash of epiphany, Rictus realised something about Corvus.

That is how he sees it, all the time. That detachment, that clear-sightedness.

The enemy spearmen were breaking ranks by centon, sending out detachments to try and come to grips with Druze's men, but the lightly armed Igranians evaded them like wolves dancing away from the horns of a bull. As the centons withdrew again, the Igranians closed in. For a few minutes they had actually closed with the enemy hand to hand. Fornyx whistled softly at the sight.

"Those bastards have balls like walnuts."

"An Igranian must kill a mountain-lion before he is considered a man," Corvus said. "They belong to an older time, when the Macht did not feel the need to congregate in cities. Igranon itself has no walls; it's little more than a glorified trading post."

"A hard people to tame," Rictus said, raising one eyebrow.

Corvus shook his head. "I did not tame the Igranians, Rictus; I merely earned their respect. Their trust." He watched the distant fight with his curious pale eyes. "You have that, and they will follow you anywhere."

The Igranians broke off the battle, wheeling away from the League army. They had cut several centons to pieces; Rictus had been able to make out men running back to their own lines without shields.

In rear of the enemy battle-line, there was now a strong column marching from north to south.

"He's reinforcing his right," Corvus said. "Good." He turned to one of his aides, seating on a snorting horse. "Marco, go to Teresian, and tell him it is time."

"Yes Corvus." The fellow kicked his horse into a whinnying canter and the mud from its hooves spattered them all as he took off.

"The curtain rises," Corvus said. "Look, brothers. We finally woke them up."

The enemy army was on the move, that vast snake of men undulating forward over the plain. Faint at first, and then louder, there came the sound of the Paean.

The advance was ragged, halting. Some of the League's contingents were better ordered than others and had to mark time while their comrades caught up. In the middle, a great body of spearmen remained in good order throughout, many thousands. They were the core. The men on the flanks were not as well drilled, but they presented a fearsome sight for all that.

"That is Machran, in the centre," Corvus said. "See the sigils?" It was too far for Rictus to make out, but he nodded.

"Their polemarch is Kassander, an ex-mercenary and close friend of Karnos himself. He has trained the spearmen of Machran well – so far as a citizen army goes. Karnos is wise enough to know he is an orator, not a soldier, but he's a good judge of men, by all accounts, and he can charm the birds off the trees when he has a mind to.

"I want him to die today."

"I'm sure he feels the same way about you," Fornyx drawled, and Corvus laughed.

Their own army had begun to move now. On the left, Teresian was taking forward the veteran spears, four thousand men in eight ranks. Their line extended some half pasang, and they too began to sing the Paean as they advanced. Rictus watched their dressing with the close attention of a professional, and he had to grudgingly admit to himself that they were not half bad.

The conscript spears under Demetrius remained immobile, stubbornly refusing to move. Alarmed, Fornyx grabbed Corvus by the arm, his black beard bristling.

"Half your spearline is still asleep, Corvus."

"No. This has all been set in train by my hand, Fornyx. Be patient. Enjoy the view. When was the last time you were able to stand and watch history being made?"

It was quite a sight, indeed. Thirty thousand men were on the move now across the plain in various formations. To the south, Druze's Igranians were pulling back, and the League's reinforced right wing was making good time, though their ranks were not all they might be; the soft ground was scrambling them. Teresian's veterans were marching out to meet them, veering left as they advanced. An oblique. Only good, disciplined troops could accomplish such a manoeuvre.

Finally, Demetrius's conscripts began to move. Their line was as untidy as that of the enemy, and there was a widening gap between them and Teresian. The two bodies of spearmen advanced separately on the enemy. In the centre there was nothing but a growing hole.

"Phobos," Fornyx whispered.

Valerian joined them, out of breath. He hauled off his helm, his lopsided face burning with urgency. "Rictus – Corvus – for the love of God, look at the line! We're broke in two before we even begin!"

Corvus held up his hand. "Do not concern yourself, centurion – get back to your men and stand-to. I shall be wanting you presently."

His whole attention was fixed on the moving bodies of men out on the plain. There was none of his flashing levity now; he was as solemn as a statue.

But his eyes blazed, like a gambler watching the fall of the dice.

"Rictus!" Valerian protested.

"Do as he says," Rictus said quietly. "Shields up, Valerian."

The young man stamped off unhappily, but a few moments later the order rang out and the Dogsheads lifted their shields onto their shoulders, donned their helms, and worked their spears side to side to loosen the sauroters in the sucking ground. Rictus's heart began to quicken in his chest, pushing against the confines of Antimone's Gift. He and Fornyx stood silent, watching as Corvus sent couriers out to right and left, young men on tall horses beating the animals into gallops that sent clods of muck flying through the air like birds.

"Rictus," Corvus said, turning back to the mercenaries. "What is it the Dogsheads can do that citizen soldiers cannot?"

"We can die needlessly, that's for damned sure," Fornyx murmured.

"We can advance at the run," Rictus said.

Corvus nodded. "I like to read. Have you heard of Mynon?"

"He was a general of the Ten Thousand. He made it home."

"He wrote it all down, some fifteen years ago, before dying in some stupid little war up near Framnos. I read his story, Rictus; they had it in the library at Sinon, copied out fair by a good scribe. He talked of Kunaksa, how it was won, what you all did that day."

The Paean rose and rose, tens of thousands of voices singing it now all across the plain. Druze was taking his men in again, harassing the enemy's southern flank once more, and Teresian's spears were going in alongside him. The enemy line was skewed and slanted to meet this threat.

A gasping courier reined in before them.

"Ardashir is ready, Corvus."

Corvus cocked his head to one side, like a crow eyeing a corpse.

"Tell him to go."

The courier galloped off like a man possessed, a youngster bursting with the enthusiasm of his age.

"At Kunaksa, the Kefren had thousands of archers, who should by rights have shot the Ten Thousand to pieces before they closed – am I right?"

"What is this, a fucking history lesson?" Fornyx demanded.

"We went in at a run. They hit us with the first volley, but by the time they'd readied a second we were already at their throats," Rictus said. He had not been a spearman that day, but he remembered watching, seeing the morai go in.

"Citizen soldiers cannot advance at the run, or they lose their formation," Corvus said, and he shrugged.

"Now watch."

THERE WAS A long line of movement out to their right, in the ranks of the dismounted Companions. Ardashir led a solid mass of his command forward, following in the wake of Demetrius's slowly advancing conscripts. There was something odd about them, Rictus noted.

"Kufr," Fornyx said. "He's taking in all the Kufr. Corvus, this won't –"

"Shut up," Corvus said.

Some sixteen hundred Kufr, tall Kefren of the Asurian race, who had, like all their fellows, been brought up to do three things. They had been taught how to ride a horse, how to tell the truth... and how to shoot a bow.

They cast aside their brightly coloured cloaks, left them lying on the mud, and from their backs they pulled the short recurved composite bows of Asuria. They had quiver-fulls of arrows at their hips, and at a shouted command from Ardashir they nocked these to their bowstrings.

Ardashir raised his scimitar, a painfully bright flash of steel. He held it upright one moment, watching the battlefield to come, the advancing League spearmen on the plain before him. They were perhaps four hundred paces away.

In front of him, Demetrius's gruff voice rang out, and the conscripts halted.

A shouted command in Asurian, the tongue of the Empire, and following it a heartbeat later came the sweeping whistle of the arrows, some one and a half thousand of them arcing up in the air over Teresian's spears, to come down like a black hail on the advancing enemy.

That is the sound, Rictus thought. *That is what I heard that day.*

A staccato hammering as the broadheads struck bronze, the individual impacts merging to form a hellish, explosive din of metal on metal.

Scores of men went down. The line of advancing shields buckled, faltered, the ranks merging, breaking, gaps appearing up and down, men tripping over bodies, men screaming, cursing, shouting orders.

And moments later the second volley hit them.

It was like watching a vast animal staggered by the wind. Some men were still advancing, others had halted and were trying to lift the heavy shields up to counter this unlooked-for hail of death. Others were standing in place with the black shafts buried in their limbs, tugging on them, looking to left and right, shouting in fear and fury. Centurions were seizing the irresolute, thumping helmed heads with their fists, moving forward out of the mass of stalled spearmen, urging them on.

A third volley.

The ground was thick with the dead and the wounded. These soldiers were small farmers, tradesmen, family men. There were fathers and sons on the field, brothers, uncles. Some of the untouched spearmen were dropping their arms to help relatives, neighbours. Hundreds fell back, but a core came on regardless of casualties. They were Macht, after all.

Corvus was watching it all with a kind of grim satisfaction, but at least he did not seem to relish the developing massacre. If he had – if he had shown any kind of pleasure at the sight – Rictus would have killed him on the spot.

"And now, Demetrius," Corvus said quietly.

Rictus had lost count of the volleys, but the others had not. The conscript spears began advancing again, five thousand of them moving to meet what had been a line of six thousand League troops. The odds were evened out now, but more than that, the League forces were little more than a mob, a snarled-up confusion of armed men struggling in a mire which their own feet were deepening with every minute.

"That should do it on our right," Corvus said. He turned to look south.

Teresian was about to make contact with the enemy right, and Druze was supporting him, worrying at the end of the enemy line, his cloud of skirmishers partially enveloping it. He was working round the back of the League army while they advanced steadily to meet the spearmen to their front.

Even as they watched, they heard the roar and crash as the two bodies of heavy spears met, bronze smashing against bronze, spearheads seeking unprotected flesh. Two bulls meeting head on – Rictus could feel the ground quiver under his own feet at the clash of armour.

As soon as the enemy was committed to the attack, Druze led his men north behind the line. The Igranians split in two. Half pitched into the rear of the enemy phalanx that was now irretrievably entangled with Teresian's veterans. The other half – almost fifteen hundred men – kept going north, parallel to the League battle-line – towards the rear of the enemy centre.

That centre was now almost upon them. These were the best of the League troops, the levies from

Machran under Kassander. Seven thousand men in good order, they had paused as Corvus launched his army on the wings, seemingly unable to believe that there was nothing facing them but the empty plain. Now they were advancing again. They could pitch in to either one of the two separate battles that were now raging to north and south.

Corvus turned to Rictus. "I have a job for you, brother, you and your Dogsheads." He pointed at the long line of shields bearing the *machios* sigil.

"I want you to take your Dogsheads and hit those fellows as hard as you can."

"You're not serious," Fornyx breathed.

"You have only to halt them in their tracks, hold them a little while, bloody their noses a little. You have to buy me time." He gestured to the north and south. "We will beat them on the flanks, and then come and meet you in the centre. And Druze is already in the rear of the Machran morai – as soon as he sees you going forward, he will attack. And Ardashir will support you also."

"I'm like to lose half my men," Rictus said, staring Corvus in the face.

"Fight smart, Rictus – don't get enveloped. All you have to do is poke them in the eye."

The thunder of the battle rose and rose. The critical point of it was approaching – Rictus could feel it, like he could feel the loom of winter in his ageing bones. Was Corvus trying to have him killed? He did not believe it. No – he was simply moving the knucklebones on the board, using what he had. Sentiment did not even enter into it.

Rictus pulled on his crested helm, reducing his world to a slot of light.

"Very well," he said.

"One more thing," Corvus added, tossing up his hand as though it were an afterthought.

"What?"

"I'll be going in with you."

FOR KARNOS THE world had become a strange and fearsome place. He was the fifth man in an eight-deep file, one cog in the great machine that was the army of Machran, which in turn was but part of the forces assembled here today. He alternated between an inexplicable exhilaration and bowel-draining apprehension.

This, the greatest clash of armies in a generation, was his first battle.

In earlier years he had drilled on the fields below the Mithos River along with the other men of his class, but since his elevation to the Kerusia he had not so much as lifted a spear. He was Speaker of Machran, as high as one could be in the ruling hierarchy of the city, but on the battlefield he was the same rank as all the other sweating men in the spear-files. Here, Katullos the Cursebearer commanded a mora – Kassander, the entire levy – but he, Karnos, commanded only himself. He found it unbelievable now that he had overlooked something so basic – incredible that he was included in this anonymous horde like every other citizen.

Gestrakos and Ondimion, who had set the world

alight with their intellect and their art, had fought as humble foot-soldiers also, so he was in good company. But that did not ease the weight of his armour, the burden of the bronze-faced shield and the dozen aches and scratches that his barely-worn cuirass inflicted on his torso.

He was fat, unfit, and desperately aware of his own martial ignorance. His only consolation in all of this was that he was fifth man from the front. No-one had ever told him that the men in the middle of the files took the heaviest casualties, which was why the most inexperienced were placed there, sandwiched between the veteran file leaders and closers.

And around him was the army, these myriads which surely no –

"Advance! On me – one, two – left!"

Kassander's voice, somewhere in front and to his right. He was only a few paces away, but packed in the ranks of the phalanx he might as well have been on the far side of the world.

The man behind Karnos cursed him. "Get in step, you fat fuck. And watch that sauroter; you poke me with it one more time and I swear I'll break it off and jam it up your arse."

Laughter rattled along the files. "Ostros, don't you know who you're talking to?"

"That's the Speaker, you stupid fuck!"

"Karnos – tell us – how many slave-girls do you have a night, eh?"

"You horny old bastard – I hear tell you've nothing but naked cunny to wait on you night and day!"

Breathing heavily, Karnos found the air to shout,

"they smell better than you rotten bastards, that's for damned sure."

"I'll take a bath, Karnos, and then you can suck my cock."

The anonymity of the crowd, the faceless helmeted heads; here was the citizenship of Machran, where all men were equal under bronze. It made Karnos remember a time when he had been nothing more than a quick-thinking slave dealer with a big mouth and a memory for faces. For a few minutes, tossing the filth and the insults back and forth, he was almost enjoying himself.

A great sound erupted from the front ranks, like a massive groan. The men in the rear began shouting forward. "What the fuck's going on – you lads – what do you see?"

"They have archers," someone yelled back. "The Afteni and Arkadians are getting hammered."

"Phobos! They're really getting fucked! Where the hell are the Arienans? Bastards should be on our right."

They were still advancing, but slowly now, stop and start. Finally the halt was called. Karnos could see nothing but the men in front and to either side – he could not so much as turn around, and the close-fitting helm filled his head with a sound like the rush of the sea. As he stood, he worked his feet in the mud, feeling himself sinking into it. His feet were numb with cold, but despite that the chiton he wore under his cuirass was soaked with sweat, and his throat was parched – and the battle had not yet begun.

Yes, it had. He could hear it now. A surf of noise rising up around him – it was almost impossible to guess which direction it came from. He heard sharp above the roar the screams of men in a last extremity of pain and fear, and a hammering of metal.

"Front rank, level spears!" came the order. Kassander again. "Centurions, hold together – prepare to advance – advance!"

And they were off again, but more quickly this time, the files shuffling into a fast march with the centurions calling out the time. "One, two, one, two – pick it up there!"

"It's redcloaks – mercenaries!" someone shouted at the front.

His head bobbing from side to side in the bronze helm, Karnos caught glimpses of the world beyond the phalanx, and saw something coming towards them, something with glittering teeth and shining in bronze and scarlet. He heard the Paean being sung – but not by his own side. What in the hell was –

An enormous crash. He was brought to a full stop, piling into the man in front. Behind him, the weight of the three men of the file crushed him, the cuirass fighting the pressure. He thought he would faint. He could see faces – helmed men facing the wrong way – Phobos – they were facing him! And then the adder-strikes of spearheads. He saw an aichmé come lancing through the ranks in front of him to bury itself in a man's head and then snap off. The man was borne along by the press for a few minutes, and then slid out of sight. The file closed the gaps, the pressure unrelenting.

This is it, Karnos thought. This is what the stories are for, what the poetry is about. I am here in the middle of it at last.

The pressure and the fear emptied his bladder, and the piss ran hot down his legs, but he barely noticed.

"Level your fucking spear!" the man behind him shouted, and he hefted the weapon horizontal on his shoulder, feeling the sauroter tear into flesh behind him as he brought it up. He rested the long weapon on the wing of the file-leader's cuirass for a second, getting used to the balance of it, and then thrust forward into the red-cloaked mass that faced him. The spearpoint jarred, the whole shaft quivering in his fist as he struck a shield.

He tried again, aiming for a helm-slot, but struck empty air. A spear came the other way, the two shafts clashing together as they met. The aichme dunted him in the forehead, rasped along the crestbox and snapped his head back. He would have fallen were it not for the men behind him pushing into the small of his back. His eyes were full of tears. There was something wet inside his helm and he did not know whether it was blood or sweat.

He stabbed again, angry now, and from his chest there came that hoarse animal roaring that had no thought behind it but was a base response, a defiant bellow of rage. Thousands of men were making it – it was part of every battlefield. It rose now and filled the air above them, as deafening as the blacksmith's clatter of iron on bronze. This was the *othismos*, the bowels of war itself.

They were advancing, step by step, and mixed in with the wordless bellowing were cries of triumph. Karnos stepped over a body, glanced down quickly and saw a red cloak on the ground. He stepped on the man's body and it moved under his feet, still warm.

He vomited, with the sensation and the heat of the press and the singing sound in his head. The vomit ran down his fine ornate cuirass unheeded, one more stink among many. The fluids of mens' insides were running into the muck at their feet, and making of it a terrible mire. They plunged their dogged way through it, calf-deep.

The sandal was sucked off Karnos's right foot, but trailed behind him, its strap entangled in his greave, until someone behind him trod on it and snapped it free. They were still advancing. Up front, someone shouted, "They're pulling back!" and a growl of triumph tore through the files. But seconds later someone else shouted, "Arrows – they're shooting at us!"

The long black clothyards of the Kefren poured down upon them. As if in a dream, Karnos saw an arrow strike the helm of the man in front and flick up into the air, jerking his head to one side. Most of the men were wearing cuirasses of stiff, layered linen, and Karnos watched in horrified fascination as the arrows came arcing down like black snakes and clear through the wings of the armour, burying themselves in men's shoulders, smashing collar-bones.

A new cry, from behind this time. A javelin flew over Karnos's head – he saw the cold gleam of the iron point not a foot from his eyes. The file-closers were shouting. "About face! The bastards are behind us, brothers!"

The phalanx was losing its cohesion, men turning this way and that, desperate to see what was going on. The advance stalled and the lines intermingled. Packed close together by the threats to front and rear, the men of Machran stood irresolute, frightened, angry. The centurions were bellowing orders like men possessed, but the spearmen in the ranks seemed as unresponsive as cattle.

The sweat running down the small of Karnos's back went icy cold. This was not how it was supposed to be. There was no order now, and even the centurions were beginning to look about themselves in growing panic. How had –

A crash to the front – the fearsome red-cloaked mercenaries had hammered into their face again, laying on the pressure. The air was crushed out of Karnos's chest as the crowd tightened, recoiling on itself. Some men tripped and went down, unwounded, and were then trampled to suffocation in the deepening mud at their feet.

Karnos looked at the sky, the black arrows raining across it. The press of men tilted this way and that, battered on all sides. He heard the roar and clash of a fresh onset off to his left, and the entire phalanx shuddered as though it had taken a body-blow. Someone shouted that the left wing had been routed, and then a few moments later some other idiot insisted it was the right wing.

It did not matter – they were pinned here like a turtle on its back. The cohesiveness of the phalanx might have gone, but the pure brute weight of meat and metal remained. It was being packed tighter on itself.

Karnos's feet were dragged from the mud, sucking as the press shifted and took him with it. He gasped for air, and beat down the impulse to scream for space, for room to move and breathe. For the first time, the reality of his own death began to crowd his mind.

And the pressure began to ease. The sea-roar of noise in his helm changed, picked up a note. Oh, thank Antimone, the crowd was opening out. The tide had turned, it seemed; this was the way it was supposed to happen after all. Victory was still there, in the air. In his relief, he felt he could almost taste it.

Men were throwing down their shields and tearing off their helms, shouting about betrayal and defeat. The phalanx, which a few moments before had seemed a brute, packed, immovable thing, now began to fall apart. As men abandoned their bronze burdens, so they became more mobile, and somewhere out at the edges of the formation, or what was left of it, they were running.

They were running away. Karnos stared in disbelief so utter that it cancelled out the bowel-draining fear. "No! No!" he screamed. All Machran was here in front of him, seven thousand men, the heart of the greatest city in the Macht world – and it was bleeding to death in the churned muck, or in flight right in front of his horrified eyes.

He sagged as the men about him moved away. A shield, dropped by his neighbour, struck his anklebone an agonising blow. He raised his head to shriek his pain and his anger at the cold sky, and the falling arrow lanced cleanly through the right wing of his cuirass, sinking into his shoulder with an impact that sent him reeling on his back into the bloody mire below.

TWELVE
LONG NIGHT'S JOURNEY

RICTUS WATCHED THE blood dripping from his fingertips with a kind of morbid fascination. He was clenching a filthy clout about his arm at the elbow, twisted tight as he could make it, and the trickle had slowed at last. Even so, the torchlight in the tent seemed incredibly bright to him, splintering in shards and blades, like ground glass in his eyes. That would be the thump on the head, he supposed. He had already been sick once, and were there anything left in his stomach he had no doubt he would be so again.

Fornyx's face swam into view, shadow in light. He felt the weight of his friend's hand on the numb meat that was his forearm.

"I got the carnifex."

"There are men hurt worse than me," Rictus said muzzily.

"That artery wants stitched shut, or you'll bleed white. Now shut your mouth before I slap you."

Rictus smiled. He leaned back, was caught by Fornyx before he toppled off the blood-slimed wooden table, and drifted into a hazier place in his mind. Aise was there, young and smiling again, and Rian had flowers in her hair, a marriage-crown of primroses and forget-me-nots. But who was the man in shadow beside her?

He felt a stab of sharp pain that jolted him awake again. They were holding his arm down and old Severan, one of the Dogsheads' two carnifexes, was working a blood-brown needle through his flesh. Another scar for Aise to find, Rictus thought.

His gaze drifted. The great tent was full of the stink of death, a slaughterhouse reek. Men were lying on sodden straw or were being pinioned upon stout wooden tables as the army physicians went to work. A strange and horrible calling, to spend one's days delving into the living flesh of other men.

Rictus dragged himself back to the present, putting to the back of things the pop of the needle as it threaded through skin and muscle and dragged the slashed halves of his arm back together.

"What's the butcher's bill?" he asked Fornyx.

The dark little man bent close and looked in his eyes. "Lucky you had a good helm, or that spear would have drilled a hole through to the bone."

"Fornyx –"

"Forty-six dead on the field, nine from our own fucking arrows. Ninety-six wounded, of whom – Severan?"

The grey-haired man working on Rictus's arm grunted. "Thirty or so of those will be back in scarlet within a week or two – like the chief here. But of the rest, there are a dozen who will take longer – broken bones and the like. The rest are done with soldiering for good."

"A third of us," Rictus said in a cracked whisper.

"A hard day's work," Fornyx said. "He gave us the worst job on the field."

"He gave it to us because he knew we could do it," Rictus said.

"That's pretty fucking magnanimous of you."

"It's the truth, Fornyx. You know it too. He gave us the hardest job because we are the best he has."

A bleak smile flitted across Fornyx's face. "It is a distinction which could well prove the death of us all."

"Not today," Rictus answered. He closed his eyes, nausea rising like a blush in his throat. He clenched his teeth shut until his jaws creaked, let it pass.

"I'm done here," Severan said, rising with a groan and pushing his fists into the small of his back in the way Rictus often did after rising in the mornings.

"Keep that arm slung for a week, and stay awake for the rest of the night – Fornyx, don't you let him sleep – I've seen too many men with a knock on the head sleep their way through Antimone's Veil. You hear me now?"

"I hear you, you old bugger."

Severan slapped him on the shoulder and then stumped off to the carnage of the tent without another word.

"No sleep. Ah, Phobos take it," Rictus groaned.

"You heard him. Let me get you to Corvus's tent. He wants to see all his underlings tonight, and it's as good a way to keep you awake as any."

"Fuck you, you evil-eyed little scrawny bastard."

"Careful, Rictus; you know I love it when a girl talks dirty."

ANTIMONE WAS WEEPING. It happened often after a battle, especially a large one. The more blood on the ground, the more tears she shed, it was said. The rain came down in a soft cold shroud to fill up the rutted footprints of the living and the dead, to patter on the eyes of the corpses littering the field. At least at this time of year, the process of decay would not set in so quickly as during the usual summer campaigning.

Rictus leant on Fornyx's bony shoulder as they made their unsteady way through the camp. He could remember little of the battle's end. The Dogsheads had charged into the mass of Machran warriors once, withdrawn, and then charged again. The next thing he remembered was fighting to keep his head out of the mud while men stood on him.

Well, the thing was done now, at least. The camp was full of drunken men reliving their own versions of the day's events, pouring thankful libations of wine into the ground for Phobos, for Antimone, in thanks at having survived with eyes and arms and balls intact.

The Dogsheads were more subdued. They had lit two huge fires kindled from broken enemy spears, and were standing around them in their red cloaks passing wineskins with the thoughtful purpose of men who mean to drink deep. They raised a cheer at seeing Rictus, however, and the mood around the fires brightened. Valerian and Kesero were there, Kesero limping with a linen rag knitted about the big muscles of his right thigh, Valerian untouched and as earnest as always.

"You had us worried when we saw you taken into the butcher's tent," he said to Rictus. "For a second, we thought you might be in trouble."

"No trouble," Rictus assured them. "An aichme's love-bite is all."

"Our employer has his victory," shaven-headed Kesero said. "I hope it makes him happy."

"Machran is finished now," one of the other men put in: Ramis of Karinth, Kesero's second, a high-coloured strawhead who was already drunk. "We must have killed or maimed half the men they had on the field."

"I believe we did," Valerian said with a half-smile. "Now I know what a great battle is like. And I know why the stories make of them such glorious and terrible things."

His mutilated face gave the smile a bittersweet cast. Rictus set a hand on his shoulder. Yes, he thought, I believe Rian could do worse.

"What's our story now, boss?" another voice broke in. Praesos of Pelion, a good steady fellow like to make centurion in a year or two, if he survived.

Rictus collected his swimming thoughts. "I'm on my way to Corvus now. We'll see what's what. There will be a shitload of clearing up tomorrow, for one thing – we must police the battlefield, burn the dead, collect what arms were left on them, and reorganise."

"Not many of us made it into the enemy camp," Praesos said. "Every other bugger in the army was there before us, leaving their wounded on the ground. By the time we got round to it, it was picked clean or under guard."

"We don't fight for plunder," Valerian snapped at him. "We look after our hurt and dead first of everything – it's the way it is done."

"Well said, brother," Kesero grinned, "but you can't blame the lads for being a little put out. We do the right thing, and it leaves us with empty purses while Demetrius's fucking conscripts raped the place."

"Aye – what about some pay?" someone called out, back from the firelight and the golden shimmer of the flame-caught rain.

"I'll see what I can do," Rictus said.

"He threw us into the biggest shithole of the day," Kesero said, "and we came out smiling. I think he owes us a bonus."

There was a growled murmur of agreement about the fires.

"He came in along with us," Valerian said. "Remember that. He was in the front rank right beside me. He did not do it for a joke – that's why he was there."

"We're mercenaries," Rictus said quietly. "We voted for the contract. Our job is to kill and be killed; to look after one another when alive, when hurt and when dead. That comes first of everything. A man who has issue with that can take off the red cloak and walk away when this contract is done – but not before."

"And when is this contract done, Rictus? On the fall of Machran?" Keșero asked.

"That's what I agreed with him." At that moment, Rictus could not quite remember the terms of the agreement, but it sounded right enough to his addled mind.

Kesero winked. "Then we're going to be rich men very soon," and he grinned so that his silver-wired teeth glittered white in his face.

The tension about the fires broke in ribaldry and laughter. After all, they were alive and standing, and they were victors of the greatest battle ever fought in the Harukush. In their minds they had already begun to bury the worst of the day's memories, leaving what could later be polished up and made part of a better story.

Rictus knew this – he had done it himself. But he knew also that the black memories were kept by Phobos to fester in the depths of a man's heart. He could never be rid of them; they became part of who he was.

"THE SUPPLY WAGONS will be emptied and will take the more severely wounded back to Hal Goshen," Corvus said, pacing up and down as was his wont. "The looting of the enemy camp is to stop – Teresian, you will see to that. Post more men – your oldest and steadiest. Karnos has stockpiled several day's rations, and we will use them ourselves while our supply train is away."

He paused as Rictus and Fornyx emerged from the

darkness beyond the tent-flap, and his face broke open into a grin of delight.

"I knew a little thing like a slashed arm would not keep my old warrior down. Rictus, you look as pale as Phobos's face – Teresian, give up your seat there. Brothers, the wine is standing tall in your cups; we can't have that."

Rictus sat heavily in the leather-framed camp chair. Corvus's scribe, a plump, powerfully built little man named Parmenios, came forward with a waxed slate, his stylus poised.

"Marshal, how many of your men are still fit to fight?"

"Three hundred, give or take."

Parmenios scratched the slate. His black eyebrows rose up his forehead a little. "A heavy accounting," he said.

"I've heard it called worse," Rictus snapped. His mind was a throbbing bruise. More than anything else he longed to lay his head down upon his arms on the map-strewn table in front of him.

Teresian offered him a cup of wine. "Drink with us, Rictus."

They were all holding their cups off the table, looking at him. Poised for a toast, he realised. One-eyed Demetrius, the grim ex-mercenary, spoke for them.

"Today we saw how men fight, and die." He lifted his cup higher.

"To the Dogsheads."

"The Dogsheads," the others repeated. Humourless Teresian, the suspicion gone from his grey eyes. Dark, smiling Druze, with his arm in a sling to match

Rictus. And Ardashir, his strange long face solemn. They all drained their cups and then flicked out the dregs for Phobos, mocking Fear itself.

Rictus caught Corvus's eye, and the strange young man winked at him.

The Dogsheads had been sent on a suicidal attack for sound military reasons; it was harsh, but rational. But Corvus had also thought this far ahead. Their obedience, their self-sacrifice had finally won round the doubters among his officers. Rictus had at last earned his place as one of Corvus's marshals.

You conniving little bastard, Rictus thought, and he raised his empty cup to Corvus in a small salute.

"Back to business," Corvus said briskly. "The roads are turned to soup with this god-cursed rain, and men who have abandoned their armour can run faster than those who have preserved it. The Igranians have done what they can, but I've no wish to scatter the army on a wild hunt along the Imperial road. We're fairly certain that Karnos was expecting reinforcements before battle commenced. It remains to be seen if they will now remain in the field or return to their cities."

"What of Karnos? Any news?" Rictus asked.

"Their dead are out there in heaps," Ardashir said. "If he is one of them he will take time to find."

Corvus waved his hand back and forth. "Dead or alive, he brought the League here to its destruction. At least a third of the enemy army is still on the field, and Machran lost most heavily of all the League cities, as I had intended. If we appear before the city walls within the next month, I will be surprised if they do not accept our terms."

"Machran itself," Demetrius said, with an odd look of awe on his face.

"Machran folds, and the rest go down with it – they will not fight on once we have our feet planted on the floor of the Empirion," Corvus said. "We are very close, brothers."

Even through the haze of his exhaustion, Rictus found himself wondering; *close to what?*

KARNOS OF MACHRAN *is dead.*

Karnos has been slain on the field of battle.

Karnos died heroically – no, no, damn it, that's not it.

He lay in the wet crushing darkness and listened to the rain tap on the stiffened bodies which lay atop him. He was more thirsty than he had ever been in his life before. In fact it seemed to him that he had never really understood the true nature of thirst before. When the rain came he opened his mouth and let it trickle in, foul-flavoured from the corpses on top of him, but wet.

Life.

Karnos is alive, in the midst of the dead.

Men had gone back and forth across the battlefield in the aftermath of the fighting, looking for their own wounded, for enemy wounded to slay, for some trinket which might make their labour worthwhile, or perhaps a better weapon – or, if the gods were smiling, one of those miraculous finds, a black cuirass.

The expensive armour which had so impressed Karnos in the confines of his villa, he now knew to be inferior, gimcrack shite, and these men had seen it as such also. That had saved his life, for they had not tried to strip it from his very much alive and terrified body. And thus he lay here with his fellow citizens sheltering him from the rain.

And pinning him to the ground.

His arm was numb from the shoulder down, and he could not bring himself to look at the black shaft which protruded grotesquely from his flesh. It was a Kufr arrow, fired from a Kufr bow, created by a Kufr fletcher in some far-flung portion of the world which knew nothing of him. And yet it was now inside his flesh, intimate with the very meat of him. All that way, across the sea, in some strange foreign creature's quiver, then laid against that bow, to flash through the cold air of the Harukush, and end up inside him, Karnos of Machran.

He started at his task again; that which had preoccupied him since the fall of darkness and the departure of the battlefield scavengers. He was inching the bodies of the dead off his own in increments a child could measure with their fingers. In this he showed a patience which he had previously not known he possessed.

As he did, his mind wandered. He remembered squatting in the heat and dust of Tinsmith's Alley in the Mithannon, scratching at the scabbed-over burns on his bare feet where the sparks from his father's hand-forge had landed.

He was seven years old, and a passing aristocrat in a himation as white as snow had dropped him a copper obol. He was staring at the little green coin, which would buy him a stick of grilled meat from a foodstall, or a pear-sized cup of wine from one of the shops at the bottom of the alley. It was the first time in his life he had been given something for nothing, and he liked the feeling.

One of the corpses toppled over, as stiff and unlike a living man as an overstuffed sack of flour. Karnos smiled, grunting at the pain, but swallowing it down, as he had swallowed down the beatings he had received as a child. Even then, he had known his father loved him, but knew also that he'd had to lash out on occasion at the nearest thing to hand.

If it were not Karnos, it would be one of the starving strays that littered the city alleyways, and Karnos pitied them even more than himself. They were used and discarded by the slumdwellers who had spawned them, feral little beasts who could barely speak, whose sex was indeterminate, whose eyes held nothing but fear and greed. If they survived they would grow into whores and thieves and beggars, and beget the curse of their existence on another generation. Thus were the slums of Machran renewed.

Karnos began to breathe more easily. He was feeling the cold now, and a warm lassitude came creeping over his battered frame.

They think I have so many slaves because I love lording it over them; me, the boy from the Mithannon, making his own little kingdom. Kassander knows better.

I keep them slaves to protect them. No man or woman wearing my collar will ever be abused in

Machran. They are safe with me. Pollo knows that. He knows me better than anyone.

He wanted to shout for Pollo now, to tell him that his bed was damp, that he needed an extra coverlet. He raised his hand to push back the wet covering that was stealing his thoughts away, and his hand settled on the cold wax-hard face of the dead man whose body lay upon his own. The jolt of that snapped him out of his reverie, and the pain came flooding in, clearing his head. He ground his jaw shut and pushed the chilled meat away from his face, found a leg loosened, and ploughed himself through the mud on his back.

He was freezing cold, but free, staring up at the invisible rain, the teeming dark. How far to Machran? It must be over a hundred pasangs.

Machran, the sun of his world. He loved his city more than he would ever love any wife. One could walk there upon stones that had been shaped in the dawn of his race's existence. It was rumoured that below the circle of the Empirion were caverns in which the first of the Macht had lived, sealed chambers which housed the dust and dreams of millennia.

My city.

The rain was easing, and in the tattered dark of the sky he could see glimpses of the stars peering through the cloud as the wind picked up and began to harry them away. Phobos was long set, but the pink glow of Haukos could still just be made out, and to one side, Gaenion's Pointer, showing the way north. He fixed it in his mind, and some almost unconscious part of him made his fist dig a hole in the mud pointing north.

I think my father taught me that. He lived his life in a half dozen narrow streets, and yet he knew about the stars – how is that?

Because even the poor can look up past their next meal. Even the drunkard pauses now and then to cast his face to the sky and hope, and wonder.

We are beaten, Karnos thought. He beat us fair and fully, outnumbered and in the muck of winter when his horses could not run.

I should have offered Rictus more. His men were in front of me today – or yesterday – his Dogsheads. Corvus did that on purpose. What a marvellous bastard he must be. I wish I knew him.

I hope Kassander got away.

And with that thought the rags of the present came back to him. The League he had spent years building was cast to the wind, and the flower of Machran had been slaughtered here, around him.

How many died here today?

He sat up, and the pain became something quite novel in its intensity. He had heard old campaigners say that the worse the wound, the less the pain. He hoped it was true.

Pollo, I need a bath. Who knew that war would stink so bad?

Karnos of Machran stood up, a fat man in a gaudy cuirass, barefoot and slathered in mud and blood, a black arrow poking from his right shoulder. He was the only thing moving upon the flooded mere which had been a battlefield.

The Plain of Afteni, they will call it, he thought, for Afteni is not twenty pasangs away along the road. That is where they will be, those who are alive. That is where I must be, if I am to live.

He began walking west.

THIRTEEN
THE HIGHLAND SNOWS

PHAESTUS – ONE-TIME SPEAKER of Hal Goshen, until Rictus had shown up at his gates – had always been a man who prided himself on his appearance. He liked the attention of women; his wife, Thandea, had been a noted beauty in her day and was still a handsome matron. More to the point, she was an amenable adornment to his life who kept his household running smoothly in conjunction with his steward, leaving Phaestus to consider the weightier things in life, be they the running of a great city or the pursuit of other men's wives.

That was all in the past.

To become ostrakr was a blackened distinction within the Macht world. It meant a man had no city, no citizenship, and hence no redress for wrongs done to him.

He might own taenons of good land, but the

moment he was ostrakr, that land became anyone's to own. He might try to defend it with the strength of his own arm, but what is one man to do when three or four – or fifty – walk onto his farm and declare their intention to take it from him? He dies fighting, or he leaves it all behind.

The same applies to his house, his slaves, all his possessions. And if some stranger takes a fancy to his wife or his daughter, then it is his own spear, and that alone, which will preserve their honour. There is no recourse to the courts, to the assembly, or even to the assistance of friends and neighbours. He is ostrakr – he no longer exists.

Mercenaries forsook their cities when they took up the red cloak, though there were far fewer of them around now than there had been – so many had died with the Ten Thousand that a kind of tradition had been lost, and even now the true, contracted fighting man who fought by the code of his centon was something of a rarity. Such men were ostrakr also, but they at least had the brotherhood of their fellows to fall back on. They exchanged one polity for another.

A man who had nothing to fill up the framework of his world was naked in the dark, and must subsist with the tireless wariness of the fox until he somehow found a way to become a citizen again, to come in from that darkness.

That is what Phaestus had meant to do.

He stood now wrapped in bear-furs which he had bartered from a group of drunk goatherder men over the campfire of the night before. They had been good men, rough and ready as all were who lived up in the highlands with no city to call their own. Up here it was still the world of the clan and the tribe, a more ancient place. But still, men belonged to something. They looked after those of their own blood.

It was a white, frozen world this high in the hills, and the Gosthere Range was a marching line of blinding-bright giants all along the brim of the horizon, the sky as blue and clear as a robin's egg above them. Here, winter had already come into its own, and the drifts were building deep, the dark pinewoods locked down in frozen suspension, and the rivers narrowed to fast flowing black streams between broadening banks of solid ice, the very rocks bearded with foot-long icicles.

The goatherder men had been bringing their flocks and their families down into the valleys for the winter, and were glad to trade: furs and dried meat for wine and pig-iron ingots. They had haggled hard over the wine and then shared it out liberally afterwards, for such was their nature.

These were the original strawheads of the high country, from whom Phaestus's own people had come. The dark-skinned lowlanders might sneer at them, but they at least did not burn down cities and enslave populations. All they wanted was grazing for their animals, a place to pitch their dome-shaped tents of weathered hide, and room to roam. They were a picture, perhaps, of how the Macht had lived in the far and misty past. Perhaps.

Phaestus watched them go, and raised his spear to answer the headman's departing salute. Ten families, perhaps thirty warriors and a hundred women and children and old folk. A unit more cohesive than the citizenry of any city.

If only life were that simple, Phaestus thought.

He had grown a beard to keep the wind from his face, and it had come out as grey as hoar frost. His plump wife had lost some of her padding and had stopped complaining about having to sleep on the ground. And his son had become a man right in front of his eyes, discarding the preening sulks of the adolescent in a few short weeks.

Exile had been good for him, young Philemos. Dark like his mother, and inclined to amplitude like her, he had become an angular young man who took to this life of exile as though he had been waiting for it to happen. There was that much, at least, to be thankful for. The two girls were a different matter.

Phaestus turned in his tracks to regard the straggling little column on the slope below him. One mule had died already, and the rest were overburdened. They would have to dump more of their possessions, pitifully few though they were. His complete collection of Ondimion was already in a snowdrift two days back, a sacrifice which had wrenched his heart. But there was no need to read of drama in a scroll when it was the stuff of their daily lives now.

Tragedy, revenge; yes, that is what life hinges around. The poets had it right after all.

He looked north, at the furrowed valleys and glens of the Gostheres, white in a dreaming world of snow.

That old word they used, from the ancient Machtic – *nemesis*. That is what I am, Phaestus thought.

His son joined him, scratching and grinning. "These bearskins have lice in them, father. Are we to become barbarians to survive?"

"Yes," Phaestus said. "That is exactly what we must be. But not forever, Philemos."

"I hope not – I can't listen to my sisters carp and moan for much longer. I love them dearly, but I would also love to clash their heads together."

Phaestus laughed, his white teeth gleaming in his beard. "Now you know how I have felt these last few years. The women are unhappy, and rightly so – this is not their world, up here. Everything they have known has been taken away from them – the least we can do is bear their carping without complaint. That is what men do."

"We're soft. I had not thought so until we were with the goatherder people last night. I think their women are tougher than us."

"They breed them hard, this high," Phaestus said, and his smile faded. "Your mother and sisters are folk of the city, lowlanders, but my people came from the highlands, and it is in your blood too. It's well to remember that. The clans of the mountains are not savages – not like the goatmen, who are worse than animals. They are ourselves, in a purer state. What we write down, they keep in their heads, and their sense of honour is as refined as our own. As soon as they sat across a fire from us last night, we were part of their camp, and had some threat come upon us, we would all have fought it together."

"And if we had cheated them in the bargaining?"

"They would have considered themselves fools for

being cheated – that is what such barter is about. But you cross them in a matter of honour, Philemon, and they will kill you without mercy, and all your family. You must remember that."

"I will." The boy sobered.

"Good lad. Now, get back down and help with the repacking and, for Phobos's sake, don't overload the mules. They have a long journey still to make. Send Berimus up to me."

"Yes, father."

Phaestus watched him go.

Seventeen years. old, and ostrakr. It's still an adventure to him – he has no real idea what it means.

Berimus stood silently for some time before Phaestus spoke to him, and when he did his tone was entirely different, harsh and cold as the mountain stone below the ice.

"Are all the preparations made?"

"Yes, master."

"I am no longer your master, Berimus. You are no longer a slave."

He turned around. Berimus was a small man, built as broad as an oak door, with a nut-shaped head of dark hair and lively grey eyes. The same age as Phaestus, he looked ten years younger, a compact, muscular version of the tall patrician with the pepper-grey beard, who looked him in the eye.

Phaestus handed him a clinking pouch of soft leather.

"That is all we have left, but it should be enough. You won't need it up here in the hills, and do not show it – it will only make trouble."

"I know."

"Once you reach the lowlands, show someone in authority this." Phaestus produced a sealed scroll of parchment. He rubbed the red wax with one finger.

"This is the seal of Karnos himself. Any official of the hinterland cities will recognise it, and will assist you. Make due west – it's four hundred pasangs to Machran. Do not let the ladies tell you otherwise. My wife will think to command you – do not let her. You are a free man now, but still my steward, and the man I trust most in the world."

"Master, your family is my own – you know that."

"I do. Berimus, we will come out of this thing. When I bring Karnos what I seek we will be citizens again, of the greatest city in our world. I will see you right, I swear."

Berimus bowed his head.

"You remember when we were boys together, and we came up here hunting with my father?"

"The day the boar felled him – I remember."

"We stood over him that day, shoulder to shoulder like brothers. That is what you have always been to me. I am entrusting my family to you now – stand over them as you stood over my father."

"I will, master."

"I am called Phaestus, my friend."

Berimus looked solemn as an owl. "Phaestus. I will deliver your family to Machran, or I will die trying. You have my word on it."

They clasped forearms as free men do.

"Philemos and I will join you before midwinter. Karnos will look after you until then. Give this to him." Another scroll, another waxed seal.

"Be careful, Phaestus," Berimus said. "These hills are a strange and dangerous place."

"Dangerous?" Phaestus smiled. "Don't worry, Berimus. I only go to call on the home of a friend."

TWO SEPARATE LINES of people, one family. They moved apart from one another, mere dots on the white spine of the world. Phaestus was throwing his life into the hollow of a knucklebone, and with it, those of all he loved.

Let me show you how it feels, Rictus, he thought.

HE HAD HUNTED in these hills for decades; he knew them as well as any city-dweller could. In the winter he had tracked wolf, in the summer deer. North of the Gostheres, in the deep Harukush, there were mountain leopards with blue eyes, and enormous white cave bears. So it was rumoured, though Phaestus had never seen one, or met anyone who had.

It was an ancient place, the Deep Mountains. The legends said that the Macht themselves had originated there, migrating south and east out of the snows and the savage peaks, leaving behind them a lost city – the first city – whose walls had been made of iron.

The first Macht had all been Cursebearers, according to the myth, and had known Antimone herself. She had descended to the surface of the world to dress them in her Gift, and then had left for her endless vigil among the stars with only her two sons for company.

And God had turned His face from them all, from the goddess of pity and the race on whose behalf she had intervened upon the face of the earth.

So said the legends. Phaestus was nothing if not a rational man, but he was astute enough to know the value of myth. The black armours which dotted the Macht world were an undeniable reality, and had not been made by any craft that now existed. So there was that seed of truth at the root of the legends. If there was one, there might be others.

He had talked to Rictus of it, back in the days when he had been an honoured guest at Andunnon and the two had sat by the fire after a few days' hunting in the hills. Together, they had speculated idly that they might one day make an expedition into the lost interior of the Deep Mountains, to look for that lost city with walls of iron. Something to occupy their retirement.

Antimone, Lady of Night, Phaestus thought, how did it come to this?

THEY KEPT TO the high ridges to steer clear of the drifts, and found themselves in a blue and white world, where the wind took their breath away and set the snow clouding in a blizzard off the rocks and stones at their feet. The sky was empty except for the pale red disc that was Haukos, always reluctant to quit the sky in winter, but to the north the great peaks of the Harukush – legendary even among the Kufr – barred the horizon like a white wall. Down from them the wind swooped, and the bite of it was as bitter as a plunge into a midwinter sea.

There were six of them: Phaestus, Philemos, and four others who had come out of Hal Goshen with them. One of these, Sertorius, had been at various times in his life a mercenary, a hunter, a slave-dealer, and a pimp. It was in this latter guise that he had come to the attention of Phaestus, in his duties as chief magistrate of the city.

The two had known each other for many years, and from their confrontations there had arisen a grudging mutual respect. In his own way, Sertorius was as proud and stiff-necked as Phaestus, and as disgusted by the tame surrender of his city. It was he, and his silent little band of henchmen, who had smuggled the Speaker of Hal Goshen, his family and some of his household out of the city – and with a surprising degree of discretion.

Ostrakr, the sentence had been, but Phaestus had no doubt that he was not intended to survive. His rival, Sarmenian, had ached for the chief magistracy for too long to be magnanimous in victory.

Sertorius had been well paid for his troubles, but this current exploit he was doing for free. Like Phaestus, he was a man without a city now, and were he to walk through the gates of Machran, he wanted to do so with something to show for his trouble, something which would ease the transition.

He was a lowlander, a black-haired, brown-skinned man with eyes the colour of a thrush's back and a convict's gall-marks on his wrists. His face was seamed and scarred with knife-fights and wickedness and he had a wide gap between his front teeth. He was not the company Phaestus would have chosen for a trip into the highlands in winter – still less the three hulking street-thugs that were his companions – but the choice had not been wide, and Sertorius had at least a brassy, hail-fellow-well-met way of getting along with others which had come in useful with the goatherder folk the night before.

What Sertorius and his men lacked, however, was a knowledge of the mountains, and they stumbled in the wake of Phaestus and his son, holding onto the tails of the mules and complaining endlessly about the cold.

"Two good day's travel," Phaestus told them, reining in his contempt with the practice of a politician. "That's all. Two days, and then we shall have a roof over our heads, for a day or two at least."

"If the weather holds," Sertorius said, the words hissing through his gapped teeth. "I hope the prize we seek is worth it, Phaestus."

"Believe me, my friend, it will be well worth the trip. But we must make it to Machran as quickly as we can. The last I heard, Corvus was banking on a swift winter campaign. The fighting is going on even as we speak."

"Then we're well out of it," Adurnos, one of Sertorius's henchmen muttered.

"If it hurts the little fucker who took our city, then I'm all for it," Sertorius said. "But remember, Phaestus, I was paid only to get you out of Hal Goshen. This here trip is my own charity."

"And your own self-interest," Phaestus told him. "This way you turn up at Machran with something that Karnos wants. You arrive there empty-handed, and you'll be starting at the bottom again."

"The bottom's where I feel comfortable," Sertorius said with a laugh.

Struggling along the knife-ridge later in the day, with the sun setting at their left shoulders and the wind masking all conversation, Philemos drew his father close.

"I don't trust them."

"Nor do I. But so long as their interests and ours coincide, they will serve us faithfully. Sertorius is a rogue, but he has a keen sense of what's good for him."

"They're animals, father; scum from the sewers. What's to stop them turning on us?"

"Philemos," Phaestus said, smiling, "I am their introduction to Karnos, to the fleshpots of Machran. And more than that, look at them. They're lowland city criminals – if you and I walked away from them now they would perish up here. They need us as we need them. They are outside their own world."

"So are we," his son said. "Father, I would sooner we had gone to Machran and joined the League army – to fight in open battle. What we're doing here –"

"What we do here is worth a thousand men on the battlefield," Phaestus snapped. "Not everything comes down to standing in a spearline, boy. And you'll get your chance at that before we're done." His face softened at the look on his son's.

"Philemos, you were born to be more than phalanx-fodder, as was I. If you are to be a man, you must learn from me. A man cannot always follow the dictates of what he perceives to be his honour – sometimes that will lead him to his ruin."

"Father, you could have been ruler of Hal Goshen under Corvus – it was your honour that has brought you here."

Phaestus smiled. "Well said. I shall make a rhetorician of you yet." He turned away, and the smile curdled on his face.

It was not honour. It was ambition, and outrage, and bloody-minded hatred. To be offered something like that, like a coin dropped on a beggar's plate – and by Rictus, who despite everything was nothing more than a brute mercenary.

It could not be borne. It was the manner in which the offer had been made, as much as the offer itself.

I am a better man than Rictus, he thought. And I will prove it.

FOURTEEN
TEST OF LIFE

THERE WAS SOMETHING in Aise which responded to winter. She respected it, with the good sense of a woman who had lived her life in the blue and white world of the high hills. But there was more to it than that.

It was not that she enjoyed the sensations of the season – although she did – it was more that the vast labour of the year was done, at long last, affording a chance to stand and look around, and to lean back from the earth upon which she threw all the life she had within her, year upon year.

She did not like winter – no fool could – but there was a certain satisfaction about it, seeing all which had been set in train throughout the year lead up to the moment of truth. That was winter in the highlands; the test of life itself.

The barley had been scythed, threshed and

winnowed, and the grain stored in the three-legged wooden bin at one end of the yard. When Aise felt cold, or out of sorts, she would open the bin and scoop out a bucketful, then pound it to flour in the great hollow stone that Rictus and Fornyx had dragged out of the river years in the past. They had been two days getting it from the water to where it now sat, and every time she thumped the iron-hard log into it she thought of them that summer, sitting grinning at one another with the muck of the riverbank all over them and that great stone between them. Now it sat in the yard as though it had been there since time immemorial, a totem of their permanence here.

A clinking of bronze bells, the nattering bleat of the goats. Rian was walking slowly across the yard with a leather bucket of goat's milk, which was steaming in the chill of the morning. Ona chattered along beside her, bright as a starling, and around the two girls the dogs flounced like puppies, sure of their share of the milk.

In the house Styra was tending the fire – at this time of year it was never allowed to go out. Garin had been chopping wood since dawn, and was sat before the hearth, talking to her. The talk ceased when Aise entered, and Garin rose with a sullen look about him. He and Styra had become a couple very quickly – slaves were wont to do such things, casting around for what comfort they could in life – but he had never forgiven Aise for selling Veria, and his work was falling off. He spent more time out in the woods now, trapping and tree-felling and hunting, sometimes with Eunion, sometimes alone.

It is Rictus he stays for, Aise thought. My husband has a way of garnering loyalty, even when he is not trying.

Eunion came to the table with a cloak wrapped about him, a few strands of white hair standing out from his head like a dandelion gone to seed. He was yawning, and in the morning his face seemed as wrinkled as a walnut.

"You should not sit up so late," Aise said, kneading the barley dough into flat cakes for the griddle. "You read too much, Eunion." She hated that Eunion was getting old. She could not imagine life here without him. She would be lost, and that made her all the more terse.

"I was reading. One of these months I will go to Hal Goshen for a better lamp, a three-flame one with a deep well. My eyes smart like blisters."

"They look more like cherries. Have some milk. I will have bannock made soon. Rian!"

Rictus's daughter stuck her head in the front door. "Yes, mother?"

"Draw me a gourd of oil from the jar, and set the plates. Where is Ona?"

"Playing with the dogs."

"Bring her in."

The household gathered about the table. When Rictus and Fornyx were not here they all ate together, slaves and free alike. Aise rose, flushed, from the fire with barley bannock hot to the touch, and poured the oil over the pale, flat cakes. There was soft cheese to go with them, and goat's milk with the animals' warmth still in it. Eunion munched on an onion, and winced as his ageing teeth met their match in the purple bulb of it.

"I was reading about the Deep Mountains," he said to the table.

"Which story? The one about the city of iron?" Rian asked eagerly.

I will have to brush her hair tonight, Aise thought. It is as matted as a horse's mane – and I do not believe her face has felt water this morning.

"Yes," Eunion went on, gesturing with the onion. "It seems to me there's something to be said for the theory that the first Macht wanted to keep themselves hidden, hence the remote location of the legendary city of iron.

"But more than that. When I read the myths, I find that Antimone is there with them at the beginning, not just as the goddess we know and pray to, but as a creature who lived upon the face of Kuf in their midst. Who knows – she may even have been one of us – a Macht woman of great learning and wisdom that subsequent generations imbued with the godhead. When it comes to the black armour –"

"Eunion, you read too much that is not there," Aise said, looking up from her bowl. "It's one thing to spend the whole night ruining your sight in front of a bunch of old scrolls, but quite another to be filling the children's heads with – with –"

"Blasphemy?" Eunion said.

"Well, yes. Antimone watches over us all eternally. She was never a mortal woman; that's absurd. You're just playing with ideas, and Rian has enough of those in her head already."

Eunion grinned. "Aise, I merely flex my mind. It is a muscle, like those in your arm. If you do not exercise it, it will atrophy, and we would all be no better than goatmen."

"Drink your milk, old man, you talk too much." But she smiled.

"Goatmen! Tell us, Eunion," Rian wriggled in her chair, "how was it that they came to be?"

"Gestrakos tells us that –"

The dogs growled, low in their throats, and padded away from the table towards the open door of the farmhouse. Eunion fell silent.

"Maybe they smell wolf on the wind," Garin said.

The family sat quiet, listening. The two hounds both had their hackles up and their teeth bared. They walked stiff-legged outside, and began baying furiously.

"We have visitors," Eunion said, and rose up from the table with a swiftness that belied his years. Garin rose with him, wiping his mouth.

"Spears?"

"Yes – go get them."

"The pass is closed," Aise said. She could feel the blood leaving her face.

"Perhaps father has come back!" Rian said.

"The dogs know better," Aise told her. "Stay here."

Eunion and Garin were lifting their spears from beside the door, short-shafted hunting weapons with wide blades, made to fight boar and wolf.

"Aise –" Eunion said, but she shook off his hand.

"I am mistress of this house."

She stepped outside, into the brilliant snow-brightness of the blue morning.

Just in time to see the death of her dogs.

The baying was cut short. Half a dozen men stood black against the snow on the near riverbank. As Aise watched, she saw one raise his arm again and spear one of the animals through and through. Blood on the snow, a colour almost too vivid to be part of this world. Aise stood frozen. Eunion and Garin surged out of the doorway behind her, saw the black shapes of the men scant yards away, and the bodies of the two hounds. Garin gave a wordless cry of grief and rage. The men looked up. Wrapped in winter furs, they were unrecognisable. A voice said, "That's her," and they came on at a run.

Eunion and Garin shouldered Aise aside, hefted their spears, and stood to meet the incomers. Two of the strangers held back, and the taller yelled, "Alive! There is no need for killing here!"

Garin charged like a bull, knocked aside an aichme with the deftness of a man who has faced down wild boar, and thrust his own spear into the belly of the man in front of him. There was a high pitched gurgling cry, and the man fell to his knees. The spear went down with him, clutched by his intestines. The other men roared with fury. A spearhead flicked out and transfixed Garin through the eye. He fell backwards, off the blade, a bright arc of blood in the air following his body to the ground.

Aise scrabbled for his weapon, but was kicked in the ribs once, twice –

"Fucking cunt," her attacker snarled.

Eunion barrelled into him, smashing the shaft of his spear into the man's face, thumping the butt of it into the chest of a second. The third stabbed him at the base of the spine, grunting with the effort of the thrust. Eunion fell to his knees, startled. He looked down at Aise as she lay gasping for breath in the snow.

"This is not –"

Two more spearheads were pushed into him. One was thrust so hard it exited his chest, a grotesque spike under his chiton. He looked down at it in utter bewilderment. Then the man behind him set his foot in Eunion's back and booted him off the end of the spear. He fell over Aise, warm, twitching, his blood hot and coppery over her.

She heard Rian shriek and tried to rise, pushing Eunion to one side. His eyes were still moving and his mouth opened, but nothing came out except the smell of the onion he had eaten for breakfast. His face went still.

Someone kicked Aise again, hard in the back.

"Stay down there, bitch."

She tried to rise regardless. Rian was screaming, and she could hear Ona sobbing. The man set a boot on her breasts and leant on her. He looked down, a black shadow against the blue sky.

"Nice looking cunt, Sertorius. Things are looking up."

"Keep her there. Adurnos, go check the house. How's Fars?"

"He's dead. That fucking slave killed him, and that bald fucker broke my nose."

"Makes you prettier. Now, go do as I say. Let the filly loose; she won't leave the mare."

Aise heaved for breath, the man's foot crushing it out of her.

"Their own fault, Phaestus – don't you give me that look. They came at us first, so fair's fair. Anyway, we have what we came for."

Phaestus? Aise scrabbled through the white panic in her mind.

"Phaestus?" she croaked aloud.

"Get your foot off her, Sertorius. I'll see to her." An older man's voice, familiar.

"Leave that girl alone!" Another voice shouted, a boy's yell raised in outrage.

"Philemos – get the daughters, bring them to me."

There was a cry inside the farmhouse, and Aise heard Styra scream. The men laughed and whooped.

She closed her eyes. Setting out her hand she touched Eunion's head, the feather-soft tendrils of white hair about the ears. Her eyes burned. But she would not weep.

A shadow over her, a new one that did not smell as bad as the last.

"Aise, let me help you up."

She laboured to her feet, and Rian was hugging her, white face streaked with tears. Ona was clinging to her skirts, silent, empty-eyed with her thumb in her mouth.

She knew this man in front of her: a friend of Rictus, an important figure in Hal Goshen. She knew him as vain and proud and full of himself, but a man of probity and wit. A guest-friend. He had eaten at her table. He had drunk wine with Eunion, whose corpse now lay on the snow between them.

Eunion –

Her face hardened. "Phaestus," she said, and her voice was steady, as cold as the stone in the frozen river. "What is this evil you do here?"

There had been something like remorse on his face – dismay at least. Now that fled. His face matched hers, stone for stone.

"I revisit on the family of Rictus the evil he has done mine," he said.

"What has my husband done to you, his guest friend?" Aise asked, and her voice cracked on the last word.

"He has made us ostrakr, robbed us of everything we had and set us on the roads like vagabonds. He has brought my city to servitude and shame. And all for a mercenary's purse."

"Hal Goshen?" Aise asked, shaking her head.

"Corvus now owns my city, like a paid-for whore."

Aise looked down at Eunion's body. She wanted to take the old man in her arms, to kiss his eyes shut. For twenty years he had been like a father to her, a more constant companion than the husband who had brought them here. Now he lay like slaughtered meat in the snow. His half-eaten onion was still on the table inside.

The tears brimmed up and burned like acid in her eyes.

"Did Rictus do this to you?" she asked simply, and opened her hands to the dead man.

"This was unforeseen, an accident," Phaestus said.

"I had not meant it to be like this."

A shriek from inside the house. Styra's voice.

The young man standing beside Phaestus looked stricken. "Father, we must stop them."

"She's only a slave," Phaestus said.

"But –"

"No!" he roared, face flushed red. "Be silent, Philemos. The world works like this – as well you see it first hand at last. If you can't hold your tongue then go and get the mules – not another word!"

Rian had stopped sobbing. She knelt in the bloody snow and closed Eunion's eyes, then bent and kissed him as Aise had wanted to do. She straightened.

"I know you," she said to Phaestus. "So does my father. When he hears of what you have done here he will find you, and he will kill you. This I promise."

Her eyes were grey, like Rictus's, and in them was some of the same wild fury. Phaestus stared back at her a moment. His mouth opened. Then he swung his arm and back-handed her across the face. Rian tumbled into the snow. Aise knelt at once and gathered her into her arms. Ona let out shrill scream.

"Sertorius! – get out here! Sertorius!"

The gap-toothed brigand came out of the farmhouse with a wineskin in one hand, grinning. "Got everything you want, Phaestus? Who'd have thought there'd be such fine flesh up here in the arse of nowhere?"

"Take these three and tie them up, hands in front of them. But let them get some things out of the house first – travelling clothes. And take whatever you can from the place in the way of food."

"Whoa there, my fine friend – aren't we going to hole up here for a day or two? That was the plan. We could be pretty snug here; they have a whole winter's supplies squirreled away."

"Take what you need and what won't slow us down – we move on at once."

"Listen, chief –"

"Do as I say, Sertorius, if you want that big welcome in Machran."

"What of the dead meat lying here?" Sertorius asked, surly now.

"Throw them into the house, and then burn it."

Aise moved through the familiar rooms in a fog. In a normal, everyday tone she told Rian to dress in her best woollens, and the fur-lined cloak her father had brought back from Machran.

Everything inside the house had been kicked over and picked through, things broken for no reason. The little aquamarine pot in Aise's room was smashed in blue shards upon the floor. Rictus's battered old farm sandals lay to one side.

I wish you were here, husband, she thought. *Though it is you that has brought this upon us.*

In the back room, Styra lay naked and sprawled like a broken doll. Her face was beaten into a swollen fruit, a pulp of bone and blood, and she had been stabbed below her left breast.

Aise stood looking at her for a long time, standing square in the doorway so Rian could not see.

This is what awaits us all, she thought.

One of Sertorius's men came up behind her, his mouth full of the barley bannock Aise had baked that morning.

"Bitch had a knife on her, cut me good – you see what she did?"

Aise turned. He was heavily built, and the hair from his chest rose up to join with that of his beard. He had a fresh wound at the side of his eye, a finger-long slice with the blood already dry upon it.

"All we wanted was some sport," he said, shaking his head. "Fucking waste." He smiled at Aise. "You make good bannock. Tasty." His grin widened, and he slapped Aise on the rump. "High and mighty, aren't we? Wife of the great Rictus." He took another bite of bannock, and held it up to her. "Hope you can suck cock as well as you cook."

When they were outside again with a pitiful collection of belongings furled in blankets upon their backs, Sertorius grabbed their hands and bound them with rawhide strips cut from the milking buckets.

He leaned in close to Rian as she stood there and sniffed at her neck. She flicked her head as though a fly had settled on her, and he laughed – then straightened as Phaestus and his son approached.

"The bodies go in the house," Phaestus said.

"What does it matter, for Phobos's sake, if they burn or the wolves have them?" Sertorius protested.

"Wouldn't you want someone to do it for you?" Aise asked him.

Sertorius looked at her. "Don't speak to me, cunt."

"Just do it," Phaestus said quickly. "One of your own is lying here."

"Fars was always a slow lazy bastard – oh, all right. Adurnos, Bosca, you heard the fellow – trail this rubbish in the house before we fire it."

Aise looked up at the sky. It had been such a beautiful morning, a blue, still winter's day. She wished it had not been so beautiful; now, when there were other days as fine as this, she would be remembering the events of this morning, and they would taint every blue winter's sky for her.

If she lived long enough to have the memories.

I wronged Garin, she thought. I should not have sold Veria, for she was his wife in everything but name. I got rid of her because she reminded me too much of my own hurt, of the boy we lost. For that at least, I am paying now.

Lord, in thy goodness and thy glory, let me take it all upon myself, what remains ahead of us. Let it all be mine, the hurt and the evil to come. Protect my girls, and let the pain be on me alone.

She smelled smoke, heard a crackling, and turned round to find the thatch of the farmhouse on fire. Phaestus's son, Philemos, was shooing the goats out of their bothy while the roof broke into flame above him.

"What's with this, goatherder boy?" Sertorius asked.

"No need for them to burn," Philemos said. His colour was up and his eyes were shining dark. "There's been enough death here for one day." He looked over at Aise and Rian and then looked away again quickly.

They gathered together in front of the farmhouse as it went up and the two mules brayed in fear at the smell of smoke and the massive rush of heat. All the outbuildings were on fire also, and the goats were streaming away in panic from the blaze. Sertorius was wearing Rictus's spare soldier's cloak, mercenary scarlet, while his accomplices were loading down the mules with hams, barley-flour, oil-jars and skins of wine.

"Not an obol in the place," Sertorius said, staring at the burning house. "Where did the famous Rictus keep his money, is what I want to know? The bastard lives simply – there's hardly a damn thing worth stealing."

"The moneydealers in Hal Goshen have it all," Aise said, "Safe in one of their cellar-vaults. He is not stupid enough to keep it here." Sertorius looked at her with an eyebrow raised.

"We have what we came for," Phaestus said. "It's the best part of three hundred pasangs to Machran, and winter is on us. When we deliver these three to Karnos, you won't want for money, Sertorius. I'll see to that."

"See that you do," Sertorius said. "I am a man of many virtues and vices, Phaestus, and one might say that the one weighs in the balance against the other. Don't try to leave your thumb on my scales."

Then he grinned. "Ah, the warmth! Let us hope our campfire tonight will keep us as warm! But to the logistics of today. Adurnos, you will lead the spitfire girl. I will take the woman –"

"No," Phaestos said. He stepped forward and grasped the long lashing of hide that hung from Aise's wrists. "I'll take her. Philemos, you lead the girl, and you, Sertorius, the child."

"Fuck that," Sertorius said. "Adurnos, the brat is yours. At least she'll be light, carried. Shall we leave then, brothers and sisters? The day is trailing on and I want to get past the drifts at the top of this dungheap valley before darkness finds us."

They set out. Sertorius led the way, and Aise was jerked into motion behind Phaestus as the older man tugged on her bonds. Philemos came next, Rian walking at his side as though he was escorting her for a ramble through the woods. Then came the big man with the broken nose, Adurnos. He settled Ona up on a mule with a curse, while Bosca, whom Styra had marked with her knife, brought up the rear, leading another heavily laden mule.

They crossed the river, their feet breaking through the snow-covered ice that had thickened on the surface of the water. The bite of the stream cleared Aise's head somewhat. She heard a great crash behind her and looked back to see the roof of the farmhouse cave in with a rush of black smoke and scattered sparks. In the bright day, the flames were saffron-dark and solid as swords, drenched in sunlight.

Smoke the colour of an autumn storm rose in a high pillar in the air above the valley. It loomed over them all, casting its own shadow on the snow, and smuts from the burning floated over the trees like ethereal carrion birds.

At least you had a pyre worthy of you, Eunion, Aise thought. Now your ashes will be in the air and water of this place, like my son's.

And Rictus, your precious gold is under the hearthstone where we put it.

Aise bent her head and followed her captors through the snow to the woods that hung dark and deep on the slopes of the glen above.

Behind her the home that she and Rictus and Fornyx and Eunion had made blazed into destruction, the stone walls toppling as the heat cracked them open, the hoarded grain, the oil, the olives and the wine – the very stuff of life – taking light and combusting in a boiling tower of black smoke that blighted the morning.

And in the flames at its base the bodies of the dead lay darkening into ash and dust; a grey taste on the wind, no more.

FIFTEEN
MUD AND WATER

THE CITY OF Afteni, famous for its metal-workers, was now an island in a shallow sea. Built, like most Macht cities, on rising ground and surrounded by a twenty-foot wall, it found itself surrounded by water also, a knee-deep lake extending for two thirds of the city's circumference.

Since the Battle of the Afteni Plain, which had seen the scattering – if not the destruction – of the army of the Avennan League, the clouds had gathered, black over the lowlands at the foot of the Gosthere Mountains, and had released their burden upon already saturated farmland. The Imperial Road had disappeared, sunk in brown water, and the entire plain had gone with it. There was only the endless dreary expanse of rain-stippled floodwater, with groves of olives and bedraggled vines and sodden trees straggling above it, cowering from the endless downpour.

And that had proved a salvation.

Karnos stood on the battlements of the citadel with a soldier's oilskin cloak thrown round him, his own little tent against the wet, and peered east, striving to pierce the rain-curtain. Unconsciously, his arm came up and he began carefully kneading the bandaged flesh of his shoulder.

"It itches, Kassander – that's a good thing, isn't it?"

"It doesn't smell, which is even better. You are a fast healer, Karnos. You heal like a young dog, as my mother used to say."

"And what about the rest – how are they healing?"

"The last wagon train left for Machran only this morning, though they will need Phobos's horses in the traces to make more than a few pasangs a day in this mire. I pity them."

"They're men of Machran – that's where they belong."

"They're going back with a tale of defeat. You should beat them to it."

"I will, as soon as I am done here. One man on a horse will travel faster. I wish to speak with Katullos first."

"Antimone may have words with him before you do."

"Nonsense! That old bugger? If seeing me become Speaker did not kill him, then a spear in his throat won't."

"He wishes to see you in any case. We must decide what to do with what's left of the army."

"I couldn't keep the Pontis men here. I tried – I spent all last night talking to that fish-livered bitch

Zennos – but he wasn't having it. So there's a thousand men pissed away."

"He's not the only one."

"Come on, let's get out of this fucking rain. It's our friend at the moment, I know, but it's like a friend you owe money to: uncongenial company."

"Admirable candour from someone who has borrowed money from me more times than I care to remember."

"Ah, don't be such a girl. Come, have some wine."

They retreated to a tall portico which ran around the base of a tower. There was a brazier burning there, a table covered with papers, and men were coming and going, adding to the pile.

"You have become newly fond of fresh air," Kassander said, throwing back the hood of his own cloak.

"I like the view. I can see half a dozen pasangs down the road when the rain lifts a little – it means I'll see that bastard coming."

"By all accounts he's not on his way just yet – the road is washed out in half a dozen places, where it's not wholly underwater, and rumour has it there's sickness in his camp. He's afloat in a sea of his own shit some ten pasangs back down the road, long may he remain there."

Karnos poured some wine with his good hand. "Meanwhile we sit here in relative comfort. It warms my heart to think on it."

"He did the right thing with the dead – sent Greynos of Afteni's body forward under a green branch and burned the rest with all the proper rites."

"Yes, he's quite the fucking gentleman. In the meantime we are sitting here on a castle of sand, leaking centons by the day. Kassander, we must think of Machran now. The League has snapped in our hands like a wishbone."

"You think we're on our own?"

"Stop and listen."

Kassander sighed and nodded. Below the endless patter and hiss of the rain was another noise, a vast hum, like a hive of angry bees.

"That's the Afteni assembly in session, ten thousand angry, frightened men standing in the rain at the bottom of this rock, making a debate about something they have already decided. They lost six hundred of their best down on the plain, and Greynos, the only one of their Kerusia with any stones. They are finished, and they know it, but must spin out the argument while Machran and the other contingents are still within their walls looking on. It's like observing the decencies at a funeral pyre. The eastern cities of the hinterland are lost, Kassander. The rest are waiting to see what Machran can do."

"Machran will never capitulate," Kassander said, his big, good-natured face darkening. "Not while I live."

Karnos touched him on the arm. "Well said, brother." He set down his winecup. A young man in the black sigil-embroidered chiton of the Machran staff coughed politely behind him.

"Yes, Gersic?"

"Sir, counsellor Katullus requests that you meet with him at your convenience. He is –"

"I know where he is, Gersic; tell him I'm on my way. And Gersic –"

"Sir?"

"How is his voice?"

The young man, dark and earnest and with a stitched-up stab wound on his arm, considered. "He can whisper, sir."

"Good enough." Karnos turned back to Kassander.

"It has come to something when I view Katullos as an ally, of like mind to myself."

Kassander raised his winecup. "Being wounded and left for dead has done wonders for your reputation."

"I should have done it years ago," Karnos said.

A SMALL, BARE room, austere enough to satisfy even an ascetic like Katullos. There were no windows, and a single lamp burned by the bed. In a corner, the black cuirass sat upon its stand like a silent spirit, not a mark upon it, though Katullos had been at the very heart of the fighting.

The old man had taken an aichme to the throat. They had closed the wound with a hot iron and it blazed below his chin now like a second, purple-lipped mouth. His magnificent beard had been shorn off by the carnifex, and his face looked absurdly small without it. His skin was flushed with fever, but his eyes were clear. His big, mottled hands picked at his blanket ceaselessly as Karnos took a stool beside him.

"Lean close," Katullos said, a zephyr almost

drowned out by the sound of the rain outside and the rumbling from the assembly.

"Here." A letter, folded and sealed. There had been three attempts at the seal before it had taken – he had done it himself.

"For the Kerusia. It may help."

"What does it say?"

Katullos smiled. "To trust you."

Karnos sat back again, frowning, holding the letter like a trapped bird in his hand. "How do I know that? You have never been a friend to me, Katullos. I may break the seal and look."

"Then it is worthless."

"Better that than –"

"Trust me." Spittle was leaking from the corner of the old man's mouth. A few days before, he had led a mora into battle while wearing the Curse of God. Now he was reduced to this. Karnos felt a sting of pity.

"We have been adversaries all our public lives, you and I. What has changed?"

Again, the death's head smile. "I once told you I would be there to cheer the day you fell. Now I see that to do so would be to cheer the fall of my own city. You did the right thing, fighting when you did. You had your blood spilled for Machran. You love the city as I do. I did not see it before. I thought you loved only your own ambition."

"A man can love both."

"No, Karnos, not now." He coughed, a long wet rattle in his chest. Karnos could feel the heat radiating off him, as though his life were burning out in one last, guttering flare.

"Keep fighting," Katullos rasped. "Machran must never surrender. This man means to make himself king of us all. If Machran falls, he will have his foot on our necks for a generation." He sagged. "You see it – but not all men do."

"I see it – I have known it a long time."

"We were at cross purposes. I was wrong. You are Speaker of Machran; you speak for us all. Break him before our walls. No other city can do it."

"We cannot face him in open battle again, Katullos. The League is falling apart."

"The walls, Karnos. Hold the walls. Bleed him white. No-one can take Machran if men are on her walls, not even Corvus."

Karnos took one of the big, restless hands in his own. A jet of pain ran through his shoulder as he leaned over the dying man in the bed.

"Katullos, you have my word on it."

Katullos smiled again. "That is worth something – I know that now."

"I'll have you on the next wagon heading west – you'll see the city again, I promise you."

"I'll be dead before then. But take me home, Karnos. Burn me at the Mithos River and scatter my ashes in the water. Carve my name on the catafalque of the Alcmoi."

"It shall be done."

"My cuirass – see it goes to my family."

"I will."

Katullos stared closely at him. "You are a disgrace to the Kerusia, a demagogue, a rake and a philanderer. But you are all we have. The rest are sheep."

Karnos chuckled. "You flatter me, Katullos...
"Katullos?"

The old man remained staring, but the breath
was running out of him in a long, hoarse sigh. He
was still, the grip of the liver-spotted hand relaxing.
Karnos shook his head.

"Stubborn old bastard." He closed the still-bright eyes
with his fingers and bowed his head a moment. Then
he looked up, and stared across the room thoughtfully
at the Curse of God which sat silent in its corner.

THE MEN OF Machran marched out the next day,
weighed down with all their gear. The roads had
become so bad that no wagon could take to them, so
the battered morai splashed through the mire with
all their wargear on their backs and as much in the
way of scanty rations that Afteni could spare. It was
almost two hundred pasangs to Machran, and they
would be hungry long before they were home.

Other contingents of the League were marching
out also. The men of the hinterland cities had called
their own assemblies in Afteni, and voted on what
to do next. The Arkadians and Avennans, who had
been keen supporters of the League and allies of
Machran for time out of mind, voted to stick with
Karnos and Kassander.

Murchos, polemarch of the Arkadians, was a
burly man with a face like that of a pink, startled pig,
but he was a guest-friend of Kassander and would
follow him anywhere, as his own men would follow
him – especially since he was also a Cursebearer.

The Arkadians had always been a froward, reckless bunch. They threw their knucklebones high when they gambled, as they were gambling now. They would hold true, all three thousand of them.

The Avennans were much the same, though they liked to see their city as the true heart of the civilized Macht, the place where laws were made. The thought of it being ruled by an upstart warleader of no family, who employed the Kufr as soldiers, was anathema to them. They, too, would march with Machran. Two thousand men under Tyrias, who liked to call himself the Just, but who was known more commonly as Scrollworm, for he was more at home in a library than on a battlefield, despite his polemarch's helm.

All told, some nine thousand men marched out of Afteni with Kassander leading them west. Nine thousand men who meant to man the walls of Machran to the end. It was enough. It would have to be enough.

The rest had gone their separate ways, the mauled contingents from the other cities trailing out of Afteni in a less martial fashion, for many of them had thrown away their arms on the field to aid their flight. And it was understood that Afteni itself would capitulate to the invader when he finally got his army moving again through the mud.

It still wanted a month to midwinter.

KARNOS BENT LOW in the saddle, hissing with the damnable pain of it. He dropped the reins and shook Kassander's hand.

"March them hard, brother. The longer we have to ready the city the easier the thing will be."

"You should have an escort, Karnos. You're not near healing, and if you fall off that horse it'll take a file of men to push you back up on it again."

"I'm thinner than I was, I'll have you know." Karnos tugged the oilskin soldier's cloak closer about his neck. "Gersic is enough. He's a good boy, over-eager, sincere, and none too bright; just the type I like to have about me. I mean to do it in four days at most."

"You have my letters."

"Next to my heart, Kassander. Whatever rumour has run ahead of me, I bear the first official news. And I will tell it my way."

"If you have time, look in on my wife and sister – let them know I'm not ash on the wind."

"I will, brother." Karnos straightened, swore viciously at the pain angling through his shoulder, and then kicked the barrel-chested lowland cob into a trot. It flailed its way through the floodwater, like a boat chopping through a heavy swell.

He raised his good hand in farewell, and at the head of the long column half a dozen centons who recognised him set up a cheer. Then he disappeared into the mist of the rain.

KARNOS WAS NOT a man attuned to the natural world. He was more at home on pavement than pasture, and while he loved to eat red meat, he saw no virtue in killing it himself. The debating chamber, the bedroom, the marketplace – these were the places he felt at home. He still had his father in him, he supposed – in all three places the essence of the thing was a kind of haggling.

Now, as the land rose under his horse and the floodwaters began to recede, he pushed the animal hard, cantering to one side of the stone-paved road that led all the way to Machran with young Gersic shadowing him on a lighter, more spirited animal. Karnos's horse was a dogged bay with a rolling gait that was less aggravating to the jolting pain of his wound. He liked the animal – it had a stubborn heart, and it ploughed through the muck of the roadside as though it would never stop.

The natural world. It was a world shaped by the Macht, cowed by millennia of occupation, ploughed and planted and pruned to meet the needs and fashions of men. This was the finest farmland in all the Macht lands – sometimes they brought off two harvests a year in the hinterland of Machran. One could feed an army here, if one timed it right. And even in winter, the farms which dotted this country would have storehouses and byres and smokehouses full of grain and oil and meat on the hoof.

That was the problem.

Whatever Corvus's logistic woes were at the moment, they would vanish as soon as his army came this far west. He could live off the land for weeks, perhaps months, without worrying about his supply lines back to the east.

It was going to come down to an exercise in endurance. Karnos did not believe it was possible to assault the walls of mighty Machran so long as they were defended, but Machran was a great city with over a hundred thousand mouths to feed. The problem would come when they grew hungry faster than Corvus's army.

There would have to be something done about that, and no-one was going to like it.

They stopped for the night in a village off the road, some nameless little place with a noisome wine-shop and a menu painted on the walls. Karnos spent coin liberally, silver obols with the *machios* sigil upon them, and held court in a corner by the fire while Gersic rubbed down the horses and did whatever it was horseriding types did to keep the animals on all four legs.

The local population gathered in the smoky musk of the place and listened to Karnos tell of the battle lately fought, a hard-clenched affair according to him, in which both sides had suffered horribly, and it had been a near-run thing who should be declared victor.

He told them that the men of Machran and Arkadios and Avennos would be marching through soon, that the war was not over, that they were to keep faith with the customs of their fathers and pay no mind if the usurper Corvus came their way; he was a passing catastrophe, like an earthquake, or a summer thunderstorm.

He had not convinced them – he could see it in their faces. Not even his heavily edited version of the truth could disguise the fact that the League forces were in retreat. He slept that night with his pack beside him on the floor of the louse-ridden best room, and scratched at the sodden dressing wound clammily about his shoulder.

He and Gersic were on the road before dawn, the night's wine hammering at Karnos's temples, the village left buzzing with apprehension behind them. For once in his life, Karnos found himself wishing he had kept his mouth shut.

More days, grey with rain and fatigue, the horse under him the only thing of warmth in the world. They stopped in Arkadios, halfway to Machran now, and here Karnos was welcomed by the Kerusia, given leave to speak before the assembly. He measured his words here more carefully, and did not gloss over the defeat.

He spoke bluntly of the carnage on the Afteni Plain, the fact that their menfolk were marching back west, not to defend Arkadios itself, but to add to the defence of Machran.

He liked the Arkadians. They were a bright, sophisticated people much like his own, and if one could give an entire city a certain character, then Arkadios would be a rakish younger son. The Arkadian assembly was known to be mercurial and volatile, and Karnos had both abuse and praise thrown at him as he stood there in the marble amphitheatre off the agora. But he gave as good as he got, relishing the opportunity to indulge his wit, playing upon his wound, talking up the bloodiness of the battle which was becoming more and more a settled series of pictures in his mind.

He did not win them over, but he won their respect. He had to make one concession, though; if

Arkadians were to defend Machran, then Machran must take in those Arkadians who chose to flee their own city and put their trust in Machran's walls. To this he agreed, knowing that he had committed himself to an unwise move. He had tried too hard with his last knucklebone, and knocked some of his own pieces off the board.

Well, he thought, you want to eat eggs, you got to break eggshells.

The road again, the sturdy uncomplaining horse under him to whom he talked as he rode. His shoulder pained him less, and under the bandages his wound was closed, and the heat was leaving it.

The rain stopped at last, and all across the vast lowland bowl of the country about him the sun caught in a thousand splashes of white reflected water-light, and green came into the world again. He and Gersic passed through the towns of the hinterland: Lomnos, Verionin, Mas Gethir, Gan Brakon. This was the most thickly populated area of the world that Karnos knew, and the people here counted themselves citizens of Machran, and had the vote in her assemblies. He was almost home again, and the thought of a hot bath and his own bed and Pollo to see to his needs was a potent spur to his tired frame. He drove his horse harder, thinking of the men on the road behind him, the things that must be done on his arrival.

But even so, he reined in his blowing mount when Machran itself finally came into view across the rolling farmland to the west, the Harukush rearing up in the gem-bright sky behind it. At the side of the road was an ancient stone waymarker, carved with writing so ancient that men no longer understood it. The view of the city from this point was famous, and bumpkins from the east had been known to stand here and gawp at the sight.

Machran of the White Walls, the city had once been called, though most of the marble which had given it that name had been stripped away over the centuries. Those walls were the height of five tall men, and the towers along them twice that. Sixteen pasangs, the walls ran, enclosing a close-packed space the shape of an elongated egg. There were two hills within them, massive mounds which had been built over again and again since time immemorial. To the west, the Round Hill, a conical height upon which the richest districts of the city were clustered in well-spaced streets. To the east, Kerusiad Hill, upon whose slopes Karnos himself had his home.

Legend had it that the two hills had once been two separate villages which quarrelled with one another until some bright soul had suggested they meet in the hollow between them to settle their differences. This marshy hollow had become a meeting place for the two communities, until they grew and merged.

There had been a river there once, which flowed north into the Mithos, but it had been covered over long ago, and was now the main sewer for the city. And in deference to ancient tradition, the Empirion stood in that hollow, whose dome Karnos could see now shining in the winter sunlight. A place of learning, of entertainment, and – more prosaically – somewhere for the assembly to convene when the weather was especially bad.

Not far from it was the Amphion, the Speaker's Place where the assembly gathered in ordinary session to hear their leaders debate the issues of the day. The marshy riverbottom had become the seat of power and government for the greatest of all the Macht cities. The only one, legend had it, which had never been conquered, by siege or assault.

The city had five gates, and Karnos was facing the South Prime, also known as the Avennon for the Quarter in which it stood. The gates were ancient, made of oak faced with bronze. Such was the prestige of Machran that Karnos could not remember in his life ever seeing those gates closed. Even at night, the wagons and carts of the country people went in and out of them, bringing their goods and their chattels, their pumpkins and their slaves and their hunting-dogs and their greed and dreams to the • richest markets of the hinterland: the Mithannon, the Goshen, the Round Hill. These were places where all things could be had for a price, from a tinsmith's scoop to a woman's virtue.

And now, in this great city, this teeming walled hive of commerce and endeavour, there was something in such short supply that it had become almost beyond price. The courage of fighting men.

They had left a thousand spears behind when they marched out to meet Corvus west of Hal Goshen, and Karnos had entrusted his fellow Kerusia members, Dion and Eurymedon, with the task of recruiting more. But the true red-cloaked mercenary was a rare beast these days. One might hire any number of so-called warriors from the scum and vagabonds who came and went through the city like corn going through a man's bowels, but these were not the disciplined, drilled centons of a generation ago. The genuine redcloak was just not to be had anymore, not in any numbers.

But I have my ten thousand, Karnos thought, just as Rictus had. It must be enough – it will be enough.

He kicked his horse, and cantered down the long slope towards his city, the fatigue of the road forgotten.

SIXTEEN
THE AFFAIRS OF MEN

On the move at last, Corvus's army did not present a very martial sight. Except for the absence of women, it looked more like a mass migration than a military formation. The men were bundled in their cloaks, most of them barefoot despite the cold, and scores were dropping out of the column to relieve themselves, squatting in the muck and rain-stippled water of the floodplain. Even the Companion Cavalry were afoot, leading their hangdog mounts off to the flank of the main column, the gaudy cloaks of the Kefren drenched and mudstained so as to blend in to the drear landscape.

The main column straggled along the line of the Imperial Road for over twelve pasangs, and the baggage train was even further back. Only in the van were there compact bodies of formed-up troops, like a fist kept clenched at the end of a withered arm. These were Rictus's Dogsheads, and Druze's Igranians. They plodded along with skirmishers thrown out in scattered clumps to their front. The Dogsheads had doubled their red cloaks over their shoulders to keep the hems out of the water, and their shields were slung on their backs, the bronze faces greening in the wet.

"All things considered, Fornyx said, "I prefer winter in the highlands." He scratched his beard, squeezing the rain out of it.

"No good will come of him pushing the army like this," Rictus said. "If it were up to me, I'd go into winter quarters in Afteni. It's rich land around here. We could improve the roads back east and consolidate our hold on places like Hal Goshen, do the thing thoroughly."

"Teresian hanged three deserters he caught yesterday," Fornyx said. "Conscript lads from Goshen, been in the army about ten minutes, and missing home. He's a bloody-minded bastard, that one. Reminds me of you, fifteen years ago."

"Rules are rules," Rictus said dryly, rubbing his wounded arm. "Corvus makes his own."

"Well, they've brought him this far I suppose."

Druze joined them, leaning on a javelin as though it were a staff. Pain had pinched lines about his eyes that had not been there before.

"Hear the news? Karnos is alive after all."

Rictus was not surprised. "A born survivor, that fellow."

"He's on his way back to Machran, it's said. The Afteni may have surrendered, but some of the hinterland cities are sticking by the League and marching their men back with him."

"How many?" Rictus asked.

"Enough to make a fight of it."

"Looks like our triumphal entry into Machran will be problematic," Fornyx said, and spat into the mud.

"What does he mean to do, Druze?" Rictus asked.

"What do you think? He's Corvus. He'd chase them to hell if they were still thumbing their noses at him. You mark my words, brothers, before the month is out we'll be sitting in front of Machran looking at those big white walls and wondering how to get on top of them."

"You can't assault Machran, it's never been done. It's the strongest city in the world," Fornyx protested.

Druze grinned. "All the more reason for him to try." He patted Fornyx on the shoulder. "Cheer up! This is what it takes to make history."

THE ARMY SLOGGED onwards. Rolling out of their sodden blankets and fireless, cheerless camps well before dawn, the men were on the road while still chewing on salt goat and mouldy biscuit. They would march all day, though *march* was a euphemistic term for their mudsucking, agonising progress.

Then, as night fell, they would go into camp – another euphemism for lying huddled together in knee-deep mud with their cloaks and blankets drawn round their shoulders, their feet spoked towards whatever pitiable fire they could coax into life through the rain.

Corvus shared it all with them. The tents had been left behind with the baggage train, but a team of mules carried his along with the main body. He had it set up each evening with braziers burning bright and hot within, and he would spend part of every night rousing up those who seemed worst off with the flux or the cold, or carrying old wounds, and he would set them on clean straw in his tent, ply them with his own stock of wine, and a store of stories no-one had known he possessed. He did not seem to sleep at all.

The men who were brought to his tent for the night were few in number, considering the size of the army, but they would go back to their comrades with fresh heart, telling of how the general of them all had sat down beside them and poured them wine, piled their plates with fresh meat and bread, and taken the time to hear the stories of their lives.

Good news and bad travels faster through an army than a man can run, and these efforts on Corvus's part put new heart into the men. It was deftly done, and Rictus, for one, marvelled not only at Corvus's handling of his many thousands, but at the stamina of the man, who never admitted to weariness, never lost his temper.

Youngsters from Hal Goshen, Goron and Afteni, conscripted into an army which had extinguished their city's independence, would look up to find the man who had done it all to them enquiring after the state of their feet and their stomachs. After a half hour's banter, Corvus would slap them on the shoulder as though they were old campaigners he had shared a thousand campfires with, and disappear.

They would be envied by their peers, pressed for stories of the encounter. They would begin to feel part of the massive bristling, brutal mass that was the army around them.

The army needed that boost to its cohesiveness. More and more of the spearmen in the ranks were now conscripts. Some of them had even fought against Corvus in the last battle. His treatment of conquered cities might be lenient by Macht standards, but the levies he imposed upon them were rigidly enforced. Demetrius, marshal of the conscript phalanx, was not a man to take no for an answer. When he enforced a levy, he split up the city centons of the men who had been pressed into service, scattering them throughout his morai, breaking up the identities of cities in the ranks, embedding loyalty within the formations he created to replace them.

It was an efficient but harsh process, and almost every morning when the army moved on they left behind them a gibbet with bodies swinging from it. To be left for carrion was the worst thing a Macht could imagine happening to him after death, and the lesson was quite deliberate – and it had been sanctioned by Corvus, the same smiling fellow who came round the campfires at night enquiring after the state of his new conscripts' feet.

HE APPEARED AT Rictus's campfire one night, walking in noiselessly from the teeming dark like an apparition.

About the struggling flames were all the usual suspects of Rictus's acquaintance, plus a few more.

Valerian was there, and Kesero, as always; Fornyx, and Druze, who often dropped by with gossip once the army bedded down for the night. Rictus had come to like the dark Igranian, and he and Fornyx had become like bantering brothers, unable to say anything to one another that was not in some sense a goad. Each knew it, each enjoyed it. They were all listening intently to a particularly vile story that Fornyx was telling, interrupted with great relish every so often by Druze, when they realised that Corvus was just on the brim of the firelight, watching them, his face a white mask with a smile painted across it.

"Fornyx, don't look at me like that. I'm not your mother."

"Not with those hips," Fornyx shot back. "Lord high and mighty – why don't you pull up a knee and have some wine – I found a skin of it on the road today. It tastes like piss, but so does the water we've been drinking this last week."

Corvus squirted wine into his mouth and swallowed. "That's an Afteni vintage, if I'm any judge."

"I think it followed the army a while before it lay down to die," Fornyx said with a wink.

Corvus handed over the skin. "Here and there, if a skin of wine goes wandering, there's no harm I suppose. So long as it does not become a habit. This army is made up of soldiers, not thieves." He smiled.

The lazy drunken light left Fornyx's eye in an instant. He sat upright, his splayed fingers sinking into the mud as he rose. "*Thief* is an ugly word. Not one to be thrown around lightly."

The men around the fire fell silent, watching. The

rain was hissing about the logs farthest from the flames, and beyond them the hum of other conversations about other fires went on, a background murmur. But here it seemed as though a silent bell had been struck, and they were listening to its echoes.

Druze broke it. "Tell the truth, I think I pissed in that wineskin earlier. My cock is so shrivelled these days, the neck just about fit. You ever tried to fuck a wineskin, Rictus?"

Rictus smiled, still watching Fornyx and Corvus. "Not me. I'm hung like a donkey. Ask Fornyx – you ever wonder why he's such a bow-legged bastard?"

The men about the campfire lit up with laughter, and even Fornyx threw his head back with the rest of them. Rictus and Corvus caught one another's eye, each smiling falsely with their mouths.

"Chief," Rictus said, rising with a loud groan, "let me escort you away from these degenerates. They're ill-educated runts. The best part of them ran down their mother's leg."

Another chorus, laughter, feigned outrage. The skin tossed about the campfire. Rictus took Corvus by the arm; his bicep was as slender as that of a girl, but made of steel wire.

"Let's walk the camp, you and I."

Corvus came with him, the rain falling on them both in the darkness. Rictus was as drunk as cheap wine and short commons could make him. He set his good arm about the younger man's shoulders, and for some inexplicable reason thought that moment of Rian, and how he had kissed her hair in the upland pasture while they sat there with Eunion talking about the slight young man now walking beside him.

I'm getting old, he thought. Those tall enough to bear the spear are now young enough to be my sons. This boy here, he is a thing of genius, and he teeters on the edge of disaster. I see it now.

Phobos, how I miss them.

The drink set his mind running down courses he would as soon as left alone. He gripped Corvus tighter.

I had a son once, dead and burned. He would not be much younger than this boy here, if he had lived. Is that what I'm doing here?

"I hanged two men tonight," Corvus said. "For looting and rape. Some farmer's daughter they dragged back to camp." His voice was a strained croak. "A time is coming when this army will have to live off the land like a host of locusts. I know that, but there are some things I will never tolerate. That discipline must be learned now, if it is to hold later, when this thing becomes harder."

"You need to sleep," Rictus told him.

Corvus smiled. "Sometimes I am afraid that I will go to sleep, and when I awake, the army will be gone, scattered to the winds. It's getting harder, as we come west. In the east we were more tightly knit. I wish you could have seen us."

"I wish so too," Rictus said, honestly. "Tell me something, Corvus – how did it all begin? What was it that brought you to this?"

The smaller man halted and turned to look at him, the strange eyes with that light in them in the night. "This is what I was born for. I was conceived in war, and I am my father's son."

"And who was your father?"

"Do you not know – have you never guessed? Rictus, I thought you more acute."

"I'm tired and more than a little drunk, Corvus. Indulge me."

They began walking again, round the perimeter of the sprawling camp. Corvus nodded to a sentry, spoke to the man and called him by his name.

"My father was once of the Ten Thousand, Rictus. From what my mother tells me he was a great leader, a good man who died needlessly.

"His name was Jason of Ferai."

Rictus's arm slipped from the younger man's shoulders. He halted in his tracks.

"Tiryn," he said. "Antimone's pity, she was your mother."

He remembered. He remembered. Almost a quarter of a century gone by, and still he could recall the happenings of those days in gem-sharp images. This boy's mother was a beautiful Kufr woman who had been Arkamene's concubine, abandoned and abused after Kunaksa. Jason had fallen in love with her, and she with him – as unlikely a pairing any story ever saw. Jason had been about to retire, to forsake the red cloak and the Curse of God, and buy a farm somewhere east of the sea, to live out his days in some obscure corner of the Empire, in peace.

Rictus shook his head, baffled with the bright glittering memory of it all.

"Your father," he said thickly, "He was like a brother to me."

"And it was because of you he died."

"Yes, it was. I was a stupid boy, a young fool who had no self control."

"My mother told me. She never forgave you, Rictus."

"I do not blame her for that. Is this why you came seeking me, Corvus? Is this some kind of –"

"Revenge?" Corvus laughed. "My friend, I have been hearing stories of you since I was of an age to speak. I hold no ill will for the death of a father I never knew. But I counted always on meeting the famous Rictus, to face the legend and see what truth there was behind the stories."

Rictus shook his head. "You of all people should know that stories are never anything more than an echo of the truth."

"I have met the man, and he measures up to the stories, Rictus. If he did not, he would be dead by now."

Corvus walked away, until the darkness was near swallowing him up. "You are a man of honour, and you know what excesses an army can commit, in victory or defeat. You think as I do, Rictus – you hate the things I hate. I need men like you right now. In the times to come I will need you even more."

He wiped his forearm across his eyes, and seemed like nothing so much as some lost boy standing in the dark.

"I have fallen between two worlds. I have had to fight to find my way with the Macht – my own people. And yet Ardashir and the Companions see me also as one of their own."

"You are lucky in your friends, Corvus. As lucky as I once was."

"That may be. But I still do not belong in the world as I find it, so I have decided to refashion it. The Macht are – we are – ignorant barbarians, compared to the civilization that exists on the far side of the sea. And the Empire is tired and decadent, for all its riches, its ancient culture, its diversity. I think something better can be made of both."

Rictus blinked, the last of the wine leaving his mind. "What are you saying?"

Corvus turned round and grinned. At once, he had that unearthly look about him again, and the tortured boy had vanished utterly.

"I am thinking aloud, daydreaming in the night. Pay me no heed, Rictus."

He advanced on the older man. "If you had command of the army, what would you do now – how would you proceed against Machran?"

Rictus rubbed his chin, collecting himself. Corvus's eyes on him were unsettling.

"I would take the hinterland cities, first off. They're broken up at the moment, demoralised. They should be ripe fruit. Then I would sit out the winter in them, divide up the army to garrison the major cities and prepare to attack Machran in the spring. By that time the new levies will have settled in and the men will be rested and ready for another fight. Machran will be a hard nut to crack open. We must prepare ourselves for it."

"I agree on that. But if we wait until spring, the untaken League cities, and Machran itself, will have time to recover from the shock of their defeat. In all likelihood, we would have our work to do all

over again. Given time, Karnos will reconstitute the
League – he is a resourceful man."

"Then what would you do?"

Corvus smiled. "Were I Rictus, I would do what
you suggest. It is the sensible thing. But I am Corvus.

"We will move on Machran with all we have, at
once, invest the city through the winter if we have to.
I want the thing over and done with by the spring.
We have them on the run right now – let us keep
them that way."

Rictus shook his head. "We don't have enough men."

"Numbers aren't everything, if an army is all
motivated by one spirit, one idea. There is a thing
I have found about the Macht since I began leading
them and fighting them; something that is different
from the peoples of the Empire. They will fight for
an idea, an abstraction – if that idea is powerful
enough. It is what makes them a great people."

"It will take more than an idea to scale the walls
of Machran."

"Oh, I know. Parmenios is working on it. For a fat
little man with inky fingers, he has some ideas that
would startle you." Corvus turned to walk away.

"Best continue with my rounds. I have not yet
spoken to Ardashir this evening..." He paused,
turned about. "Rictus, do you know why Fornyx
hates me?"

The question took Rictus off guard. "I –"

"Because he loves you, and he thinks I have
brought you to this by threat of death. You and I
know different. There is nowhere in the world you
would rather be right now than here with this army."

Corvus raised a hand, almost like a salute, and then walked off into the darkness.

IN THE DAYS of marching that followed, the land rose under their feet and the rain began to ease. They came upon signs of the retreating League army: broken wagons, dead mules and discarded items of personal gear littering the roadside.

With the improvement in the weather the men's spirits lifted, and they made better time. By now, all the food that they had raided from the League camp's stockpiles had been eaten, and they were on short rations. Corvus finally sanctioned a series of foraging expeditions, led by the mounted troops of the Companions. The two thousand cavalry split up into half a dozen strong columns and criss-crossed the countryside for pasangs on either side of the Imperial road.

They were gone for several days, though couriers were sent back to the main body by Ardashir to keep Corvus informed of any enemy movements he had sighted.

The army had become a vast, hungry, short-tempered horde, kept in check by the personality of its leader and his senior officers. Those who had campaigned before were philosophical about the shortages, but the new conscripts were especially restive. Watching Demetrius at work in the camp during the evenings, prowling his lines like a cyclopean schoolmaster, Rictus was reminded of his own efforts to keep the Ten Thousand in check on their long march west. It was like holding a wolf by the ears.

Ardashir's columns returned in time for the first lowland snow of the winter, a skiffle of white that was soon trampled into the earth by the passing thousands.

His horse-soldiers made their way into camp on foot, leading their mounts, for the big animals were weighed down with the pickings of the countryside round about. Herds of goats and cattle and pigs trotted with them, and that night the army feasted as though it were a festival; the men erected spits above their campfires and gorged on fresh meat, baked flatbreads, and the fragrant green oil of the Machran hinterland. Morale lifted, and centons gathered about the night-time fires began to talk of the riches of Machran and what their share of them might be.

Arkadios hove into view on their horizon, and the army formed up for battle before its walls. The usual terms were offered, and accepted with stiff formality by what remained of the city's Kerusia.

But it was a hollow gain. The fighting men of the city had left for Machran, along with a large part of the population. Arkadios was a shell of itself, and the garrison that Corvus left there was met with sullen hostility. The woman of the city spat at the soldiers of Corvus, and assured them that their stay would be short.

The army marched on, making good time now, and the conscript spears were at last beginning to cohere in their new morai. They kept pace with the veterans, listened to their stories, and began to take something like pride in themselves. After all, they were part of something grand and important, witnesses to one of the great moments of history.

More than that, they were now part of an army which had a tradition of victory. The Macht had been fighting amongst themselves for time out of mind; it was no unnatural thing to make war against their own kind. And they were at least on the winning side.

They had not yet considered where victory might take them, or what it might do to the world they knew.

Corvus was hurling the army across the hinterland like a spear. On all sides, cities whose men had been bloodied in the battle of Afteni stood unconquered, but he ignored them all, even ancient Avennos to the south. He had momentum now, and they were shackled by the inertia of their defeat.

Ardashir's foraging columns reported no sign of organised resistance in the lands round about. The hinterland cities had shut their gates and were awaiting events. They were waiting to see what would happen before the walls of Machran.

RICTUS AND HIS Dogsheads were in the van with the Igranians as usual, when a mounted patrol came cantering down the long slope ahead and reined in just in front. Corvus was there, and Ardashir, the two of them as bright-eyed as if they had been drinking.

Corvus threw up a hand. "Rictus, come forward. There's something over the hill you have to see!

Fornyx, pass word down the line – all senior officers to the front of the column at once."

Fornyx raised a hand. "Off you go," he said to Rictus. "Don't keep the little fellow waiting."

"Go piss up a rope, Fornyx," Rictus said, and took off up the hillside at a trot, his heavy shield banging on his back.

He stopped, gasping, at the crest of the hill. A knot of horsemen had gathered there, and Corvus had dismounted. Rictus knew the spot – there was a stone waymarker here at the side of the road.

Machran loomed in the distance, a vast stain upon the land, the smoke from ten thousand hearths rising up to cloud the air above it. A famous view – Ondimion's plays had scenes set on this spot, and Naevius had made a song about it.

Corvus and Ardashir stood marvelling at the sight.

"Machran at last," Corvus said. "After all this time."

Rictus suddenly realised. "You've never seen it before."

"Never – just read the plays and heard the songs and listened to men speak of it over their wine. I have maps of this city; I know its geography as though it were written across my dreams. I know the men who rule it, their names and families. But this is the first time I have seen it for myself – Ardashir too. I have been travelling years to stand at this spot, Rictus."

"I wish you joy of the sight," Rictus said with a smile. Here was the boy again, alight with the wondrous marvels of the world. There was something... unspoilt about Corvus. It was more than the mere enthusiasm of youth – it was a kind of appetite. He would always find the new experiences of his life to be vivid and memorable and worth the cost, like a man who has a fine nose for wine, who finds in it subtleties and fragrances that others miss. What was the line Gestrakos had used? Eunion was fond of quoting it.

"*A man who has a passion will always find life to his taste,*" Rictus said aloud.

Corvus turned to him at once. "*A man who cares for nothing is a man already dead,*" he said, finishing the couplet. "Rictus, you surprise me. I had not thought you a philosopher."

"A friend quoted me that, a long time ago."

"Then he was a wise man. For soldiers, the sayings of Gestrakos are a window on our lives."

The head of the column reached them, and Fornyx raised a hand to halt the Dogsheads. Behind them, the line of marching men ran as far as the eye could see, and the weak winter sun ran along it, raising sparks and flashes off spearheads, helms, the brazen faces of shouldered shields.

"We are what – four pasangs from the walls?" Corvus estimated. "I will pitch the command tent on the slope ahead. Rictus, your men shall bivouac forward a pasang, and Druze's Igranians with you. The rest will file in behind. I must inspect the line of the walls close-to before I decide how to post the rest of the army."

"They've seen us," Ardashir said. "Look; they're closing the gates."

Rictus could just make out the fall of shadow in the wall as the massive South Prime Gate was slowly pushed shut in the distance. It was something he had never seen before: Machran shutting its gates. He looked at the endless snake of the high fortifications running across the land for pasangs, and shook his head at the thought of assaulting such a place.

"The countryside is empty," Ardashir said, shading his pale eyes with his hand. "There's not a man or a beast to be seen for pasangs. It would seem Karnos has prepared the city somewhat."

"I expected no less," Corvus said. He mounted his horse, and the animal – a coal-black gelding which made him look small as a child on its back – threw up its head and snorted as it caught his mood.

"Bring up the baggage train, and deploy the army along this ridge, just in case he wants to come out."

"He won't come out," Rictus said.

Corvus nodded. "I know – but we must show willing, and besides, it's a grand thing to see an army file into line of battle. It will give the men on those walls something to think about."

He bent and patted the neck of the restive gelding, crooning to it with words of Kefren. Then he straightened and flashed a wide grin at them all.

"Brothers," he said, "today the siege of Machran begins."

SEVENTEEN
THE GATES CLOSE

KARNOS STOOD ON the heights of South Prime Tower, in whose bowels the great gate was grinding shut, groaning and screeching like a sentient thing. There were two dozen men down there with their shoulders set to it, and half a dozen more were ladling olive oil over the seized up hinges.

To left and right, the walls of the city were crowded with people, thousands of whom had climbed the battlements to catch a sight of the army forming up in the distance. For months it had been a mere idea to them, a subject for gossip and speculation and argument. Now it was there, assembling on the lip of the great bowl-shaped vale in which Machran stood. A man might walk briskly from the walls to the front ranks of the enemy in half an hour.

It had come to this at last, this brutal reality.

Dion and Eurymedon stood beside Karnos on the

tower's topmost outpost. Two old men who looked even older this bright winter's day as the undefeated army of Corvus deployed in line of battle before the city, as if to taunt them.

Behind the trio of Kerusia members were Murchos of Arkadios, whose city was already lost, and Tyrias of Avennos, or Scrollworm to his friends. Kassander was down at the gates, cursing and cajoling the men working there.

"I do not know what he is thinking," Dion said, and there was the quake of age in his voice. "He forms up as though we're about to give him battle."

"Or invite him in," Murchos grunted, striding forward to lean on the grey stone of the battlement. He rubbed shards of snow off the stone irritably. "Arrogant bastard. He means to begin the investment right here and now, in the middle of winter."

"He has never been one to dawdle," Karnos said. "Ah, the impetuousness of youth."

"Let him sit there while the snow comes down on him, and see how he likes it," Tyrias said. "He's overreaching himself. We can sit here all winter and watch him shiver."

"Have the messengers gone out?" Eurymedon asked. He was a cadaverous, grey-bearded man with a long red nose. He looked as though he either had a cold, or liked to stave one off with wine.

"They went out last night," Karnos said with a touch of impatience. "What good they will do us remains to be seen."

"They're a fart in the wind," Murchos said. "Those who are willing to fight are already here within the walls. The rest will wait on events. There will be nothing done now until the spring, perhaps even later."

"Agreed," Karnos said. "We're on our own, brothers, for a few months at least. We put up a good showing through the winter, bleed this boy's nose for him a little, and the hinterland cities will get over their fright and see that their fate rests here with us as surely as if they were standing on these stones."

"There are many cities that would like to see Machran humbled," Eurymedon said with a sniff.

"We'll see how they feel once this conqueror's foraging parties start faring afield for supplies," Karnos told him. "Once their granaries get raided a few times, things will turn around, you mark my words."

He hoped he sounded more convincing to the others than he did to himself.

ALL AFTERNOON THE army of the conqueror marched and counter-marched. When his challenge was not taken up, Corvus put his host into camp square across the Imperial road, and as the winter afternoon dwindled swiftly into night, so the people of the city looked out to see a second city come to life in a thousand gleaming campfires to the south and east.

Stragglers from the outlying farms hammered on the East Prime Gate that night and pleaded to be admitted to the city, but were denied entry for fear that they were in the pay of the enemy. They were told to try the Mithannon Gate, which was farthest away from Corvus's camp, and they cursed the men on the walls and held up their children to show the cautious gatekeepers. The Goshen road was cut, a mora of spearmen encamped across it, and their farms were being raided for food and livestock. If they stayed outside the walls they would starve, they shouted up. They were told to wait for daylight, and try the Mithannon, and some kind soul threw a few flatbreads and a skin of wine down to them.

Karnos remained on the walls until well after dark, unwilling to be seen to leave before the city crowds. Eventually the numbers on the walls thinned with the advent of night and the growing chill in the air, and soon there was no-one about the battlements except the armoured men whose job it was to walk them.

Kassander joined him. His face was thinner than it had been, but he still had the slow easy smile which belied the quick workings of his mind.

"I'll be bored to death before this thing is done," Karnos said. "Especially if the Kerusia keeps those two ancient vultures hanging at my heels."

"Anyone would think they didn't trust you," Kassander said.

"They're afraid. Frightened men feel a need to try and know everything. When they were ignorant they were happier."

"Then from the sounds in the streets, there are a lot of ignorant people abroad tonight. Can you hear them?"

Karnos nodded. "The Mithannon is teeming like a puddle full of spawn. The incomers from Arkadios and the other cities are intent on seeing the fleshpots while there's still some flesh to be had."

"It's what men do."

"And a damned fine idea!" Karnos exclaimed. He clapped Kassander on the shoulder. "Join me for dinner. Bring your sister. I'll have Pollo hunt out the good wine. We'll get drunk and I'll make an arse of myself – it'll be like old times."

Kassander smiled. "I accept your gracious invitation."

"Good! I'll ask Murchos and Tyrias too. Murchos can hold his wine and Scrollworm always has a poem or two on hand to help preserve civilization."

Kassander jerked his chin towards the distant campfires. "You don't think he'll try anything tonight?"

"Tonight? That would be rude – he's only just arrived. No, Kassander, our friends across the way will be busy making plans tonight. They've cut two roads into the city, and have three more to go. Tonight Corvus will be talking to his friends as we will be, plotting our destruction. And if they've any sense, they'll be doing it with a drink in their hands too. I'll have Gersic stay on the walls and report to us later on; he's too excited to sleep tonight anyway."

"Aren't we all?" Kassander drawled.

KARNOS'S VILLA ON the slopes of the Kerusiad presented a fortress-like face to the world. Built around the fountain-courtyard, it looked in on itself rather than out at the city, a fact which Kassander had remarked upon more than once.

In summer, Karnos threw parties centred on the fountain, and drunken guests had been known to end up in it. So had their host. But with the advent of winter the long dining tables were laid athwart the second hall, further inside, so that the sound of the falling water was lost, and in its place a fire spat and crackled on a raised stone platform at one end of the room, the smoke sidling out of a series of louvred slats in the roof. The long couches upon which the guests sat or reclined according to their preference were set out facing one another, and slaves brought food to the diners on wooden platters and in earthenware dishes.

It was the way the rich ate, and Karnos was nothing if not rich. He had never forgotten the communal pot-meals of the Mithannon, with a dozen people dipping their hands in the food at once and grabbing it by the fistful in an echo of the mercenary centos. He had sworn never to eat like that again.

The meal was plentiful but plain. Karnos had developed expensive tastes in many things, but food was not one of them. He still relied on the country staples of bread, oil, wine, goat meat and cheese. The wine, however, was Minerian, one of the finest vintages ever trodden. Tyrias exclaimed as he tasted it, and held up his cup in salute. "As sieges go, this one certainly begins with promise," he said.

"I thought it fitting to mark the day," Karnos told him. He raised himself up off his elbow and turned to the plainly clad woman seated apart from the men on an upright backless chair of black oak.

"Kassia, are you sure you're quite comfortable? These couches were made by Argon of Framnos – it's like lying on a cloud."

The woman, a handsome dark-eyed lady with Kassander's broad face, smiled at him. "It would scarcely be proper, Karnos. And besides, I've spent enough evenings here to know you will probably end this one on your back."

The men laughed, Kassander as loud as any. "My sister knows you too well, Karnos," he said.

"She does." Karnos raised his cup to her. "Her honesty is as refreshing as her beauty is intoxicating."

"Your flattery is like the wine," Kassia shot back. "It needs to be watered down a little."

"Forgive me, Kassia. When a man is so dazzled by the exterior, he sometimes forgets what treasures sparkle within."

"And now you're becoming shopworn, Karnos. I have heard better lines in street-plays."

"It's true I have not attended to the classics as much as I should. But it was Eurotas who said that a woman's face holds no clue to her heart."

"Ondimion once said that to quote from drama was to sully the air with someone else's fart."

"He did? And I thought him a dried up old pedant. Still, you have proved his point."

"There is a concept called irony – let me explain it to you."

"Enough!" Kassander cried. "I wish you two would just get married and have it over with."

"All intelligent conversation ends with marriage, Kassander – you know that," Karnos said, waving a slave over for more wine. "Once the woman has her feet in the door the talk is all of budgets and babies."

Kassia looked the slave-girl pouring Karnos's wine

up and down. "It seems to me you have too many wives already, Karnos."

"I have an enormous heart, lady," Karnos told her gravely. "It craves affection, but wilts like a flower when confronted by the brutalities of everyday domesticity. I have constructed my household to shield me from such indelicacies."

The eyes of every man in the room followed the willowy girl with the wine-jug as she padded back into the shadows. Kassia sighed.

"You are a massive boy, Karnos. The woman who married you would be yoked to a lifelong project."

"And that," Karnos said triumphantly, "is the very definition of marriage. I thank you, lady, for putting it so pithily."

Kassander lay back on his couch. "If the building were on fire, you two would stand inside arguing over who had started it."

"Argument between a man and a woman is lovemaking without the orgasm," Tyrias said with a raised eyebrow.

"Ah there we are – someone else farts," Karnos said. "Can't educated people converse without digging up the bones of dead men?"

"You're a trivial bunch," bull-necked Murchos grunted. "The world is on fire around us, Machran besieged, our fates cast to the whims of the gods, and you sit here sipping wine and indulging in sophistry. I'm glad the men on the walls don't have an ear in this room."

"Given half a chance they'd be doing the same, though with a little more raw gusto," Karnos said dismissively. "Tomorrow we'll stand on the walls and look Phobos in the eye. For tonight" – he poured a scarlet stream of wine onto the exquisite mosaic of the floor – "here's a libation to gentle Haukos of the pink face, god of hope and men who drink too much. His pale-faced brother can kiss my hairy arse – saving your presence, lady."

"Your piety is charming," Kassia said. She stood up. "Gentlemen, I shall take a turn about the courtyard to clear my head." She lifted her veil from her shoulders and wound it about her hair.

"Ah – the sun goes in!" Tyrias cried. "Sweet Araian, how canst thou veil thy bright face from me?"

"Put your cup to your mouth, Tyrias," Karnos said, and rose in his turn. "Lady, will you lean on my arm?"

"Is it steady enough to bear me?" Kassia asked.

"I am a rock," Karnos told her, swaying slightly. "Kassander, I will walk your sister in the shadows by my fountain. I assure you I am of innocent intent."

Kassander waved a hand. "Take her, take her."

The cold air struck Karnos like a splash of water as the pair left the firelit room for the blue shadow of the outer courtyard. The fountain splashed white moonlight in its pool and, looking up, Karnos found himself staring full into the pale face of Phobos, leering over the city like a rounded skull. Kassia shivered and drew closer to him. He could feel the warmth of her skin through the thin silken peplos.

"Phobos is full," she said. "This is his season."

Karnos put his arm about her and nuzzled the silk-covered fragrant hair at her temple. "Kassia, we are alive and well and there are ten thousand valiant men standing between you and the barbarians beyond the gates." He bent his head and kissed her through the veil.

For a second her mouth responded to his, coming to life, and then she withdrew, patting his arm.

"I had always heard that men take liberties in wartime," she said. And then, "It seems like bad luck, with Phobos looking on."

"Marry me, Kassia," Karnos murmured, his hands running up and down her arms, sliding the silk across her skin. He could feel the raised stipple of goosebumps on her flesh.

"That old saw? You have laid siege to my virtue for years, Karnos – what makes you think my walls will yield to you now?"

"You love me, as I have loved you all this time. What better moment to finally admit it than now, when the world is liable to come crashing down around us?"

She looked up at him, that strong jawline he loved, the courage in that broadboned face, the moonlight making the veil covering it as translucent as mist.

"And is the world to come crashing down, Karnos?"

He hesitated a moment, his face sombre, his eyes fixed on hers. Then the old buffoon's grin flashed out. "You think this city can fall while your brother and I defend it? We are the Phobos and Haukos of Machran."

She set a hand across his mouth. "Don't talk like that."

"The gods can laugh too, Kassia," he said, kissing her cold fingers. "And Antimone loves those who chance everything for the love of another, whether it be a soldier shielding his brother on the battlefield, or a man risking all for the regard of a good woman."

She lifted her hand and set it on his shoulder, atop the padding which still covered his wound.

"I would have died, had you not come back to me, Karnos. You will not make me love you more by bleeding in some battleline."

"I know. And that's why it is you for me, Kassia – you alone. It always has been."

She walked away from him, a slim upright shadow greyed by the moonlight.

"You play the fool to win the heart of the mob; but I hate to see you do it. And you surround yourself with slaves so you will not be alone – the only people in this world you trust are old Pollo and my brother."

"And you."

"If you trusted me you would do as I asked."

He shook his head helplessly. "This is who I am. The way I live –"

"Is a scandal which makes your name a topic in all the wineshops of the city. You find that useful – I detest it."

Karnos's shoulders sagged. "I cannot discard my people. They depend on me."

"They are your slaves, Karnos."

"You have never been poor, Kassia. You don't know."

She whirled on him. "You damned idiot. You're too frightened to let go of your past for fear of ridicule. How the mob would marvel if Karnos of Machran became respectable!"

"It's all appearances, nothing more."

"It is not – it goes right to the heart of you. You will always be the child of the Mithannon. You are Speaker of Machran, Karnos, leader of the greatest city west of the sea. You have nothing to prove."

"Except to you."

"Except to me," she said quietly. She stepped close to him again. "My dear, you are a better man than anyone knows."

"I am a coward and a buffoon."

"It is not cowardice to feel fear. You do not need to wield a spear to show me your courage. I know your quality, Karnos – I only wish more people did."

She stood up on her toes and kissed him. "Now go back to my brother. I will ask Pollo to escort me home."

KARNOS RETURNED TO the warmth of the inner hall, where the men on the couches reclined with their cups to hand, and the slaves stood about the walls like attentive statuary. He held out his own cup without a word, and Grania came forward to fill it. She smiled at him, but his face felt like wood.

"Karnos," Kassander said, "Tell these fellows about the time you and I won that drinking contest in the Mithannon. They won't believe me – they have to hear it from your own mouth."

Karnos blinked. His face came slowly to life. The old grin spread across it.

"It was last summer, as I recall..." he said.

EIGHTEEN
THE GROVE OF OLIVES

THE WHITE, CLEAN world of the highlands was behind them, and they were trudging downhill now, always downhill, through the small farms and olive groves of the Machran hinterland. The olive trees were black in the winter light, and seemed scarcely alive at all; gnarled relics of a forgotten summer.

They camped beneath them when they could, for shelter against the rain, and Aise cupped her bound hands full of the dead leaves of the year gone by, brittle shavings with the shape of spearheads. She smelled them, inhaling a last scent of the world's warmth.

The party grouped about the fire, Ona and Rian huddling up to her like pups seeking warmth. Ona was pale and empty-eyed, but now and again her furious barking cough would make the men start and curse.

"Shut that fucking brat up," the one named Bosca

snapped. He rubbed the scar at his eye where Styra had exacted payment for her rape and murder. "Boss, do we really need to be hauling that little shit with us? She's not even of an age to fuck."

Sertorius was rebinding the straps that bound his thick-soled sandals to his feet. He did not look up. "Take it up with Phaestus, or stow it."

"If we have to move quiet, she'll be the bane of us all."

Sertorius raised his head at that. He looked at Aise, then shrugged. "We'll see when the time comes."

Phaestus stumbled into camp, his son at his elbow. His face had become ossified, a skull in which his bright eyes burned. He half-fell in front of the fire, and Philemos reached for the flaccid wineskin.

"Easy on that," hulking Adurnos said. "It's the last one."

"He needs some warmth in him," Philemos protested, and uncorked the skin, holding the nozzle to his father's mouth. Phaestus choked and swallowed, the red liquid running down his neck in trickled lines.

"You've done well to get this far," Sertorius said to Phaestus. "For a while there I thought we'd be leaving you for the kites and ravens."

Phaestus mastered his heaving breath. "I have enough in me yet for the job to get done."

"He should be on the mule," Philemos said, wiping his father's mouth.

"The mule can barely manage that barking brat as it is," Adurnos grunted. "Another few days and it'll go the way of the last one."

"Good eating, though," Bosca said with a grin. Adurnos and Sertorius laughed.

Philemos stared across the fire at Aise and her children. They were hollow-eyed scarecrows, flesh worn close to the bone, hair matted with filth. The company had been ten days on the road, and the pasangs had left their mark upon them all, but the three captives had fared worst.

He scrambled through the grey leaf-litter and knelt in front of Aise, holding out the skin.

"It might help her."

Aise nodded, her eyes flickering with gratitude. She held Ona in her arms and put the spout of the wineskin to the child's mouth. Rian raised the skin, almost empty now. She looked at Philemos.

"Thank you." The words a cracked whisper, no more.

"That's your share you're giving her, boy," Bosca said loudly. "You want to waste it on the little rat-cunt, it's your affair, but don't expect no more."

"Fair enough," Philemos said without turning around. His dark curls hung in mud-fastened strings either side of his face. He looked at Aise, at Ona, swallowing the wine and whimpering, and lastly at Rian, who returned his gaze squarely, her eyes grey as the shank of a spearhead.

His mouth worked, but he took the skin back from Aise without saying anything.

The day died about them, the fire brightening against the blue darkness of the world.

"There's farmers here have places for pigs to have a roof over their heads, and yet here we are sleeping on dirt for I don't know how many nights," Bosca said. "I don't see the wisdom of it, is all – we're not up in the fucking mountains anymore."

"We don't know what's been going on since we were up in the hills," Phaestus said. "Or how far Corvus's army has come." He wheezed wetly as he breathed, and when Philemos set a hand on his arm he managed a laugh.

"I've been hunting in the highlands these twenty years, and now a two week jaunt has me like this. Phobos must have a sense of humour."

"Phobos hates all men," Sertorius said, chewing reflectively on a strip of roast mule meat. "Not just you. You're old, Phaestus – that's all there is to it. You were a right hard bastard when you were younger, but I think Antimone's wings beat over you now."

"My father will outlive you all," Philemos said fiercely, the fire glinting out of his eyes.

"Maybe he will, but I doubt it," Sertorius said, tilting his head to one side. "Phaestus, we're back down in civilized lands now – how far do you make it to Machran?"

Phaestus pushed his son away, sat up before the fire, drew his knife, and began pushing the unburnt butts of the sticks into the bright core of flame.

"Two days. Maybe less, if we make good time."

"Well, Antimone's tits! That's some news to savour at least. I take it back, Phaestus – you have years of life in your bones yet. Two days! It's enough to warm a man's heart." Sertorius grinned. He leaned over and clapped Phaestus on the shoulder.

"What way lies Machran?"

Phaestus's jaw worked. The air sawed in and out of his mouth. "You see the tree to my right, Sertorius? That way is north, by Gaenion's Pointer."

Sertorius kept looking at him.

"You can make your way in the world by that star. For us it means that west is to my left. Where Rictus's wife sits – that is the way to Machran."

Sertorius's head jabbed from one side to another, like that of a blackbird eyeing up a worm. He winked at Phaestus.

"And it's just like that."

Phaestus nodded. "Just like that." He seemed like a man too tired to care.

"Old friend, this calls for something beyond the ordinary." Sertorius stood up, strolled to the edge of the firelight and took the mule by the halter. The animal blew through its nose and he stroked it. "My little secret-keeper. Give us a kiss." He nuzzled the mule's nose.

"You are one funny bastard, boss," Adurnos said.

Sertorius ran his hands over the mule, his eyes dark as sloes in the firelight. Then he stood leaning against it with an arm across its withers. The emaciated animal stood patiently, ears down.

"I trust this poor beast more than any of you – you know why? The fucker doesn't talk."

He whipped around, reached into a pack on the ground, and began rummaging through it.

"That's the last of the food, chief," Bosca said, uncertain, frowning.

"That's why I said no-one should touch it but me," Sertorius retorted. He straightened, grinning. "Look what I brought from the great Rictus's country retreat, boys. Been saving it until we were well out of all that fucking snow."

It was a full skin of wine.

Sertorius tossed it towards the fire. "Go on, lads – I'd say we've earned it."

Bosca and Adurnos cackled like huge girls, scrabbled over the wineskin for a few moments until Bosca gave in to Adurnos's snarling bulk. The big man's broken nose made him snuffle and snort as he squeezed the skin into his mouth, eyes closed.

"Go easy on that friend," Phaestus rasped. "There's enough for all."

Adurnos paused for breath, the wine dribbling red across his teeth.

"Fuck you, old man," he said.

AISE SAT WITH her back to the tree. The firelight still touched her feet, but the rest of her was in darkness. Ona slept, snuffling and whimpering, against her, while on her other side Rian was as taut as a strung bow.

Aise and Rian were bound with ropes of rawhide, strung to long wooden pickets hammered deep into the ground at Sertorius's side. Their wrists were bloody and inflamed, scabbed and welted like raw meat, but they scarcely felt the pain any more.

Phaestus was asleep, wrapped in his own blankets and those of his son. He moaned and muttered in his sleep, muscles working in his face, every sinew tight against the skin. He had taken the flux a few days out of Andunnon, and Aise knew that he had been passing blood for some time now. Philemos hovered over him like a protective hound, watching the three other men at the fire.

They were all drunk now, these three, the wineskin drained almost flat. The strong yellow wine that Aise and Rian had trodden out in the big tub the summer before, the grapes popping and breaking under their bare feet. A last remnant of a life destroyed.

Sertorius, Bosca and Adurnos. They were sat side by side, their boasting and horseplay done with, the wine working in their minds, setting their thoughts to other things.

A silence fell across the little campsite, broken only by the snap and spit of the wet wood in the fire, Phaestus's stertorous breathing, and the whimpering of the sleeping child at Aise's side.

"What's so special about this Rictus fellow that his bitches will make a difference to Machran?" Bosca asked. In the firelight, his bearded face was a mask of fur.

"You never heard of the great Rictus of Isca?" Sertorius said. "Ignorant fuck; he led the Ten Thousand. He's a hero, a stone-hard red-cloaked mercenary with his own army."

"So he'll chuck it all away for the sake of these?" Bosca asked. "What is he, soft in the head or something?"

Sertorius grinned. "He's a thing you can't understand, Bosca, a family man. A man of honour. Phaestus here reckons Rictus would do pretty much anything to keep his women safe."

Big Adurnos was running his eyes over Aise and Rian. "They're not so pretty as they was, but I like the young one. I bet she's never been popped. They start late, the girls up in the hills."

"You think?" Bosca said with a yellow grin. "Phobos! I can't remember the last time I dipped into a virgin's cunny." He turned to Sertorius. "What do you say, boss? We've been good boys – how about allowing us a little taste before we have to hand them over?"

Sertorius blinked slowly. He looked at Aise and Rian across the fire, his eyes black and cold as stones. He seemed to be rolling the idea around in his head.

"I can't see what the harm would be," he said at last.

Philemos shook Phaestus violently. "Father – father, wake up!"

Rian shrank closer against her mother. Her face was set and white beneath the filth encrusting it. "No," she whispered.

The three men on the other side of the fire got to their feet.

"You can go first, boss," Adurnos said. "Fair's fair – you held on to that wine for us."

"We'll do the older one while you have the girl," Bosca said. "She's got a nice face on her yet."

Aise and Rian struggled to their feet, constrained by the rawhide ropes anchoring their wrists. Ona woke up and uttered a thin cry, then clung to her mother's knees.

"No!" Philemos shouted. He slapped his father about the face. Phaestus stirred sluggishly.

The boy rose with a snarl, drawing his knife.

"Don't you touch them, you fucking animals!"

Sertorius grinned. "Careful, son – you might nick yourself with that thing."

"Out of the fucking way, you little shit," Bosca growled.

Phaestus was awake. He struggled to his hands and knees, saw what was going on, and levered himself erect using his spear. Then he stood holding the aichme out level.

"What's all this, Sertorius?"

"Nothing to get in a twist about, my friend. Call off your son. His heart's in the right place, but I don't like having a knife pulled on me by anyone, and if he don't put it away there will be blood. I warn you fair and square."

A second's silence. Sparks cracking in the fire.

"Phaestus," Aise said calmly. "Are you going to allow this?"

Phaestus stood still. The weight of the spear made his arms quiver, and there was sweat running down the side of his face.

"Father –"

"Shut up, Philemos. Put the knife away. You stand against Sertorius and you'll be dead before you can so much as blink."

"Listen to the old man, boy," Sertorius said. "You have quality in you – I can see that. This is not worth the fight."

"Father," Philemos said again. He stared at Phaestus and there were tears in his eyes. "You cannot allow it."

"This is a time of war, Philemos. These things happen. It is the way of the world."

Philemos turned and looked at Aise and Rian. They were frozen, mute.

"Not the girl," he said at last, desperation cracking his voice. "Leave her alone."

Bosca guffawed. "So that's his game, eh? He wants the tenderest meat for himself."

Philemos walked over to the women crouched on the far side of the firelight. He knelt beside them.

"I'm sorry," he whispered to Aise. Then he took his knife and cut the bindings that anchored Rian to the pickets. He grabbed the stub of the rope and dragged her after him, standing by his father. Raising his voice, he said; "This one's mine."

"You cocky little bastard – you think you can keep the choice cut for yourself?" Adurnos snapped. He started forward, reaching for his own knife.

The spearhead swung round, bringing him up short. Phaestus stood holding it out at waist height.

"My boy knows what he wants. Let him have it." Phaestus's face was set and hard. "Take the woman, if you have to. The girl is Philemos's."

Sertorius slapped his thigh. "Good for you, lad!" he chortled. "I didn't think you had it in you!"

He strode past the fire, lifted Aise to her feet and slashed her picket-rope. He looked into her eyes. "You'll have to do us all."

"Mother!" Rian screamed, and Ona began to wail.

Aise bent and kissed her youngest daughter. "It's all right, honeybun. Go to Rian. It'll be all right."

Rian tried to lunge at Sertorius, but Philemos held her back. "Don't, for God's sake." Ona tottered over to her sister and Rian buried her face in the child's shoulder, sobbing.

"Come on, sweetheart," Sertorius crooned. "Come

out into the dark with us. We're not barbarians; we'll spare your brats the sight."

The three men gathered around Aise. Bosca gripped her dress at the shoulder and pulled at it. There was a ripping sound, and the material slid down her torso.

"Nice," Adurnos said. He grabbed at one of her breasts and dug his fingers in.

"I'm first," Sertorius said.

The three of them dragged Aise beyond the firelight, out into the wet darkness of the olive trees.

PART THREE

HEART OF WAR

NINETEEN
LAST OF THE MERCENARIES

RICTUS KNELT ON one knee in the freezing mud. The timber under his hand creaked as he leaned his weight upon it. His breath frosted out in the moonlight.

"Wait," he said in a low voice. "The cloud's coming again."

The wind high up above his head tumbled a broken fretwork of black cloud about the sky. Through rents in the cloud, pale Phobos leered down, and Haukos glowed red and low on the horizon, almost set.

He gripped the rough-hewn wood of the ladder on his left and turned his head this way and that, nodding as he caught the bright feral glow of Ardashir's eyes beside him. The tall Kufr smiled, a gleam of teeth in the flickering moonlight. Rictus's vision was heavily circumscribed by the bronze shell of his helm. He longed to take it off, but knew he would need it for the work ahead.

To his right, Druze crouched with a line of men along another ladder. For hundreds of paces, a host of men were kneeling in the frozen mud, formed along the siege ladders like legs on a centipede. Half a pasang to their front, the walls of Machran loomed up huge and black in the night, as solid as a cliff-face.

Rictus stifled a shiver.

"The lazy bastards must be half asleep," Druze whispered. "One good flash of moonlight and we're as plain as a turd on a tabletop."

"Let's go, Rictus," Fornyx said behind him. "Druze is right – any second now they'll wake up on us."

"Wait for my word," Rictus said. "Remember the plan."

A splurge of shouting in the night, off to their left.

"That's Corvus," Ardashir said. "He's starting."

"Give them a moment," Rictus hissed to the men around him. He could sense their eagerness, the impulse in all soldiers to get it started, to get the thing over with.

The tumult to the south and west broadened, rising to break apart the stillness of the winter night. They could see torches running along the walls now, and someone began beating on a bronze gong.

"That's their alarm," Fornyx said. "Rictus, you want me to piss myself? Let's go."

Rictus grinned inside his helm. He rose to his feet, hauling at the heavy wood of the ladder. "All right, girls, up you get. Move quick and quiet."

The ladder-bearing files of men climbed off their

knees and brought the siege-ladders up to their shoulders. Rictus led off at the head of his and the rest followed. They spread out as they approached the walls; a bristling crowd of men, centons intermingled. Dogsheads, Igranians and Companions, all creeping together in the dark under the walls.

They were perhaps a hundred paces from the base when they were spotted. Someone yelled and held a blazing torch over the battlements, looking down, waving his arm.

"Fuck," Rictus said. "Pick it up, lads. The party's begun."

Ardashir darted aside from the line of ladder-carriers. He lifted his bow from his shoulder and reached calmly for an arrow from the quiver at his hip. The rest ran past him.

The man on the walls with the torch cried out, dropped it, and staggered back from the battlement. The torch fell to the ground below and Rictus fixed his eyes upon it, a reference point in the night, something to keep him focused.

They were at the base of the wall. Rictus dropped his end of the ladder. "Lift!" he shouted. "Move in as you push!"

The heavy iron-frapped timber of the siege ladder rose up as a score of men manhandled it upright. They moved in as it rose, until it thumped against the wall above them and they were all in a huddle at its foot.

"Spread out a little, for Phobos's sake!" Fornyx rapped out.

Rictus took a breath, hearing it hoarse and loud inside the helm. He drew his sword – he was carrying a heavy drepana – and settled his shield on his back. The bronze-faced weight of it seemed almost impossible to manage as he set a foot on the first rung and began to climb. He was glad of the helm now, and instinctively hunched as he ascended, expecting at any second to feel the impact of a stone or arrow.

The ladder flexed and bounced under him as it took the weight of man after man below. The quiet of the night was entirely ruptured now, with men's voices raised all along the walls in fear and fury. In battle, men would scream themselves hoarse and not even be aware they were making a sound. Rictus had done it himself. But not tonight. He was concentrating too hard on climbing one-handed in full panoply. For the men below him it would be even harder, as there would be muck on the rungs to make their feet slip.

Other ladders on the walls to left and right. They had sawn out fifty in the past two days, chopping down a grove of fine old plane trees for the timber, and hammering out the iron reinforcing brackets in the field-forges of the army using spare horseshoes.

Back over the rise that led down to the city walls, Corvus and Parmenios – his plump little secretary – had set up a cross between a factory and a lumberyard, and men worked there in shifts, night and day. They had felled taenons of woodland and gathered every piece of scrap iron the countryside had to offer, everything from knives to ploughshares. No-one was quite sure what they were at; a bigger thing than these ladders, that was for certain.

But the ladders were the most economical way of getting men upon the walls of the city. They had to attempt a quick assault before settling down to the siege, Corvus had said. Even if it did not succeed, it would rattle the defenders, and give the attackers experience.

Experience, Rictus thought, gasping and gripping the wooden shank of the ladder so hard his bones hurt. Experience is overrated. If you want men to do this kind of thing with a willing heart, they're better off ignorant.

He raised his head and looked up, a gesture of courage in itself. There were heads framed in the battlements above him. He saw a pair of arms raised.

Phobos! He jerked to one side and the heavy stone clipped the edge of his shield, struck the man behind him full in the face. The fellow did not even manage a scream out of his shattered mouth before he soared backwards and disappeared. In his fall he had thumped against the man below him on the ladder and knocked his feet from the rungs. The second man hung on by one hand – Rictus saw the terror in his eyes, bright in the T-slot of his helm – and then he was gone also, plummeting into the press below.

Rictus felt heavy, drained and weak, cold fear diluting the very blood that pumped madly through his heart. As he began to climb again, he uttered a guttural snarl, and his teeth bared like those of an animal.

A javelin glanced off his helm, clicked against the great bowl of the shield on his back, and was gone. His sandals slapped upon the flattened wooden rungs of the ladder. He held the drepana above his head as though it were some kind of talisman.

And he was there, level with the battlements – looking into the faces of the men who were trying to kill him.

One was pushing at the ladder, trying to lever it off the wall. Rictus flicked out the wide point of the drepana and dropped him with a pierced throat. He climbed higher up the rungs, set a hand on the cold stone. It felt as reassuring as a rope flung to a drowning man. He swept the drepana in a wide arc, missing his blow, but forcing the men in front of him back.

He was off the ladder, perched on the top of a merlon like an immense crow. He lunged forward, keenly conscious of the great long drop at his back; the weight of the shield still liable to drag him towards it.

He tumbled, felt a strike on his shoulder which slid off his black cuirass. A spearhead punched him in his chest, a heavy blow which would have transfixed him were it not for the Curse of God. He straightened, still snarling, his feet planted securely on Machran's stone, and sent the drepana licking out like a snake, not trying for damage, just unbalancing his attackers, gaining room. With his left arm he angled his elbow into the bowl of the shield and swung it forward, slid his forearm into the centre-grip, and at once felt safer. "Dogsheads!" he bellowed. "Dogsheads to me – on the walls, boys!"

Someone had dropped onto the battlement behind him. A shield was tucked beside his own. He felt a surge of new energy, the bowel-draining fear leaving him.

More of his men were up at the lips of the walls, their heads popping up all down the line. The defenders were being pushed back. Corvus's diversion had worked; the enemy was very thin on the ground here.

Rictus smashed forward, butting his shield into the face of the man in front, stabbing the drepana low at his knees. He felt the blade shear through flesh and the gristle of a joint. The man cried out, his mouth a wet hole under his helm. Rictus shouldered him hard and he flew backwards, off the catwalk.

More men behind him now. The assault was succeeding – they had a foothold.

"Who'd have thought it?" Fornyx yelled. "Ladders!"

"Keep them coming," Rictus shouted back. He saw Kesero there under the banner, and Valerian was further along the wall, standing in an embrasure and holding fast to a tottering ladder. Dogsheads were fighting side by side with Druze's lightly armed Igranians.

Rictus looked west, the world spanning out below his gaze.

To his right there rose the vast dark bulk of Kerusiad Hill. Below him were the narrow contoured streets of the Goshen Quarter. All Machran lay before him, speckled with lights, a vast beast rolling out to the horizon in the fitful moonlight. Corvus's attack was marked by a long cluster of blazing torches down in the Avennan Quarter some two pasangs away.

Phobos – I hope he keeps the bastards off our back a little longer.

The Dogsheads and Igranians fought along the walls, the heavily armoured mercenaries locking shields and battling forward foot by foot, the Igranians darting in and out with stabbing javelins and drepanas. Rictus saw one of his own men trip over a corpse and go flying into the air – he tumbled off the wall and struck the roof of a house below with an explosion of clay tiles, then slid down the incline, scrabbling for a hold, before pitching to the street below, the shattering impact of the cobbles breaking the body within the armour.

Rictus's eye was drawn to the streets on his left. Some kind of torchlit procession was pouring along it, like a flame-crested serpent of immense size.

"They're bringing up reserves!" He shouted. "Make some space, lads – we need more men up here!"

A ladder was shoved back from the walls, a Machran soldier pushing it off with his feet. It swung sideways with a dozen men still clinging to it, and went down with a sickening crash, crushing a whole file of men below.

The troops at the foot of the walls were frantic to ascend the ladders and help their comrades above. A crowd of them clambered up one while more held it steady at the top of the wall, urging them on, pulling them over the battlements as they reached the top.

Then there was a tearing crack, and the ladder broke in the middle. It went down in pieces, men still clinging to it.

One of the men in an embrasure caught a friend by the arm as he fell, held him for a moment, and then was pulled down with him, the two soaring into the crowded carnage below with their fists still locked together.

"Steady, boys!" Rictus shouted, dismayed, "Ten to a ladder, no more!"

The press on the walls was tightening again. One of the great towers of Machran loomed over them to the west; they were fighting towards it under a hail of stones and javelins. The defenders were even throwing shields and helms down upon them. Rictus felt his feet slithering in blood. He raised his shield instinctively as something came at him, a half-guessed shadow of a lunge. A blade clanged off the bronze face and he sent the drepana under his attacker's guard. It went in below the man's cuirass.

As Rictus pulled the weapon free he felt the stitches in his arm open up and a hot flow of blood ran down his fist, gluing the sword to his fingers.

There was a whoosh of air over his head – he felt it tug at the transverse crest of his helm – and something flew through the night above him. A clang, and a knot of men behind him went down as though flattened by a giant fist.

He stared uncomprehending for a long moment, disbelief sawing the breath in and out of his throat. A massive spear or bolt, thick as a man's wrist, had skewered three of his men, bursting through their armour as though the bronze were gilded paper.

"Ballistas!" Fornyx shouted across at him. "I thought those bastards didn't work anymore!"

Another tore overhead, like some raptor stooping for the kill. On the crowded battlements it could not miss. Rictus saw two Igranians pinned to a Machran spearman, the three joined by the long barbed shaft of the missile.

Men were pouring out of the tower, and more were fighting their way up the stairs to the catwalks, a flood of them with torchlight and moonlight splintering across their armour, playing across it in gleams and flashes. There was open space around Rictus. His own men were falling back to the remaining ladders. The tide of battle had shifted. The ballista bolts hammered into the ranks and knocked men down like skittles.

Fornyx was at his side, supporting Druze. The dark Igranian had a death mask for a face. His bound arm gleamed black with blood.

"Let's ask them if they want to surrender," Fornyx said, his teeth white in his beard.

"Get back to the ladders, Fornyx – this isn't working."

"Not those fucking ladders again," Druze groaned.

"Where's Valerian?"

"Down the wall towards the other tower – same story down there." Fornyx spat. "The towers are killing us."

Rictus stood up straight. The ramparts had been flooded with his men and Druze's. Now the tide had gone out. There was only a wrack of flotsam and jetsam left – and bodies, so many bodies. They choked the catwalks so thickly that they were entangling the feet of the living. The Machran troops who had manned these walls were nearly all dead, but more were on their way, hundreds more.

"The attack has failed," he said. He looked around.

Some two dozen Dogsheads were standing in a tight phalanx. Stones and arrows were raining down on them, clanging off their helms and shields. Everyone else was making for the ladders. The Companions in the second wave had not yet climbed them in any numbers. The traffic was all the other way now.

"This is the rearguard. I stand here. Fornyx, get the rest back down the wall. Have good men at the ladders – for Phobos's sake don't overload them, or we'll all die up here."

"Don't play it the hero, Rictus – Phobos!" They all ducked as another ballista bolt soared over them.

"We've got to get us some of those," Druze said wryly.

"Go, brother," Rictus said. "And try not to fall on your ass."

Back to the task at hand. The strength was going from Rictus's right arm, the blood hanging from it in snot-thick threads. He butted his attackers back with the heavy shield, the drepana darting out in quick, economical lunges, wounding more often than killing. A jet of anger as he regretted his cheap stabbing sword, still back in camp.

THE MEN AT his shoulders stood with him unquestioning. In the dark and chaos of the fighting he could not even be sure of their names, though they saved his life again and again, as he saved theirs.

They worked together, fighting for each other against the flood of foes that came barrelling down the catwalk. They fell back step by stubborn step, retreating over their own dead, closing up the gaps left by the fallen. It was a kind of fighting they knew well, and they understood also that behind them their brothers were queuing up at the ladder-heads on the walls.

To break now would mean the end of them all. They bargained away their own lives for the sake of the army, for the Dogsheads, for their centon.

For none of those things. They did it for their friends.

Finally they could retreat no more. Of the men who had climbed up the ladders with the setting of the moon, perhaps half made it back down again. The last ladder broke, and fell in shattered bloody splinters amid the terrible wreckage at the foot of the wall.

On the battlements above, Rictus stood at bay with a pair of bloodied companions, the dead piled around their feet. There was a grey in the air that heralded the dawn, and he could see the vast city that was the cynosure of the Macht world rising in front of him on its hills, brightening moment by moment.

He tossed down his broken sword, his arm almost too numb to feel it leave his fist. His shield followed, and finally he lifted off his battered and pitted helm, feeling the cold air on his face, cooling the sweat upon it.

The enemy soldiers halted, panting. One of them, a centurion by his crest, raised a broken spear.

"Nicely fought. Toss that fine black cuirass over here and we'll let you live."

Rictus looked at his two companions, who had

also doffed their helms and were breathing in the cold air like thirsty men gulping water.

"Fromir. And little Sycanus of Gost. I thought it was you."

"I think they have us, chief," Sycanus said.

"It doesn't look good," Rictus admitted. "I thank you, brothers, for standing by me."

"It seemed like the right thing," Fromir, a bulky man with thick, curly hair said.

"Mention it if you get out of this – you're due a bonus."

"Fuck the bonus," Sycanus said with a mirthless grin.

"Hand over the armour!" the enemy centurion shouted. He raised a hand.

Rictus looked up and saw the men at the top of the overlooking tower cock back their arms with javelins in their grasp. Even now, the defenders were wary of coming to grips with three men who wore the scarlet.

"Alive or dead, I'm having it, old man – your choice."

My choice? I suppose it is, Rictus thought.

He looked over the wall at Corvus's retreating, broken centons as they straggled back over the plain to their camp; hundreds, thousands of them.

He climbed up onto a merlon and balanced there, a welter of memories pelting through his mind. Aise, Rian and Ona – the sweetest joys he had known in his life.

Fornyx and Jason. His brothers.

The Ten Thousand singing the Paean, marching in time to face their deaths.

Rictus looked at the centurion, and smiled.

"I gained this armour at a place called Kunaksa," he said. "If you want it, you can come and take it."

He stepped out into empty space, and plunged from the tall stone wall of Machran.

TWENTY
FLOTSAM OF WAR

"Dead?" Corvus repeated. "He cannot be dead."

Fornyx stood in front of him, his blade-scarred helm in one arm, his tattered scarlet cloak folded over the other, and the Curse of God slathered with blood across his chest. He looked like some sculptor's ideal of war incarnate.

"The last ladder broke before he made it down off the wall. If he had been captured we would have heard of it by now." He bowed his head a second. His voice was raw. "Rictus is gone."

Corvus sank back onto the map-table, eyes staring at nothing. He had a bloodied linen clout tied about his upper thigh, and another on his forearm.

"Druze, what do you say?" he asked.

Druze stood like a whey-faced ghost, his arm strapped to his side. "Fornyx got me down, or I would be dead too. We were among the last. When we took to the ladders Rictus was still fighting with maybe a dozen of his men, covering the retreat. None of them made it."

Corvus rubbed his forehead. Fornyx glared at him.

"When the Dogsheads took your contract – if you want to call it that – we numbered over four hundred and sixty, Corvus. Today, rather less than a hundred of us are still standing. And Rictus is dead. Did you mean to destroy us, or was it something you had just not factored into your deliberations? I'm curious. Tell me."

Corvus looked up. In the tent about him all the senior officers of the army were gathered, as sombre as men at a funeral. He looked their faces over one by one.

"Where is Ardashir?" he asked.

"He has not been found," Druze said heavily. "But there are very many bodies out there at the foot of the walls."

"Phobos," Corvus whispered. His eyes filled with tears. He turned from them and leaned on the map-table, the dressing on his forearm darkening as fresh blood stained it.

One-eyed Demetrius stepped forward. "It was a close thing, Corvus – the diversion worked. When they saw your banner at the South Prime they rushed every man they could there – had we possessed more ladders, I think Rictus's assault would have succeeded."

"It was meant to succeed," Corvus said with a strangled groan. "Fornyx, despite what you think of me, I do not send men out to die for nothing."

"These things happen in war," Teresian spoke up. "Now we know better what we face."

"The towers," Druze said, "And the machines they

have upon them. They crucified us on those walls."

"Parmenios," Corvus said. He wiped his eyes. "Do you have numbers yet?"

The fat little secretary came forward with a waxed slate and a stylus. Despite his paunch, he was powerfully built about the shoulders, and he had the hands of a man who built things. He tapped the slate. "These are provisional – such is the confusion –"

"Tell me!"

"Just under a thousand men, dead or so badly wounded as to be lost to the army for good. The Dogsheads and Igranians suffered worst, though Demetrius's conscripts also took heavy casualties."

"They fought well," Corvus said, collecting himself. "Demetrius, I congratulate you. Your command is a thing to be proud of."

Demetrius bowed his head slightly in acknowledgement, his single eye shining.

Corvus approached Druze. "Forgive me, brother," he said brokenly.

Druze smiled, that quicksilver darkness. "There is nothing to forgive. This is the first time I have known defeat under you. It is Phobos's doing – he means to humble us."

Corvus leaned over the table again. He raised his voice slightly.

"I cannot afford to lose the services, or the example, of men such as you, Fornyx. Since you and Rictus joined this army I have given you the hardest post of all; but it was the post of honour. I thought there was a possibility we could end this thing with one quick assault. It had to be tried, and I knew that I wanted my best at the tip of the spearhead. I miscalculated, and you paid for it with your blood."

He turned around. His eyes were bright and rimmed with red, and the high angular bones of his face seemed more pronounced than ever in the shadow of the tent. "You all paid for it, and I will not forget that. We were beaten last night, but we are not defeated. We will prevail against Machran – the city has shown that she is a worthy adversary."

He laid a hand on Fornyx's chest, and wiped some of the dried blood off the black cuirass. "I made you pay too high a price. Rictus was a man none of us could afford to lose." He smiled, and his eyes welled up again.

"Fornyx, I loved him too, more than you know."

Fornyx's face remained hard as flint and his voice when he spoke was harsh as that of a crow.

"I wish to send a green branch to Machran to ask for his body. His wife would wish it of me."

"Do as you think best."

"It is an admission of defeat, to ask for the dead," Demetrius rumbled.

"Then it is stating no more than the obvious," Corvus replied. "The men of Machran fought well last night – let them have their triumph. If they now believe themselves invincible, then by Phobos we will use that against them."

"They have one more Cursebearer on the walls of the city today," Fornyx spat. "Think on that, if you will."

*   *   *

A THIN VEIL of sleet came slanting down out of a blank sky as winter settled itself comfortably about the lowlands surrounding Machran. On the horizons the mountains were white, their peaks lost in cloud. It was a day when a man prefers to set his back to the door and stare into a good fire.

Karnos stood in the arched shadow of the South Prime Gate as the huge oak and bronze doors were swung back by a dozen armoured men. Behind him, a centon in full panoply stood in ranks, most with the sigil of Machran on their shields, but Avennos and Arkadios were represented too. Murchos of Arkadios stood beside him wrapped in a piebald goatskin cloak against the cold. He wiped his nose on the fur and stamped his feet to keep the blood flowing.

"I don't like this – he's a tricky bastard, Corvus."

"It's three men, Murchos – what can three men do, even if they wear the scarlet? We have a hundred here – and the rest of the bugger's army is back in camp nearly two pasangs away. Unless they grow wings and fly, they're not going to interfere. And besides, I want to know what the great Rictus has to say."

"Nothing good. It was he who brought the surrender terms to Hal Goshen, don't forget."

"After last night, I hardly think they're here to demand that. Relax yourself, Murchos – you're worse than Kassander."

The gates were wide open now, and Karnos walked through them, close-wrapped in a wool cloak of his own. Murchos followed him, a bear of a man made more feral by the rough goatskin. And behind the pair the centon of spearmen advanced, some ninety armoured men in close ranks.

Three men in red cloaks stood awaiting them in the shadow of the walls, one holding aloft a branch of olive wood with a few thin leaves clinging to it. Around them, scores of corpses still lay contorted on the cold ground, the residue of Corvus's diversionary attack of the night before. The three looked like the sole survivors of some disaster as they stood there amid the tumbled bodies of the dead.

None of them were Rictus, Karnos noted at once, disappointed. He slid his good arm out of his cloak and raised his hand.

"Close enough, friend – what is it you've come to say?"

The branch-bearer was a lean, wiry man with a black beard. He walked forward a few steps, his feet cracking the ice which had gathered in the frozen rutted mud of the roadway. Blood, too, had frozen in puddles hard as gemstones, but he avoided stepping on it. He let his cloak fall back and Karnos saw that he was a Cursebearer; he studied the man's face more intently.

"Fornyx?"

The man smiled. "You have a good memory for faces, Karnos. We only met the once, I think."

"You're Rictus's second, aren't you?"

"I was." A spasm of pain crossed the lean man's features. "I come here to ask you a favour, one soldier to another."

Karnos's eyebrows shot up his forehead. "After last night, I find this a strange time to –"

"Rictus of Isca died on your walls last night. I have come to ask you for his body."

Karnos's mouth opened, but nothing came out. He looked like a landed fish. Murchos sprang forward. "What's that you say?"

Fornyx's face was a study in sinew and bone. His eyes flashed. "You heard me. I ask your permission to search through the bodies on your walls." His jaw worked as though he wanted to bite back the words as he spoke them. "I lay no claim to his armour. I want only to be able to burn him decently, for his wife's sake."

The news had run through the ranks of the spearmen in the gateway. Their voices were a low buzz of wonder.

"Quiet!" Murchos shouted.

"This could be a trick," Karnos said, more for form's sake than anything else; he could read a man's face, and he knew that Fornyx was telling the truth.

"I will enter the city alone, if you like. I'm not a spy – I know Machran well in any case. I wish only to do the decent thing by my friend."

Karnos nodded. He saw something else in Fornyx's eyes, an anger smouldering alongside the grief. That was interesting. He turned and looked at Murchos. The big Arkadian seemed torn between astonishment and glee. He made a show of considering the matter a moment.

"Very well, then. You can enter – you alone. Your companions can wait here. The gate will be shut, and I will escort you myself."

Fornyx bowed slightly. He nodded to the other two mercenaries who accompanied him, handing the olive branch to a young man with a scar that tugged his face askew, and then stepped into the shadow of the South Prime Gate.

The spearmen made a lane for Karnos and Fornyx, while Murchos ordered the gates shut in a voice of brass. They clunked shut with a boom, and Fornyx stopped and looked at them in wonder.

"First time I ever saw them shut, close to," he said. "You must have had a hell of a time loosening those old hinges."

"It took enough oil to drown an ox," Karnos said. "But then, we've plenty to spare. Perhaps you'd care for some wine before we begin your sad task? I'm sure I can lay hands on a skin."

Fornyx's mouth twisted in a half-smile. "You are a shifty bastard, Karnos. But I make a point of never refusing wine, especially on a morning like this."

"I'll have some sent to the wall. We can pour a libation for the dead."

THE DEAD STILL lay in heaps. Many hundreds of men had died on the walls of the Goshen Quarter and the clean-up process had only begun. The bodies of the enemy were first looted, stripped of arms, armour and any trinkets of value, and then the defenders tossed their stiff, stripped carcasses over the parapet to lie like gutted fish in the street below. Waggons waited there, and municipal slaves with the *machios* sigil painted on their tunics were loading the corpses upon them like cords of wood.

Fornyx drained his wine-cup while standing beside Karnos on the battlements he had fought atop the night before. They were treacherous with frozen blood. It was splashed about the stone of the merlons as liberally as paint. Karnos raised his voice and called a halt to the grisly work.

"What will you do with them?" Fornyx asked him.

"Our own dead will be burned on a pyre outside the Mithannon with all the proper rites, if Corvus will allow us to do so without harassment."

"He will. He has authorised me to promise that."

Karnos inclined his head. "Your people are your own affair. They will be hauled north separately, and left on the banks of the Mithos."

"You would leave them there like carrion?"

"You are our enemy, Fornyx. I will not use up the city's resources to make you a pyre."

"Fair enough. Give me some more, will you?" He held out his cup.

Karnos filled it himself from a wineskin. Soldier's wine, as raw as vinegar. Fornyx downed the cup in a single throat-searing swallow.

"It was a good enough way to die. At least he did not fall in some poxed little skirmish somewhere. The walls of Machran are a grand enough stage even for Rictus."

"He could have been defending these walls. I asked him – you know that," Karnos said.

"I know. In the end, it was his curiosity that killed him."

"How so?"

Fornyx smiled. "Come, Karnos – you must have felt it yourself. This phenomenon, Corvus. Tell me you would not like to meet him."

"I would," Karnos conceded. "But the price of his fame has been too high."

"Yes it has," Fornyx said. And then: "More wine."

The cup was refilled and emptied again. Fornyx's eyes were bloodshot and watering with the potent stuff, but his face remained as hard as ever. Karnos merely sipped at his own cup, watching the mercenary closely.

"Your men died well," he said, "but there cannot be many of the Dogsheads left now. They are a dying breed."

"They are dead. They died here with Rictus. I am done with this war, Karnos. I am going home. Rictus's wife is a woman –" he halted, looked into his cup, frowning.

"Yes?" Karnos looked as prick-eared as a cat.

"Nothing. All I want now is to walk away from this." A twisted smile flitted across his face.

"The fun has gone out of it, you might say. I care not a damn now whether Machran stands or falls."

"You are lucky to be able to do so. For us within these walls, there is no such choice."

"That is war. A man cannot always have what he wants." Fornyx let the last of his wine trickle over the bloodstained stone of the walls. "For Phobos, who has the last word on us all."

Karnos did the same. "For Antimone, who watches over us in pity."

Fornyx tossed his cup away. "I must get started," he said.

*　　*　　*

THE SHORT WINTER'S day ran its course, and as night came on the corpses lay contorted and hardening at the foot of Machran's walls amid a wreckage of broken timber and iron, the ghastly flotsam of war. The bodies on the battlements were slowly cleared away, the waggons trundling into the night with their grisly loads, but no-one as yet had gone near the mounded charnel house piled up outside the city. Those who had died going up and down the ladders lay where they had fallen.

Rictus opened his eyes.

All day he had lain as still as the corpses surrounding him, drifting in and out of the world. His wounds had stopped bleeding, and he was almost beyond feeling the cold. He knew there were things broken in him, but he could not quite make out what they were. His black armour was so slathered with blood and gobbets of flesh that it had lost its unearthly darkness and was a dull red, the colour of a clay tile.

He smiled. He was still a Cursebearer.

There were other things moving in the mound of bodies, and small mewling sounds from men who were still alive deep in that hill of decaying flesh. One of the last to fall, Rictus was near its crest. He had tumbled from the walls and landed on a mattress of dead and dying men, and Antimone's Gift had stopped the impact from killing him. When he breathed, he could feel the broken ends of bones grating in his chest, but he was breathing.

Alive, but not quite of this world, not yet. The cold had numbed him, and the reopened wound in his arm had bled him almost white.

Better the cold than the putrefying heat of the summer.

There was a snuffling and yapping at the base of the corpse-mound, animals growling and snapping. The vorine had come out in the night to feast upon the dead.

That galvanised him. He bit down on his own agony as he struggled over the wood-hard limbs and snarling faces that surrounded him. There was torchlight on the battlements high above, and periodically a sentry would lean over an embrasure and study the sights below. Once, one threw a stone at the feeding vorine. Each time, Rictus went limp, staring up with the open eyes of the dead at the men above.

He was not the only survivor with the strength to move. As he slithered downwards over the bodies here and there a hand clutched feebly at him, a desperate stare met his own. He ignored them, intent on his own salvation, on beating down the pain and keeping the languor of the cold from carrying him out of the world.

Someone was coming. It was not yet moonrise, but even so, Rictus could make out a crouched shadow working its way about the foot of the mound. He fell still, but the mound shifted under him, and he slid helplessly across the face of a bronze shield, and was jabbed in the thigh by the blade of a broken drepana. He emitted a sharp hiss of new pain.

The shadow paused, then approached. The vorine turned to meet this new threat, snarling, unwilling to leave the hill of bounty they had found. There was a swift, sharp sound, and one of the beasts yelped.

Torchlight over the battlements again. All went still. The yellow eyes of the vorine reflected back the light as they drifted off in the darkness, angry and afraid. The light left, the sentry walking on.

The shadow came closer. Rictus lay paralyzed with sudden terror, as keen a fear as he had felt on any battlefield. Something was climbing up the serried limbs of the dead, standing on their joints and fingers, ascending a ladder of meat.

Rictus could hear it breathing right beside him, see the warm air it exhaled in a white cloud. Then it set a hand upon his face.

He lurched, the pain in his chest screaming. The hand forced him down easily.

"Be quiet, you bloody fool. Lie still."

A strange voice, but familiar.

An eye came into view, a glow about it similar to that which lit the eyes of the vorine.

"Bel be praised. Rictus!" the voice whispered. "How are you hurt?"

"Who are you?"

"It's Ardashir." The face came closer, and Rictus could see it was that of the tall Kefren. One of his eyes was swollen closed, and all that side of his head was black with blood.

"Ardashir..." Rictus fell back.

"Can you walk? Are you much hurt?"

"I don't know, Ardashir. What happened to you?"

"I got hit on the head by a stone, right at the start – I never even made it to the ladders."

"You were lucky," Rictus said. He closed his eyes. The world was moving under him, as though he

were too drunk to stand. He grunted as the pain
bit into him again, and realised that the Kefren was
pulling him down over the dead, grasping him by
the wings of his cuirass.

"If your legs still work, time to start using them,"
Ardashir whispered. "It's a long way back to camp."

"My head is stuffed with wool. No, keep going.
For the love of God, get me out of this."

His legs worked, albeit sluggishly, as though they
had gone unused for days. Finally Ardashir and
Rictus lay on the cold ground beyond the mounded
bodies. Rictus struggled and swayed to his feet,
while Ardashir set another arrow to his bow and
shot it at the vorine pack which hovered scant yards
away.

"Get yourself a spear, or something to swing at
those fellows," Ardashir said. "They seem rather
intent on us."

Rictus found a bloodied drepana, but it was too
heavy for him. His right arm was a bloodless lump
of meat. He found the sauroter-end of a broken
spear, and stood with it in his left fist, swaying.

"I could do with a drink," he said.

"You and me both – here, lean on me, and wave
that thing at our hungry friends. We've a way to go
before moonrise."

The mismatched pair began limping and stumbling
away from the walls of Machran, the tall Kefren half-
carrying the dazed Macht. The vorine watched them
from a safe distance, and then left off the pursuit for
easier pickings among the dead of Corvus's army.

TWENTY-ONE
THE SHADOWS
ON THE PLAIN

"LOOK AT IT," Philemos said in wonder. "It's like a city. Father, do you see?"

Phaestus lifted his head, as weary and lean as a dying vulture. "It's his army. His curse upon the world."

Sertorius looked out across the darkened landscape at the vast crescent of campfires which extended for pasangs to the south and east of Machran. He whistled softly. "Phaestus my friend, were I a believing man I would echo you. Never seen anything like it."

Bosca spat upon the sleet-thickened pelt of the earth. "Machran still stands, and from what I see this fellow has no campfires to the north of the city, up at the river. Looks like a way in, boss."

"Agreed. We'll follow the riverbank and try for the Mithannon Gate. Come, people; we're nearly there."

He turned to the three huddled figures behind him, scarecrows with hair as wild as brambles and eyes sunken into their heads. He bent and grasped one face in his filthy hand, turning it this way and that.

"Bosca, you are a slap-happy prick, you know that? Can't you fuck a woman without using your fists?"

"She needed a little encouragement," Bosca said with a shrug. "Wasn't putting her heart into it."

"It makes us look bad, like thugs from the gutter."

"That is what you are," Philemos said evenly.

Sertorius drew close to the dark-haired boy, smiling. "Careful, lad – we're not in Machran yet. I've indulged you, because I like your spirit. Even gave you the girl to moon over all you want. But don't you press me too hard – I get cantankerous, this close to the end of a job."

"The boy means nothing by it," Phaestus croaked.

"Well make sure you speak up for us in Machran, Phaestus – make me look good. I've not come all this way for a pat on the head and a bronze obol set in my hand. Me and mine have earned something substantial, getting these bitches this far."

"Get us into the city and you shall have your just deserts, Sertorius, I promise you," Phaestus said.

"Very well, then. Up, ladies! The last leg lies before us."

He bent over Aise again. "Soon that sweet cunny of yours will get a rest, wife of Rictus. You can spend what's left of your days looking back on the fond memories we ploughed you with."

Then he turned and set his face close to Rian's. "I

only wish I had tasted you, my little honey-pot. I would have given you dreams to remember me by."

He straightened. "Let's go. Adurnos, carry the brat, and keep it quiet."

The little company moved out. Sertorius led Aise on a leash, and she stumbled in his wake, her once beautiful face bruised and swollen and bloody. Then came hulking Adurnos, carrying Ona on his shoulder as though she were a sack. The child's eyes were dead as stones, and when she gathered breath for a cough he set his fingers over her mouth and smothered it.

He was followed by Philemos and Rian, half-dragging Phaestus with them. Bosca brought up the rear. He amused himself now and then by shoving Rictus's eldest daughter in the back, his grin a yellow gleam in the darkness.

They straggled through the night, a haggard company of travellers at the end of their journey. As they drew nearer to Machran they could smell burning; not woodsmoke, but a putrid, sickening reek that hung heavy in the night.

"That's a funeral pyre," Sertorius sniffed, "a big one."

"There's been a battle," Philemos said.

The river was loud and pale to their right. The open plain about Machran seemed deserted, the city and the conqueror's army facing each other across it as though separated by a gulf of shadow.

"Phobos is rising," Phaestus said. He fell to one knee. Philemos hauled him up again. Phaestus leaned his weight on the shoulders of his son and Rictus's daughter.

"Forgive me," he murmured to Rian.

"Shit," Sertorius said. "Someone's out there – I can see them. Down, all of you."

They lay in the broken crackling rows of a winter vineyard. The plants had been slashed and trampled flat, but were still high enough to conceal them. Sertorius and his men drew their knives.

A pair of shadows lurched by not two hundred paces away to the south, one supporting the other like a man helping a drunken friend. They were making a painfully slow progress across the plain to the camp of Corvus's army.

Sertorius breathed out. "Just stragglers, that's all. Nothing to worry about. Up, up – let's go before the night gets old."

Aise stood staring at the retreating shadows for a moment before the leash at her throat jerked her into motion. She trudged after Sertorius again, head down, her feet bare and bloody and the white skin of her naked shoulder shining like a bone under the rising moons.

THE PYRE WAS still burning as they passed it, flames licking here and there in fitful tongues. There were people coming and going between it and the open gate of the Mithannon, and centons of spearmen standing in ordered ranks. Women were keening and sobbing, an eerie chorus in the night, and the torchlight made of it all a dark tableau of shadow and fire, a dramatist's invocation of grief. The company made their halting way to the looming gateway of the city, and there were stopped by men in full panoply, one bearing a centurion's transverse crest.

"Your names and district."

"Phaestus," Sertorius said, "This is on you, now."

The old man straightened and seemed to find some last reserve of strength. He stood tall in front of the centurion.

"I am Phaestus of Hal Goshen, and I bear news for Karnos, Speaker of Machran. You must take me and those with me to him at once."

When the centurion did not move, he barked out in a much louder voice, "Do as I say!"

The strength left him. He sagged, and was seized with a fit of wet, bloody coughing.

The centurion turned to one of his men. "Get Kassander here."

FROM THE MITHANNON Gate to Kerusiad Hill was two pasangs as a crow might fly, half as long again by the meander of the Mithannon's cramped streets and alleyways. Phaestus and Aise had nothing left in them, nor any strength to trudge over the hard cold cobbles of the city amid the night-time crowds. When Kassander arrived he looked over the travellers one by one. As he saw Aise's condition his eyes widened and anger made of his mouth a wide, lipless slot.

"What has happened to this woman?"

"She tried to escape," Sertorius said. Standing by the burly armoured polemarch he seemed like a jackal cowering before a lion. "She's been difficult from the start. We've travelled over half the Gostheres to get here, through snowdrifts as high as your head. Been near three weeks on the road."

Kassander flicked a hand at the centurion. "Cut her free. The other one too." He looked down at Sertorius and a muscle in his jaw flickered. He turned.

"I know you, Phaestus. We have met in the past."

"You know me," Phaestus agreed. He lay on the cobbles with Philemos supporting him. "I must see Karnos."

"Can you walk?"

Phaestus smiled faintly. "I've walked this far."

"I will have a cart brought here. Centurion!"

"Aye, sir."

"Stay with these people. When transport arrives escort them to Karnos's villa on the Kerusiad. Then set a guard about the house."

He turned to Sertorius, leaned in so close that the bronze face of his helm was misted by the other man's breath.

"I don't give a fuck who she is; you'd better have a good reason for treating a woman that way."

For a city under siege, Machran did not lack liveliness, even at this hour of the night. The mule-drawn cart sent for them had to have a path cleared for it through the crowds by the escorting spearmen, and by the time it had meandered across a third of the city, Phobos was almost set and Haukos was high in the sky.

Pink Haukos – to the Macht he was the moon of

hope, but across the teeming Empire of the Kufr, he was called *Firghe*, moon of wrath.

Word had gone ahead of them. When the mule-cart finally completed its clattering ascent of the Kerusiad Hill, the doors of Karnos's villa were already open in a blaze of torchlight, and the master of the house stood wrapped in a woollen chlamys against the cold, his household all about him. He saw the condition of those in the cart and clapped his hands. Half a dozen slaves congregated on the vehicle. Phaestus lifted his head, but could not speak.

Karnos bent over him and took his hand. "My friend, be at ease. Your wife and daughters arrived here over a week ago. I have them quartered in comfort further up the hill. I shall send word to Berimus." Phaestus closed his eyes, and tears trickled down his face. Karnos patted his shoulder.

"You must be Philemos," he said. "A fine looking young man. I salute you for seeing your father to safety." Philemos bowed his head, looking more than anything else ashamed. Karnos sucked his teeth a moment.

"You three," he said to Sertorius and his comrades. "What part did you play in all this?"

"We were the escort," Sertorius said with a grin that flickered on and off in his face. "Without us, Phaestus would be dead in the drifts of the Gostheres."

"Is this true?" Karnos asked Phaestus. The older man's eyes opened and he nodded.

Karnos ran his gaze over the brutalised captives in the cart. Rian met his eyes with a glaring, tearstained defiance, holding Ona in her arms. Aise sat with her head resting on her elder daughter's shoulder, eyes shut, barely conscious.

"You are to be congratulated," he said at last to Sertorius. "It's not a time to be on the road." He raised his voice slightly. "Pollo."

"Master?" The old steward was also staring at the women in the cart, his white beard quivering.

"We must find a space for these three fine fellows to lay their heads. Water for washing, food and wine – whatever they want. Have the cook run something up."

"How about a plump little slave girl?" Bosca leered.

Karnos looked at him. "Centurion?"

"Yes, Speaker."

His eyes were still fixed on Bosca. "I want four men to stand guard over our guests here. Make sure they do not wander round my house and lose themselves."

"Yes, Speaker."

"Now listen here, Karnos –" Sertorius exclaimed.

"Ah, I have it. Grania, show these gentlemen to the grain store. You will forgive me, my friends, but I am a little short on space." Karnos jerked his head to one side and the spearmen clustered around Sertorius, Adurnos and Bosca. The slim slave girl led the way.

"Phaestus – you tell him!" Sertorius shouted over his shoulder. "You'd be dead were it not for me!" The spearmen shoved him along in Grania's wake with the relish of angry men.

Karnos was still staring at Rictus's brutalised family. "*Phobos*," he seethed under his breath. He and Pollo looked at one another.

"We couldn't stop them," Philemos said miserably. Karnos looked at him with contempt, then shook his head and touched Rian gently on the arm.

"Lady, you are in my house now, and here I swear no man shall touch you."

Rian bent her head and began to sob silently.

THE SLAVES WENT about their business in unaccustomed silence. They had rarely seen their master in such a mood. He was not shouting, ranting or throwing winecups at the walls, as they had seen him do many a time on returning from the Amphion. He was not drunk, nor was he impatiently shouting orders as was his wont.

He sat in his chair before the fire of the main hall and stared into the flames with unblinking eyes as though he were waiting for something to appear there. The long room was almost in darkness, a few single-wicked lamps glowing in the corners. His chlamys lay on the floor at his feet, and no slave had yet dared approach to pick it up.

It was Pollo who broke his dark reverie.

"Master, the lady Kassia is here."

"*What?* Fuck!"

"Shall I show her in?"

Karnos stared into the fire again. He had lost weight, and as the flesh had melted from his face so the bones beneath had become more prominent. He was no longer the florid fat man he had been before Afteni.

Pollo cleared his throat. "I believe Kassander sent her. She has two servants with her, and baskets of linens."

Karnos nodded. "That's Kassander's way. I was going to send for a carnifex to look at them, but the last thing they need is another fucking man pawing –" He clenched his teeth shut on the words. "Let them in, Pollo."

Before Pollo could move away, Karnos set a hand upon the older man's fingers and gripped them.

"Thank you," he said.

Pollo raised his eyebrows slightly. "You do not need to thank me for a thing, master."

"Perhaps I will before this is done. What about Phaestus and the boy?"

"They are sleeping."

"Let them sleep then. And send in that bloody woman."

He bent and tossed another log on the fire. Pine wood, hewn from the forests north of the Mithos River. The resin in the timber oozed and spat and flared up in little knots of white fury.

"Sitting in the dark?" Kassia's voice said behind him.

"The dark seems best, for now."

She bent and retrieved his cloak from the floor. "Kassander told me, said I might be needed here. I brought two good women. One's a midwife. They will look after them."

Karnos nodded.

"What are you going to do with them?"

He looked up, and laughed. "What would you have me do? They were brought here because they are the family of a dead man. Their suffering has no significance, no sense to it."

"Most suffering doesn't."

Karnos clenched one fist in another. "What a filthy world we live in, Kassia."

She sat in the chair across from him, picking at the threads of his chlamys, teasing out the wool. "There are a thousand women like them in the city."

"I am responsible for this, Kassia. Me." He stood up, began pacing the room, in and out of the dark and the firelight and the lamplight, up and down like something caged.

"I encouraged Phaestus to do this thing. It was his idea, but I wrote, urging him on. Get them, I said. Bring them here. We will hold this over the great Rictus's head and cleave him from Corvus. I was so fucking clever about it. My seal on a scroll of paper is what brought them to this."

Kassia stared at her busy fingers picking the wool in her lap. "I see."

"It is one thing to face a man on a battlefield, or on the floor of the Empirion for that matter. But this is pure poison, even had it worked."

"You love your city, Karnos," Kassia said simply. "You would do anything that would help preserve it."

"You have not seen them, or the leering bastards that brought them here. I would have killed those animals on the spot, except I am no better. It would not be justice, unless I had the same done to me – I am complicit."

"You did not know this would happen, Karnos."

"A man's *family*, Kassia."

"Do they know he is dead?"

"What? No – not yet. I must tell them, I suppose."

"Not tonight, for Antimone's sake. They have been through enough."

"You are right not to marry me. I am not fit for a decent woman."

She stood up and blocked his path, took him by the arms as he tried to sidestep her. "If that were so I would not be here, and this would not be tearing you up the way it is. You made a mistake, Karnos. But you are leader of a great city in desperate times, making a hundred decisions a day. You will be wrong some of the time, and because you have power in your hands, your mistakes will bring misfortune and misery to people. That is the nature of your position."

Karnos stared at her and managed a strangled laugh. "By God, Kassia, you can be a cold-blooded bitch when you want to be."

She slapped him across the face, eyes blazing. "You are Speaker of Machran. You do not have the time to indulge your guilt. The thing is done. That's all there is to it."

He glared at her, and for a moment they measured up to one another in a crackling silence. She lifted her hand again and touched the reddening welt on his face.

"Kassander is right – we should marry and get it over with. Then we could make up like married people do."

The fire in his eyes smouldered. He took her by the

upper arms and kissed her, hard enough to blush her lips into a bruised rose.

"I am a big-bellied slave-dealer with a streak of drama running through me. At heart I am still only that. I mind these things. I cannot play the great man and put them to one side."

"Machran is lucky to have you."

"I wish I could believe that." He kissed her again, gently this time, then turned and faced the fire, watching the smoke rise up to be sucked out of the slats in the roof. The moonlight was red outside, the smoke taking colour from it as it left the house.

"Will you go to Rictus's wife in the morning Kassia? Tell her about her husband. I cannot do that. Maybe I am Speaker of Machran, but I cannot stand in front of that wretched woman with such news."

She nodded. "I will."

"And Kassia, tell her that she is safe here. She can come or go as she pleases."

"You want her under your roof, knowing you had a hand in her fate?"

"I deserve it. I too must pay."

She stood beside him and twined her fingers in his.

"Karnos, they burned a thousand men on a pyre today, and it was counted a victory. The times we live in are full of blood. Before this thing is done, we will have it on all our hands."

"I wonder sometimes if it's worth it. To fight like this – and for what? So we can tell ourselves that we are free men? What did freedom mean to my father? He was more a slave than Pollo is. Freedom is a word, Kassia."

"There has to be something worth dying for. Remember what Gestrakos said: *a man who cares for nothing is a man already dead.*"

Karnos grimaced. "There's another saying, about ends and means. Let me show you something."

He led her down to the end of the long room. At the bottom a tall cabinet of dark wood stood, barely lit by the oil lamp in the corner. Karnos touched the bottom of the cabinet and there was an audible click. A door opened, taller than either of them.

"I had Framnos make this, the same time he built me my couches," Karnos said. "Now you know how it opens, as only he and I did before." He swung open the door. There was a darkness within, and in that darkness a deeper black.

"Reach out and touch it."

Kassia put her hand out hesitantly, then recoiled. "I can't see – what is it?"

Karnos brought the lamp over and held it high. Set within the cabinet was a black cuirass. It seemed to soak up the light of the flame, like a hole in the fabric of the world. And then they saw a gleam run over it here and there, like a delayed reflection.

"The Curse of God," Karnos said.

"Karnos – I never knew – how did you find this?"

"I stole it," he said with a crooked smile.

Her mouth opened. "You cannot steal this, Karnos. These things –"

"It belonged to Katullos. I was with him when he died. He wanted it given to his son, but his son is not twelve years old. So I took it for myself. I, the Speaker of Machran."

"It's not right. His family –"

"Call it fortune of war." Karnos reached out and touched the lightless contours of the armour. "I shall wear it on the walls, when the end comes, for good or ill. It will do the city more good on my back than in the family vault of the Alcmoi."

They stood looking at it, until Kassia shivered. "I don't like these things – they are not of this world."

"You may be right. But they are part of what we are. They cannot be pierced, damaged or destroyed. They simply exist. As long as they do, so shall we."

He closed the cabinet door again. "You think me a thief now, I suppose."

She looked at him closely, studying his face, the mark she had left upon it. Tears welled up in her eyes.

"What is it, Kassia? Are you ashamed of me?"

"No – not ashamed. Afraid."

"Afraid of what?"

"I know you, Karnos. You are many things, but a thief is not one of them.

"You stole that armour because you see yourself dying in it."

WITH THE MORNING came the light in the room, a bright winter sun edging over the Gostheres to the east. She lay and watched it brighten the blue slots above her, breaking in the slatted windows up on the wall. With it came the smell of woodsmoke, of bread baking, and the unfamiliar sea-surf sound of the waking city beyond.

Her daughters were with her in the bed, Ona curled up in her arms, Rian spooned against her back. For a few moments, Aise was able to lie and listen to them breathe, and be herself again. She could put out of her mind the pain of her blistered feet and throbbing face, the dull ache of her insides. There was not a part of her they had not touched.

The moment was gone, so quickly lost it had not truly existed. She lay in the clean bed breathing quickly, heart hammering, no longer seeing the sunlight on the wall. Her mouth was full of dirt, her face pressed into it, and they were holding her down, entering her in the darkness, filling her body with foulness, the hot filth jetting out of them to find its way to her very heart.

She drew breath deeply, listening to the sleeping heartbeats of her daughters, blinking her way back to the present. It was over, it was finished with.

And yet the men who had done this to her were still in this house, mere yards away.

She sat up in the bed. Rian and Ona stirred, but did not waken. She wriggled out from between them and pulled the blanket over their shoulders, smoothed the hair from their faces.

I made the bargain, and the gods kept it. I took the worst thing on myself, and they allowed me that grace. I must be thankful.

She kissed her sleeping daughters one after the other.

There was a pile of cloaks and clothing on the other bed in the room. She selected a heavy peplos, a woman's winter garment, and wrapped it around her shoulders. The stone floor was cold underfoot, but it soothed the ragged tears in her feet. She limped out of the room, closing the door without a sound.

She was in a tiny courtyard with a pool in the middle, a colonnaded walkway all around, and plants in pots. In *pots*. She touched a pungent juniper, smelled lavender, bay, and mint. All dying back, all past their best, but easing her mind with their scents and their memories.

How marvellous it was to be free of fear, just for now. To stand and feel the winter sunlight on her face and rub lavender between her fingers...

The smell of the clothes chests at Andunnon.

A slave entered the courtyard with a basket, looked at her, startled, then bowed and scurried away. Aise sank back against a pillar, not sure what this might presage. It was only a few moments before a well-dressed woman appeared in the slave's place. A dark-haired lady with a broad, handsome face, her hair braided up behind her head. She was young, perhaps not yet thirty, but she had a direct gaze, and there was nothing hesitant about her as she approached.

"I am Kassia, my dear. My people looked after you last night. Did you sleep well? How are the children?"

Aise folded her arms inside her cloak. "We are well," she said.

"Perhaps you would like to break your fast? Karnos's cook baked bread fresh this morning, and there is honey to be had, and clean water."

Aise stood as if rooted to the spot. At last she said, "I'm sorry. I am not –"

The woman called Kassia took her arm. "It's all right. You're safe now. You brought your children through this, and you are all alive. The rest is a matter for time and Antimone's mercy."

"I must go back to them. They're sleeping," Aise said, edging away.

"Let them sleep," Kassia told her. "Please. Come with me, Aise. There's a fire burning and a table laid."

Eunion, biting into a purple onion at breakfast, the last thing he would ever eat.

"No, I cannot."

"Listen," Kassia said, and her eyes left Aise's face for the first time. "I have news you need to hear, something you should know. And it were best I tell you now, while your children are asleep."

Aise's face became blank. "Tell me, then."

"No, please, not out here. Come join me at the fire. We'll have some wine."

"I will not drink wine," Aise said.

"Then I will." Kassia smiled, flustered now. "Please come with me."

Unwillingly, Aise allowed herself to be tugged along by the arm. They left the courtyard and entered a room in which the walls were painted the colour of an earthenware pot. There was a small corner hearth, its beehive interior full of fire – olive wood, by the smell. And a balcony. Aise stepped over to it in wonder. There was a thick wooden balustrade the height of her thigh, and beyond it, a soaring view of Machran. She caught her breath at the sight.

Kassia joined her, lifting a winecup off the table that sat like an island in the middle of the room.

"It's quite something, to see it all from here," she said, smiling. "We are high up on Kerusiad Hill, and you're looking west. There's the Empirion, and Round Hill rising behind it. All of Machran at your feet. I never tire of looking at it."

"I've never seen it like this, like a view through the eye of a bird."

"The Kerusiad is a tall hill. At the top of it is the citadel of Machran, an old fortress where the Kerusia meet in session. They're repairing it now, just in case we..."

"In case Corvus and my husband breach your walls," Aise said. She turned around. "Lady, you seem a kindly woman. Of this Karnos I know nothing except that he has a reputation as a womaniser and an orator. Tell me, what does he intend to do with my girls and I?" Aise stared at Kassia unblinking. The white of one eye had half-filled with blood, and its socket was a purple hollow.

"Karnos is a good man, whatever you've heard of him," Kassia said earnestly. "He detests what was done to you. He has told me that you and your children are welcome to make his home your own for as long as you wish."

"He sounds like a man with a guilty conscience," Aise said. "I know we are not here on a whim. He seeks to use me against my husband."

Kassia set down her wine carefully on the tabletop.

"Aise." She glided forward and took the older woman's hands in her own, looking her full in that beautiful, broken face.

"Rictus died yesterday in an assault upon the walls."

Aise stood very still for perhaps three heartbeats. Then she jerked her hands out of the younger woman's grasp and backed away.

"That is a lie."

"I am so sorry."

"I do not believe you."

"I would not lie about such a thing. Aise, yesterday morning Rictus's second, Fornyx, came to the city under a green branch and asked to retrieve his body."

"Fornyx?" Aise backed away further. One hand came up and covered her mouth.

Kassia followed her, opening her arms. "Believe me when I say Karnos has no hidden plans for you. With Rictus gone –"

"With Rictus gone I am without worth," Aise said. And spoke his name again, so softly it could barely be heard.

Tears burned bright in her bruised and blood-filled eyes. She drew a breath that was part sob, part snarl.

All this time the knowledge that he was there in the world, a black-armoured invincible pillar of her life – it had kept her on her feet. The fact of his very existence had made her take one step after another when she wanted nothing more than to give up, to lie down and shut herself away from the memories poisoning her heart. Rictus would find her. Rictus would set things right, if he had to tear Machran stone from stone to do it.

A childish belief, but it was the last hope she had possessed.

And now he was dead.

"Aise –" Kassia began, her face twisted with pity.

"*Stay away from me.*" The look in Aise's eyes halted Kassia in her tracks.

She walked to the balcony and stood there with her hands on the reassuring wood of the balustrade. All Machran loomed out below her, a surf of noise and activity that filled the world. Men shouting, dogs barking, mules braying, the rattle of cartwheels, and unending, ceaseless chatter. Tens of thousands talking, talking.

She set her hands on her ears, the tears trickling down her face, thinking of Andunnon, the quiet world of the hills, making bread that last morning before it was all destroyed. She would never know peace again, now. She knew that.

Even in the most silent hour of the night, she would hear them laughing as they violated her, and see their faces. Rictus would have killed them. He would have made things right.

Rictus was dead. Her world was destroyed.

"Aise," Kassia said. "In time..."

She had made a bargain with the gods, and they had kept it. *Let it all be on me,* she had prayed, and her prayer had been answered. Her daughters were alive and whole.

"You say you will look after my children."

"Yes – of course."

She had done enough. All her life she had been doing things for others. Now she would do one last thing for herself.

"Aise!" Kassia screamed, and lunged forward.

Too late. Rictus's wife leaned out over the balcony and let herself fall. A flash of turning pictures galloped past her mind, bright leaves from a forest of memories; and then there was a shattering blankness. And she knew true peace at last.

TWENTY-TWO
DEATH AND
THE GODS

LIKE A SLUGGISH beast, the army of Corvus came awake in its camps. As the first snows came and went in the dilatory way of the lowland winter, so the morai of the conqueror began marching again.

The baggage train was up at last, and gangs of labourers were set to improving the washed-out sections of the Imperial road that led east, thousands of the inhabitants of the hinterland rounded up and put to work felling trees and quarrying stone. The main camp astride the road took on a more permanent look as the brown army tents went up in neat rows with corduroyed roads laid between them. And the army spread out to north and south, an octopus with arms of barbed spearmen.

Teresian led two morai west, marching the whole length of the city walls, and set up camp opposite the West Prime Gate. Demetrius and three thousand spears ensconced themselves to the south, cutting the Avennon road. Druzè led two overstrength morai of spearmen and Igranians north, and began constructing a stockaded fort outside the Mithannon, on the banks of the Mithos River. One of the first things he did was to retrieve the mouldering dead of the army's last assault and gather them into a pyre, to burn alongside the ashes of the defenders.

Corvus remained facing the East Prime Gate with the main body, the cavalry and the baggage-park.

Stockades of sharpened logs went up in great skeins around the walls, dotted with watchtowers, and beacons were stacked up at key locations, ready to be lit should the defenders decide to sally forth and challenge the tightening grip on the city.

Machran was wholly surrounded, every road blocked, every means of egress from the city overlooked by men in arms. It was cut off from the outside world.

"WHAT IS IT this morning? More of that damned barley broth? Get it away from me," Rictus snapped.

Fornyx blew on the steaming bowl. "At least it's hot. Most of the army breakfasts on stale bread and goat meat so high it bleats as you put it in your mouth."

"I could do with some of that."

"Severan says nothing with a taint in it – you're still too weak. Now be a good boy and eat your fucking broth."

Rictus grunted in pain as he sat up in the bed and

took the bowl from Fornyx. "How's a man supposed to heal without a bit of meat or a splash of wine?"

"You have me there." Fornyx leaned back in the leather-strapped chair and closed his eyes a second. The brazier to one side gave off a shimmer of heat, and the air in the tent was close.

"Open the flap, will you? I can't breathe in here. That smoke-vent hardly lets any air in at all."

Fornyx opened his eyes again. "You want to take the lung fever? Last week you were flat on your back coughing up green slime and talking to people who weren't there. Another fever will carry you off, Severan says. You're not the young buck you used to be, made out of rawhide and horse's piss. None of us are."

"Then talk to me, Fornyx. Tell me the news."

Fornyx looked at his friend closely. Rictus had been pared back to the essentials of life; sinew, bone and corded muscle. His skull seemed too large for his body now, despite the broadness of his shoulders, and he had lost the outdoor ruddiness of wind and sun and snow. His face had the pallor of an invalid, and there were blue rings beneath his eyes that had not been there before.

He looked old. For the first time, Fornyx saw the elderly man in him. The youth who had joined the Ten Thousand all those years ago was utterly gone.

"There's not much to tell. No spearwork to speak of; our tools this last while have been the spade and the axe. The men spend what free time they have scouring the frozen wasteland they've made for a turnip or an onion that's been overlooked. There's not an olive tree or a vine left standing for twenty pasangs, and even the grass seems to be withering. Ardashir has had to move some of the horselines ten pasangs back east. Those big Kufr horses are starting to look like rag and bone. By the time the last of them die they won't even be worth eating."

Rictus coughed over his broth and winced, a hand set to his side. "And the men – our men?"

Fornyx frowned. "Corvus has taken them as a kind of bodyguard. Now that he's cut us down to size he finds use for us as mascots. We have one under-strength centon still in the scarlet. Those here now are here to stay – Kesero has his heart set on the plunder of Machran. Valerian doesn't say much. I think this kind of warfare is not to his liking."

"Is it to anyone's? What's going on in the city? Do we have any inkling?"

"Machran is a different place now, Rictus, a world apart from ours. There's no coming or going; the place is sealed up tight. If we're hungry here, with supplies still coming in from the east and the foraging parties out night and day, then think what it's like inside those walls, with a hundred thousand and more mouths to feed."

"If all they had to eat was this shit they'd open the gates tomorrow," Rictus said, setting the bowl to one side. He lay back in the bed – it had been made specially for him on Corvus's orders – and looked at his old friend.

"Druze tells me you were going to leave the army when you thought me dead."

Fornyx shrugged. "There didn't seem to be much point to it any more."

"You were the one so keen to find yourself part of history, Fornyx. This is it – we are inside it right now. There were times in the Empire I wanted to lie down and die, many times –"

"I told you once I thought it must have been like some black dream of Phobos. I was right."

"Well, then."

"At least in the Empire you knew where you were going, Rictus. Here, I look around and wonder what it's all in aid of. Are we here to make Corvus into a king?"

"I think so."

"And you're happy with that? That half-breed boy lording it over all the Macht like a Kufr tyrant?"

"He's not as bad as you make out."

"Oh I know – you and he are like family now. I see it, Rictus. He was half out of his mind with joy when Ardashir brought you back from the dead."

"He is Jason's son, and it was my fault his father died."

"That's not a debt he can hold over you all his life – he never even knew his father."

"I knew him," Rictus said firmly. "He was a better man than either of us, and his mother a fine woman."

"A Kufr."

"A Kufr, yes – does it matter?"

"Most of the clodhoppers in this army have no idea their beloved general has Kufr blood in his veins. What do you think they'd do if they found out?"

"Nothing. He has luck on his side, Fornyx. Knowing him, it would only add to his mystery."

Fornyx lowered his head. "All right, all right. I hear myself and I sound like some bitching recruit missing his mother's tit. This grand scale of war, it's new to me. There are too many faces missing around the centos, Rictus, men you and I had marched with for years. They fell in windrows up on that wall, and at Afteni."

"There will be others, Fornyx. The faces have always changed. Doesn't he have you recruiting?"

Fornyx laughed. "He does. He has given permission for any spearman in the army to try for us. Valerian and Kesero have them lined up outside their tents every morning, young fellows with a hankering to wear that scarlet cloak and call themselves a Dogshead.

"There was a time, Rictus, years ago, when there were mercenaries in every city, and the red cloak was nothing more than a badge of shame. Now, since the return of the Ten Thousand, and with this campaign, it's something else."

"An honour," Rictus said.

"Yes. Who'd have thought it?"

"We'll take the best of them, and build the Dogsheads up again, Fornyx," Rictus said, patting his friend's hand.

Fornyx grinned with a flash of his old vulpine self. "We're drilling them till they puke."

To THE REAR of the camp which sprawled across the Goshen Road, east of Machran, a fenced-off lumberyard and ironworks had been set up. Within it, Corvus's secretary Parmenios was lord and master, and he had conscripted every carpenter and blacksmith to be found from Machran to Afteni.

Every day the waggons poured into the enclosure, bearing lumber and scrap iron and charcoal, and the forges sparked and hammered there day and night. Tall structures began to rise up in the middle of them, rising higher day by day, and new orders went out across the countryside. Herds of cattle were brought in, slaughtered for the beef that the army would eat, and then stripped of their hides.

Soon the reek of a tannery was added to the smoke of the roaring forges, and Corvus set sentries about this strange enterprise of Parmenios's, most of them Kufr from the Companions. They turned away every curious soldier who ambled over the hill to see what was going on, and the army buzzed with speculation as the last days of the year ran out, and the dark night of midwinter came upon the earth.

ALMOST TWO HUNDRED pasangs to the south and east, the city of Avensis rose on its crag to dominate the wide plain between Nemasis and Pontis. A great trading settlement, a hub of the caravan trails which converged before joining the Imperial road, it was also the richest member of the Avennan League after Machran itself.

The men of Avensis had fought at Afteni and fallen by the hundred. Now the Kerusia had decided to wait upon events, so advised by Ulfos the polemarch, who had been at Afteni and seen the prowess of Corvus's army first hand.

They were meeting in the citadel of the city, an airy colonnaded space that looked out over the fertile plain below. Ulfos stood upon the grey mottled marble, blowing into his hands.

Winter was here; even this far south it had its bite, though there was no snow on the ground as yet. The circle of the Kerusia was a fine place to meet on a summer's day when the sky was a cerulean blue overhead, but today the place had a bleakness to it that matched the mood of the men taking their seats on the stone semi-circle of benches.

Parnon, the Speaker of Avensis, rose in the classic fashion, himation caught up over one forearm. He extended the other to Ulfos.

"General, you said you had news. Best to present it quickly." One of the elderly Kerusia behind him sneezed, and there was a muttering, swiftly silenced by a look from the stately Parnon, his white beard jutting like a brush.

Ulfos turned around and beckoned at the antechamber beyond. At his signal, a scrawny, bedraggled figure limped into the Kerusia circle, a filthy shock-haired youth, his cloak in rags and his bare feet bloody.

"This can't be good," one of the old men muttered to his neighbour.

"Speak up, lad," Ulfos said. "Give what you carry to the Speaker here and then tell him what you told me."

The boy looked the Kerusia over, then reached into his cloak and produced a tattered, rain-spotted scroll. He handed it to Parnon.

"Your honour, that is a message from Karnos of

Machran himself, with his seal upon it – and it ain't broke, I made sure of that."

Parnon looked down at the scroll as though the boy had placed a turd in his hand. His gaze swept the Kerusia circle, and then he broke the seal, unrolling the paper. His lips moved, and his face grew set and hard.

He looked up at the boy again. "How did you get here?" he asked.

"I ran, your honour."

"You ran? What – all the way?"

The boy laid an open hand on his chest as though feeling for his own heartbeat. "All the way. I swear. Karnos made me promise to stop for nothing, to talk to no-one on the road."

"Did he send any other message?"

"He told me to tell you there would be no more messages."

Parnon nodded. "What's your name?"

"Fidias, your honour."

Parnon drew near the boy and set a hand on his shoulder. "You have done a thing of great worth, Fidias. I thank you for it." He looked at Ulfos, who stood biting his thumbnail, his cloak bundled around his arms.

"Look after this young fellow. He has quality in him. Go now, Fidias – you look as though a bath and a hot meal would not go amiss."

The boy's face lit up. "Thank you, your honour!" At a gesture from Ulfos he trotted out of the room, his gait a peculiar limping shuffle, at once sprightly and painful-looking.

Parnon threw the scroll down upon the marble floor of the circle.

"Machran is under close siege. The failure of the first assault has not dented Corvus's determination. He has the walls surrounded and is building a circumvallation to seal off the city entirely. Karnos tells us that the city can subsist perhaps a month before starvation sets in. He asks that the forces of the League reassemble for a relief attempt as soon as possible."

He bent and retrieved the scroll again, his eyes dark.

"That's it then," one of the Kerusia said, his breath rattling in his throat. "Machran is finished."

"Without our help," Parnon said.

"We gave our help already, and saw our men burned outside Afteni," another said bitterly. "We have done enough. Do you forget that Machran offered us no help fifteen years ago when Pontis attacked?"

Parnon lifted his hand. "Let us not dig up the past. There's enough here to occupy us right now."

"I thought Machran had greater reserves of food," another said.

"They had." It was Ulfos who spoke up now. He worried at his thumbnail like a terrier after a rat. "So many refugees came into the city from Arkadios and some of the other hinterland cities that the numbers went beyond normal reckoning. Too many mouths to feed."

Parnon tapped the crumpled scroll against his upper lip. "How many spears can we still turn out, Ulfos?"

"Maybe three thousand, if we leave nothing behind."

"You think we could persuade the other polemarchs to meet here? Pontis, Arienus?"

"They've already been beat once by Corvus, Parnon. What makes you think they'll stake another throw of the knucklebone?"

Parnon held the scroll out. "Corvus lost a thousand men in his failed assault. He has had to detach more to hold down Arkadios, Afteni, and the other hinterland cities. He has nothing like the numbers that faced us before. If we do not try again now, then it is over for Machran."

"If Machran falls, then no-one can stand against him," one of the Kerusia said, an old man who banged his olive-wood walking stick on the floor with a crack. "The cities of the Planaean Coast have no armies to speak of; Minerias grows wine, not fighting men. They're soft – useless! There's us, the Pontines and the Arienans. That's all the backbone left in this part of the world. By Phobos, were I young again –"

"Therones is right," Parnon said. "All the best of the Macht fighting cities are either already gone, or were at Afteni with us. We must reassemble them – it has to be worth a try. I will go to Pontis myself."

"Then you'd best run as fast as that brave boy with the bloody feet," old Therones barked, and he banged his stick again.

NORTH, ALONG THE ancient caravan trails which ran in the hollows of the hills and followed the fastest path like the flow of water. The roads were brown now, rutted with hardened mud, and there were few people upon them at this dark heart of the year.

The southern hinterland of Machran had not yet seen the host of Corvus in all its might, but they had endured the foraging parties he sent out to keep his army fed, and the people of the small farms and towns south of Machran had marvelled at the sight of the Companions on their tall black Kefren horses, beasts bred from the Niseians that bore the Great King himself.

The Kufr who rode them spoke Machtic, after a fashion, and sometimes they even paid for the grain they took and the animals they herded away. They never cleaned out a district entirely, but left the seed-corn and the makings of a new flock or herd behind when they left.

The small farmers of the plain about Gast and Nemasis and Avennos did not quite know what to make of them; they possessed better discipline than the citizen armies that had tramped over their lands from time immemorial, and their outlandish appearance lent them a kind of alien glamour.

There were those who grew hot-headed at the thought of Kufr looting the country of the Macht, but for the most part these kept their thoughts to themselves, as did so many in these days.

NORTH AGAIN ALONG the ancient caravan trail, and the land grew empty. The foraging parties of Corvus would find nothing to glean here, for Karnos had already stripped the country bare in preparation for the siege, and the local people had fled their farms rather than starve. What had once been well-tilled farmland was now bare and sere, and scattered houses lay empty to the rain and snow.

And finally the city itself, the centre of the winter world, a subject of conversation in every wineshop from Sinon to Minerias.

Machran had always been a crowded city, even before the siege, but with the addition of the refugees who had followed their retreating spearman rather than live in their own occupied cities, the condition of the place had deteriorated. What open spaces that existed within the walls had over the weeks been transformed from parkland and gardens to shanty-towns, and thousands lived in cobbled together shacks packed into every space available.

The first deaths had begun. Not the normal everyday passing of the old and the very young, but deaths caused by sickness and exposure. The old died as they always had, but they died in greater numbers, unable to afford food or firewood at the inflated prices now soaring all over the city. The Kerusia had tried to stamp out profiteering, and hanged the worst offenders from a gallows newly erected near the Amphion, but a thriving black market existed in the Mithannon and was too widely patronised to be shut down.

The Kerusia met infrequently now, and when it did there was little Karnos asked of them that they did not agree to. A council of older men with their wisdom and their insight might be a fine thing in time of peace, but in wartime hope withered in the old more quickly than the young.

In most respects the city was ruled by himself and Kassander, with help from Murchos and Tyrias. Due legal process was quietly set aside for the duration, and the edicts of the quartet went unquestioned, backed up as they were by all the fighting men of the city.

The ground barley and oats that were held in the city granaries were doled out once a week in the open area around the Amphion where the assembly had usually been convened in happier times. Now it was a fight to keep the hungry people in line, and the gravelled walkways were becoming ever more constricted, hemmed in by the jerry-built slums of the refugees from Arkadios.

The ground in the Avennan Quarter had always been low-lying, and soon it became infamous for the miasma which hung around it, the effluent from thousands of people living more or less in the open, squatting to relieve themselves wherever they could find a quiet corner.

Karnos went everywhere in a nondescript box chair now, borne by four of his most trusted slaves. When he walked on the streets openly he would not get a hundred paces before some woman would be holding her sick baby up to him and shrieking. So he went through the streets of Machran – his city – looking out from behind a twitching curtain while the slaves negotiated a way through the febrile crowds, aided by a file of spearmen who were unafraid to use their shields to bowl the stubborn or bloody-minded out of the way.

He watched as day by day the great capital of the Macht, with its towering marble buildings and soaring domes, became a cesspool of the desperate and the wicked. Little could be done about public order, because the spearmen were needed on the walls – even so, they had put out two major fires in the last week.

He climbed out of the box-chair in front of his house, and Pollo was waiting for him, slamming the heavy doors behind him, and shutting out the close-packed chaos of the streets outside. Like water, the people seemed to gather in the hollows of the city in preference to the hilltops, and the Kerusiad Hill was quieter than the districts around the Empirion and the Amphion.

As for the Mithannon, it had become a law unto itself, and gangs were operating there with relative impunity. Not the old, well-established street-tribes of Machran, but new, disorderly, vicious bodies of desperate men who would not pick up a weapon to defend the walls, but would fight to maintain control over the few wretched alleyways they considered theirs to rule.

No doubt that was where Sertorius and his henchmen were now.

The three had broken out of the villa the day after they had arrived and had disappeared into the vastness of Machran. There was no point in trying to find them again; they would fit well into the anarchy prevailing in the Mithannon. Karnos was glad they were gone, in a way that made him feel ashamed. He had wanted the three of them dead, for the brute animals that they were, but his own part in the death of Rictus's wife left him with dirty hands. He did not feel he had the right to sit in judgement over anyone anymore, no matter what Kassia said.

He was not the only one, either. Phaestus had joined his family in a rented villa further down the hill, and Karnos had not spoken to him since the day after his arrival in the city. He was failing fast, at any rate, coughing his lungs out of his mouth piece by piece. Antimone's wings beat over him now, and from what Philemos had told Karnos, the old man did not seem to mind. He had led a blameless life, but had ended it with one brutal act, and seemed to feel that his painful death was punishment for it.

We all think more and more in terms of death and the gods these days, Karnos thought. We flick out our libations and make light of it when we have wine inside us and the wolf is far from the door, but break down our world a little, let us glimpse the eyes watching us from beyond the firelight, and we call on the gods like children wailing for a parent.

"Any trouble?" he asked Pollo automatically.

"No, master. The guard's day shift was just relieved. There is nothing to report."

Twice in the last fortnight, prowling mobs had sallied up the hill looking for the house of Karnos, to let him know just how much they resented his mishandling of the city's administration. Twice, Machran spearmen had beaten them back, and killed several of their own citizens in the process.

Law and order, Karnos thought. In the end it all comes down to who has the biggest stick.

"Have we visitors?"

"Master Philemos is here, and the lady Kassia is waiting for you. Polemarch Kassander sent word by runner that he will be here for dinner."

"Dinner!" Karnos laughed. "Very well. Thank you, Pollo."

He looked in on Rictus's children. They had a suite of rooms at their disposal, and he had hired a quiet, middle-aged Arkadian woman to look after the youngest.

She was kneeling on the floor now with the little russet-haired girl, Ona, and the two of them were assembling wooden blocks in front of a meagre fire.

For weeks now, the child had withdrawn from the world. She cried silently night and day, and would speak to no-one except her sister, but would become absorbed at the sight of a trinket or crude toy, crooning over it for hours.

The room was warm, at least, and there were a couple of lamps burning. He met the eyes of the nurse and shook his head when she made to lift the little girl for him to look at, then walked past the doorway without a sound, feeling like a thief in his own home.

Rian, Rictus's beautiful eldest daughter, was in the inner courtyard, sat on a bench with a blanket round her shoulders. Philemos stood in front of her, chattering away. He was quite a talker when he got going, Philemos. Karnos liked the lad; he had courage, though he would never be physically formidable, and he was clearly besotted with Rian.

Karnos stood silently behind a pillar and watched

the pair of them. Rian's skin was pale as a hawthorn bloom, and her ordeal had brought out the exquisite bones of her face. Sadness made her features even finer. Philemos had told Karnos of their journey to Machran, and he knew there was a strength in Rian that matched that of her dead mother.

You had a fine family, Rictus, Karnos thought. You should have kept out of all this, stayed in the hills and left your spear by the door. How could a man not be happy with what you had?

Rian looked up and saw him there. Philemos paused in mid flow, and gave her his hand. They came towards him side by side, and Karnos suddenly realised that the affection was not all one way.

It was Kassia who had drawn their eyes. He could smell her perfume as she came up behind him and slid her arm through his.

"The master of the house returns. How went the day, Karnos?"

He set his hand on hers, smiled at Philemos and Rian.

"It goes much better now than it did. What say you we all take a seat by the fire, and I'll tell you about it?"

TWENTY-THREE
MOON OF WRATH

THE FORAGING PARTY was two hundred strong, strung out along two pasangs of track, its column broken up by lumbering waggons and the braying stubbornness of a mule train. At its head a knot of horsemen rode with their cloaks pulled up over their heads, and the tall Niseians plodded below them in gaunt doggedness, their coats staring and as muddy as the harness of their masters.

"Old Urush here is near the end of his rope," one of them said in Kefren, patting the corded neck of his mount. "It's been nothing but yellow grass and parched oats for him these three weeks past."

"The Macht eat horses," another said. "They think nothing of it. How can a race pretend to civilization when they will eat a horse?"

"You might be glad of a taste of it ere we're done," a third said, a grin splitting the golden skin of his long face. "Ardashir, what say you?"

Their leader reined in and held up one long-fingered hand. "Shoron, you have good eyes – look south to where the track goes round the spur of the hill, maybe seven pasangs."

"I can't see a thing. The rain is like a cloud in this country."

"Wait a moment, it will shift – there. You see?"

The Kefren called Shoron dug his knees into the withers of his horse and raised himself up off the saddle. He shaded his eyes as though it were a summer day.

"Mot's blight, that's infantry, a column marching this way. I count... blast the rain. Maybe five thousand – the column's at least a pasang long. Could be more."

"Bless your sight, Shoron," Ardashir said. He looked back at the long train of horsemen and waggons and mules behind him. His mount picked up his mood and began to lumber impatiently. He hissed at it. "Easy, Moros, you great fool." He shook his head.

"It's no good. We must leave the waggons – even infantry can outmarch the damn things. Bring the mules along. We must pick up the pace and get back to the city. Arkamosh, head back down the column and tell the rest. Break off back the way we came. Make all speed."

"I thought we had all the Macht beaten or penned up in the city," Shoron said.

"They are a stubborn people," Ardashir replied. "Defeat does not come easy to them."

* * *

THE MEN AT the head of the infantry column saw a fistful of horsemen in the distance, half hidden by the rain; they disappeared over the crest of a hill and were gone. The rain turned icy, and the day closed in on them. Steam rose from the men tramping along in their armour. Their shields bore the *alfos* sigil of Avensis, and further back in the column, the *piros* sigil of Pontis. They marched in their stubborn thousands, their faces set towards the north, and the siege-lines of Machran.

"EMPTY YOUR POCKETS, gentlemen. Let's see what we've all brought to the pot," Sertorius said.

The gang about the battered table muttered and did as they were told, like hulking children obeying a schoolmaster. Onto the burn-scarred wood fell scraps of root vegetables, a rind of salted meat, cheese blue with mould and some crusts of flatbread, hard as the wood of the table itself. A pause, and Sertorius ran his eyes over them one by one. A second shower of scraps followed, much like the first.

"Now the other. Don't hold back, brothers – we are all in this together now."

There was a clinking little waterfall of coin. Bronze obols for the most part, but there were threads of silver in it, and at the end Bosca grinned yellow in his beard and set a single gold obol atop the pile. There was a silence as the other men about the table looked at it.

"Bosca, how in the world?" Sertorius began.

"I ventured up Kerusiad Hill last night, boss, and a fine-looking lady gave me this to escort her home."

"You fuck her?" Adurnos asked. A professional enquiry, nothing more.

"She was older than my mother, and hardly a tooth in her head."

"He did, then," Sertorius said, and the table broke into laughter.

People walking by the group of men at the crossroads stopped and stared a moment at the mirth, then walked on hurriedly.

They were gathered together under a tattered cloth awning in the front of what had been a wineshop. But the shop had been looted and burnt out weeks ago, and was now little more than a shell, a fitting base of operations for Sertorius's new venture in Machran.

He had seven men under him now, a tight-knit gang who had all been strangers to the city until the siege. Apart from Adurnos and Bosca, there were a pair of brothers from Arkadios, and three Avennan soldiers who had pawned their armour for food long ago and were now intent only on avoiding starvation, as the siege drew near its end.

Food, or the procurement of it, was what obsessed them all, as it did every person still alive within the walls. The grain-dole had been halved, and was barely enough to keep a child standing, let alone a full grown man. Antimone was hovering over the city now, waiting for the end. There were wild-eyed prophets who haunted the shanty-towns and swore that they had seen her gliding on black wings around the dome of the Empirion at night.

There was no longer any wood to be spared for burning the dead, and the corpses were tossed over the walls each morning by details of men who were paid in bread. Women were selling themselves for a crust, offering their children to strangers for some morsel that would keep the life in them another day.

Lurid rumours of cannibalism ran through the Mithannon, but Sertorius for one did not put much stock by them. There were still rats to be had, two obols apiece, and enterprising archers had started to shoot down the crows and ravens that circled the city as though it were one vast carrion pit. They were not such good eating, but they kept the life in a man.

Sertorius lifted up the gold obol, and clapped Bosca on the shoulder. "You see this, boys? Right now we would pay this for a boiled chicken, or a half skin of wine. But this here means something. We get clear of this shithole, and this piece of gold is worth a horse, or some cattle, or a slave. We got to remember that, if we're to come out of this smiling."

"I'd rather have the chicken," one of the Arkadians said.

"Right now we all would. But think on it, lads – there's houses up on the Kerusiad that are stuffed with these. When the whole thing turns to ratshit, we all have to stick together, and think of the future. One day very soon, that Corvus is going to come in over the walls, and when that happens, we'll be ready. There will be a shower of gold for those who keep their heads, and maybe other things too." His face hardened. "I hear tell that Phaestus, the old bastard, is still alive, and living in comfort in a house not far from Karnos's."

"Fucker," Adurnos said with feeling.

"And we know where Karnos's house is, don't we? He's the richest bastard in the city – think what he has stowed away up there."

"That little black-haired bitch," Bosca said, running his hand through his matted beard. "By Phobos, boss, I'd die a happy man if I could get a cock in her before I go."

Sertorius brought a fist down on the table. "There you are, then. We wait this out, boys, steer clear of the other crossroads-gangs and keep our heads down. Then, when the big show begins, we make our way up to the Kerusiad, settle some old scores, and fill our pockets. We play this right and the whole thing can end happy. Are you with me?"

Around the table, the men growled in agreement.

THERE WAS HUNGER on the other side of the walls also. The supply waggons trundled in ceaselessly from the east, but there was never enough to go round, and the men in the various camps of Corvus's army grew restless.

Desertions had begun, conscript spearmen who had had enough and were sick of the tented lines, the huddled campfires, and the persistent hunger. This was not how they had imagined war.

Corvus toured the camps with an escort of Dogsheads, and Ardashir's Companions patrolled the stockade-lines ceaselessly to deter those who had had enough from putting their discontent into action, but despite the arrival of fresh levies from some of the eastern cities, there was a growing disquiet in the army, a feeling that their general might have miscalculated.

Rumours flew abroad like crows – Maronen had rebelled, and the uprising had been put down by its garrison only after a bloody battle that had seen the streets run red. Hal Goshen and Afteni were simmering with discontent, and reinforcements meant for the army surrounding Machran had been diverted to reinforce their garrisons.

Most unsettling of all, there were scattered reports that the Avennan League had recovered from its mauling of the year before, and was now assembling an army for the relief of Machran. It was already on the march, camp gossip said. Soon Corvus would be caught between two fires, and the besieger would find himself outnumbered and surrounded.

"There is truth in some rumours," Corvus said. He stood in front of the map table with his father's black cuirass gleaming dark and menacing on its stand behind him. In front of the table stood all the senior officers of the army, except one.

"I have had word from Ardashir this evening. He's in the hills twenty pasangs to the south of our lines, a foraging trip with two hundred of the Companions and a train of waggons." Corvus let his strange bright eyes range over the silent men standing before him. Rictus was there, hollow-cheeked and lean as a winter wolf. Beside him stood Fornyx, and then Teresian, one-eyed Demetrius, dark Druze, and Parmenios, not so plump as he had been, and wearing armour now like the rest.

"It would seem our friends in the League have used the winter months to some advantage. They have taken heart, and rebuilt an army of sorts. That army is even now marching to the relief of Machran."

The men he faced said nothing, but stared at him. There was no speculation; there were no questions. They had been at their trade too long for that. Corvus smiled at them, his white face shining like a bone.

"It will be here in the morning."

Now they did stir. Frowning, Rictus spoke up. "How many?"

"Ardashir reckons on some seven thousand, all spears."

"The defenders will sally out, when they get wind of this," Demetrius grunted. "Even if they're half-dead with hunger, they will come out."

"Yes, they will," Corvus said. "And therein lies our hope." He leaned over the map table. Once, it had been covered with maps of the entire eastern Harukush, with cities dotted over it like cherries, blobs of red wax with ancient names. Now there was one large sheet of paper, the corners held down with empty winecups, and drawn across it were the outlines of Machran's walls.

It has all come down to this, Rictus thought, looking down on the map. One lone city, and tomorrow: one single day. Like the point of a spearhead.

Corvus met his eyes, and grinned. He seemed to be thrumming with barely suppressed energy; there was almost a gaiety about him. Always, he seemed happiest when on the cusp of great events, be they good or bad.

"Take a look at our lines, gentlemen. We're spread thin, to contain the city. That job is done. After tomorrow it will not matter any more, one way or the other. So I intend to consolidate the army once more, but only to make a fresh division of it."

They raised their heads and looked at him, puzzled. His hand skittered over the map.

"Druze, you will abandon your camp on the Mithos, and bring your command back here, to the main body. Teresian, you will take your morai south, to join with Demetrius. Ardashir will concentrate the Companions on you as well. Rictus, you will take your Dogsheads –" he raised his head. "How many have you trained up now?"

"Six hundred."

Demetrius's face darkened. "That's why Teresian and I have understrength morai – we've been leaking our best men to Rictus and Fornyx for weeks. Every bastard wants to get himself one of those red cloaks."

"I want the Dogsheads opposite the South Prime Gate," Corvus said, cutting short any further exchange. "When Karnos sallies out, it will be from there, to meet up with the army marching north. Rictus, you will meet him, and drive him back into the city. That is your job. Demetrius, Teresian, you will each detach a full mora to Rictus's command."

Both marshals straightened at that. "Corvus," Teresian began.

Corvus held up a hand. "We do not vote on these things, brother. Those are my orders." He turned to Druze.

"You, my friend, will also detach a thousand of your Igranians to help Rictus. You will then take command of the reminder, plus the other two morai we have here in this camp, and you will work with Parmenios and his machines."

Druze looked thoughtfully at the little man who was Corvus's secretary, now clad in a linen cuirass reinforced with bronze scales. It was ill-fitting, made for a taller man. But Druze only nodded. "I am with child to finally see these things you've made in action, Parmenios. Will you join me on the wall?"

Parmenios met Druze's black eyes. "I will be supervising the advance of my command from the rear. I am not a soldier."

"Well, we're agreed on something then," Druze said, and winked at him.

"I will be with Demetrius and Teresian and the Companions, south of Rictus's positions," Corvus said. "I will meet the relief army and defeat it, and then turn around and help Rictus's command force an entry to the city." He watched the men about the table. They were all staring at the outline of Machran on the map as though picturing to themselves the blood and chaos of the morrow.

"If you have questions, brothers, I'll listen to them."

"Not a question, but a fact," Fornyx said. He stared at Corvus with undisguised hostility. "If you are defeated by the relief army, then Rictus's

command will be utterly destroyed – it cannot
retreat."

"I'd best not be defeated then," Corvus said.

THAT NIGHT THE army abandoned its camps to the
west and north of the city, the men leaving their
tents standing and the campfires burning behind
them. They marched in quiet columns through the
darkness, following the lines of the stockades that
ringed the city. They carried only the arms and
armour they would be needing in the morning, skins
of water, a few dry flatbreads to gnaw on before the
sun came up.

The position of the army and Corvus's plans for
it had been disseminated to all centurions, and it
filtered down to the men in the long files in whispers
as they marched. Slowly, the knowledge seeped
through the army that this was the end. In the
morning they would either take Machran, or they
would face utter defeat. But one way or another the
long siege would be over.

"THE RUMOURS ARE true, then?" Kassia demanded.
She clasped her hands together, knuckles as white
as her face.

"They are true." Karnos kissed her. "Parnon
must have the oratory of Gestrakos. A boy from
his column made it through the lines yesterday. The
League army will be before the walls in a few hours.
When the sun comes up, we will open the gates and

go out to meet it. Corvus will be caught between us like a nut for cracking."

The light in her eyes faded. "You're going out with them? I thought Kassander –"

"I will be with those men, Kassia. I would have it no other way."

She leaned against him and buried her head in his chest. "There is no need for it – what is one more man?"

"I have been hiding in a box-chair for weeks now, afraid to walk the streets of my own city, Karnos, the Speaker of Machran. But I am also a citizen of this place. I am entitled to carry a spear in its defence."

Kassander appeared in the doorway. "Karnos!" he stopped short at the sight of his sister in Karnos's arms.

"Kassia, for God's sake leave him alone – you can kiss him all you want after you're married. Karnos, we must go. The morai are assembling down at South Prime."

"You go on, Kassander. I have one or two things to clear up here."

"Well, make it quick – it's two hours until sunrise." He disappeared from the doorway, and was back again two seconds later. He clanked into the room, already in full armour with his helm in the crook of his arm. He bent over Kassia and kissed her on her forehead. "You be safe, sister."

"Look after him for me, Kassander."

Kassander snorted. "He's big and ugly enough to do that for himself. Karnos, hurry!" He was gone again.

"You might have wished your brother well too, you know," Karnos said with a smile.

"He knows me, and all that I wish him, Karnos."

"Come with me." He took her by the hand. "I want your help with something."

The long room, with the cabinet of Framnos at one end. Every lamp in the house had been lit, and the household were all up and about though it was still the middle of the night. Pollo was there, and all the household slaves. In a corner Rian stood with Ona at her side, and by them was Philemos. He wore a soldier's cuirass.

The cabinet door was open, and the Curse of God that had belonged to Katullos stood within like some icon of shadow. Karnos lifted it from its place and held it out to Kassia.

"Help me put it on."

She was reluctant to touch it, but as he settled it over his shoulders, she clicked shut the black clasps that held the halves of it together, and pulled down the wings that settled snug into place over his collarbones.

Karnos exhaled. The cuirass seemed to settle on him. He was no longer fat, and the black stuff of the armour closed in against his torso and gelled there, a black hide matching the contours of his chest perfectly.

"Now you are a Cursebearer at last," Kassia said. There were tears in her eyes.

He gripped her arm a moment, and stepped forward to the table upon which the rest of his panoply lay. A plain bronze helm, a shield emblazoned with the sigil of Machran, a spear, and a curved drepana in a belted scabbard. But he did not touch these, taking up instead a small iron key.

He walked over to Pollo, and set the key in the old

man's slave-collar. With a click, he loosened it, and carefully took it from his neck.

"You are free, my friend. I am only sorry I did not do it sooner."

Pollo rubbed his throat. He looked down on Karnos like a stern father. There was a gleam in his eye, though his face never changed.

"I was never a slave in this house," he said.

Karnos gave him the key. "Free them all, Pollo – they can come or go as they please. I will own no more slaves."

Something like a smile crossed Pollo's face. "You have grown, Karnos."

Karnos tapped the side of his black cuirass. "I thought I had shrunk."

The two men stood looking at one another. Now that Karnos had become thin and gaunt they could almost have passed for father and son.

"I shall be here when you return," Pollo said. "This is where I belong."

Karnos nodded.

He turned to Philemos and the children of Rictus. "Stay here. The streets will not be safe – better to stay behind stout walls tomorrow, whatever happens."

"I'm coming with you," Philemos said, and Rian clutched at his arm.

"You are needed here," Karnos told him. "Stay in my house, and look after those you love. You will do more good here than in a spearline." He half-smiled. "That is my order, as Speaker of Machran."

Then he went back to the table, and set the bronze helm on his head.

* * *

THE SUN BEGAN to rise, and with the dawn a stillness fell across the city. The walls were lined with spearmen of Machran and Arkadios and Avennos, and gathered together in the square within the South Prime Gate a mass of spearmen, thousands strong, had formed up and stood silently, looking at the grey lightening of the sky.

On the blasted plain before the walls, the army of Corvus formed up, massing to the east and south of the city. They stood in ordered ranks, waiting like their foes within.

And over the hills to the south a third army came into view. It shook out from column into line of battle, and as the sun cleared the Gosthere Mountains to the east, so the men who marched in its ranks took up the Paean, the death hymn of the Macht, and the sound of it rolled over the plain and filled the air like the thunder of an approaching storm.

TWENTY-FOUR
ANGER OF THE GODS

ARDASHIR HUMMED LIGHTLY under his breath, a cradle-song, he had learned back in the Empire. The tune came to him now and again, on sleep or waking, and reminded him always of a warmer world, of blue skies and heat shimmering across yellow fields. It seemed like a dream from another life, but there was comfort in it.

The horses of the Companions shifted and pawed at the ground restlessly. They were on the left of a line extending just under two pasangs, facing south across the vast brown bowl that had once been the famed fertile hinterland of Machran. To their front, the army of the Avennan League was approaching, a line of bronze shields which the rising sun caught and set alight in sudden, blazing ripples of yellow light. Ardashir looked at the sky. At least there would be sunshine today, something to give colour and warmth to this drab country.

Corvus sat his horse beside him, his banner-bearer behind him. The leader of the army had doffed his tall helm with its flowing white crest, and was smiling, the light catching his eyes and kindling in them a violet flame. He looked today more like a fine-boned Kefren than one of the heavy, stolid Macht. His mother's bones in him, Ardashir thought. He must have his father's spirit.

Corvus turned to him as though he had caught the thought. "Good hunting, brother," he said.

The Macht spearmen to their right had taken up the Paean, the men of Teresian and Demetrius's morai booming out the ancient song in time with their kinsmen across the way. It stirred the blood, a dirge which was nonetheless a challenge to battle.

The horses in the ranks of the Companions knew the sound, and began to prance and nicker under their riders. They were ill-fed and overworked, but still they had the Niseian blood in them, that of the finest warhorses ever bred, and the loom of battle made them sweat and stamp where they stood. The brightly armoured Kefren riders spoke to them and called them by their names. Soon they would be let loose on the singing men drawing nearer minute by minute.

Ardashir turned to his left. Shoron had his lance in one hand, his reins in the other, and a bronze horn hanging from his cuirass.

"You think you'll have enough spit to blow that thing?" Ardashir asked him, grinning.

"I'll blow it in your ear and let you be the judge."

"Good hunting, Shoron."

"Good hunting."

Corvus rose up in his saddle, balancing on his knees. He turned right and waved his arm. "Xenosh – the signal. Give it now."

Behind him his banner-bearer lifted up the streaming raven-flag and moved it forward and back.

A moment where nothing happened, but then a series of orders rapped out through the ranks of the Macht spearmen. Centurions in transverse helms moved forward of the main line, raised their spears, and bellowed to their centons.

The commands of Teresian and Demetrius began to move, three thousand heavy infantry. The Paean sank a little as they started out, and then rose up strong again, the beat of the song marking their footfalls. The phalanx moved out to meet the challenge of the men approaching from the south, who outnumbered them better than two to one.

"The anvil is on its way," Corvus said. "Brothers, we are the hammer."

ALMOST SIX PASANGS away, the defenders of the East Prime Gate were craning their necks to watch what was going on to the south, when someone shouted out in astonishment.

Their attention shifted to the enemy troops along the Imperial road. These were not yet advancing, but behind them something else was. Looming up out of the early light came six huge towers, the rumble of their progress audible even on the walls of the city. Each was the height of ten tall men or more, topped with battlements, and encased in hides of all colour and hue. And they were moving on wheels.

Perhaps two hundred men drew each tower, and there were more pushing from behind.

As the six behemoths reached the lines of Druze's men, so the infantry moved forward with them. On the towers of the city, crews began to crank back the immense bows of the ballistae.

AT THE SOUTH Prime Gate, a centurion shouted down to the waiting centons and morai below.

"The enemy is moving out to engage the League army!"

Kassander was walking through the waiting ranks of men. "This is it, lads," he said calmly, "Move out nice and quick, but don't bunch up in the gateway. Form up on your centurions outside."

Then he bellowed at the men in the gatehouse. "Open the gates! Machran, we are moving out!"

The gates swung screeching on their ancient hinges, pushed by straining soldiers. Kassander went to the head of the lead centon and raised his spear. The troops of Machran and Arkadios and Avennos began to follow him out of the gates, close on four thousand men in full armour.

Karnos was in the third mora. His heart was thumping high in his chest as he shuffled forward, and as the pace picked up he began to march, keeping his spear snug against his side to avoid entangling the man next to him. No-one was talking now, and every man had that hard, distant stare which comes at the onset of battle. They could hear the Paean being sung by the formations out on the plain, and deeper yet, the low rumble of thousands of horses.

The Companion Cavalry of Corvus' was on the move.

"STAND FAST," RICTUS said, raising his voice to be heard. "Hold your positions until I give the word."

He was standing out in front of the Dogsheads, as were all his senior centurions. His men were assembled in an arrowhead. The leading ranks were all red-cloaked mercenaries, trained up by the original Dogsheads over the preceding weeks until they were deemed worthy of the colour.

Behind them were the morai on loan from Teresian and Demetrius, a mixture of veteran spearmen and recent conscripts, though the distinction between the two of them had faded with the duration of the campaign. And on their flanks, hanging back like scavengers, were hundreds of Igranian skirmishers.

Fornyx had the left, Valerian the right. Kesero stood close by Rictus, holding aloft the ancient banner of the Dogsheads, entrusted to Rictus by Jason over twenty years before. Jason, whose son was now leading two thousand heavy cavalry out to the east of the approaching League army, and dropping off centons of horsemen as he went. Whatever plan he had for dealing with the League forces, Rictus was not privy to it.

The city garrison was still pouring out of the South Prime Gate and spreading out in a ragged line. Rictus counted the sigils, and nodded to himself. No surprises there. Karnos was taking half the garrison out on this sally, risking all for the opportunity to link up with the League morai. He would have done the same himself.

"I never saw such a complicated fucking battlefield," Kesero said, his voice hollow inside his helm. "Look, Rictus: Parmenios's infernal machines are on the move. I had a bet with Valerian he'd never get them past the wagon park."

Maybe five pasangs away, the tops of the siege towers could be seen over the city walls. They ground forward like sullen titans, and now Rictus could make out motes of fire sailing through the air towards them.

"They've set light to the ballista missiles. They're going to try and burn them down."

"Phobos," Kesero said. "I'm glad I'm standing on my own feet and not cooped up in one of those damn things."

"Look sharp, Kesero," Rictus said, as he walked up and down the line, peering this way and that. "Nearly time."

He took his place at the apex of the arrowhead. He was not quite himself, not yet; the strength he had lost had not been regained.

I don't heal as fast as I used to, Rictus thought.

He could not help but wonder how many more days like today he had left in him.

Over half the Machran morai were now outside the walls and in formation, maybe two thousand men formed up in line, and two thousand more still inside the gate, pushing through.

"Brothers," Rictus said loudly, "Remember your drill. Watch the man in front. Keep together, and don't think about anything else than what's ahead of you. Other battles are being fought around us, but for now all you have to think about is this one.

"To those of you who wear the scarlet in war for the first time today, do not disgrace it, either in the thick of the fight or afterwards. The colour has been worn by both good men and bad for centuries, but it has never been worn without courage."

He raised his spear. "*Forward!*"

To THE SOUTH of the Dogsheads, the spearline of Teresian and Demetrius was the first portion of Corvus's army to make contact. The Paean was snuffed out as they crashed into the morai of the Avennan League, three thousand men in a compact phalanx in a head-on collision with seven thousand others. The appalling clatter of the impact carried clear across the plain to the walls of the city.

To the east of this clash, Corvus was leading the Companions at a fast canter round the enemy flank. Every time he raised his hand, the centon next to him would peel off from the main body and remain behind, reining in their horses and stabbing their lances into the ground alongside them as if they meant to be there for some time. Then the Kefren riders swung their deeply curved compound bows off their backs, already strung, and began fishing for arrows from the quivers hanging at their thighs.

The overlapping morai on the eastern flank of

Teresian's spears had begun to move in on the flank to roll up the enemy line, but they hung back at the sight of Corvus's cavalry flashing past. Periklus of Pontis jogged forward of the hungry advance. The men at the front could see only that they were about to outflank their foes, and it took him several minutes of shouting, grabbing centurions, and banging his spear on the shields of the file-leaders before they came to a ragged halt, the open flank of the enemy right in front of them, as inviting a sight as any spearman on a battlefield could wish for.

But the men on the outside of the formation had seen the cavalry, and were turning to meet it. The right wing of the League forces curled in and then out again, a great swirl of close-packed men. Orders were shouted and then countermanded. The lines within the formation began to merge. File-closers found men behind them, and file-leaders looked over their shoulder to see strange faces there, their own file dislocated by the momentum of the confusion.

And then the first arrows came raining down on them.

THERE WAS NO dust to cloud the air, and the ground was cold and firm for the horses. Corvus cantered two lengths ahead of the rest of his cavalry, trailed by his banner-bearer and Ardashir. He looked back quickly and saw the growing confusion of the League right wing; that end of the line had bunched up and halted, the senior officers bellowing at their men, the first casualties slumping in the press with arrows in their necks.

"Pick up the pace, brothers!" he shouted in Kefren, the language of the Great Kings. The remaining Companions broke into a gallop, the big Niseians rocking under them like boats on a stiff swell. He still had some fourteen hundred cavalry following after him like a great thundering cloak of flesh and bronze trailing across the plain. He was in the rear of the League line now, a pasang from the file-closers. The Kefren on their massive warhorses leaned forward in their saddles and braced their lances on their shoulders, following the slight figure and his raven banner at their head.

DRUZE WIPED THE sweat off his face and exchanged a grin with the man next to him. It was close-packed in the confines of the tower, and the massive structure creaked and rumbled under them. They were in the belly of a beast, a rancid darkness stinking of green hides and pitch and newly sawn wood. The whole structure lurched, and the men inside fell against each other, swearing and wide-eyed as hunted deer.

"This ain't no way to go to war," Druze's neighbour said.

"Make way there, lads – I'm going to puke," another snapped out.

There was a massive crash full on the front of the tower. Druze leapt back instinctively as the broad blade of a ballista bolt smashed through the wooden ramp in front of his nose. Sparks and gledes spattered into the interior with it, and men began stamping them out feverishly. The reek of burning was added to the other stinks and men began to cough and heave for breath.

"Phobos help us – the thing's on fire!" someone wailed.

"It's just the hides on the front," Druze said. "Stand still, you fucking girls. "Show these westerners how Igranians can take the pain. We'll be on the walls before you know it."

They stood in the lurching darkness as the smoke rose around them, blind men in a box. There were three stories to the towers, and fifty men on each, packed as tight as arrows in a quiver.

The tower halted. To its front the wood was thumped and rattled as unseen missiles cascaded against it, and there was the crunch and splinter as another bolt struck the side of the structure. This one punched straight through and impaled a man standing by the right hand wall. He screamed and thrashed while his comrades tried in vain to pull him off the great barbed arrowhead transfixing him. Finally he died, held upright like a puppet with only one string.

Panic rose in the dark interior of the tower, a reek as heavy as their sweat.

"Steady, boys," Druze warned. "We get this wrong and we're stepping out into empty air."

There was the sound of a horn-call from outside.

"Now!" he shouted.

Two men cut the ropes holding up the heavy ramp. It swung down with a crash, and the light and cold air of the winter day flooded in.

"On me, brothers!" Druze yelled, blinking madly, advancing blind into the sudden white winter light with his drepana raised. The men poured out of the tower in a torrent of raging faces and upraised iron, intent only on getting out of the panic-stinking darkness of the compartment. Below them the tower rocked and shook, while the men on the lower levels were climbing ladders to follow off the ramp in their turn.

So tall was this contraption of Parmenios's that the ramp had swung down square on the topmost battlements of the tower abutting Machran's East Prime Gate. Corvus's bald-headed little secretary had judged the measurements correctly to within the span of a man's hand, the result of days of observation and calculation. The men on the ropes below had pulled it into perfect position, their determination marked by the trail of bodies leading all the way out of bowshot.

Of the six towers, four had made it to the wall. Two more were standing burning within a hundred paces of the masonry, and screaming men flooded out of them with the bright hungry flames blackening their flesh. But in the four which had survived were six hundred others who were desperate to get out, and who would not be halted. They flooded the tall towers of the East Prime Gate and overran the ballista crews on the battlements, slashing at the hated weapons and tossing the unfortunates who operated them over the edge. There was no quarter asked or given.

The rest of Corvus's forces at the eastern end of Machran had not been idle. They surged forward now in their thousands, bearing hundreds of scaling ladders. Now that the ballista towers had been neutralised, the ladders went up in a forest of timber too thick to be thrown back. But the defenders of Machran did not retreat. They stood and fought on the walls, toppling ladders and skewering Druze's men as they made it to the embrasures. They died hard, fighting for every foot of stone.

FOUR PASANGS AWAY, the scarlet arrowhead of close-packed spearmen that was the Dogsheads broke into a run. The men loped along with spears at the shoulder, each shield covering the man to the left, the tall horsehair crests bobbing on their helms. Rictus was at the apex of that rumbling mass of meat and metal, a conspicuous figure in his black armour. He did not speak – the Dogsheads had dropped the Paean and were now powering forward, so that all six centons of them seemed to be one single huge organism, breathing hard and the sound of their breathing attuned to a kind of rhythm in itself.

In the moment before impact, Rictus saw the ranks of the enemy recoil before him, the line of citizen spears fracturing right in front of the gate. They had never seen a spearline advance like this before, and the redcloaked mercenaries had acquired a fearsome reputation during the course of the siege. Half-starved citizen spearmen of Arkadios and Avennos and Machran itself flinched at the moment of impact, backing in on themselves.

The Dogsheads struck. Rictus lifted his spear clear of the melee in the first moments to keep it from shattering. So great was the pressure of the advancing men behind him that he was propelled into the ranks of the enemy. An aichme broke in pieces upon the breast of his cuirass. Another struck his shield so hard that it penetrated the bronze facing and broke off in the oak beneath. There were snarling, terrified faces inches from his own. One man had lost his helm, and Rictus head-butted him at once, the heavy bronze of his own helm mashing bone and flesh, one eye glaring out of the red ruin before the man went down, lost underfoot.

The Dogsheads kept their formation, a red lance aimed square at the open gateway of the South Prime. Men were trying to push the massive gates closed, but so great was the press of bodies in the gatehouse that it was impossible; they succeeded only in packing the crowd of shouting spearmen tighter.

Here the work began, and the discipline told. The Dogsheads settled in to the fight, choosing their targets, jabbing overhand at helm-slots, glimpses of flesh at the necks of cuirasses. Rictus saw an enemy spearman's arm pierced clean through by the spear of someone behind him. The man jerked his flesh off the aichme and the keen blade sliced him open like a cut of meat, exposing bone.

Blood sprayed through the air, hot and steaming in the cold. Rictus stabbed one man through the eye-guard of his helm, and his own spearhead snapped off as the fellow went down. There was no way to switch to the sauroter, not in that packed mass, so Rictus continued to stab out with the splintered shaft of the spear, grunting as he did so like a man at heavy labour in his fields.

The roar of the othismos rose up, enveloped them all. The struggle in the gate had become a different kind of world, a place of bronze and iron and lacerated flesh, men screaming, men underfoot, men pushing on the armoured torsos of their fellows. It was a dark, sodden universe of carnage.

But it was moving inexorably backwards, into the shadow of the walls. The deep formation of the Dogsheads, all that massive concentration of power, shoved the line of the defenders in on itself. The mercenaries maintained their ranks, while those of Machran disintegrated. The defenders fought bitterly, but they were fighting now as individual men in a mob, and only the brute mass of their numbers held their attackers in place.

And they were dying fast. The Dogsheads had lost scores of their number, the defenders of Machran many hundreds, shunted backwards, stumbling into the press to be trampled and suffocated, or stabbed by the aichmes and sauroters of the attackers. They could not present a coherent front, and the struggle in the gateway became a business, an exchange of lives for space. It was pure and simple killing.

Rictus found himself struggling uphill, and could not quite account for it until his foot slid on the convex bowl of a shield. He was stepping on a mound of the enemy dead, and the Dogsheads were climbing it. The men of Machran were dying where they stood, all training and drill forgotten. They were fighting for themselves, but conscious also that the gates were open wide at their backs, and the way into the city lay open.

They were building a new wall in front of the tall stone of the city, a breastwork of corpses.

The Dogsheads ascended it, their formation growing tighter as they closed ranks over their own dead. The weak winter sun was cut off, and Rictus found himself in shadow. He was inside the gateway itself, and the ancient gates of Machran loomed on either side of him like indifferent totems, their black oak now splashed red and glistening.

"One more!" Rictus shouted. "One more push, brothers!" and he felt behind him the surge of bodies, heard the animal roar of his men as they answered him.

"FORM LINE ON me!" Corvus cried. He held his lance up so the sunlight sparked off it, as though it had flashed out in white flame above his head. His white horsehair crest streamed behind him, and the black horse half-reared as he reined it in.

On either side of him the Companions formed up, wheeling in by centon, extending their ranks to left and right. They formed a line almost a pasang long, two ranks deep, the big horses sliding in next to one another foaming and snorting, their manes like black flags. The armour of their riders glittered as the winter clouds cleared and Araian looked down upon the battlefield.

Before them, the army of the League was closely engaged in the business of destroying the morai of Teresian and Demetrius. The right wing of the League was trying to wheel to meet the challenge of the bow-armed Companions that Corvus had dropped off to harass them, but the main body was committed wholly to the fight in front of it, a raging conflict of close-quarter spearwork.

The file closers at the rear of the line were turning around, and men were running up and down the back of the line frantically, warning their comrades of the sudden appearance of the Kefren cavalry, but the main body of the army was like a fighting dog in the pit, its jaws locked in its opponent's throat. Only death would loosen that grip.

Corvus turned to Shoron. "Brother, sound me the charge."

Shoron shared a look with Ardashir, wet his lips, closed his eyes, and put the horn to his mouth.

Clear and shrill over the battlefield the long ululation of the horn-call rang out; the shrill notes of the call to hunt, a sound heard on battlefields across the lands beyond the sea since the Empire had existed. Now it was ringing out in the heartland of the Macht.

The line of the Companions began to move, fourteen hundred brightly armoured riders on fourteen hundred tall black horses. They broke into a trot and then, as Corvus spurred his own mount, a canter.

The ground seemed to echo with the trembling impact of that mass of horseflesh, and the sound of it rose to challenge every other noise on the battlefield, to be heard even by Rictus and his men fighting in the gateway to the north.

It echoed across the earth. Druze heard it in the midst of the great slaughter at the east gate. It carried clear across the city, so that Sertorius and his men lifted their heads and paused a second to listen as they stood at the foot of the Kerusiad Hill. Kassia and Rian heard it as they stood upon the balcony from which Aise had leaped to her death, and peered out across the teeming bulk of Machran to the battling formations on the plain beyond the walls, wondering what it signified. It did not seem like a sound made by the agency of man. It sounded like the muttered anger of the gods.

The Companions broke into full, tearing gallop, and their lances came down, the wicked points held out at breast-height. Too late, the morai of the League realised what was thundering towards them from the south. Some managed to turn and present their spears; others simply stood and stared at that rolling mass of murder approaching, that black line of death.

The Companions smashed into the Macht battle-line with the impact of a flash-flood. The Niseians had been trained not to flinch from men, but to use their bulk, their iron-shod hooves, their teeth. They were warriors as much as the Kefren who rode them, and their sheer weight and momentum was irresistible.

The charge broke upon the rear of the League army like an apocalypse and broke clear through it, chopping the fighting centons of Avensis and Pontis to pieces.

Hundreds of men were bowled off their feet, and the big horses trampled them into the bare muck of the earth while their riders stabbed out with the long lances, a flickering hedge of darting iron.

Parnon died there, still struggling to make himself heard. The flower of the fighting men of two cities were annihilated in a few minutes. The League army, which had been on the cusp of routing the foes to their front, simply ceased to exist.

Men threw down their shields and tried to squirm out of the press any way they could. Some died fighting, clustered together in stubborn knots and clots, battling back to back. More died without the opportunity to strike a blow, crushed in the deadly space between Corvus's anvil and the hammer he had sent galloping upon it.

The men on the walls of Machran who were able to lift their heads and look south saw a long vast rash of men and horses embroiled in a formless mob, pasangs long: the sun glittering across it, catching spearpoints, the flash and gleam of helms and shields tilted to the sky. And then the teeming crowd opened, and across the plain men were running for their lives, hundreds, thousands of them, heading south away from the walls.

But the horsemen reformed their line and, before them, so did a long battered formation of spearmen. They dressed their ranks, and began to advance north towards Machran to join their comrades fighting and dying in the shadow of the walls, and they were singing as they came.

TWENTY-FIVE
MACHRAN

Something had changed. Some kind of current had gone through the men fighting and dying in the gatehouse of the South Prime, like the hide of a horse twitching at the bite of a fly. Rictus felt it – he had known it before on other battlefields, but so tight and entangled and brutal was the fighting here that it almost went unnoticed.

The packed mass in front of him seemed somehow to ease a little. He heard men shouting – not the wordless baying of the othismos, but some kind of news that travelled through the ranks of the enemy like fire on a summer hillside.

Fornyx was at his side now, brought close by the murderous attrition of the battle. At the beginning of the morning they had been separated by a full centon of men, but those were all gone now.

"The League is in flight, Rictus," he yelled. There

was blood on his mouth and all down his neck, though they were all slathered in it. Impossible to tell until the thing was done whether it was one's own or other men's gore.

"You hear them? Corvus has done it – he's beaten off the relief army."

The pressure slackened. Men were backing away now, the desperation still in them, but with these tidings they knew the beginning of despair. They were fighting automatically now, and hope was leaving their eyes – it was a thing impossible to explain to any man who had not been in the belly of a hard fought battle, but Rictus felt it too.

"Dogsheads!" His voice was a gravel-hard croak. He reversed his broken spear at last to use the sauroter. There were weapons aplenty lying at his feet, but they were all broken. Men were fighting with swords now, but there was little room to swing, and the slashing drepanas were hard to manipulate in the crowded phalanx.

"Dogsheads, on me – advance!"

Fornyx was on his left, Kesero on his right. The Dogshead banner was five feet above their heads, but splashed with blood all the same. Rictus saw Valerian off to one side – he had lost his helm and his mutilated face was streaming blood. All the old veterans of the Dogsheads seemed to have moved up through the ranks and were in the forefront. The newly trained men were good – better than any other spearmen on the field – but they were still not the hardened veterans of Rictus's old command, and they were not bound to him in the way that these men were.

"Same old faces," Fornyx said with a grin. "You just can't get rid of us, Rictus."

"Same old game, brother. One more push, and we're over the hump. Can you feel it?"

The Dogsheads surged forward. Before, it had been like setting their shoulder against a stone wall. Now it was as though they were pushing on a rusted gate. There was movement. The fight shifted, the men of Machran backing away foot by foot, dying with every step. The fearsome crush in the gatehouse lessened.

Then the sun was on their faces again. They were through the gates, into the open square beyond, and Rictus's men were opening out into line, centon by centon. Centurions stood only paces apart, so worn down had their commands become. But there were enough red cloaks to hold one side of the square.

Rictus looked up and saw to his left the white dome of the Empirion rise up out of the maze of streets before him, untouched and inviolate, whilst to his right was the bulk of Kerusiad Hill in the distance, whitewashed villas clinging to it like tiers of swallow's nests. The gates were taken, and behind the Dogsheads fresh morai of spearmen were moving in support.

But the men of Machran were not yet beaten. They reformed on the far side of the square, and began to advance again. They were led by a Cursebearer, whose black armour was like a hole in the sunlight. He raised his spear and shouted for them to advance, and hundreds followed him, roaring.

"We need that bastard dead," Fornyx said. "They see a Cursebearer go down, and I think we'll have them."

The Dogsheads lowered their spears, those who still had them, and charged. They kept their lines intact as they moved, where the enemy hurtling towards them had lost formation, becoming a mob of crazed men in bronze.

But they had momentum. As the two sides crashed into one another the Dogsheads were halted in their tracks by the savagery of the Machran assault, and all up and down the square the thing restarted in earnest.

The struggle in the gatehouse had been bitter; this one verged on insane. As men went down dying they clutched at the legs of their enemies, reached up under the short chitons to tear at their genitals. Rictus had a sandal pulled off his foot and brought his heel down on a snarling face, then stabbed the sauroter into an eye-socket.

The enemy Cursebearer was almost opposite now, and he left his own line and hurled his spear-butt in the man's face. It clanged off his helm, making him look round. Rictus swung his shield and smashed it into the torso of a soldier opposite, kicked him in the knee-joint and drew his drepana. He stabbed downwards as though it were an oversized knife, not looking to see the damage it did. He hauled it free of quivering meat, trusted Fornyx to finish the job, and lunged into the enemy line, utterly unaware of the animal snarling from out of his own mouth, intent on coming to grips with the man in the black cuirass.

Their shields clashed. The other man stabbed down with his spear-butt and the sauroter point struck the rim of Rictus's shield, clinked off the bronze, and skittered from the surface of his armour. The press had tightened again, and Rictus could not raise his sword. He let go of it, reached up and caught the Cursebearer's spear. The sauroter sliced open his palm, but he was able to wrest it out of the other man's grip. The man was tired. His neck was corded and gaunt under the helm, a big vein pulsing blue in the shadow of the cheek-guard.

Rictus flipped the spear-butt round, the two of them swaying breast to breast in the packed mass of the melee. He looked into the other man's eyes through the helm-slot, felt a strange flash of recognition, and then stabbed downwards, into the man's neck. The sauroter went so deep as to bury the bronze, and the Cursebearer slid bonelessly to the ground.

Something like a wail went up from the Machran men all around. "Karnos is dead, Karnos is dead!" they shouted.

It was the breaking point. The line fell apart, and into the gaps the Dogsheads lunged with methodical professionalism. Men were speared as they turned to flee, tripped up and stabbed before they could get past the reach of the spears, hemmed in by the mass of men boiling behind them. The battle in the square disintegrated; in moments, heartbeats, it transformed, became a slaughter.

"Fornyx," Rictus said, panting. "Keep the push on – don't let them reform."

"Are you all right?"

"I'm fine. Go on. I'll catch up."

Fornyx led the Dogsheads up the square with a roar that belied his wiry frame. The Machran defenders were in rout, and the Dogsheads broke formation to take up the pursuit. Behind them came hundreds more of Teresian's and Demetrius's centons, and looking back Rictus saw horsemen in the gateway now as well, the lead elements of Corvus's cavalry.

He bent over and vomited onto the bloodsoaked stones, dropped his shield, and dragged off his helm, gasping for air.

Then he staggered over to the dying Cursebearer lying amid a mound of his own men, the spearshaft protruding obscenely from above his collarbone and his blood running down the black armour in a steady stream.

He knelt down and pulled off the man's helm.

Karnos looked up at him with wide, white eyes, and after a moment, he smiled, blood oozing from his lips.

"Rictus of Isca? Am I dead already?"

"Karnos." The round face was gone. Karnos had become a different man, familiar and changed all the same. A gaunt warrior who wore Antimone's Gift as though he had been born for it.

"You will be soon," Rictus said. He took the dying man's hand, feeling an indefinable sadness. He had not thought much of the silver-tongued slave dealer who had once tried to employ him, but the man who lay before him now was someone else. "You fought well. I did not think you had it in you."

"Rictus?" Karnos's white face twisted into a picture of astonishment. The blood gurgled in his throat. He gripped Rictus's hand until the bones creaked. "But you died, weeks ago. On the wall."

"Almost. I made it off the wall the quickest way I could."

Karnos shut his eyes a moment. "Oh, Phobos, you filthy swine."

"What is it, Karnos?"

"Listen to me." Karnos coughed up a gout of blood, choking on it, and Rictus wiped it from his mouth, leaned close to catch the man's failing breath.

"I have your children in my house. Your children, you understand? I am sorry, Rictus. I sought to use them against you. They are on the Kerusiad Hill."

"My children?"

"Forgive me. Phaestus and I, we thought –"

Rictus's face was a white, bloodstained mask of shock and fury. "My family?"

"You know the house – the big villa with earth-coloured walls. They are there, safe."

"My wife!" Rictus said, his voice rising. "What about my wife? What have you done, Karnos?"

But Karnos was already dead.

THE PANIC SPREAD across the city in waves. Broken remnants of the Arkadians and Avennans were already streaming off the walls, heading for the Mithannon, whist the men of Machran fought on hopelessly.

Their polemarch, Kassander, rallied a dozen centons below the towering dome of the Empirion itself, and led them back into the fray, but Corvus's forces were already in command of most of the Avennan Quarter, and the siege towers had broken the defence to the east, in the Goshen.

Fully half the circuit of the walls had been taken by the enemy or abandoned by the defenders, and more of the besiegers were pouring through the gates by the minute, a tide that seemed unstoppable. The citizens of Machran began flooding north and west, away from the fighting. Tens of thousands of people were on the move in the streets, in places packed as tight as the ranks of a fighting phalanx.

"THE CITY HAS fallen," Sertorius said. "That's it, lads, I'm telling you. The whole thing is about to come crashing around our ears. Bosca, for Phobos's sake, clear a way there – Adurnos, help him."

They were going against the flow, a small determined fistful of men battling against the current of the panicked crowds, clearing a path for themselves with the threat of their drawn swords, and sometimes with the flat of them slapped into someone's face. The streets leading into the Goshen Quarter were a madhouse of screaming women and shrieking children, bloodied men fleeing the lost battle of the walls.

Above them, Kerusiad Hill rose on its crag like a vision beyond the smoke and roar of the streets below. They were under two pasangs from Druze's siege-towers.

"Left here," Sertorius shouted above the din. "Up this way." They turned off the main thoroughfare, and the crowd was less packed. Men and women were trundling handcarts down from the hill piled high with their belongings and wailing children too small to keep their feet. Sertorius led his men against the current of the exodus, feeling the hill rise under him.

"It's not far now," he said. "Phaestus is in that house on the right, up ahead, the one with the yellow roof tiles. We do him first."

"And that little shit of a son he has," Bosca snarled. "I want some fun with him before he goes."

"As long as we make it quick," Sertorius said. "Remember, the real prize is at the top of the hill. And don't forget the slaves – I want them too. They're gold on the hoof, brothers."

The men around him growled in anticipation.

The rented villa had stout doors of iron-studded wood, locked shut against the chaos of the streets. At a nod from Sertorius, Bosca and Adurnos swooped on a family pushing a handcart, tossed the children off the vehicle, and when the man protested beat him down, leaving him a broken bundle in the street with his family shrieking around him.

"Now, lads, after three," Sertorius said.

They crashed the handcart into the heavy doors, running it up with a roar, and the bolt wrenched free of the wood. They whooped happily, and poured inside with drawn swords. A dark-haired man who was in their path stood frozen and was cut down with barely a pause.

"Phaestus! Phaestus, you cheating bastard. It is I, Sertorius, come for you!"

They careered through the house like mad children, kicking over furniture, pawing through drawers and cupboards. Not a lamp was lit in the place; aside from the dead man near the entrance the place seemed deserted.

It was Adurnos who found him, and shouted for the others to join him. They crowded at the door of the room, breathing heavily.

"The fucker got away from us boss," Adurnos said moodily.

Phaestus lay like a wax image on the bed, a blanket drawn up to his chin. His face was white as old ivory. Sertorius leaned over and touched it.

"Cold as a fish. Antimone got to him before we did."

"Let's torch the place," Bosca suggested. "There's not so much as a mouse in it – they've cleared out long since."

"No, no burning," Sertorius said. "I'll not give this son of a bitch a pyre. Let him lie here and rot." He straightened.

"Let's get us that cart again, lads, Karnos's house is just up the hill a ways, and I don't mean to be done out of my fun a second time."

They turned and ran back through the empty house like a dark, flapping gale, a curse spoken by Phobos and given form.

RICTUS WAS EXHAUSTED, but kept going out of pure will. He had thrown away his shield and helm, picked up a discarded drepana, and was fighting his way east through the streets like a salmon wriggling upstream. In his wake followed Valerian. There had been other Dogsheads with him, but they had become separated.

Fornyx was still leading the bulk of the men in the destruction of Kassander's last stand.

There was no other kind of ordered resistance left in the city, but the entire population of Machran appeared to be on the streets, most people trying to make their way north, to the districts Corvus's army had not yet captured. They had no plan in their minds beyond that. Half-crazed by hunger and fear, they had no kind of plan at all.

The red cloak and the Curse of God cleared a path for Rictus, people recoiling from him as he strode along. Or perhaps it was the look on his face. He no longer cared if Machran stood or fell, if it went up in flames and was burnt to ash. He knew only that he had to find out whether Karnos had been speaking the truth. If his family were in this city he would tear the place down brick by brick to find them. He would have struck down Phobos himself if the god had stood in his path.

KASSIA AND RIAN closed the door shut, slid the heavy bolt across and leaned their backs against it.

"Better in here than out there," Kassia said, setting a hand on Rian's shoulder. "The slaves were fools."

"They weren't slaves any more," Rian said. "It was their choice, to stay or go as they wished."

Philemos stood to one side with a short stabbing sword, his soldier's cuirass too big for him. His eyes were red-rimmed. "We'll stay here until things settle down. I can go out and look, later, see what's been going on."

Pollo shook his head. "Young master, do you hear that?"

They went quiet. The agony of the city rose up Kerusiad Hill, people wailing and screaming in their tens of thousands, their feet raising a murmur from the earth.

"That is the sound of a city's fall," Pollo said, and his face gnarled with grief. "Karnos has failed. Have you looked to the east? They brought towers to the walls. But the fighting there is over now – the enemy is inside the city."

He drew a deep breath. "I will abide here, and wait for Karnos. If he is alive, he will return. For the next few days, there is no more dangerous place in the world than the streets outside this door – especially for the women. Ladies, you must trust to these walls."

"My mother wants to leave as soon as it's dark – we have people we know in Arienus," Philemos said. He looked at Rian.

"You are the head of your household now," Pollo told him. "It is for you to decide what is to be done. Your mother must realise that, Philemos."

The boy nodded. "It comes hard. It's new to me."

Rian reached out and took his hand.

Kassia stood with tears running silently down her face, but she managed a laugh. "Listen to us, conjuring up the worst picture we can! Pollo, if ever any two men were going to live through a disaster, then they are Karnos and my brother. They'll be back here, you'll see. Even if Machran falls, those two cannot be kept down."

Pollo nodded gravely. "Lady, I believe you're right."

"So what do we do?" Rian asked. "Sit tight and wait for order to be restored?"

"Yes," said Pollo. From the folds of his snow-white himation he produced a long iron knife. "One more thing – all of us should arm ourselves."

"A kitchen knife will not do much," Kassia said.

"Better than nothing," Rian told her. "Kassia, even if the city is lost, my father's men will be out there. Fornyx and Kesero" – she darted a swift, strange look at Philemos – "and Valerian. The Dogsheads will find us."

"Friends in both camps," Kassia said with a small, bitter smile. "I'm sorry, Rian – I forget sometimes. You have ties to the men outside the walls."

"I have ties within them also, Kassia," Rian said.

CORVUS RODE ACROSS Avennan Square with an escort of Companions. Ardashir was beside him, and thronged throughout the square were hundreds of spearmen from the commands of Teresian and Demetrius. These were too spent to join in the general pursuit careering through the streets of the city.

Many of the men were sitting on their shields with their helms off, mouths hanging open. At the moment, they were too glad to be merely alive to yet feel the triumph of the city's capture. But as Corvus entered the square and took off his helm, they scrambled to their feet, and began to smite their spears on their shields and cheer.

Hundreds of them, perhaps thousands, standing cheering in that great corpse-choked open space, the Empirion rearing up white behind them and the agony of the city a backdrop to their delight. Corvus raised a hand and the cheers redoubled. They began chanting his name. The sound carried across the city in a wave, unmistakeable, crushing the hope out of the last few defenders still fighting despair.

Fornyx pushed through the mass of cheering spearmen. He had his hand on the shoulder of a tall, broad-shouldered fellow who had the sigil of Machran painted on his armour. The crowd of spearmen made way for them, shaking their spears in the tall man's face. He ignored them, walked along as though in some kind of reverie, and only when he stood before Corvus did he look up and seem to snap out of it.

"Corvus," Fornyx said, his face split wide in a grin. "I have a prize for you. This fellow here is named Kassander, and he is the polemarch of Machran. His men laid down their arms at the foot of the Empirion not ten minutes ago. They were the last. I promised them their lives and their freedom, for they fought well. I trust you will respect my promise."

"Gladly, Fornyx," Corvus said. He bent in the saddle and grasped the Cursebearer's hand. "It was well done. I should have done the same thing myself."

He turned to Kassander, who stood stolid and uncaring, though he did look up at the youth on the black horse with a wistful kind of curiosity.

"I am glad to see you alive, Kassander," Corvus said to him. "I have heard you are a good man."

Kassander grunted. He was a picture of carnage, soaked in blood, and he was missing the upper part of one ear. The blood from the sliced flesh had formed a black bar down the side of his neck.

"What of your friend Karnos? Do you know where he might be?"

The question seemed to pierce the fog. Kassander swallowed, looked up at the sky, winter-blue. There was not a cloud to be seen, but Phobos was a pale round wisp high up in it, a ghost with a cold smile.

"Karnos is dead. He is lying here somewhere. Your mercenaries killed him. He wore a black cuirass, but I suppose that will be stripped off him by now."

Corvus's face fell. "That is a pity. There was a time I would have wished him dead, but not now. You and he put up a rare fight, Kassander. I salute you for it."

Kassander turned bloodshot eyes upon Corvus. "The city is yours now, and we are all in your hands. They say that Antimone shows us the hearts of men not only in defeat, but in victory also. Your name will be tied to this victory forever, Corvus, and what you and your men do to Machran now will follow you for as long as there are Macht to remember it."

Corvus nodded. "I know this – it is something I have always known. You need not fear for Machran, Kassander. It will be my capital now, and its people are my people also."

Kassander cocked his head to one side, squinting in the sun. "Are they?"

"We are all one people," Corvus said softly. "We've been fighting amongst ourselves too long."

Kassander rubbed a hand over his face, streaking it with blood. "Then let us put an end to it," he said.

TWENTY-SIX
THE HOUSE ON
THE HILL

THE FIRST CRASHING impact on the door had startled them more than the roar of the city's fall. It was immediate, personal, and on a human scale. Their fear, which had been an ill-defined dread before, now lurched into something closer to terror.

No sound outside, no shouting, nor clamour of a mob. Just the crash on the stout doors of Karnos's house, as though a giant ram were charging it with blind malevolence.

Philemos's mother became hysterical. She and her two young daughters were locked away in a far corner of the house. As Philemos shut the door on them, he heard the sound of furniture being dragged and piled up against it on the inside.

The wide front doors of the house were solid, oak and bronze. Kassia, Rian, Ona, Philemos and Pollo began hauling furniture in their turn, dragging the beautiful couches made by Framnos, Karnos's pride and joy, across the fountain courtyard and wedging them tight against the gate. Now they heard the grunt of men outside, the rattle of wheels on the cobbled street before every crash.

"There are armed men in here!" Philemos shouted. "Come through those doors and we'll cut your throats!"

The only response was a burst of laughter, and then the gates were charged again. The heavy doors moved inwards, and white cracks opened and closed in the black wood.

"Perhaps we should go shut ourselves in different rooms," Kassia said, her face white and bloodless with fear. She was thinking of Aise the night she had arrived, that look in her eye. She could not imagine what had been done to her to make her look like that, but now it was going to happen. To all of them.

Rian stood calmly, a kitchen cleaver in her hand. She hugged Ona close to her.

"You have to try and hide," she told her sister. "Ona, can you find some little space where no-one will find you?"

A timber was smashed free of the doors and skittered across the flagstones of the courtyard.

"Can you do that? I'll come and find you later, I promise."

The child looked at her dumbly, great dark eyes under a mass of red-brown hair.

"I promise," Rian repeated, and her voice quavered on the word.

Ona put her arms around her sister's neck, solemn,

but eerily untroubled. Then she turned and ran away. They could hear her feet pattering through the house. Then there was a moment's silence. Philemos set a hand on Rian's arm. She wiped the tears from her face.

"I wish I had died at Andunnon, with Eunion. We should all have died there together."

"I will not let them touch you," Philemos said fiercely. "I protected you once before, and I will do it again."

The door crashed inwards, the bolt tearing free of the wood.

They stood side by side, four people brought together by some whim of Phobos. A sister, a daughter, a slave and a son.

The doors sprang open, the iron bolt that held them together flying off. The heavy couches grated backwards on the flagstones, their legs splintering. They saw what looked like the bed of a handcart. It was hauled, grating, backwards out of the newly made entrance. Men's voices in the street outside.

They came in, a group of lean, hungry-looking vagabonds, filthy and bright-eyed. Sertorius led them, and as he entered the fountain courtyard Rian shrank backwards in horror and Philemos seemed to stagger. He saw them standing there, and his face stretched in a wide grin.

"What's this, a welcoming committee? People, I am touched! Look at this, lads – don't it make a picture?"

Six other men entered the courtyard in his wake, dusting off their hands and wiping sweat from their faces.

"There's my little black-haired sweetheart. Girl, I have something for you – we all have. I've been saving it since we turned you over to Karnos."

"The other one's not bad either," Bosca said, running his fingers over his mouth.

"I told you there'd be nice pickings in this place, didn't I?"

The men spread out in a crescent. The four people in front of them backed away until their heels were against the lip of the fountain pool.

"Get behind me," Philemos said to Rian.

"There is money in this house," Pollo said loudly. "I can take you to it, save you some time. This is the house of Karnos, remember. He's a powerful man. If you harm us, gentlemen, he will find a way to make you pay for it."

"Karnos is dead, you old fuck," Bosca snarled. "It's all over the city. This Corvus is in charge now. He'd probably thank us for doing his work for him."

"Dead?" Kassia repeated. "Karnos is dead?"

"What's this – are you pining for him, my lovely?" Sertorius smiled. "That's tragic, that is. Let us comfort you in your time of sorrow."

"Enough," Adurnos snapped. "Fucking do it, and leave out the talk, chief."

They moved in like wolves. Pollo advanced to meet them, lashing out with his knife. Adurnos caught his wrist; one of the Arkadians grabbed his other arm. They stretched him like that between them, struggling, until Sertorius stabbed him in the heart. The old man went down without a sound, his beard white as sheep's wool on the stone, his eyes still open.

Two more of Sertorius's men seized Kassia, and ripped the clothes from her back. One held her from behind while the other stripped her, laughing as she kicked and screamed at him.

Philemos stood still with Rian at his side, and behind them the fountain. He held out his sword and waved it back and forth as Sertorius and his men closed in on him.

Sertorius seemed in a high good humour. He stood looking at Philemos with a kind of amused tolerance. "I always knew you had spirit in you, boy – the way you fought for that little morsel behind you, up in the hills. The thing is, you got to learn when to walk away from a fight. Your father should have taught you that before he died.

"You got no more time for learning, now."

Philemos was not looking at him. He was peering over Sertorius's shoulder, at the broken doors behind, and his face was a picture of astonishment. Sertorius frowned, and turned himself.

Two men stood in the tall doorway of the house. They wore chitons and cloaks of scarlet, and one was armoured in the Curse of God. Naked drepanas glittered in their hands and their armour was covered in blood.

"What the fuck?" Sertorius said. His men all turned with him. The two manhandling Kassia released her and she ran to Rian, naked and weeping.

Rian stood with her eyes shining, full of tears.

"Father," she said.

Rictus and Valerian advanced into the courtyard. There was a light in Rictus's eyes that made the seven men in front of him back away.

"Rian?"

She stared brokenly at him. The breath sawed in and out of her as though she had suddenly come out of deep water.

Rictus looked over the men in front of him, saw Philemos.

"Where is my wife?"

Sertorius jerked his head at Adurnos, and the big man began sidling around Rictus with the two Arkadians.

"He raped her!" Rian screamed. "They raped her and she killed herself!" She broke down, sobs tearing out of her throat. "Daddy, they killed her, they killed her. She's dead, she's dead." She sank to her knees.

Rictus's eyes narrowed to slots of pale murder.

"Go left," he said to Valerian, an animal's sound, barely words at all.

"There's better ways to end this, friend," Sertorius said. "What's done is done –"

Rictus leapt forward, his red cloak whirling up around him like a bloody cloud. The drepana leapt in his hand, a flash as swift as a hawk's strike.

One of the Arkadians fell sideways with his throat slashed open. The other swung madly and missed as Rictus side-stepped, catching him off balance. He brought up his knee and slammed it into the man's face, breaking bone. The Arkadian went down.

Big Adurnos charged like a bearded bull, punching Rictus in the mouth and stabbing with his own sword in the same moment.

The blade clicked off the Curse of God. Rictus soaked the blows up, backed away a step with blood running down his chin, and stepped in again. One, two, three flashes of cold iron, the clang as his drepana clashed with Adurnos's sword, and the big man's blade was knocked down. Rictus flicked up the point of the drepana and it ran smoothly into Adurnos's groin.

He stopped, stock still, his mouth open and a look of sheer disbelief on his face.

Rictus twisted the blade and pulled it out and up, and Adurnos's body opened up like a sack full of steaming meat. His insides fell down onto the flagstones of the courtyard with a wet slap. He looked down at them, scrabbling at the great rent in his body as the sight left his eyes, and he toppled.

Valerian had downed one of the Avennans, but the other one, along with Bosca and Sertorius, was pressing him back to the entrance, hacking at him. The remaining Avennan suddenly went down with a bitter cry of pain; Philemos had come up and stabbed him from behind.

Sertorius shouted with fury and turned on the boy.

Rictus shouldered Philemos out of the way, charging into the fight like a scarlet avatar of wrath. Sertorius's sword slid off the black cuirass and Rictus swept his own blade down with a grunt, chopping through Sertorius's arm close to the wrist. He cried out, raised the spurting stump and gripped it with his free hand. "No, no!" he screamed.

The sound distracted Bosca and Valerian stabbed him through the ribs, and as the man folded in on himself he raised his sword and brought it down two-handed, stabbing Bosca at the base of his neck. The drepana sliced through meat and bone. The head fell slack, attached to the body only by strings of sinew and skin and Bosca slumped to the ground, twitching. For a few seconds his eyes rolled in his head, and then he was still.

Sertorius had sunk to his knees, still clutching the stump of his arm. His face was chalk-white.

"The great Rictus!" he said, and managed something like a laugh. "Well, it's something to have met a legend."

Rictus stood panting in front of him, and wiped the blood from his chin. He looked over at Rian. Philemos was holding her in his arms, and she was staring at him with wide, bloodshot eyes. Beside her, Kassia was kneeling, naked, numb and silent.

Valerian was staring at Rian also. He saw how Philemos was looking at her, and closed his eyes a second.

Rictus wanted to ask Sertorius what he had done to Aise – for some reason he had to know. The great searing pain in his chest had to hear something, know something of Aise's fate, no matter how bad it might have been.

"What did you do to my wife?" he asked Sertorius, and his voice cracked with strain, a grief he had not known he was about to feel. Agony, more raw than anything he had felt since he had been a boy.

Sertorius sneered. "Phaestus was right – Rictus the family man. Well, my friend, we used your wife like a little whore. We –"

The blade of the drepana silenced him, sliding easily into his mouth, chopping through his tongue and opening his cheeks, a last, wide smile. Sertorius gargled, choking on his own blood.

Rictus stood there, holding the blade, keeping the thief upright while he drowned and flailed in front of him. Finally it ended. Rictus tilted the sword, and Sertorius slid off it like meat off a skewer.

He turned around, unutterably tired, unwilling to contemplate the desolation that was being unveiled before him.

One of Sertorius's men was still alive, the one with the broken face. Rictus nodded at Valerian, and the younger man killed him, a single clean thrust. Then he stared at Rian, but no longer with any hope in his eyes.

Rictus knelt in front of his daughter. "Where is Ona?"

"Hiding."

"Rian," Rictus said. His voice broke.

His daughter moved into his arms and he held her close to him, burying his face in her hair, crushing her against the black unyielding breast of Antimone's Gift.

"I'm here," he said, "I'm here. It's all right. Everything will be all right now."

TWENTY-SEVEN
THE TURNING OF
THE ROAD

THE HALLS ECHOED with his footsteps, the nails in his sandals clicking on the marble. In alcoves set every few paces, the great leaders of Machran stood hewn in more marble. Dead faces, empty eyes, white stone.

All meaningless now. Whatever Machran had been to these men, it was something different today. Tonight. This quiet night near the tail end of a long and bloody winter.

Fornyx met him at the junction of the corridors and the two appraised each other for a moment.

"What do you think he wants?" Rictus asked.

"Why ask me?" Fornyx demanded. "You're the father-figure here."

They stood looking at one another, a tall, fair man with a haggard face, and a short, wiry black-bearded fellow some ten years younger. Both wore black cuirasses and scarlet cloaks. Both bore the marks of old wounds on every limb.

"Spring is almost here," Rictus said. "Planting season."

"The snows will be melting," Fornyx told him. "Another few days and the hills will be clear enough to walk."

Rictus nodded as though they had both just agreed on something. Then they turned as one and continued walking down the cavernous corridor.

A pair of sentries stood holding spears before a deeply recessed wooden door. They, too, wore scarlet cloaks.

"Athys," Rictus said to one of them. "How's the leg?"

"Barely a scar, chief. I can run as fast as ever."

"It's all right. He's expecting us." Rictus opened the small door. He had to stoop to enter.

There was a fire burning in a round hearth, lamps hanging from the ceiling, and papers scattered over every available surface: chairs, tables, in cascades upon the floor.

"Corvus?" Rictus said.

Something stirred. There was an anteroom off to one side, a simple bed in the corner, an armour stand with a black cuirass perched upon it, and Corvus, dressed in a red chiton.

"You wanted to see us?" Rictus asked.

Corvus nodded. He was looking at the Curse of God with his arms folded. He had lately had his hair cropped short, and the thick black shock of it stood up like a brush. He looked more like a Macht than he had; flesh had been added to his slender bones.

Since the end of the campaign, the hard riding and marching had become a memory, and he slept now in the echoing maze of the Empirion, his tent packed away with the rest of the army's baggage.

In this room as in the next, papers and maps covered everything. Parmenios had offices here in the Empirion, but kept them stacked and ordered like the ranks of a well-trained phalanx. This disorder was Corvus's own.

Rictus saw a map of the Empire lying on the floor. He picked it up, old vellum that sagged in his hand. For a second he ran his finger across names and mountains and rivers that had seen the blood of his youth spilt across them, five thousand pasangs and twenty years away.

"It's a big day tomorrow, chief," Fornyx said breezily. "A bit like getting married. You ask me, you should either be drunk, or asleep."

Corvus smiled. "You're right, Fornyx; I suppose it is a kind of marriage." He reached down and lifted something from beside the cuirass, something that glittered in the light of the lamps.

"Look at this. Silver from a mine on the slopes of Mount Panjaeos itself. Tomorrow Kassander of Machran will place it on my head, and I shall be a king."

He tossed the circlet up into the air, caught it as though it were a gleaming child's toy, and then set it down again.

"What do you think of the chiton?" he asked Rictus.

"I like the colour," Rictus said with a raised eyebrow. "From now on, all the army will wear scarlet.

It will be as much a symbol for us as the raven sigil. We'll train up every spearman to match your Dogsheads, and we'll teach Macht to ride horses and use bows like Ardashir and the Companions. We'll have a siege train, designed by Parmenios. We will make an instrument of war, brothers, such as this world has never seen before."

Rictus and Fornyx looked at one another.

"You're to be crowned king of the Macht in the morning, Corvus," Rictus said. "Who else is there left to fight?"

Corvus turned and smiled. "The world we live in is a big place, Rictus. You look hard enough, and you will always find someone willing to fight."

He stepped forward and ran a hand down the lightless surface of the armour in front of him.

"But I didn't ask you here to listen to me rant about the future. I wanted to ask you a favour, Rictus."

"Just ask."

Suddenly Corvus looked as wide-eyed and young as a boy confronting his father with a confession.

"Help me put it on," he said.

He touched the armour again gently, as a man might stroke the arm of a woman too beautiful to notice him.

"I must do it now, tonight. I intend to be crowned wearing it tomorrow, and I must know – I have to know that I can wear it. Do you understand?"

Fornyx looked mystified, but Rictus understood perfectly.

"Let me see, then."

The armour came up off its stand, light as leather,

harder than any stone. Rictus opened the two halves of it and Corvus slid his arm into the gap. He was sweating.

The clasps snapped shut, and then the wings came down and clicked into place. Corvus stood tugging at the neck of the cuirass. "It's too big," he rasped.

"Wait a second," Rictus said, remembering the first time he had donned his own cuirass, on the Kunaksa hills. This boy's father had told him to put it on.

Corvus's face changed. "It's shifting. I can feel it."

"It will mould to your body. It only takes a second."

Something lit up in Corvus's strange eyes. "It's done, Rictus. It fits as though it was made for me."

Fornyx clapped the shoulder of the youth's black armour. "There you go; a Cursebearer at last. What a vision we are, three men in black and scarlet."

Corvus wiped his eyes. "Thank you, Rictus. I have been travelling a long time, to feel I have the right to this. I was never sure –"

"You are Macht. It was made for you to wear," Rictus said. "After tomorrow you will be our king. Be worthy of the armour and the crown."

Corvus looked up at him. "These last weeks, since we took Machran, I have been receiving delegations from every city worthy of the name. Men that reviled me now put their signatures to edicts congratulating me."

"They've had enough of war for a season," Fornyx said. "They're ready for something new, anything so long as the fighting ends."

"I trust men like Kassander more – men who

fought me openly, who kept trying until the very end. Men like that are worth something."

Rictus thought of Phaestus, of Karnos. If they were alive right now he would kill them himself. And yet he had a daughter who loved Phaestus's son.

"I've heard it said that only Antimone truly knows the hearts of men," Rictus said, "and that is why she weeps."

"When I turned up at your farm that morning, Rictus, I never thought that it would lead to where it did," Corvus said. "I wish it could have been different."

"It's been a long road," Rictus said. "None of us know what's around the next bend in it."

He thought of Jason, this boy's father. Eunion, that good and gentle man. And Aise, whose life had ended in torment. All because of him.

Their lives, their deaths; they would be with him always in a blackened corner of his soul.

"We just keep marching," Rictus said softly. "That is what we do. We carry the Curse of God on our backs and go into the dark together."

"There are times when I am not sure what it means, to be one of the Macht," Corvus said. "And I know I do not yet know what it means to be a king.

"Tomorrow the leaders of the Macht will all be there to see the circlet put on my head, men from fifty cities, a crowd of thousands. But what that means, for me and them, I am not yet sure."

Rictus looked down at him, this terrible, earnest young man with the strange eyes.

"It will come to you," he said. "In time."

EPILOGUE

THE SNOWS WERE gone from the deep glens, though the mountains still blazed white on the blue horizon. They waded across the river, feeling the bite of the water, the ice not quite done quickening in it.

Rictus walked through the ruined doorway of what had once been his home. The walls still stood, blackened and broken, stone upon stone. He picked his way through the wreckage and knelt in front of the beehive hearth, in which Aise had baked the bread. The hearthstone was still in place. There were blades of grass rising through the joins between the flags.

He lifted aside a beam and it crumbled to charcoal in his hands. Broken pottery crunched underfoot. He startled a blackbird, which launched itself from the ruin with an indignant clatter.

He passed through what had been the side door, to the space where he and Aise had slept.

And knelt there, remembering. Something glittered in the sunlight, and he stooped and rummaged through the ashes. A piece of aquamarine blue glass, a shard of memory. He clenched it in his palm and bent over with the sudden pain of the pictures it conjured up in his mind.

At last he rose again, breathing hard, his eyes burning. He looked up, and there were swallows in the air above him, carving gleeful arcs out of the sky. They were dropping mud as they swooped, building in the crevices of the walls.

He left the house, walked out to join the others in the sunshine and the placid glimmer of the river. Above him the woods hung on the slopes of the glen, new leaves unfurling green-tipped on the beech and oak and birch thickets. The place was alive with birdsong.

Rian took his hand. He lifted Ona up into his embrace, and the child put her arms about his neck.

He looked at Fornyx and Philemos.

"We'd best get started, I suppose. There's a lot to be done."

The End

GLOSSARY

Aichme: A spearhead, generally of iron but sometimes of bronze. The spearhead is usually some nine inches in length, of which four inches is the blade.

Anande: The Kefren name for the moon known as Haukos; in their tongue it means *patience*.

Antimone: The veiled goddess, protector and guardian of the Macht. Exiled from heaven for creating the black Macht armour, she is the goddess of pity, of mercy, and of sadness. Her Veil separates life from death.

Antimone's Gift / the Curse of God: Black, indestructible armour given to the Macht in the legendary past by the goddess Antimone, created by the smith-god Gaenion himself out of woven darkness. There are some five to six thousand sets of this armour extant upon the world of Kuf, and the Macht will fight to the death to prevent it falling into the hands of the Kufr.

Apsos: God of beasts. A shadowy figure in the Macht pantheon, reputed to be a goat-like creature who will avenge the ill-treatment of animals and sometimes transform men into beasts in revenge or as a jest.

Araian: The Sun, wife of Gaenion the smith.

Archon: A Kufr term for a military officer of high rank, a general of a wing or corps.

Bel: The all-powerful and creative god who looks over the Kufr world. Roughly equivalent to the Macht "God," but gentler and less vindictive.

Carnifex: An archaic term for an army surgeon, or any would-be healer who travels with armed men. Its ancient meaning denotes a butcher or executioner; an example of Macht humour.

Centon: Traditionally the number of men who could be fed from a single centos, the large black cauldron mercenaries eat from. It approximates one hundred men.

Chamlys: A short cloak, commonly reaching to mid-thigh.

Chiton: A short-sleeved tunic open at the throat, reaching to the knee. The female version is longer.

Drepana: A heavy, curved slashing sword associated with the lowland peoples of the Macht.

Firghe: The Kefren name for the moon Phobos, meaning *anger*.

Gaenion: The smith-god of the Macht, who created the Curse of God for Antimone, who wrought the stars and much of the fabric of Kuf itself. He is married to Araian, the sun, and his forges are reputed to be upon the summit of Mount Panjaeos in the Harukush.

Goatherder tribes: Less sophisticated Macht who do not dwell in cities but are nomadic hill-people. They possess no written language, but have a large hoard of oral culture.

Goatmen: Degenerate savages who belong to no city, and live in a state of brutish filth. They wear goatskins by and large, and keep to the higher mountain-country of the Macht lands.

Hell: The far side of the Veil. Not hell in the Christian sense, but an afterlife whose nature is wholly unknowable.

Himation: A long, fine cloak, sometimes worn ceremonially.

Honai: Traditionally, a Kefren word meaning *finest*. It is a term used to describe the best troops in a King's entourage, not only his bodyguards, but the well-drilled professional soldiers of the Great King's household guard.

Hufsan / Hufsa: Male and female terms for the lower-caste inhabitants of the Empire, traditionally mountain-folk of the Magron, the Adranos and the Korash. They are smaller and darker than the Kefren, but hardier, more primitive, and less cultured, preferring to preserve their records through storytelling rather than script.

Isca: A Macht city, destroyed by a combination of her neighbours in the year before the Battle of Kunaksa. The men of Isca were semi-professional warriors who trained incessantly for war and had a habit of attacking their neighbours. Legend has it the founder of Isca, Isarion, was a protégé of the god Phobos.

Kefren: The peoples of the Asurian heartland, who led the resistance to the Macht in the semi-legendary past, and then established an Empire on the back of that achievement. Throughout the Empire, they are a favoured race, and have become a caste of rulers and administrators.

Kerusia: In Machtic, the word denotes a council, and is used to designate the leaders of a community. In mercenary circles it can also refer to a gathering of generals, sometimes but not always elected by common consent.

Komis: The linen head-dress worn by the nobility of the Asurian Empire. It can be pulled up around the head so that only the eyes are visible, or can be loosed to reveal the entire face.

Kuf: The world, the earth, the place of life set amid the stars under the gaze of God and his minions.

Kufr: A derogatory Macht term for all the inhabitants of Kuf who are not of their own race.

Mora: A formation of ten centons, or approximately one thousand men.

Mot: The Kufr god of barren soil, and thus of death.

Niseian: A breed of horse from the plains of Niseia, reputedly the best warhorses in the world, and certainly the greatest in stature. Mostly black or bay, and over sixteen hands in height, they are the mounts of Kings and Kefren nobility, and are rarely seen outside the Asurian heartland.

Obol: A coin, made of bronze, silver, or gold.

Ostrakr: The tem used for those unfortunates who have no city as their own, either because they have been exiled, their city has been destroyed, or they have taken up with mercenaries.

Othismos: The name given to the heart of hand-to-hand battle, when two bodies of heavy infantry meet.

Paean: A hymn, usually sung upon the occasion of a death. The Macht sing their Paean going into battle, to prepare themselves for their own demise.

Panoply: The name given for a full set of heavy infantry accoutrements, including a helm, a cuirass, a shield and a spear.

Pasang: One thousand single paces. Historically, one mile is a thousand double-paces of a Roman Legionary, thus a pasang is half a mile.

Peplos: A woman's garment, very like a cloak but generally finer and lighter.

Phobos and Haukos: The two moons of Kuf. Phobos is the larger, and is pale in colour. Haukos is smaller and pink or pale red in colour. Also, the two sons of the goddess Antimone. Phobos is the god of fear, and Haukos the god of hope.

Qaf: A mysterious race native to the mountains of the Korash. They are very tall and broad and seem to be a strange kind of amalgam of Kufr and ape. They are reputed to have their own language, but appear as immensely powerful beasts that haunt the snows of the high passes.

Rimarch: An archaic term for a file-closer, the last

man in the eight-man file of a phalanx, and second-in-command of the file itself.

Sauroter: The lizard-sticker. The counterweight to the aichme, at the butt of the spear, generally a four-sided spike somewhat heavier than the spearhead so the spear can be grasped past the middle and still retain its balance. It is used to stick the spear upright in the ground, and also to finish off prone enemies. If the aichme is broken off in combat, the sauroter is often used as a substitute.

Sigils: The letters of the Macht alphabet. Usually, each city adopts one as its badge and has it painted upon the shields of its warriors.

Silverfin, Horrin: Silverfin roughly correspond to a kind of ocean bass, and horrin to mackerel.

Strawhead: A derogatory term used among the Macht for those who hail from the high mountain settlements. These folk tend to be taller and fairer in colouring than the Macht from the lowlands, hence the name.

Taenon: The amount of land required for one man to live and raise a family. It varies according to the country and the soil quality, a taenon in the hills being larger than in the lowlands, but in general it equates to about five acres.

Vorine: A canine predator, mid-way between a wolf and a jackal in size.

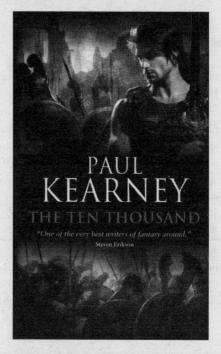

PAUL
KEARNEY
THE TEN THOUSAND

"One of the very best writers of fantasy around."
Steven Erikson

UK ISBN: 978-1-84416-647-3 • US ISBN: 978-1-84416-573-5 • £7.99/$7.99

On the world of Kuf, the Macht are a mystery, a seldom-seen people of extraordinary
ferocity and discipline whose prowess on the battlefield is the stuff of legend. For centuries they have remained within the remote fastnesses of the Harukush Mountains. In the
world beyond, the teeming races and peoples of Kuf have been united within the bounds
of the Asurian Empire, which rules the known world, and is invincible. The Great King of
Asuria can call up whole nations to the battlefield.

His word is law.

But now the Great King's brother means to take the throne by force, and in order to do so
he has sought out the legend. He hires ten thousand mercenary warriors of the Macht,
and leads them into the heart of the Empire.

 WWW.SOLARISBOOKS.COM

Follow us on Twitter! www.twitter.com/solarisbooks

ALSO FROM PAUL KEARNEY

THE MONARCHIES OF GOD – VOLUME 1
HAWKWOOD AND THE KINGS

UK: ISBN: 978 1 906735 70 8 • £8.99
US: ISBN: 978 1 906735 71 5 • $9.99

For Richard Hawkwood and his crew, a desperate venture to carry refugees to the uncharted land across the Great Western Ocean offers the only chance of escape from the Inceptines' pyres.

In the East, Lofantyr, Abeleyn and Mark – three of the five Ramusian Kings – have defied the cruel pontiff's purge and must fight to hold their thrones through excommunication, intrigue and civil war.

In the quiet monastery city of Charibon, two humble monks make a discovery that will change the whole world.

THE MONARCHIES OF GOD – VOLUME 2
CENTURY OF THE SOLDIER

UK: ISBN: 978 1 907519 08 6 • £8.99
US: ISBN: 978 1 907519 09 3 • $9.99

Hebrion's young King Abeleyn lies in a coma, his capital in ruins and his former lover conniving for the throne. Corfe Cear-Inaf is given a ragtag command of savages and sent on a mission he cannot hope to succeed. Richard Hawkwood finally returns to the Monarchies of God, bearing news of a wild new continent.

In the West the Himerian Church is extending its reach, while in the East the fortress of Ormann Dyke stands ready to fall to the Merduk horde. These are terrible times, and call for extraordinary people...